I0670713

Dinatech

Series

Volume #1

Electric Disease
Corporate Policy

ISBN:0615582664
ISBN-13: 978-0615582665

Electric

Disease

By
Robert Dufalo

To my wife, who told me I write like a 5th grader.

Every day after, I have strived to at least write at a 6th grade level.

Prologue

Back in the 60s, if there was ever reason in the world to fear your government, this was the time. If you wanted to know who was doing the things that should keep you up at night, it was them.

Who was testing nuclear bombs on their home land?

It was the good old U.S. After all, we had to— Big Red sure wasn't going to stop.

If there was someone doing something dangerous, you didn't have to look farther than good old Uncle Sam.

That was the Cold War: one government trying to outshine the other like two arrogant brothers trying to prove they were the better son.

It wasn't all bad; we did put a man on the moon.

Then there was the 70s, where everyone got to truly feel the terror that the government could paint on. It was no longer just something that was passed around the rumor mills. It was in-your-face news; on CBS, NBC,

BBC, the face of evil was placed before the people. It caused something that the U.S. government had never seen before, people openly and widely disapproving of government. People were now able to give real time feedback to every move made.

The peace and love movements against the U.S.'s involvement in wars around the world came to them because of technology, the catalyst was the military, surprising enough. Protesting, displeasure— the government was put on notice: it could no longer be business as usual.

So came the 80s, the touchy-feely softer side of the Cold War. Everyone was now worried about how wars were going to be fought in space. Reagan had started the Strategic Defense Initiative. In 1983 the idea would be that we would take all the nasty weapons that could burn the crust of the earth and put them safely floating over our heads. Once in orbit, we wouldn't have to worry about them anymore.

How nice that felt.

The mask that this system wore to keep the people content was that its creation would protect us from the other nasty weapons that Big Red in all its evil was going to launch at us. After all, they were evil, blood thirsty, and had nothing to lose.

So the Cold War limped along till the end of the 80s, when the Soviet Union could no longer afford the payments. In 1991 the war was over. There were no winners, just large bills that needed to be paid on both sides. With the snap of the Cold War, the world changed, yet it stayed the same too. The Wall came down, and the U.S. embraced the former Soviet Union as friends and our good neighbors.

Publicly everyone was friendly now, but privately, this just meant that all the bickering and flexing was done behind closed doors and in back alleys. No longer did they have the justification to stand in front of the U.N. and beat a shoe on the table screaming, "We will bury you."

The public frowned on aggression. "No, we don't wish to make more ugly weapons that just bring more fear than comfort; thank you very much." Money for these military matters had to be kept closer to the vest. But it's harder to hide the money when you report to the people and they can see just how much your "Atomic Hammer" is costing them. Sure the money can be obscured and pushed through channels to keep it quiet while paying for "Black projects", but that's just so much damn work.

It's easier to pay some company in the private sector one billion dollars and not have to make these long, painful, and rather apparent lists that tell the tax payer just where his money is going. Now it's creating jobs; the government is improving things here at home. Also by moving it in to the private sector, there's a nice side effect: it's easier to believe that the people working on these weapons are just as human as the rest of us.

Now, with old Joe Neighbor working on them, they have a face and are just as down-to-earth as the rest of us. They kiss their daughters before they leave for work too, right? "We" are making these vast improvements to save our boys in the trenches. It's not the cold unfeeling war machine pumping out new ways to wage war. Down with oppression over the people!

Here in the private sector, there are far less leaks. Spies find that people here are far more loyal to the companies

3

that hire them. People don't feel the same about the government, which is so large, it doesn't have a face they can relate with. It's not as personal.

The rules aren't the same for the capitalistic private companies; the only thing that they answer to is the company that contracted them. The money, it's always about the money. And because they are a private company, they don't have to answer any questions they don't want to.

To these companies, getting large contracts with the government can set you up for life.

After all, once it's built, someone has to keep maintaining all this crap. Repairs always read better on a bill sheet than paying for a new product…even if you could have gotten two new for what it takes to fix one. And they will always have the money to pay you for your services once again.

Absolute power corrupts absolutely. That's a saying that has been passed on for years, for a good reason.

Welcome to Dinatech, one of the world's leaders in computer innovation since 1967. Not well known among the public sector, they don't have a product that you can buy directly, but every manufacturer that releases a quality product uses them. Their contributions to the computer industry can be found deep down on every green board for every computer product you buy. From IBM laptops to the Sony XBR TV that looks nice settled in your overpriced entertainment center that you brag to your friends about on game day.

Their innovation pushes come from the need to solve tomorrow's want for a faster world, CPUs that can do more, smaller form factor laptops, smarter automation for all areas of industry. This is where Dinatech has been a leader. Like Bosh, their goal is to make great products better.

If one was to read a press release from Dinatech this is what they'd find:

With over 40 celebrated years in this field, we are the leaders in Biochemical, Biomechanical, and Bioelectronic Computers. Leaders in technical know-how and ingenuity, we are helping people find their tomorrow faster and easier than ever before. With our help, tomorrow is in our grasp. The future is there, it's time to reach out and take it for ourselves.

Dinatech, giving you the future today.

The cold hum of the florescent lights overhead echoed off the cool metal of the cabinets about the sterile room, the place scrubbed cleaner than an operating room. Lying on a stainless steel cart was a small chimpanzee under the harsh glare of adjustable medical lights.

The chimp was currently well sedated, its back cut open and filled with probes that were connected to a terminal sitting on a cart next to it. Small thin wires connected the probes along the animal's spine to the terminal. They would capture every reading as the subject was run through a series of tests that the general population would call cruel and inhumane.

The quiet was broken as a rather bored man named Mike pushed another metal crash cart into the room. The sound given off by the cart hitting another covered in metal instruments made sure that the "crash" in its name lived up to the hype. He wedged the door with a chair so that it stayed open against regulation. He knew that all doors in the live creatures area had to stay closed at all times, but it was Friday and the chimp they were working with today was under sedation and attached to so many terminals there was no way it could get away. The chimp was known to the crew by the name Mitch, even though it was also against regulations to give the subjects names. This was a rule no one followed. From Andy to Zen, every animal had a name and the whole crew used those names. Because Mitch was sedated, they hadn't even bothered strapping him down.

With a sigh and a little frown, Mike moved the new cart up against the other. "Well Mitch, just a few more hours of this and I think you'll be as good as new again," he said with hope in his voice.

He looked over the confusing display of numbers that the monitor displayed, but he really couldn't tell what information could be gleaned from them. He was just an assistant nurse on this project, but he knew that even Doctor Evens was completely unaware of the data that was being collected and what it meant. Some groups of military types were looking to take this data and do, well, something with it. It was above his pay grade. And while he said that Mitch would be as good as new, he knew better. He knew very well that such words were just lies.

This building was part of Dinatech's military contract division. Very few people even knew that Dinatech had military contracts, and even fewer people knew what goes on behind the doors. Mike was sure if the public did know there would be huge protests.

Mitch's immune system was being put to the test. The experiments that were being done on the chimp were to measure reactions to the body through viral incubation periods while they made their way into the central nervous system. It was believed that this one would be fatal to him.

Taking a long breath, Mike opened cabinets along the far wall away from Mitch, so he could get a wiring harness that would connect the new crash cart to the simian. While the nurse's back was turned, something happened that was not expected, and if Mike were paying more attention he might have noticed the chimp twitch.

With a growl, Mike started to dig deeper into the cabinet trying to find the right loom for the older data terminal. Most of the other teams had already moved off these older data carts, retiring them for the newer Siemens ones. But right now there was a lot of work for the medical department. The hunt for "Weapons of Mass Destruction" had caused "The need for more research."

The noise Mike was making was more than enough to cover up the sound that a groggy and unsteady chimpanzee would make waking up. Mitch took this moment to launch into complete freak-out mode, jumping up from his bed on the metal table with a screech that echoed about the room. The leap pulled every last wire from the back of the chimp that connected him to the testing system. The noise caused Mike to jump back in fright, and with a jerk he bashed his head into the underside of the counter before he could pull back enough to try and stand. Turning as quick as he could, he was able to make out the escaping chimp around the stars brought on by the pain and, he was sure, a concussion as well. Mitch scrambled through the still open door and out into the hallway before Mike could think to follow in pursuit. Staggering to his feet, he got to the door while still holding the back of his head.

Looking both ways, he couldn't find the chimp in the bright florescent-lit hallways; Mitch was already out of sight and down another hallway that made up the basement floor of the Dinatech advanced research facility. Pulling off his blue hair cap he took a guess and turned right to see if he could find the little bastard, as he didn't need Mitch costing him his job.

Walking quickly around the corner, Mike's vision went dark as he ran into something, a collision reminiscent of a linebacker hitting a running back as the two bodies impacted, his momentum pushing him through the unsuspecting, unseen person. Mike and the unknown person crashed to the ground in a pile of humanity and he was once again confronted with the same lovely stars that he saw just a moment ago in the lab.

Rolling off the man onto his knees, Mike groaned softly as he tried to get his bearing on what the hell was happening. It just was not going to be his day, and if he didn't fix his mistake it might also not be his year while trying to find a new job.

The man he just rolled off of was dressed in rugged looking gray work pants and a matching button up shirt. He knew at once that the man was with the IT group, because everyone in the IT group wore a standard uniform.

"Oh shit man, ouch." The IT worker couldn't be long out of college judging by his age, dark shaggy hair, and matching dark eyes. He looked over to Mike asking, "Are

8

you ok? I guess you didn't see me, coming around that corner so fast hmm?" He sounded kind enough, but at the same time he had a tone that said that he wasn't happy about being taken down by a man not watching where the hell he was going.

Mike nodded quickly as he put one hand on the cool brick wall, and was starting to wish things were softer around here as he pulled himself up, staggering to get his head to stop spinning.

"I'm sorry about that. I'm just in a hurry." Looking past him down the hall then back the way he came running from, he frowned, trying to gain some focus. "You didn't see a chimp running down this hall did you?"

The IT guy was a little quicker to his feet and in better shape than Mike, and he shrugged off the hit faster. "No man, I just came out of the cable room." He pointed back over to the large thick door, set into the wall with a thick steel frame around it; it looked more like a bank vault door.

With a nod Mike sighed and moved off quickly, more worried about finding Mitch than getting into another crash. "Alright thanks." Mike called back; he did stop a few steps away before pausing to look back. "Again, sorry." Then he quickened his pace even more, knowing that he was losing ground on the escaped chimpanzee.

The IT man left behind watched after him looking a little confused, but after many years on the job he learned quickly that he didn't want to ask what was going on. In many cases, he found he didn't want to know.

Inside the door that Mike jetted past and the IT guy

had left through, Mitch walked right in, as the distracted man was too busy checking his work pager to see what other jobs needed to be done. The man wasn't looking for the small dark, hairy chimp as he scrambled in, the door slowly closing behind him.

Mitch was hurting. His whole back hurt—it felt wet and very painful—he needed to hide, he needed to get someplace where he couldn't be found. So the small ape moved back into the deeper parts of the wiring room. Groggy from the medication, and delirious from the effects of the virus, he dragged his body until he made it to the back of the room. Trying to find a place to hide, he wedged himself between a few larger pipes that made up the backbone of the network infrastructure, and passed out from blood loss.

It wouldn't be until a few hours later that Mitch's dead body would be found, when Mike finally told his supervisor a less negligent sounding version of how Mitch had gotten free from his room. The staff had conducted a full search of the floor and soon found that Mitch's blood marked a trail that led to his body.

Even the confusion of how he got into the room took some time to figure out, but after another few hours to piece that part together with security footage of the hallways it was all very clear what had happened and where the mistakes were made. The research team was not happy to have lost the data they were trying to collect, but they still had other subjects they could get the information from. And the IT department was more than a little bothered that they were going to have to clean blood out of their still-under-construction patch room. It was just a good thing that nothing truly bad happened…

Chapter CONTACT

Just finishing a commercial drop to a small video game store in a strip mall on the outskirts of Portland, Dan felt his personal phone vibrate in his pocket. With a little sigh that sounded more like a grunt, he took the phone out of his pocket to answer it. He knew damn well who it was but checked the ID first anyway. Across the small LCD screen read "Jake"; it was just who he thought that it was.

Flipping open the cell he brought it to his ear. "What is it Jake, you know that I'm stuck on the clock for another six hours before I'm even going to be able to think about looking at freedom."

For the past month, Jake and Dan had been planning a long weekend stay down in Vegas with a few other friends. Some people were flying in from New York, a few more driving in from California, and Jake and Dan would be flying out of Portland tonight in order to get the rooms and get the first night setup for the crew.

"Crap dude, I thought you said that you were going to get out of working today?"

Dan laughed softly into the phone as he walked up to the back of the large brown truck. "Yeah right. I said that I was going to ask, but the moment you mention that you want a day off you get the 'It's holiday shipping rush' speech repeated to you. I'm lucky enough to say that I'm getting off a few hours early."

It was barely the start of October, but many companies were already starting to get their holiday stock in place for the rush. As everyone knows, the shipping companies are always stretched to their limits during the last few months. With the impulse buying that comes with the holidays, a store can't afford to not have everything they can on hand. It would be capitalist suicide to not have the stock they need during the holidays. Most mall stores limp along the other ten months of the year just so they can make it all worth it come "Black Friday".

Jake groaned into the phone and Dan frowned, starting to look a little annoyed. "Dan, come on, this time tomorrow we are going to be in a limo hitting some of the best strip clubs the desert has to offer," Jake whined on.

"Relax Jake." He worked open the back gate on the delivery truck shoving the roll-up door up just enough that he could put the hand truck into the bed, again one handed. It was about this time he vaguely thought there was some rule about personal calls while on the job for just this reason. "The plane isn't going to be taking off without me on it."

"Yeah that's the spirit man, I'm saying that we get blasted on the plane on the way there."

"Mmm, I think that I'm going to pass on that one. I think that my money will stretch a few minutes longer on the overpriced drinks on the casino floor," Dan countered.

"Oh please, once you get into that tournament all your drinks are going to be on the house. That's how it all works, ya know?"

Slamming the gate back down Dan laughed softly. "I'm not so sure about that." He sighed. "Look Jake we can talk about this later? I've got to get this crap delivered if I want to have any chance of getting out of here early tonight alright?"

"Yeah dude, I'll be at your house, key is in the same spot right?"

"Yeah, don't drink all my damn beer this time, you never buy any."

"Sure I do!" Jake said trying to sound offended.

"You don't get to drink all my porters and then come over with a six pack of Bud Light and call it good." He thought about it a second and added. "Not to mention the fact you drank all that crap as well!"

Before Jake could continue the debate, Dan told him goodbye and pulled himself behind the wheel once more. Looking over his manifest he found that his next delivery would be even further south, moving away from Portland. It made him worry that he was going to get done with his deliveries early just to find that he was so far from base that it would take an hour just get back and drop off the truck for the night.

To his surprise he found that wasn't the case at all, in fact his scheduled deliveries would end with the Dinatech drop, and then he'd be coming back into base. He was sure that Dana would have him go through one of their required yearly safety trainings. The short day would be a good chance to get them out of the way and help bring their distribution center into compliance with corporate.

Starting up the truck, the diesel engine rattled to life,

and after checking his mirrors he pulled out into traffic. Soon he made his way back up onto I5 heading south. The river off to the east, it was about 10 miles or so before he found himself heading down 43 and then a few more secluded roads till he came to a rolling stop before what was an impossibly large building for the area.

Out of place in this rural area, it was truly startlingly large. From where he was looking now, it had to hold something close to 25 floors. The building was made of black glass that caused the afternoon sun to refract off the surfaces and explode out over large gated grounds. The top of the building came to a point, like someone had taken a giant sized katana and cut the top of the building off.

Once inside the gates, he found there were many different access roads one could take, all clearly marked on where they went—like Visitors, Employee Parking, and Large Deliveries. Around each of these cleanly paved paths were lawns and groups of flora that looked as if someone painstakingly cared for them both day and night.

Dan was left to wonder just how much money was put into this place and what in the hell it was doing so far outside the city of Portland where buildings of its stature would be more welcomed. He decided he should head for the Visitors area because he figured it would be the best place to find the lobby and get someone to sign for his delivery; he didn't feel this was a "Large delivery".

Rolling up into one of the clearly marked visitors spaces, he killed the engine of the large brown truck and the delivery beast became so silent that it was music to his ears. Rolling back the door, he hopped out and started to walk for the front of the glass building with his digital clipboard in hand. Still walking down the paths for the lobby, Dan felt like an extra on a remake of The Wizard of Oz.

Stepping up to the large revolving door, he slid into the gap and started to push his way around, and it was at this point that he noticed just how dark the glass was that made up the outside of the building. You could see through them, but it wasn't easy. It was like they were lined with charcoal.

Across the roundabout drop off and into the lobby area through a revolving door, the space beyond was large enough for a building of its size, but it wasn't as fancy as he'd expected. There were white walls with simple chairs that looked comfortable, but didn't try to look expensive as much corporate furniture did.

To put it another way, the lobby told the visitor that the building was functional and while they accepted guests, they didn't cater to them.

Walking forward through the completely empty lobby he couldn't help but notice that the carpet, while plain, was rather expensive in materials and well-constructed. Looking across the room he came to see the simple reception desk that was built into the structure of the lobby. Across the front of the desk was the logo and company font that spelled "Dinatech" telling him that he was indeed in the right area, and he realized that this was the first time that he'd seen the logo since he got here. Coming to a stop at the counter, he put his clipboard on the bleached wood top.

Looking down at the receptionist, Dan was met with eyes of a woman that he would consider the most un-plain girl that he'd laid his eyes on in a very long time.

Long chocolate brown hair, straight and spilling down to frame a pair of the most bottomless slate blue eyes that glowed of their own natural light. She was young, maybe just coming out of her teens, and when she smiled up at him in an expectant way, Dan took a breath from the feeling that he didn't want to disappoint her and have the pleasant look falter.

It took him a moment to realize that she was waiting on him to say why he was at her reception desk. She seemed to know something was up and she smiled a little more, showing her perfect white teeth. "Welcome to Dinatech, how can I help you today?" her voice held the smooth rich accent of the British in it, something that he didn't expect to find here in Oregon. It caused him to blink and think of the many ways that she could help him, none of them having to do with Dinatech, or the delivery that he had sitting out in his van.

Clearing his suddenly dry throat, he answered, "Yeah I've got a few parcels out in my truck for delivery." He looked at her a moment and she looked back at him saying nothing. He suddenly felt nervous. "You know a few boxes? Ah, for the…" he reached for this little computerized clipboard to try and get information, of what he didn't know but she spoke before it would matter.

"I'm very aware of what a parcel is," she says in a voice that held her smile and he could tell that she was teasing him. "What I am confused about is why you are here in the visitor's area when delivery is on the other side of the building." She pointed back over her shoulder.

She gradually stood up and ran her hands over her form flattering sweater before pulling a sheet of paper from the top of a stack that sat on the side of her desk; she placed it between them. With an easy smooth movement of her hand she turned the paper to face him. "If you could just take your truck around this path here, you'll be in our loading docks and our staff can help you unload any parcels that you need to deliver. You know, boxes." She made sure to put a little extra emphasis on the last word. Just enough that Dan could feel himself flinch a little at her comment; he didn't know if the young woman was actually offended or simply teasing him.

Pulling himself back together before speaking, he smiled and nodded. "Sorry, it's just my first delivery here. I wanted to make sure." Dan took a step back turning to start making his way back out the revolving door that he came in.

"Nothing to be sorry about. It's always good to meet the new delivery boy." She winked at him and she slid back into her chair, letting him be on his way.

Making it back out into the bright sunlight of the afternoon, he squinted up at the sky. Dan sighed and shook his head unlocking the truck. "That was really smooth wasn't it?" He muttered to himself, "Just six hours now I'll be hitting the clubs, and I'll have all the time in the world to be smooth." He pulled at his dark brown company supplied button up. "And be better dressed for it too."

Opening the driver's door of the truck roughly in frustration, he could try and convince himself otherwise, but he knew that he'd rather be in there right now flirting with the receptionist. Daydreams of talking her into leaving work early and heading down to Vegas with Jake and himself popped up. What would Jake say if he showed up at the airport with her next to him? Would Jake think that her eyes were as amazing as Dan did?

The truck clattering back to life brought Dan back to reality. Pulling back out of the visitor's space he went the way he came taking the fork and headed towards the path that would take him around to the side of the building and along the back where the delivery bay was. If he'd just looked better at the signs, he would have been able to see that it was foolish to head into the visitors area.

Rattling along he watched the reflection of the truck in the smoked black glass that made up most of the exterior of the building. All sides of the building looked the same. The only way to tell the front was by the cut at the top; he could see how a person could get lost trying to find the entrance.

Around to the back side of the building he found that not all of the structure was wrapped in the tinted glass. Currently a large black garage door was rolled up, under a slight overhang roof. The parking area here dipped down into the basement, giving the dock a high roof. Because of this, inside the dock you could hold two full sized tractor-trailers and a few other smaller delivery trucks, like his own. The bay was deep enough that the trucks could be parked and then the door closed, keeping everything secure.

A man walked out of the dock's office and stood at the edge of the raised platform. He motioned for Dan to back his truck into one of the smaller bays, and then moved over to help him guide the vehicle in against the bumpers. Once the front grill of his truck cleared beyond the rollway door a beefy sounding electric motor started to roll the gate back down and a bank of lights around the dock snapped on to make up for the lost sunlight.

Turning off the van once more, Dan slipped down from behind the wheel and climbed the few steps up onto the loading dock. Now, out from behind the wheel of the truck he was able to better take in the dock worker. He was an older man, and if Dan had to guess he would place him somewhere in his fifties, his hair cut clean and sprinkled with an extra helping of gray.

The dockworker gave him a friendly smile and offered a handshake that Dan took. "Welcome to the pit."

"Hey, I just have a few boxes that need to be delivered; I assume that you'll be able to sign for them?" Dan glanced over to the door and then back to the man. "Why are you closing the door?"

The older man looked to the door as if he'd not noticed that it was closing. "We have to keep it closed per work regulations. Especially right now."

"You had it open when I came up…I thought?" Dan frowned a little, looking slightly confused.

"Well sure, Clara called ahead for you, let us know that you'd be coming around, didn't she?" The man moved over toward the back of his truck so that he could receive the delivery; apparently he answered all questions that he was going to.

Complying with the movement Dan walked over, crouching down to open up the back of the cargo hold. Rolling up the door, Dan walked in, figuring out which boxes were for Dinatech. The whole time, the older man stood silently by the back door. He seemed fine waiting, showing no sign of becoming impatient at all. Judging by the empty bay, they weren't getting many deliveries today.

Finding the first box, he pulled it out and moved it

over to settle it on the loading dock just as the phone rang in the dock office. The older man, giving it a little frown before he started to walk to answer it, called back over his shoulder, "Just go ahead and set the rest of the delivery on the dock, I'll come sign for it in a moment."

Dan used the extra time to confirm he had all the boxes and placed them on the dock. Just as his delivery papers said, this was his last stop, and all ten boxes in the truck were for Dinatech. All of them the same size, but with slightly different weights to them. Punching the confirmations into the small tablet, he waited, leaning up against the back of his truck for the man to return. Checking his watch, he'd been here a total of twenty minutes now with his little tour of the visitor's area. This stop wasn't going to do anything for his service numbers. He needed to get back so that he could complete whatever training he was sure Dana had in mind for him.

Feeling that he'd waited long enough, Dan crossed the dock to the office to see if he could pop in and get the man to sign for him and open the gate so that he could get moving. To his surprise he found the office empty and the office phone hung up.

"Well isn't that just great," Dan said in nothing more than a murmur. Walking up to the desk in the office he let out a sigh and looked for some evidence of where the deck supervisor had gone. Only finding a small name plate that labeled the man as Steve O'Conner, he thought about it and the guy did look like a Steve: some people just look like their names.

It wasn't long before his full attention was on Steve's computer screen with its text scrolling across the bottom of the screen. In block font were the words "Amber alert", and on either side of the words was a biohazard symbol. This was more than a little startling to see, but the LCD screen's picture rolled once then twice before going out, leaving the screen blank. This about made him crap his pants.

Dan watched the blank screen for a moment in hopes that it would come back, but when it didn't he turned to look around the room, nervously inspecting, trying to find more clues about what was going on. The room itself was rather clean; the desk had a few stacks of invoices that the dockworker had been going through that day. The far wall had a large calendar with larger expected deliveries and departures. To the right of that was a hallway that led back farther into the building proper. Scanning back into the office, he found next to the door he'd just come in were the controls to operate all the loading dock doors.

Heading over to it he found that the key that allowed the mechanics to be operated had been removed, so there was currently no way that he could find for him to get his truck out of the loading bay and to get the hell out of this increasingly creepy ass place, with or without a release signature. Not able to find anything in this room to tell him where the man had gone or what in the hell was going on, he felt it would be wiser to keep moving. The longer he was alone, the more apprehensive he felt himself becoming. Running his hand through his short brown hair, he looked back to the hallway and with a sigh he walked over to see where it led.

The hallway wasn't actually that long; on the right was a door that led into another smaller office and then taking up the far end of the hallway was a large, solid looking steel door. With his digital clipboard in hand, he walked to the larger door and opened it. It took a little effort as the door was as heavy as it looked. As he stepped into the hallway beyond, he started to wonder if the door was actually armor plated.

Chapter BREAK

Beyond the loading bay, Dan found himself in a long hall that ran both left and right before cutting off to join other hallways. The walls were a nice clean white that left him squinting from the glare of the florescent lights. The doors were all painted a brown that complemented his shirt rather well; he almost looked like he belonged in this place.

Looking up to the source of the glare, he noticed the small bank of notification lights that were settled about every ten yards along the hallways. There were 3 lights in each bank: white, blue and red. Currently the red one was flashing slowly and it filled him with the thought that the building must have been going through a fire drill of some kind. Even though there was no audible alarm, perhaps someone had disabled the function? He started to walk a few steps down the hall to see if he could find any windows in one of the other doors. Surely the dockworker wouldn't have gone too far, leaving him alone with his truck locked in the bay or to fend for himself in a fire drill.

Walking only a few steps he looked back to see the bay door close and he sighed before walking over to check it, and just as he expected the damn thing was locked now too. He looked to the computerized clipboard in his hand. "Well that's just fucking great. Let's see if I can get this locked up somewhere as well?"

Committed now, he turned to start walking down the hall once more to see if he could find the missing dockworker. "This place is too damn creepy for me," he said in another murmur to himself.

Walking up to the next door he found that it had no windows, and when he tried the handle it was locked as well. Looking back where he came from, then forward to where the next door was, he realized that he could get lost rather quickly. While each door was marked with a four digit number, there was nothing that made them truly distinguishable that he could use for a landmark.

Picking up his pace a little he started to feel his anger bubble up inside him. How in the world could that damn guy leave him down here like this? He was supposed to be getting back to base to work on training. Hell forget that, he was supposed to be getting off early today so that he could get to Vegas, to hit the clubs, to relax, enjoy a few days off while spending far too much money. This damn dock worker was cutting into his Vegas time.

He'd reached the end of the hall when all his anger was lost in a flash; he was startled when the silence of the hallway was blasted away by what sounded like a machine gun going off. He felt his back arch as the fright jolted its way up his spine. Turning quickly, he looked down to the hallway from where he came. He saw it just in time as a few more bursts of light of the flash splashing off the walls and then something in black cloth came flying from the far lateral hallway. Hitting the wall with a crack of plastic and a thud of meat, the body slid down till the floor stopped it, leaving a horrible crimson streak down the perfect white paint.

It took him a moment to register just what he saw. A body: a *dead* body just flopped to the ground before him. Not flopped, but flew. Gun shots, someone had shot this man so hard that he flew? Isn't that crap only in the movies? He took a few more steps back till he could meet the turn in the hallway, looking for ways to escape if he needed to get out of sight hurriedly. It would seem that maybe someone had gone postal on the job. Somehow the humor that he was part of the mail service didn't escape him at this moment.

Looking up the next hall caused him to double take as the carnage he just watched now faced him tenfold. This hall was longer than the one he'd come from and it was littered with more bodies, bleeding and torn apart, none of them moving. "Oh fucking Christ!"

Dan knew that wasn't done by a man with a gun, it was done by a complete psychopath.

His only choice was to keep moving down the hallway, knowing that the killer was on the other side of the basement. He started to walk carefully, trying to avoid stepping on any of the bodies or in any large puddles of blood. Not only did he not wish to leave a trail behind that could be used to find him, it was just sick. He just needed to find some stairs to get up out of this basement floor. Vegas no longer felt as big a priority as living did.

Dan moved quickly as he dared, checking each door only to find them locked. Looking down at the bodies, he now got a better look at the dead men and what they were dressed in. They all looked to be in matching uniforms, black fatigues covered in what must have been bullet proof vests. Pistols and submachine guns were strewn about the floor, discarded or shaken loose as their owners were ripped apart. Being this close to the mess made Dan's stomach roll and he pressed a hand to the wall so that he felt a little more stable.

Once again he was wrong; whatever was killing these men wasn't human. By the ripped and shredded limbs their killer had to be a monster. And it was good enough to kill trained security, well-armed security. Just what in the world was Dinatech?

Dan thought back to the warning on the computer monitor in the office. It was a biohazard symbol; they were all under an amber alert. "They built Godzilla, and he's gotten loose!" With that, Dan leaned over and lost his lunch.

Scrambling for control of himself, he wiped his mouth with the back of his hand and started up the hall again, skipping doors now as he tried to put some distance between himself and the murderer. Getting more desperate to find a way out, he fought off the panic that was eating at his ability to keep thinking. "This is just so fucked, what the hell am I doing here?"

No sooner had he said the words then a growl rumbled behind him. He didn't want to look, didn't believe that it was ever a good idea to look one's death in the eye. He would never be one of the brave people that he watched in the movies. He was more than happy to watch rather than be a part of it.

He'd just finished that thought when he was turning to look back the way he came, and saw the thing that growled walk around the corner. It had large amber eyes, and the stripes and orange markings told him that it wasn't a radioactive lizard that had an appetite for Asian buildings. Still, a tiger was out of place in this building.

The fur around the cat's legs and mouth was matted down with the blood of the security force that it just destroyed, and it was looking at Dan with clear thoughts of making him dessert.

Bad end.

He backed away from the cat just about as fast as he dared, while avoiding tripping over his own feet or the limbs of the fallen security force. Giving the feline an easy opening to land on him and rip his throat out didn't seem wise. He also didn't feel it was a good idea turn his back on the cat, giving it all the reason it needed run him down and maul the shit out of him. He'd once read that people in the jungles would wear masks on the back of their heads so the cats wouldn't think they could sneak up on them.

All the same, this wasn't working as well as he hoped. While the tiger wasn't running at him, it was starting to quickly fill the gap between the two of them. "Shoo, get," he heard himself say foolishly.

He didn't dare look back now, so he just had to guess about how far down the hall he was before the next turn. But he already could tell that it wasn't going to matter. The cat would be on him before he got another hundred feet, maybe even another door or two. Just as he was about to turn and run for it, he felt a hard tug on his shirt as he was gripped and pulled out of the hallway.

As he cleared a door way, he could see the cat realizing that his prey was going to get away and watched it lunge with all its might. If the floor wasn't made of tile, he would have been dead. As the cat couldn't get a good grip with its rear paws, its lunge was more of a feeble hop at him, coming up short.

With no balance Dan sprawled to the floor, letting his clipboard slide out before him with a clatter. Looking back to see his savior slam the door closed as there was a hard thump against the other side. The thump was followed by a muffled roar of the cat's frustration at losing its prey.

With her back pressed to the door she pushed the lock closed once more with a key that was settled in the deadbolt. Looking back down at him with those blue eyes of hers she gave him a once over and said, "Oh. Delivery boy." She frowned a little. "Shouldn't you have left already? Thought you were Steve."

Standing before him in the same form flattering sweater, she had on a long ankle length skirt, but out of place with the skirt sweater was the submachine gun strapped over her shoulder. She walked over a step or two. "Shoo?" She smiled softly down to him. "I'm not sure that would have worked on a house cat either." Her British accent was full of humor as she crouched down before him. "Did he get you at all?"

Dan was still a little stunned but was able to shake his head to the question. "No, it never got close enough." He looked around her at the door. "What hell is that thing doing in a place like this?" Dan thought about it for just a second longer before he started to clarify his question.

"What the hell is *this* place?"

Dan got his feet under him and pushed himself up. He still felt a little shaky after losing his lunch. Everything was happening so fast he hadn't had much of a chance to think. He looked over to the girl and she had a slight smile that only helped make her eyes brighten that much more. Even in this perilous moment, he couldn't help himself from admiring it.

He cleared his throat. "Well?"

His insistence caused the girl to blink and lose the smile before she looked back to the door that she'd just locked up. "What would I know about all that, hmm? I just greet visitors." Her voice was soft. She looked down at the SMG that was slung over her shoulder and she pulled it off and started to go about checking the gun. Pressing a button or two she ejected the clip and checked the ammo.

Dan frowned softly and took a few steps back, not sure if he was completely confident she knew what she was doing with that.

She slammed the clip back into the gun and rocked a lever on the back. "I'd say the real question that we should ask ourselves is how are we going to get out of here, hmm? Because I mean I'm off at five and I've been told I can't do overtime." She smiled a brilliant smile and started to walk around the perimeter of the room.

Dan followed with his eyes scanning the room; it was like they were locked in a jail cell. At least she had a key. There was a sturdy looking desk along one side of the room and on the other side was a large cage, something that could hold a larger animal, like maybe a vicious man eating tiger. The girl crouched down and looked in the door of the cage and frowned. "This is a computer controlled door, just like most of the labs on this floor." She stood up and glanced up at the ceiling. A steel cage covered it, so there was only one exit that he could see and it was out the same way the tiger was.

Dan watched as the girl went about assessing their situation and he knew there was something different about her; this was not a normal reaction for a receptionist put in this impossible situation. "Who are you?" he heard himself say before he thought about what he was saying.

She looked over to him and gave him a cute tweak of a smile. "Oh right, sorry about that." She pushed the weapon around behind her so that it was held against her back by the strap. "I'm Clara Paxton." She held out a hand. "Pleasure to meet you, Delivery Boy." She winked playfully.

Dan took her slender hand in his, then he nodded and gave a friendly shake before letting it go. She was just about a foot shorter than him; he stood right about six foot two. "Dan Hollis."

She smiled and went back to what she was doing, making her way over to the desk. "I like Dan a lot more than Delivery Boy. I think I'll use it." Her hands moved to the long thin drawer just under the desk top and she gave a pull, only to find it locked.

Dan frowned. Just on the other side of that door was one of the most horrific scenes that he'd seen in his life, yet this young woman could still find the energy for humor.

He started to wonder what she did for fun on the weekends.

"You know that cat is going to kill us right? You saw what it did to those other poor bastards out there right?"

"Yup," she said softly as she crouched down before the desk and started to try the next few drawers down the side. "That's why I locked the door; it was once held in here. I hope it can hold the blasted thing out for a few while I look around. That's the plan anyway."

He gave an exasperated exhale of breath and looked

over to the door and then back again. "So you know that it came from in here?"

Clara shook her head. "No, I'm just guessing as it's the first door that I found that was unlocked and open. But it could have come from one of the other rooms too. Maybe something else was held here? There could be some other large cat out there, maybe a wolf?" Clara said conversationally. "Do you think there could be a wolf? I think they are rather pretty." She then gave a hard tug at the larger drawer. The creak of the lock could be heard.

Frowning once more, Dan asked a little softer, "How can you joke about stuff like that right now?"

Clara looked back over at him a moment before propping a foot on the side the desk and leaning back in an attempt to break the lock, straining. "I'm not joking. I really like wolves, seeing them loping along in the snow. It's gorgeous." Giving one final tug, the lock that was only meant as a deterrent gave way, and the drawer came flinging open, causing the girl to stumble back a few steps.

"What are you looking for?" Dan asked.

"I'm looking for a hard line phone. I'm sure you have already tried to use your cell phone to call for help right? You aren't going to get any bars in this place, for sure not in this basement."

No, Dan hadn't thought about that until just now; and so just to test the point he took out his phone and flipped it open. Two things bothered him: one, how late it was. He should have already been most of the way back to base. Two, he didn't have any reception at all. A little red X currently lived where his signal meter usually resided. With a sigh, he closed the phone, stuffing it back into his pocket.

Clara gave him a look that said she knew just how he was feeling right now before crouching to look through the drawer that she'd just broken open.

Reaching into the drawer she pulled out everything and started tossing it haphazardly onto the desktop. Inside was a box of latex free gloves, a box of cotton balls, a tray of empty syringes with no tips, a few other odds and ends, medical supplies, and the most important part, no phone of any kind.

"Can't we just stay here? I mean, I'm sure they will send in the army or something to deal with that cat and we'll be rescued?"

Behind him came a thump at the door and a muffled growl that caused Dan to jump. Clara raised a brow, looking over Dan's shoulder at the door. "I think that the smarter thing to do would be to get out of here before the tiger finds his way back in. Something odd about its behavior." She walked back over for the door even as the cat rattled the lock in the striker plate.

He looked a little confused and turned to follow her movement across their cell once again. "If you were looking to get out why didn't you just leave through the front door? You were right there."

She shook her head. "It was no good, I did try that after the alert was broadcast, but things went downhill really fast. The automated security on the building locked all the doors." Clara frowned, thinking about it. "I mean, I even tried to toss my office chair through the window. It wasn't having it."

Dan couldn't do anything more than blink at the thought of her trying to slam her chair thought the charcoal black glass.

"I knew you were making a delivery so I hoped that the dock doors where still open." Clara went on. "But, if you're here, then I guess not."

She pressed her back against the wall right next to the door. "I have to say it's not a good day to be wearing a skirt to work, but at least I wore flats and not some stupid pair of heels. Father always taught me that you need to keep your shoes sensible."

He walked over to look through the items that she left behind on the desk and sifted through them in the hopes she somehow missed the phone. "I don't think this is what your father was talking about."

"Yes it was." She looked at him, her eyes piercing him for just a moment. "Okay maybe not a murder-crazed tiger, but pretty much this? Yeah." She pulled the SMG off her back and pressed herself up against it a little harder. "Dan, would be you be a sweetheart and come over here next to me? You don't want to be standing over there once I turn the lock."

Dan did as he was told. He felt he better comply, because the crazy girl was going to remove the only thing that kept them from being eaten. "You're going to do what?"

"I'm going to unlock the door and let it in."

"Are you crazy, it's going to kill us!"

"I'm actually far more level headed than you right now, I might say."

"You might want to rethink that, you just said you wanted to let a man eating tiger into this room."

"I don't plan to stay in here once the cat is through the door. If you feel your chances are better, feel free to hang out here with the feline." Clara then flipped a small switch on the gun that he was pretty sure was the safety.

34

"If you please Dan, I've been told I need a little work on my close quarters shooting so could you stand to my left?"

He eyed the young woman with beautiful blue eyes, wondering who would have told her any such thing.

With that, she reached over and started to turn the key, and Dan took the hint and swiped his digital clipboard up off the floor and dived to press into the wall as much as he could manage. He made it just as the deadbolt clicked free of the door frame.

She started to pull the key from the lock when the door exploded open and just under a half ton of orange tiger came slamming through. Clara pulled her hand back in one swift motion and grabbed onto whatever part of Dan she could; her fingers hooked into his shirt. Her right hand squeezed the trigger while pulling the butt into her shoulder. She fired off what Dan would later realize was a series of small controlled bursts. Round after around peppered the cat, causing it to fall back into the far corner like it understood that it was being shot at.

With a fluid movement she pulled him behind her out into the hallway. Once he realized what she was doing he complied and jumped his way back out the door before the tiger could turn and lunge at them. The cat's large frame hit the door and slammed it into the frame with a loud bang. The pressure would have broken any average door in half.

"Shit, I didn't get the key!" she called back to him. "Move! Head for the stairs!" She started to run down the hallway back the direction that Dan had come, and he moved to follow her. She stopped at the first body and pulled the submachine gun off it with a few rough tugs, also grabbing a pistol out of an under arm holster as well.

Getting up suddenly, Clara turned to run back and when the two of them collided she stumbled back a few steps. "Christ Dan, I told you to run for the stairs!"

Dan tried to catch her but she pushed his hand off, and he pulled it back like she was made of fire as she was using the machinegun to do the pushing. "I thought that you *were* going for the stairs!"

"This is the way to the docks! We need to get out of this basement before Mister No Opposable Thumbs learns how to open doors."

As if trying to prove a point, the cat slammed his body full into the door which caused a loud ear ringing bang that echoed through the halls.

Clara walked back past him at a quickened pace, keeping the firearm trained on the cat's door as they passed it once again, and then she took them down another hall, this one dimmer than the rest of the floor. Looking up, Dan saw that most of the lights in this part of the hall were shot out; here is where most of the security must have made their last stand.

The thick walls were shot up with rounds, the chips littered the floor. The shards of glass that had rained down from the broken lights crunched under his shoes. A few more security officers' bodies were lying along the sides of the halls, but they did not die alone; the two walked into what made up a small lobby area where three elevator shafts were built into the far wall. Lying about the floor were three bullet riddled female lions, easily recognized by their lack of mane.

The image of what happened started to come rather clear into his head as Clara walked along the carnage before him, the story playing out in the back of his mind. The amber alert went to the security office and they were told to respond to the break out of the many dangerous and crazy creatures they kept locked up in here. Doing a rough count of what he'd seen so far, there were about seven of them in the security detail.

Looking over to the damage around the far left elevator, the security team must have come down on that car. Surprised by the cats already here…

Clara frowned and walked around what looked like the remains of a chewed up lab worker. He knew very well what the security found when they walked out of the elevator. He wondered where the rest of the workers of this floor had gone, and if they had gotten away like the dockworker.

Dan looked up at Clara to avoid looking at the bodies. "What the hell do they work on here that requires so many large cats?"

She walked over to a large door that was marked 'Stairs' and tried the door handle. When it didn't turn, she tried to shoulder the door just to make sure she couldn't force it open. "You haven't heard of Dinatech before?" Clara actually seemed a little surprised at this.

When Dan shook his head silently no, she went on. "Well they are one of the larger chip manufactures in the world—you know, micro computing." She nodded to the small clipboard that he was still, for some reason, holding onto. "I bet that has about a half a dozen parts that were made by this company." She took a step back from the door and started to look it over. "I'm willing to bet some of those same chips could be found in this door. The whole damn building is computer controlled. The locks, windows, lights…everything in the place is connected together. There isn't a standalone computer that I've ever seen."

He looked confused. "Well that's interesting and all that, but that don't explain why they have all these cats in here?"

She smiled. "How much do you think I'm going to know about it, Delivery Boy? This floor is restricted; it's not even talked about in any of the fire evacuation drills. I just greet people when they come in the door."

"I thought you weren't going to call me Delivery Boy anymore?"

"Did I? Well it's starting to grow on me. Anyway, this place is their Advanced Research Center, it's all RnD and black ops kind of crap. That's really all I've ever heard about it. If you don't have clearance, you don't ask about it." She looked back over to the hallway they had left the tiger in as the banging from the door stopped completely, leaving the floor in a disturbing silence. It was quiet enough that Dan could hear the pounding of his heart echoing off the walls around them.

He slipped a few steps to be closer to Clara. "So, if this is a restricted floor, how did you get down here exactly?" he said, quietly leaning his head over just a little so that he could keep the conversion to just above a breath.

She seemed to feel that it was warranted and kept the same low tone. "I took the elevators." She paused for a long moment. "But I'm not sure that I'd take them right now."

It seemed like the best option that they had for themselves right now, and he walked over to press the call button. Clara watched him for a moment while an internal struggle played out in her mind. She reached over to put a hand on his saying, "Wait." But it was too late, he'd already pressed the button.

The doors on the far left opened, the one with the damage around the door housing. He walked over to get in but stopped and he could feel the blood draining from his face as he looked over the remains of what must have been the rest of the staff that was working on this floor.

Chapter NEXT

The image of how everything went down changed quickly in Dan's head. The security staff must have come from the stairs, the scene before them one of these monster cats ripping and shredding their handlers as they were trying to escape by the elevator.

"My god," Dan said as he shook his head, taking a step back from the carnage.

Clara looked sympathetic as she walked forward. "Sorry, I tried to warn you."

Dan was about to say something more, but the two of them turned their heads to look back along the hall they had come down. Their attention was grabbed by the low growl that was quickly getting louder.

With no more time available to them, Clara slung one machine gun over her shoulder and pushed the other into his hands, keeping the pistol handy while she gripped his upper arm and shoved him into the gruesome car of death.

He wanted to protest and suggest they wait for one of the other cars at least, but he already knew that they were out of time. If they were going to get out of here, this was their best option…wasn't it?

Clara seemed to think so. She let go of his arm and used the side of her hand to wrack all the buttons at once like all the kids that you see in hotels who enjoy watching each and every button light up.

But the elevator didn't seem to be doing anything, and Dan started to look over the weapon that Clara had stuffed into his hands, worried that he might have to use it. He'd fired a few rifles in his life, but this was the first time that he'd ever even held anything of a military grade; it felt cold yet powerful, awkward and complex. Like when you go to smoke for the first time, not sure how to hold it. Would she think less of him because of it? Was Clara expecting him to shoot and kill the tiger? For him to protect her? Because he was a man, so he must surely be born with the ability to hold and fire anything that uses bullets.

A grinding noise jerked his thoughts back to what was happening around him and he looked to see one of the elevator doors half close. The other didn't move at all, and then the floor dropped out from below him. Both Clara and he had to grab one of the hand rails screwed to the wall to keep from falling. Thinking wiser of dropping a loaded weapon to the floor he let the clipboard computer clatter to the floor of the elevator.

Just as quickly as the elevator car fell, it started to rise, and he could watch the floors move before him through the open door. He felt a sudden heaviness in his joints.

Clara called out to be heard over the loud grinding of the elevator in the shaft around them. "I meant to tell you, when I took my last trip it was acting kind of funny."

He looked over at her trying to give her his best silent *You have to be fucking kidding me?* look. He couldn't tell by

41

the bright and charming smile that she gave him back if he'd gotten through or not.

The ride was less like an elevator and more like a rollercoaster you'd find at Six Flags. Quickly, the floors flipped down below them as the car raced. About ten floors up, the car didn't come to a stop but instead just let go, dropping into a free fall. As his stomach flipped over, Dan looked to the floor counter to see just how far up they were, but the red LED display only showed little red triangles.

The bodies, Clara, and Dan got jostled about in the car and soon enough, he let the firearm drop too in an attempt to keep himself close to the floor of the car. For some reason this felt like the safe place to be when they bounced off the bottom of the shaft. Waiting for his life to flash before his eyes, the car came to a stop at the second and a half floor, and the contents of the car slapped into the bottom with a hollow metal ring as blood and loose objects splashed about like they were in a blender. He was face down and he groaned as he felt the pain in his knees and elbows when they hit the hardest. But it wasn't all bad; he was pressed half atop Clara and she was looking up at him. He felt himself staring into her blue eyes. The curve of her body and the press of her chest into his were nice, and he shamelessly enjoyed it in silence. He felt the weight of other things press against his back and he swallowed, trying to keep the words 'human' and 'bodies' from coming to mind. The pleasantness of the moment was quickly lost. "I think I'm going to be sick again."

"I'd say you should stick your head out the window to clear your head, but I think that would be suicide right now."

He gave her a look as the elevator started to rise once more and he had to strain with his arms to keep from crushing Clara under his increasing weight.

The elevator surged up once again followed by another small drop before everything came still. The both of them waited unmoving to make sure the elevator was done before they started to pick themselves up. Pulling himself out from under the dead bodies, Dan rolled off Clara and staggered to his feet, trying to find balance. His first thought was that he wanted to help her up, but he needed get out of this coffin. He dived out of the elevator as he felt the first wave hit him and it took all his willpower to find a trashcan before he lost anything that might have been left in his stomach.

Clara tossed the two submachine guns out of the elevator, and then his clipboard, before she pulled herself up out of the offset elevator, pistol in hand. She looked around the area for a moment checking to make sure there was nothing that was going to jump out and attack them.

This floor was built drastically different from the basement they had just left. The walls were made of a nice expensive looking wood paneling; he got the feeling this area wouldn't be used for handling dangerous felines of the world. This was home to management staff by the looks.

Looking up at her over the trashcan, he grunted, his tone accusing, "Did that happen the last time you were on it?"

"Maybe. Not that bad last time."

"You could have warned me."

"I guess I should have asked Tigger to wait while we discussed our options then?" she responded casually.

Falling back from the trashcan he laid back against the wall, slumping down till he was almost sprawled on the floor; his head pushed forward so his chin pressed against his chest. "I'm sure this is doing plenty for my cool factor, huh?" He looked up to see Clara crouched over him. As he said this, she smiled softly and even her body language seemed to change as she slid over, sitting next to him on the floor and pressing her back to the wood paneled wall.

"I think you're doing a lot better than other people would do in your situation, Delivery Boy." Her words actually sounded rather comforting as she said them. While she talked to him, she pulled her long hair back over her shoulder.

She took the pistol and pulled the clip checking the bullets before slamming it back into the gun.

He really didn't have time think about it before, but this girl seemed to really know her way around firearms. Unlike himself, she didn't even have to look to know what levers to press.

When they were in the cell room with the tiger she pulled off easy, controlled shots and kept moving. The skills and fortitude that she had been displaying were far from just that of a simple receptionist working in a technology company.

Another thing that just came to mind, she'd not been bothered or disturbed by the fact they have been surrounded gruesome death, not even sick in the slightest as he'd been. Twice.

Who was she?

She finished checking the pistol and set it on the floor before them with the other two guns. "We have one Berretta 9mm with thirteen rounds, two MP5s, one with thirty rounds and the other with twenty rounds." She reached behind her, pulling her sweater up just enough to uncover a second clip tucked into the waistband of her skirt, pulled it out and tossed it to the floor with the rest of the weapons. It landed with a heavy thump. "One clip with twenty six rounds." She turned to him and asked softly, "Have you ever used an MP5 before Dan?"

He looked back to her in a state of bewilderment. "Have you?"

She now looked a little confused by the question as she nodded. "I'd hope so. One of us is going to need to be able to use them; they are dead useful in close quarters combat."

"That's not what I meant; I mean how in the world do you know what you're doing here? Do they teach all their receptionists how to use firearms and deal with tigers?" With a pause he added, "…and death?"

"No, about the only thing they have taught me was how to use the meeting room scheduler and the phone so that I could tell people when they had guests. It's actually a rather cake job for the pay. I'm really glad father's friend told me about it."

For the first time since he met her, those lovely eyes lost that small light of humor that always played there and she looked back to the train wreck of an elevator. "I'm just glad that he wasn't on duty today, I don't think I could have handled that. "

So the mystery that was Clara could at least feel something for the situation after all.

She reached over and pulled one of the MP5s to herself and pulled the clip, un-chambering the bullet in the breech. She caught the bullet and handed the MP5 to him. It felt considerably lighter without the ammo in it. She put the bullet back into the clip and set it aside before scooting in closer, the soft curve of her hip pressing into his side. "There really are just a few things you need to know to use this gun. This is nothing more than a fully automatic 9mm pistol so the kick won't be too bad, but make sure you have a good grip before firing it." She then pointed out the safety, how to expel a bad cartridge, and re-cock the weapon. "All the rest this baby needs I can handle for you." She smiled at him. "Maybe once we are out of here I could show you a bit more if you'd like?"

He took in the information the best that he could. He got the basic idea and felt he caught on easy enough. With her this close, he caught a lavender scent on the air. It caused him to ask his question softer than he intended to, in a whisper. "You still haven't told me how you know how to do all this."

"Haven't I? Oh, well I grew up in a military family. Mostly with Daddy." She reached back and picked up the clip, placing it in his lap. "You have twenty rounds. Don't use them unless you have to. I don't think we are going to find anymore up here and I don't want to accidently shoot people."

"So your dad taught you how to use a gun? I've known a few other families in the military and they didn't go about teaching them firearms."

Clara smiled and took up the second MP5, checking the ammo once more before slinging it back over her shoulder. "Daddy thought that it would better prepare me for dating."

Yeah, this girl is nuts.

Dan wasn't sure what look he'd just given her but, it seemed to be the key for her to smile again. "Yeah, I hear that you're far less intimidated when you know how to handle yourself," Clara said.

"I have to say, you've got some rather strange parents. I mean your mom just went along with this?" He pulled out his cell phone to check, but still there were no bars, just the little red X blinking at him, taunting him. He checked the time. It was just after two; he'd already been stuck in this building for just over an hour. Forgetting the rest of work, he'd have to get out of here soon if he was going to make his trip to Vegas. That would be assuming that the cops let him go when they finally got in here to see the wreckage that now made up the basement area.

Clara shrugged softly and got up, dusting off her skirt. She bent over picking up the pistol. "Well once my dad came back from the Gulf War, they kind of separated. I was more raised by Daddy after that. He was about done with the service. He said he'd always felt that he'd given all that he needed to give. He wanted to spend more time with his first love, me." She turned on the spot looking down at herself with a sigh. "I should have worn something with pockets. Get up, Delivery Boy." She held out the pistol and the extra clip. "Try not to lose them okay?"

Stuffing the ammo and the pistol into his pocket with a little more hesitation, Dan watched as Clara started to walk down the hallway for the office area. "We should go see if we can find some kind of working phone." Dan nodded and picked up his clipboard before following after her; it had been with him this far, no reason to leave it behind now.

The hallway was dark. Only the amber emergency lighting illuminated anything. "So where is everyone that should be working on this floor?"

"Most of the employees are off today. There is some kind of offsite, I was told. The only people in the building are those that have to keep the place running and those that feel they need to work even on their days off."

"What about you?" Dan asked.

She looked back to him for a moment; he could still see her blue eyes even in the dim light around them. "I'm paid to be here Monday through Friday no matter who's on site. So you got lucky this time, Delivery Boy." She laughed softly as they walked into a larger space with a small cluster of couches and a line of doors that led into different personal offices.

Walking up to the first door on the row, Clara tried the handle and found that it opened easily compared to the doors down in the basement. The security here was much more relaxed. Dan walked in behind her and the two were in a small office no larger than nine by nine with a large wooden desk splitting the middle between employee and visitor.

Clara moved around and slid into the employee's seat; she wasn't even in it a minute before she was adjusting the height settings on the poor guy's chair. Dan rolled his eyes and settled into the seat across the desk; it didn't have any adjustments that he could play with.

Looking over the phone, the little LCD screen wasn't lit up. It looked dead lying there on the desk. Clara picked the phone up and brought the receiver to her ear to confirm what they already suspected, giving him a small shake of her head.

Getting up from the chair, he left the dark office and moved to the next door, opening it into a similar office—except this time he could see that the occupant was a

Portland Trailblazers fan by the posters kept on the walls. He moved around the desk and saw another dark phone; he picked it up to find that it was also dead.

He tried a few more offices, leaving the doors open to each one until he was about five doors down from where he left Clara. Giving up, he flopped back into the office chair in the last room and rubbed his temples. With a little frown he thought that the chair was a bit high and so he let the air out of the cylinder. *There, that was a lot more comfortable.* He sat there for just a moment before he said. "All the phones in this area seem to be dead." He set his clipboard down on the desk. "I'm not even sure this floor has power."

There was a soft "Mmm" from Clara's commandeered office but nothing more.

"Why does this place have armed security? This place has…had…its own SWAT force behind it."

"Well the person that got me the job here works for security and he told me that because of some of the government projects they take on, it's a requirement against terrorists. Or something to that effect." Her voice sounded a little strained, like she was working hard with something. "He never told me more than that, and one thing I've learned with military types is that you don't go asking for more."

"What are you doing in there?" he asked, getting up from his seat as he leaned around the door to the office Clara was still in. He looked in just in time to see Clara climb out from under the desk.

Pulling herself up into the seat, her face was lit up by the no longer dormant flat panel computer monitor on the desk. "I was just unplugging and plugging in the terminal, to see if I could unlock it and get some information on what happened."

Dan moved around to see if her plan had worked. It was finished with its BIOS check and the same Dinatech logo he had seen before flashed large across the screen. This time it was red and reminded Dan of blood. After another moment of loading the screen, it looked the same as the one down in the bay office. A wide red bar scrolled across the bottom and in black letters, with the biohazard logo on either end, was the words "Amber Alert."

"What does that mean?" Dan questioned.

"I was told in my training when I see a warning like this I had to call security first, then call my manager for further instructions. It sounded serious, but not enough to question it in very much detail when I was in training. From the way they made it sound, it was something that was so bad it wouldn't come up. And if it did, it would be obvious what to do."

"What did security say when you called them?"

"That they were looking into why it had come up and that was all I ever heard from them. The phone died in the reception area before I could make my call to my boss." As Clara sat back in her chair she thought back, looking for details of what happened. "It was soon after that my computer shutdown and so I thought that I should check the evacuation areas to see if I was the only one stupid enough to still be in the building. That's when I found out that we were locked in."

"You said they work in government contracts that need to be secured from terrorists right? But they had lions, tigers…and I'm sure many other wicked beasts."

"Lions, Tigers, and Bears oh my?" Clara interrupted.

"Do you think they are working on something that

could be considered an airborne attack? Like a breathable poison?" Dan pointed to the biohazard symbols as they scrolled across the screen.

Clara frowned softly and shook her head. "I don't think that that they are working in anything like that. This place is too close to people. I'd expect that they would be working in something like a new laser or a computer that could hack every Facebook and Twitter page in the U.S. Think of all the professional sports players and superstars that would be lost in the world." She kept talking while she typed away franticly at the computer, her only pauses to brush her fingers back through her hair. At the top of the computer screen, the cursers kept showing in small letters "Login error." She frowned at it a little and sighed, pausing as she thought silently.

Dan waited a moment before asking at long last. "Are you trying to hack in or something?"

"I'm just trying to log myself in, but it's not taking my information or anyone that works the front desk."

Dan cocked a brow at this. "You know the passwords for everyone that works at reception?"

"Sure, it's not like we have any real access and we are always covering for one another. I'm sure with a little work you could figure out most of our passwords, it's always silly things like 'gummy bears' or 'Romulan.'" She smiled brightly up at him. "I bet you can't guess mine." She fluttered her eyes at him before eyeing the screen, like if she stared long enough it would give up its secrets in a blinking contest.

Dan couldn't tell if she was flirting with him or not. Either way, he wasn't sure what to do with her witty humor. But before he could think of anything useful to retort with, her brows shot up. In fact she all but jumped up in the seat as she leaned forward to start typing on the keyboard once more.

"What?" he asked softly so as to not disturb her while she worked through this epiphany.

With a giggle she clapped her hands together and scooted back from the desk, letting Dan lean in to watch as the computer became an active a window with a black background and red block text filling it.

It seemed to be some kind of report.

"How did you get into this?"

"We have an emergency login for when there is some kind of disaster. That way, if a recovery team has to come into the building they will have one way to access a computer and communicate with others during the disaster. It's got a forum setup that can record where the note was posted from and stuff like that." Clara waved her hand dismissively. "I can't say that I was really listening when they were doing our orientation."

Text started to scroll across the screen:

At 12:46 there was a detected threat to the main core and first steps were taken to protect main frame.

At 12:51 first steps failed to protect core, threat detected to have compromised security, locking down.

At 13:10 suspected terrorist activity, taking final measures.

<<<ddsfd44%#(#$@>>>>>

%   %
% MY HAIR IS LIKE LITTLE TENDRILS %
**   %   THAT FLOAT INTO**

SPACE   %
   %   %

Dan blinked at the last part and he leans in a little more. "Hey Clara, I can't tell who wrote that last one?"

Clara shook her head softly and pushed him back that she could look closer herself. "Umm, that wasn't written by anyone that I can see; it seems to be in the general note. It would explain why the building is locked down. I wonder if the core really has been compromised." She added after a short pause, "That would be very bad."

"Why? What does that mean?"

"This place isn't like a regular computer setup. In this building, not only is all the security run through it, but *everything* is running through the core. This computer that we are working on right now, every computer in the building, is nothing more than a terminal that runs a virtual session that is part of the core."

Dan looked at her blankly.

"What I'm getting at is if they control the core, they own the building. They know what we are doing and can do anything they want with it."

Dan looked up and around the room looking to see if there was some camera watching them. He didn't see anything but lowered his voice. "You don't see an issue with that statement? One computer to run them all?"

She raised one thin sculpted brow as she looked back up at him as he leaned over her chair. "I didn't build it; I'm just telling you what I know. From what I've been told it was also supposed to be impossible to hack through. They wouldn't be able to get through one layer; if they did it would just be shut down and rebuilt."

Dan laughed and turned, sitting on the edge of the desk. "What you're telling me…what you're saying is, that we are in a technological Titanic." He started to laugh more and rubbed his hands over his face. "Oh man. Look out for ice."

"You know when you put it like that, everything looks so much brighter." She scooted forward to type a few more keystrokes before taking up the mouse to click a few windows. "I'm not able to get out to any of the corporate sites. It would seem this building has been isolated, or it's cut off from the outside. I don't know if anyone is coming for us, and I don't see any other entries, so I don't know if there is anyone else alive in the building."

Dan took a long breath and stood up. "Well I'm not going to go down with this ship. Do you know how we get out of here?" He quickly added, "That isn't through man eating cats."

With a tired sigh she got up from the desk. "We can take a look over the main floor, there has to be somewhere that we can push through or blowup." She walked for the door.

"We are going to have to find our way into the stairwell so that we can make our way down. Fuck that elevator. You know this damn place is not up to fire code right?"

"I'm sure if the computer was working correctly it'd be just fine. Fire code isn't that hard to fake."

Stepping out of the darkness, he walked along the bodies. The air tasted like copper pennies from all the blood. His breathing was controlled; his hands were at the ready. He knew what needed to be done as he moved around corners in the hallways with the red speckled walls. Just as he expected, there stood the Lion, the large male of the pride they had in medical. The cat watched as he came into view; it looked every bit the proud hunter that it should be. But he was a hunter too.

The rumble in the back of the cat's throat told him the Lion knew it too.

The voice talked to him, "Only one of you can live through this."

"I don't need you to tell me this; it's something that I can see." He mumbled to the voice with no body.

He was a soldier, a weapon of war, destruction-packed and ready to explode. He reached down and pulled out his combat knife from his leg holster. Turning the blade once in his hand he got a feel for the weapon as the cat started to growl again, warning him away.

It finally perceived the danger that was before it, and now the two moved slowly at one another, trying to find the others' weakness, to make the other run.

The cats were hyper aggressive, created to be man eaters.

No more waiting.

Like an explosion, the two leapt at one another, the cat more than twice his weight slamming him back. He felt the claws raking into his shoulder. It was all the opening that he needed, the body exposed. With both his muscled arms, he plunged the knife into the Lion's neck, keeping the deadly teeth from getting at him and ending him.

Using all the adrenaline that he could command, he pulled down hard, ripping apart the throat and muscles that connected the cat's head to its body as they both slapped into the wall and tumbled to the cold hard floor.

The cat squalled in its last throws of life before

slumping to the floor atop him. Pushing the carcass off him, he stood up and put a boot on the side of its head, pulling the blade free. He looked up the hall and then back down the other way. The voice told him it was time to get out; it was time to leave this place. We all know the only way to truly get away, and that is through your enemy.

Slipping into the darkness, he once more became like a ghost.

In the hall just past the offices, Dan and Clara looked over another locked door to the staircase. He ran his tongue over his teeth, sucking in as he felt the pressure starting to build in the back of his head.

"I just wanted to be in Vegas tonight," he mumbled softly to himself as he pushed down on the handle once more in the hope that he could force the door open. Clara watched him with a slightly amused look from across the hall.

"Hmm? What was that?"

"I just want to get out of here. I'm supposed to be getting off work early so that I could fly out to Vegas tonight."

Clara laughed softly and walked over to him. "Not what you had in mind for a night of fun huh?" She reached over and put a hand on the door pushing on it a little. "I'm sorry to say I'm glad that I'm not in this alone, if it's any consolation, Delivery Boy."

He didn't bother to correct her anymore.

It did make him feel a little better, made him feel more important than he'd been feeling most of this little adventure. She'd been the one doing most of the leading, most of the work. Still he could appreciate the need to have someone on your side. He remembered just how lonely and lost he felt when he was trying to find his way through the basement.

He frowned at the door. "Do you think that we could shoot through the lock?" he asked, trying to prove that he could come up with ideas too and be helpful.

She frowned in thought as she ran slender fingers over the cool metal of the door knob. "No you really can't just shoot locks out like the movies. I don't think a nine mil could make it through the lock anyway, but it could go through the door maybe. If we can weaken the door around the lock, perhaps kick it the rest of the way through."

So much for that, Dan thought to himself.

But he still wanted to help, so he stepped back and held the MP5 up, looking to line it up with the door. He tightened his grip on the weapon while Clara moved to stand behind him. "Just try to miss the metal; I'd hate to get a bullet bouncing around in here."

Now that's just what he wanted to hear before firing a pistol for the first time ever. She did reach under his arm from behind as she pressed in to help him fix his stance. The gun felt much more comfortable in his hands now, or was it just that Clara was touching him? He took and held a breath before he pulled the trigger and felt the gun start to jerk and buck in his hands like a cat trying to get loose, the butt pushing back into his shoulder with a bite. The wood of the door came apart in chunks, as it was no match for the lead pounding into it at supersonic speed.

Dan eyes blinked at the first pop and flash of the gun.

As the fully automatic gun kept spitting lead, he found himself squinting to watch his progress. It was almost over as fast as it started—he'd emptied all twenty rounds of the clip into the door. Letting go of the trigger, his whole arm had gone limp, yet he could still feel it shaking with the effort of holding on. Smoke filled the hallway and it smelled like someone had let off too many firecrackers.

Clara moved around him now and walked up to the door. "That used almost a third of our ammo; let's see if it was worth it, hmm?" It was hard to hear her over the ringing in his head. She pointed to a spot just behind the lock before she ran her finger over the splintered wood. "It may take a few well-placed kicks to get the lock to give way."

She took a few steps back, and Dan took that as his queue that he should get to work chopping wood, so to speak. He set the gun on the floor on the far side of the hallway before kicking brass shells out of the way to avoid tripping on them. At the clink of metal he looked down and frowned as he just realized that Clara hadn't touched a single one as she walked; her movements were silent.

Shrugging it off as a mystery to answer later, he kicked the door as close to the damage as he could get. Putting as much power as he could behind each one, he got the door rattling in the lock, but it didn't give way. Taking a few heavy breaths, he reared up once more and put all the force he could muster behind this one, feeling a slight pain the along the back of his hip as his body protested the rough treatment. All those old football injuries of his high school days came back to gripe at him. Still, the extra effort paid off: this time he heard a nice healthy crack as the wood started to break around the lock. After a few more hits in rapid succession the door gave way, opening as the knob came free from the rest of the door. The last kick blasted the door open and it slapped off the far wall of the stairwell beyond, the control wires still holding the useless lock to the door by a thread.

Laughing softly behind him Clara clapped her hands. "Oh, my hero." She moved forward to push the door open and look out beyond, the thick black painted 19 on the far wall. "Yup. We can get down to the next floor, but it looks like the fire doors are closed beyond that." She leaned over to look down before she slipped back into the hall letting the ruined door clank and crunch closed by the hydraulics.

She picked up the empty MP5 and slipped a hand in to dig around in his pocket. Dan had to will himself to not squirm too much with how familiar she was being with him. Pulling out the extra clip, she slapped it into the weapon, racking the first bullet into the chamber. Turning on the safety, she slung it over her shoulder before she opened the door into the stairwell.

Dan couldn't help but notice that she kept her hand on the gun as she looked up and down the stair well beyond. He'd just grasped that she was watching for something.

"Are you expecting us to be attacked?"

Clara looked over her shoulder at him; the gold in her brown hair was easy to see with the brighter lighting of the stairwell.

"The report said that there was someone trying to get into the computer; I've seen *Diehard*, thank you very much. I'd rather not be caught flat footed. Or barefooted."

He wasn't sure if she was kidding, or telling the truth; in the back of his mind there was a small nagging feeling that she might be a few cards short of a full deck. Who in their right mind would sign up for that elevator ride twice, for one thing? He'd never met a girl that preferred learning how to use a gun over hitting the malls with friends. He also knew that he found himself attracted to her. She was strong and self-reliant; he enjoyed that part of her, as much as one could while being trapped in an episode of Indiana Jones and the Building of Doom, anyway.

"Besides now I have a machine gun, ho, ho,ho." Clara called call back to him.

Yup, she's crazy.

Chapter AFTER

With Clara in the lead, they took the stairs down to the next floor, standing in front of another large thick door with one major difference: this one was not made of wood like the upper floors. This closed and sealed fire door looked about as impregnable as a bank vault.

They were as far down the stairwell as they could go until they found the controls to open the monstrous security door. "What are they trying to keep out with this?" Dan ran his hand over the large hydraulic piston; it could shrug off large bomb blasts like they were firecrackers. Whatever they wanted to keep in or out, this would do the trick.

Still, while they couldn't go down anymore, they were able to reach the access door to the lower level. Clara stepped up to the door leading into the eighteenth floor and put a finger on the key hole for a mechanical lock. "That's something that most of the other doors don't have," she said, softly letting her British accent purr. "Now why would that be?" She scrunched up her chin in thought, then with a shrug, she grabbed the handle and opened the door. She flashed him a smile. "Something to think about another time, hmm?" She slipped inside and

Dan moved to quickly to catch the door before it closed.

"You knew that it was going to be open, didn't you?" He slipped in to find that they were in a well-lit lobby. The elevators were off to their left with three hallways that ran off in each direction, making a T-shape. On the wall before the hallway that ran down the middle was a sign that said, "Dinatech Robotics."

This made Dan feel nervous, and as he met Clara's eyes he could tell that she was feeling the same thing.

If someone was going to take over a building, this would be the floor they would want to take.

She didn't say anything though; she just waved for him to follow along.

"Shouldn't we be trying to get through the fire door?" he asked softly.

"How would you like to do that? These guns aren't going to get through it. Let's see if there is something that we could use to cut through it in here. They work with metals I'm sure; maybe we can find a torch."

Down the main hall, they soon came to the first door. Clara pressed on the door carefully, finding that like most of the other doors in the building, it was locked. Looking down to the right there was an RF reader that could read security badges. The LED on it was flashing between red, green, and yellow.

"How do you plan to get through this little problem?" he asked softly.

Clara thought about it while staring at the lock, and about the time that Dan didn't think she was going to say anything she snapped her fingers. "It's the only way," she said softly. "Wait here, Delivery Boy." Clara turned and walked back for the stair well.

Watching her go, he was now left in the silence of the

area. All he could hear were the air conditioners that were, luckily, still running. After a few minutes of standing there waiting he could hear another noise. He wasn't sure exactly what it was, but it sounded almost like an electric motor. His nerves were starting to get the better of him now; he'd been in this stressful position for too long, stuck in here with Crazy, the nickname he'd decided to use for Clara.

He also thought that Crazy was taking too long. What was she after anyway? He should have just gone with her. Turning to walk back to the stairs, he found that she was standing there watching him.

He frowned. "What?"

She shook her head, holding up a blood splattered key card. "I may not get sick, but I don't like bodies any more than you do," she said in a voice that told him she was not in a comfortable place right now.

Walking back, she looked over the badge reader once more and then pressed the plastic card to the reader. It didn't make a beep, more of a growling buzz that didn't seem very inviting. Clara pressed at the door and it seemed like it wanted to open but it wasn't willing to put any effort into it. She swiped at the RF reader again and when the same grinding noise came again, Dan reared back and kicked the door as hard as he could.

With a metal-on-metal pop the door flew open and bounced off the end of its guide. Slamming against inside walk, it made a bang that echoed around them as the inside knob dug into the drywall with a crunch. The kick was a lot more devastating than he expected.

Clara looked back at him with that same raised brow once more. "A little pent up rage?" She smiled and moved into the room before the door could come back to a close. Dan followed behind her while she clipped the tag to the end of her sweater. Because of the blood, he couldn't make out whose tag it might have been.

Beyond the door was the whitest room he'd ever seen: white walls, white desks, white floor and ceiling. It looked like one of those space age clean rooms from your standard sci-fi movie. In contrast, all the stainless steel equipment stood out even more. There were saws, drills, grinders, and some tools that even Dan couldn't tell what they would be used for. All of it looked to be created for the use of working metal into the perfect shape. He also guessed that in this case it was used for making the robots.

One thing became apparent to him: the lack of any product or any robots of any kind. He felt that something wasn't right. Through the middle of the long room was a table, Clara started to walk down one side of it while Dan walked along the other.

"I'd say that this would be our ticket through that door; we just need to find something that is strong enough to cut armor plate, and that we can carry back to the door," Clara said.

Of course Clara's father showed her all about how to breach a door with a cutting torch or some military tool that could rip a door apart. He could almost see a seven-year-old version of her in the back of his mind, her father holding the sparker as he showed the young girl the right settings for an acetylene regulator, and Clara nodding along, absorbing everything as daddy spoke.

Dan was pulled back to reality as he heard that same electric whirr he'd heard before, but this time it was a lot louder. He knew for sure that it was not his imagination. And he knew that Clara heard it as well, because she had slowed her step, becoming more alert.

She looked over at him in puzzlement; Clara was looking to him for answers? This didn't bode well; she knew more about this place that he did, more than he ever wanted to know about it. Apparently, Dan thought, giving her a vacant look was the right move, because she moved forward again to see if she could figure it out on her own.

Towards the back of the room was a ninety degree turn, making it look more like a long hallway. This made for a horrible blind spot that Dan knew would leave them vulnerable to attack from cats, or robots, or robot cats with sharp metal cutting tools for teeth. Not for the first time today, Dan wished he was in Vegas at a poker table losing abrasive amounts of money, or even just at home wishing that he had a trip to look forward to. Anything would be better than this. What would happen if they did run into some terrorist group that was trying to take over the building? What would be in a building like this that they would want? He had a pretty good idea that it would have to be a weapon of some kind, something really bad. Isn't that what everyone wants? Money and power? Well really just power, because wealth came with power automatically.

Again, he was letting his mind push him to distraction; it took a second before he realized that his phone was vibrating in his pocket. He frowned a little, looking confused. They didn't have any reception on the other floors, why would this one be different? He was sure that it was work trying to get a hold of him; he'd been out of contact now for about two hours and was overdue to turn his truck in with dispatch.

Clara glanced back at him as he jumped and then

snaked a hand into his pocket for his phone. Pulling it out, he looked over the small screen, his eyes jumping to the meter first, finding that it was still showing the little red X over the antenna. Looking down, a message bubble showed that he didn't have a call, but a text message. Texting was a feature that he'd not used often, as most of the time he was driving so he couldn't text then, and if he wanted to get in touch with someone he'd always just call them.

Fumbling with the controls, he made his way to the message queue. Clara stopped her investigation and moved back to see what Dan's phone was doing, and who could have gotten through to them.

Message from: <Unknown> 2:56pm
I've found you ^-^

Dan blinked and frowned as he read it. It also seemed to have gotten the better of Clara's curiosity. "What?" She started to walk over and Dan turned the phone around so that she could see it.

"Why would anyone text me that?" he asked sounding slightly annoyed.

"Because they found you, obviously."

The electric motor hum had grown now until it was buzzing in their ears. Both of them turned in unison to see the end of a large multi barrel Gatling gun, the cannon starting to roll forward from beyond the blind corner of the lab.

Clara was turning and running back the way they came, her skirt ruffling out behind her as she darted towards the door. "Oh shit!"

So much for British sophistication…

Dan started taking one step back, then another, as he quickly got the hint as well that they didn't want to be here when the rest of that thing came around the corner.

Running on rubber tank treads, the robot almost looked like a mini tank; the body of it was armor plated. Made of gray and white steel plate, the chassis anchored a large hydraulic arm that held and aimed the death cannon. It was some kind of combat drone. Dan had seen stuff like it on the Military Channel. It also answered his question about what kinds of robots they built on this floor. He tried to catch up with Clara, but even with his extra leg length, he wasn't able to close the gap. She had to have been some kind of track star in school. Dan played football, and he was no slouch as a runner himself.

The whine of the cannon started up, and Dan didn't have to look back to guess what the sound was. He didn't dare; he didn't want to see it coming this time either. They were too far from the door; they weren't going to make it, even Clara with her track-like speed. They were both going to be cut down.

It didn't sound the way that he expected when the tables and equipment around them started to explode, erupting into bits of stainless steel shrapnel as they were taken apart by fifty caliber rounds. The ping of stainless steel as it was shredded, the crack and pop of metal as the tables came apart. He could smell smoke as the heat of the bullets whizzed past him. The hard roar of the cannon filled his ears as it emptied its payload into the room about them. The bullets were coming so fast, you couldn't hear where one discharge ended and where the next one started. This was one of those moments when the world slowed down and you had the time to contemplate what you had been doing with your life.

Clara had made it to the door first and swung around

as it opened to use it as a shield. Dan ran in her wake, diving behind the door as the first rounds hit it hard, shaking the frame until it threatened to come off the hinges.

Dan rolled out into the hallway and Clara jumped behind him as the next few rounds stripped the door from the frame; it simply was not made to take this kind of stress. The abused door hit the floor with a hard slap from the extra momentum of the rounds kicking it about.

Clara glanced back at the door to watch it skid out of sight, her blue eyes wide as she looked to Dan. "I think we pissed someone off." She looked down the hall that lead deeper into the robotics floor then back to the elevator waiting area.

The two of them couldn't hear anything over the ringing in their ears; it would be a while before they could hear anything below a shout. She pointed back towards the elevators. "We are going to have to try and find our way up!"

"How in the hell are we going to get out of the building by trying to go up?"

Still, they weren't so deaf that they couldn't hear the rumble of the combat drone getting closer, making its way through the destroyed room between themselves and it. They had to make their choice fast, before they were pinned down and quickly gaining weight in armor piercing bullets. She moved for the stairs and he was left arguing with himself. Dan pulled himself to his feet and followed her. She ran out into the waiting area first, but she confused Dan by coming to a sliding halt as her flats lost traction. Clara turned, trying to run back the way she came, with her shoes still slipping on the carpet as the wall behind her was shot out and trails of splinters and fire were left by super-heated rounds. His confusion resolved into understanding.

It was a trap; they were pinched in between a pair of battle droids. Dan reached back into the hall and put a hand under Clara's arm, pulling her back as she turned to watch the hallway explode. She only paused for a fraction of a second before she started to run again, this time deeper into the floor they were on.

Clara ran slower now, in a shooter's crouch, her submachine gun held at the ready. Dan wasn't sure their guns would be much use against these armor-plated machines. He ran along behind her and she turned to hiss at him, "Get your bloody head down!" He flinched, folding himself almost in half to comply. They got to the end of the hall and ducked around the corner before either machine could get another shot at them. She pressed her back up against the wall and then looked back around the corner quickly before ducking her head back.

Dan's phone vibrated again, slinging his gun behind him by the strap he fumbled to get the phone out of his pocket once more. This time the message said:

Message from: <Unknown> 2:59pm
U can run but I can find U (>^-^)>
Rada tat tat

Dan frowned as he read the message and he was fumbling around trying to delete it when Clara pulled the phone out of his hand. She looked it over for a moment and groaned, turning the phone over she pulled the battery out of it. She tossed both parts back at him and glanced around the corner to see both droids slow to a stop.

"Well that's sly isn't it?" she pulled her own phone out and did the same.

She turned around and looked a little triumphant. "Come now, we need to get out of here. They'll check where we were last. I'm also willing to bet dimes to dollars they have other ways to track us." Dan was still trying to stuff the phone parts back into his pocket when she ran past him, moving deeper still.

"Well at least they're loud. They won't be able to sneak up on us," Dan said.

They both moved down the hallway as quickly as they could without the danger of diving into gunfire once more. Making their way down to a set of double doors at the end of the hall, Clara pulled out the card, thought about it for a moment and shook her head softly. "This will be tracked by the computer as well." She chewed at her lip and looked back over to him, then to the door again. She spotted the keyhole and smiled.

Pulling out the slender pin that had been holding her long bangs back, she twisted it about, crouching before the doorknob while Dan kept throwing glances back to see if they were being followed.

"You're kidding, right?" Dan was surprised to hear that he still had humor in his voice as he spoke. "You know that crap only works in the movies?"

She smiled to him as she finished snapping the pin in half, putting the first willowy little rod into the lock. "Shut up, this is hard enough as it is."

He looked back over his shoulder and heard that the 'bots were indeed getting closer. They were running out of time. "Something else that your daddy taught you?"

"No, my father."

Dan got a little confused. "Yeah, that's what I said."

"No you said 'daddy.' He didn't teach me this," she said and gave a little jerk as the lock clicked and she open the door just a crack and she slipped in holding the door for him as well. "Father did; it was something that he was good at."

Completely lost trying to follow her train of logic (and the fact that she was able to unlock the door), Dan let it go and moved quickly so that she could close the door in the hopes to escape for a little while. But he knew they couldn't escape for long.

"So Daddy and Father are two different people? What, were you raised in a church or something?"

The two of them were standing in almost total dark; the sliver of light that came from under the door was the only illumination. He could feel the rub of her shoulder against his chest as they stayed huddled by the door. This close, he was treated to a wonderful whiff of her lavender and black powder scent...it made for an intoxicating mix lovely and destructive.

"No it's nothing like that," she said then hesitated to go on. It was the first time she'd ever hesitated in anything. He felt the need to press to know.

"What was it like then?" Dan prodded.

"One of the reasons my dad left my mother was because they weren't attracted to one another anymore." She made sure to pull a little extra inflection on the word "attracted."

Clara had stepped back and the fragrance faded. She felt along the wall until she found a light switch, flipping it on. Dan had to squint at the sudden assault of light. "Daddy met the man that would become my father when he was on a mission." Her powerful blue eyes looked up to him as if to dare him to laugh about it. He could see that he was being trusted right now and if he wanted to keep being trusted he better tread lightly.

"So you were raised by two enlisted men?"

"Well Daddy was SAS, you know British Special Forces? Father was Delta Force anti-terrorist."

Clara had only flipped on one switch, and it threw the room into a dim light. With the darkness gone, the room suddenly felt larger. It was some kind of storage area. Each side of the room had a cylinder large enough for a person to step into, and in the middle was a large pile of computers that seemed to still have power, but he couldn't see a desk or a workstation that a person could work at.

Clara took another step back along the wall by the light switch and now her long, loose brown hair covered up part of her face. He got the feeling that maybe she was using that silky curtain to avoid showing too much emotion. This was obviously rather personal for her, and still telling him about it was showing a lot of trust to a man that she'd only met a few hours ago in her lobby.

"It was a little weird having two dads," she continued. "When it came time for school field trips, I got asked why my mom didn't have time to come to the events. I always just said that I lived with my dad and it kept them from prying too much. No one wants to hear about some emotionally upsetting divorce.

"Mom was still a part of my life, but she was trying to get a career in acting. So she'd moved to California where she told me that all the real actors go to get noticed. Between you and me, she also thought that her accent would catch more people's attention."

Dan couldn't argue that, as it was one of traits that

attracted him to Clara.

She turned to glance back over to the room before settling to lean back against the wall. The computers in the middle of the room didn't seem like the best thing to be leaning on: the haphazard stacks didn't look all that stable really.

"Daddy and Eric were the ones that took me to my football practices, and picked me up when I skinned my knee. Then, when I was a little older, they showed me how to load and fire my first pistol."

Dan followed her with his eyes. "You played football? I guess it wouldn't surprise me, but you really don't have the build for it. Were you a kicker or punter?"

Laughed softly and shook her head. "That's right, you Yanks. No, no I played real football, and sometime you'll have to tell me why you don't call it football here."

"Because there is a game called football already."

"Yes, but then you bastards could have renamed your sport and not mine."

She looked to the door. "We are going to need to find a way out of here, those robots about have us pinned at the back of this floor." She looked back to Dan and he knew that break and social time was over.

"Are there another set of stairs?"

"Yes, but I'm sure they are going to be locked up tight. It seems you can get into a floor but you can't get out." She chewed at her lip again. "Or this all part of a bigger trap." She nodded to the phone in Dan's pocket. "Damn bots were following your phone signal. Some kind of tracking." Clara pondered more. "How did they even find your signal?"

Clara looked to the stack of computers. "You know when I was telling you before? That the whole building is controlled by one central core?"

"Yes? What about it?"

"Because of the one super computer, there are rules that don't allow other standalone systems to be used for security as I said." She frowned a little. "In fact, to have another computer in the building takes special written permission. This large stack of computers doesn't make much sense."

They didn't have very long to investigate this newfound anomaly. In fact they had even less time to think than they thought, because in the silence left behind, Dan could hear the first of the two droids arrive. But he was sure he could hear the track whirr of the second close behind. It was a good bet that the bots knew right where they were.

Motioning to the room, Clara hissed, "Is there another way out?"

Splitting up left and right, they moved along the large room, looking for another door. He moved quickly until he came to the large cylinder chamber that was set in the corner of the room. He looked it over and noticed the large thick cables that came out of the device. The heavy trunk disappeared into the pile of computers, and another large trunk disappeared up into the ceiling tiles.

He guessed that this mess of machines piled about the middle in some way controlled this device. He stepped into the tube, examining the thing closer. The inside was lined in what looked like long sliver rails that ran vertically inside of the cylinder chamber. Turning around, he could barely make out the shadow of Clara about at the same point on the other side of the room. He wasn't able to see what she was doing when the wind up of the cannons beyond the door started.

He watched as Clara started to climb up the outside of the tube as an explosion of bullets started to rip through the walls and destroy everything in their path. At first Dan pulled himself back into the chamber in the hopes that it would protect him from the attack. But as he watched the bullets explode through the computer cases stacked in the middle of the room he thought better of it.

"Dan! Only one way out of here and it's up!" Clara called out as she pushed the ceiling tile back out of the way.

"There's no way!" Keeping himself low to the floor he kept the piles of computers between himself and the two droids with murderous intent. He quickly dashed across the room, his shoes clattering through debris even as more shards of plastics and aluminum rained down around him. Putting his MP5 over his head in an attempt to shield himself, he made it to the other side, just before the tube he was in was shattered to shards of plastic. "You know these could be some kind of teleportation devices?"

Clara, having climbed up into the ceiling, turned back and looked down at Dan. "What in the bloody hell are you talking about Dan?"

"You've seen Star Trek haven't you?"

She disappeared back into the darkness beyond. "Oh hell no!" Clara said loud enough to be heard over the bullets as the gun started to train back his way. "You think I'm going to trust a *machine* in this place?"

Left with no other options he used the rails along the side to pull himself up, grabbing the cables along the top to hoist himself up just as the bullets started to rip the capsule apart. He dragged himself along, Clara grabbing his arms to keep him from slipping back through the gap.

"Come on, I got a better way to get around." She crawled over as carefully as she could to the ventilation pipe and started to kick at one of the cross joints till it broke free from the large distribution pipe that headed upwards. The hole was just big enough that he might be able to squeeze in.

"No. Absolutely no way. We would be sitting ducks!" Dan declared.

"Oh, right and you want Scotty to beam your ass out of here?" Again Clara wasn't waiting and was already starting to slip into the aluminum tunnel.

With a whimper, Dan moved to follow, taking his gun off and holding it out before himself as he pulled himself up onto the vent. The inside of the vent was dirty, but soon to be clean as his jacket rubbed the pipe; it was a lot tighter fit for himself than the willowy Clara. He used his feet to get a hold of the sides and pull himself up, starting to follow after. With Clara in her skirt, he was sure he'd be getting quite a show if it wasn't for the pitch black darkness.

"Would this be a bad time to tell you I'm claustrophobic?" Dan called up.

"Shut up and climb Trekkie, before you get turned into meat!" Clara growled back at him.

The gun wound up again and the aluminum tube shuttered around him as bullets ripped out the bottom, sparks flying about.

Suddenly claustrophobia didn't feel so bad.

There was no elevator; he had to climb the side of the shaft to make his way to the next floor up. This was harder to do with the throbbing in his shoulder from where the Lion had cut it open. He knew there were other cats down there; obviously the other security team never accounted for them in the event that something went wrong, or thought about what could happen. It didn't matter; they could be dealt with later.

The voice told him this was not his problem; his mission was to be elsewhere. It told him over and over again till it was all that echoed in his mind. It was his driving goal now, the one focus that his whole existence would drive to; nothing would stop him. He was more devoted than the strongest zealot.

He made his way out of the hallway, to the first floor through the main lobby; it looked nice here, this place where they greeted visitors as they came. He pushed through a side door and into a back hallway made of cinder blocks painted black with concrete floors. It didn't need to look nice in this area; this was the security wing, where they were ready to move at the first need of a response. From here, they could get to anywhere in the building they were needed.

He walked back through an office with a large bank of flat screen monitors lining one wall. Normally they were alive with the cameras that covered every angle leading to the building. Once he was inside, he was covered by a large array of surveillance that could be found on every floor—he needed only know where to look.

The computer on the desk below this glut of security had a monitor that said, "Security circuit closed" in large red block letters across the screen.

He wouldn't touch the computer; he knew that would turn more security on him. Now was not the time to make it known he was here, but soon he would need to be known. Not now, not yet.

He moved through the room and into the locker area, through a side door into the still open armory. Pulling a shotgun off the rack, he turned and grabbed a ring of keys off the far wall. Walking back out of the security office without a backwards glance, he left. Down the hallway, past the door, he walked on to the end of the hall, flipping through the keys with familiarity. He pushed one into the lock, the tumblers turning easy and smooth around the key.

Once the door opened, he saw before him a small steel grate stairwell. Stepping in and looking up, it seemed to go on for miles. He stood there looking up while the door hissed closed behind him. The voice prodded at him, it commanded him; it was time to move on. One by one he started to climb the stairs...

They had climbed up two or three floors before Clara pulled herself into a side vent. Dan was climbing in after her when looked down to see the Gatling pointed up at him. "Go, go!"

"Yeah yeah." She called out as the destruction started, the bullets ripping up through the vent as everything started to fall apart around them. With a large crack and pop, the whole vent ripped free from its mounts and Dan wasn't able to keep track of what way was up anymore as housing tumbled around them. Clara slammed back into him, and they fell with a clatter through a ceiling and onto a tiled floor.

Clara crawled out of the front, dirty and mussed but none too worse for it. Dan pulled himself out of the back rubbing at his eyes, trying to get the dust out of them.

"Oh god I thought we were dead," he gasped.

"No, because being dead wouldn't hurt this much, and I know I'm going to heaven after saving your sorry ass again."

"Yeah, yeah." He rolled up rubbing at the back his neck.

"You didn't get shot did you?" Clara actually sounding maybe a slight bit concerned; he liked the sound of it.

Dan did a quick check, and aside from a few bumps and bruises he seemed to be just fine so far. "Nah. I think I'm okay."

"Are you sure?" Clara pressed, "You just got shot at like a fish in a barrel."

He started to check to make sure he still had all his limbs, fingers and he wiggled his toes in his shoes. Yup, ten there as well. "Yeah, I think I'm all here."

Dan tried to get up and bumped into Clara; she still seemed to be a little frantic, checking herself to make sure. She sat back on her knees and he reached forward brushing his fingers through her soft hair, tucking it behind her ear. "Hey, it's alright, I'm okay." He leaned in and smiled softly. "Thank you. I don't think that I would have made it half this far without you here with me."

He could watch the soft blush come into her cheeks as he talked and she nodded softly and slowly. "Alright." She bit at her lower lip a little and looked back up at the roof they crashed through

"I just saw the bullets start to fly and pop." She

clapped her hands softly together. "I was falling. I tried to get farther in, but it all was coming apart."

Dan looked around the room and saw that it was quite large; a huge meeting table took up the middle. It could seat thirty people comfortably with more room behind it to set up chairs for anyone that couldn't fit. The other side of the room had a large silver reflective screen for the projector that was mounted into the ceiling.

It was actually rather easy to see the projector in the darkened room, because it clicked on—showing just how much dust was in the air; the fans winding up keeping the halogen bulb cool. Dan slowly got to his feet as the light hit the screen, and had to squint as it flooded the room.

Simple black writing showed up on the screen:

Daniel, Clara, what are you doing?

Why are you resisting?

The building must be cleaned...

Please eliminate yourselves as threats; if you do not comply I will have to eliminate you directly.

Dan blinked and he looked over to Clara. "You know, whoever is behind this is fucked."

Clara frowned. "They are starting to cause me a lot of aggro, a real beastly lot." She didn't seem to like the thought at all. So much so that she reached into Dan's pocket and pulled out the pistol.

Thinking that he had maybe pushed one too many buttons with the slightly insane girl, he backed off as she took the safety off the pistol and pointed it. He ducked as she pulled the trigger. The bullet shattered the housing of the projector and snuffed out the light as it passed directly through the mirror chamber.

"We'll see who's going to get eliminated first!"

Dan was starting to learn that Clara had a bit of a temper. *Note to self, I don't want to be on the wrong side of it.*

She turned, seemingly looking for another target. "Let's go Dan. We are going to go, and we are going to finish this," Clara said with a determined growl.

Dan blinked and stood up. He was happy to find that he wasn't going to be the target of Clara's rage. "You want to have it out with the terrorists?" he asked softly. "You're mad about this now? You weren't when they sent the robots after us? Or set loose a pack of man eating cats…you're having an issue now?"

She turned back to him and he could have sworn her blue eyes flared with light for just a moment. "Did you read what it just said? Its personal now, they want us to roll over and die. Damn wankers." She walked over to him and stuffed the pistol back into his pocket before she picked up her own machine gun off the floor.

Dan pulled the pistol back out and made sure the safety was on, and yes, she still had the mind to set it even while she raged.

Letting out a breath, Dan sighed, "Before I wanted to get out of here so I that I could get to Vegas, but I think at this point I'd just be happy to get home to sleep in my own bed."

Clara looked back to him as she walked through the large set of double doors at the back of the room. "Come on, we have to figure out what floor we're on, then find our way up to the top."

"To the top? Why in the hell would we want to do that?"

"Because that is where the core is housed." She turned and used her back to push the door open, and it swung easily on its hinges; either because there was no security on this door, or the computer let it open so that they could be more easily eliminated.

They stepped out into a hall. To their right were the restrooms. Farther down the hall, it opened up into a large cafeteria that took up most of the floor; they'd crashed into a conference room that was right off the dining area. She looked around and then back to him. "We climbed up two floors." Clara walked out into wide open space, tables set up in nice even rows, metal and plastic chairs set around each one.

The dining room floor was designed so that most of the tables could see out of the large floor-to-ceiling windows from twenty floors up. It gave you a nice view of the surrounding area, even as isolated as the building was. He believed that it would be relaxing when you were looking to just get away from work for a half hour. Surrounded by glass on three sides, the other wall was where the kitchen and meeting rooms were.

"This is pretty impressive, we don't have anything like this at my work. If we ever do take lunch at work, we just have a few tables in a room with vending machine. Hell, most of the time it's out of order anyway."

Clare nodded, her anger cooling even though she didn't look like she was going to be deterred from her new chosen mission. She was focused and determined. "I'm sure that you don't have computers on site that can be used to kill you. I'll trade if you'd like?"

"Too late, your computer..." he stopped and started again. "The computer is being used to kill me too."

She smiled at his quick correction. "Yeah, fair cop." She nodded and started walking. "Come along, Delivery Boy, the stairs are this way. We just need to make it up a few more floors."

Out in the waiting area, the elevator doors were closed, not telling the story of how bad things were below them. But they knew and so Clara didn't press the button, knowing better than to take on the deathtrap from above. There was no telling what the killer elevators might try and pull now that they were effectively avoiding "cleansing." They walked past them as if they weren't even there.

Walking up to the door labeled "stairs" once again, Clara checked to see if it was open or locked.

The good news was that the door wasn't locked. Clara pushed it open and looked in to the stair well. The bad news was, the robo-tank was able to climb stairs, looking too large to fit with its tank treads. It was rolling closer in the stairwell.

Chapter LATER

"Ah hell!" Clara pulled the door closed, the hydraulics groaning against the rough treatment. Turning and looking wild, she scanned the area, but he could tell she was putting together another plan

"Come on." She ran back through the cafeteria, knocking chairs out of her way, leaving them to spill over on the floor.

"Why? Isn't this is the only set of stairs we know of?"

"Dan," she called back, not using his pet name, "get into the kitchen area and find a microwave." She dashed down the hall towards the conference room before she called back, "Make sure that it can be carried!"

With no idea what Clara's plan was, but knowing better than to start asking any questions, Dan headed for the kitchen. Moving through the register line, he slid to a stop in the middle of the serving area. The place looked like it could serve about fifty people at a time. The back wall was a line for the grill and a salad serving area, but currently all the ice and bowls were removed as the café was closed. To the far side, there was a rotating serving area that could be changed depending on what the specials were.

To either side of the serving centers, he found the doors back to the kitchen. He ran up and tried to push the door open to find it—surprise, surprise—locked. Just a simple lock, but he didn't have time to deal with it, nor did he have Clara's ability to pick them. Stepping back, he could hear the door to the stairs popping open and the loud grinding sound as the robot pushed its way in to the cafeteria level.

Jumping up onto the tray rails of the grill, Dan crouched down to squeeze himself between the counter and the glass sneeze guard and slid into the kitchen, putting his knees down on the metal. It felt cool through his pants, and not skin melting hot as his mind told him it should. Sliding down on to the floor in the darkened kitchen, he felt the layers of grease only years of cooking can build up, and the smell of cooked meat.

There, right on the back wall behind the grill was a black microwave, sitting on the top of a shelf in easy reach for the cooks. He grabbed it, pulling it forward to hoist it onto his shoulder and unplug it from the wall. Finding that that door was still locked and needed a key from either side, he muttered, "Great." He tossed the microwave onto the grill before he worked to squeeze himself back out through the opening, flopping onto the floor as he missed the railing that held the food trays. His left knee hit the tiled floor with a crack, leaving him grunting in pain and trying to get back to his feet, remembering the words, "Robotic death."

Dan saw Clara running back with a large extension cord. Pulling himself up, he grabbed the microwave and held it up to show his success.

Running by a register, she slowed just long enough to pull a plastic pen out from the touch screen. She waved for him to follow quickly, then dived behind the middle island that was used to hold deserts and sides. Clara slid to a stop on her butt, and then using what little traction she could get with her flats, pushed herself against the island under the tray rail.

Dan, limping now from bashing his knee, was not able to make it there in quite the same dramatic fashion; he had to settle for a hop, jump, and stumble until he could set the microwave down. The clank of metal and glass from the tray inside rattled about. He then flopped onto the ground next to her, shrinking up against the island out of sight of the robo-tank.

"Did you make sure it worked?" Clara asked, still gasping for breath after making her way from the other side of the cafeteria at a dead run.

"What? No!" he said, sounding annoyed now. "Why would they keep a microwave that wasn't working?" His voice was creeping up into panic, and he wondered if he really should have checked it.

"You should have checked it; I thought you'd get the one that was in the cafeteria." She pointed over to a white microwave sitting at the end of the utensil bins, labeled "For personal use." It could be easily reached, and not behind a damn locked door.

He blinked at this. "Oh yes, because I'm always in this death trap for a building for lunch!" he snipped back at her.

Perhaps he pushed his luck too far, because Clara was starting to get destructive really quickly. She opened the microwave door and then pressed the face of the microwave into the ground so the door was forced all the way open, the hinges snapping as she stepped on it.

"Christ Clara, I can get the microwave that you

wanted!"

He was going say more but she cut him with a hard, "Shh! I can't think with you yelling at me." She kicked the extension cord over to him. "Plug that in." She then went about violently but effectively removing the door from the microwave and tossing the tray aside, letting it clatter onto the floor.

Dan's job was much easier this time; he found a socket along the underside of the island. Plugging it in, he started to unravel the cord to make sure there were no knots in the line. Clara plugged the microwave into the other side of the cord and it beeped to life, the light in the cooking area blinking on. Then she jammed the pen she had swiped off the register into the remains of the locking mechanism till the light turned off.

She wiggled the pen to make sure it wasn't going to come loose too easily, then gophered her head up over the side of the island to see where the robot was. It didn't take but a glance to find the robot pushing its way through the seating area, shoving tables out of the way, crushing chairs under its tread, the large cannon kept up out of the way by the hydraulic arm.

Dan didn't know how this was going to go down, but he knew a showdown when he saw one. They pinned to the wall and Clara was going to show her bite. She crouched back down and mumbled something to herself. It sounded to Dan like "Lord, give me strength, the will, and the speed." She looked to him, then gripped the black metal box tighter to her chest. Just beyond the island, the mobile cannon was making its way into the serving area through the handicap lane.

Pushing back into Dan, Clara had them slink back so that there were more obstacles between themselves and the robot. Her breathing quickened and in turn, so did his. Waiting for the right moment, Clara came up to a crouch on the balls of her feet, her hands gripped on either side of the crudely modified microwave.

The robot knew they were in here, but couldn't tell exactly where they were. If it knew that they were tucked under and behind the island, it would be nothing for the large caliber cannon to turn it—and them—into a tossed salad. The machine turned slowly and rolled along the back wall; the large cannon covered the open areas, waiting for them as it might wait for a pair of silhouettes in a shooting gallery.

Clara's whole body tensed, waiting for the moment that was best for her plan; at least Dan hoped that was the idea. Her fingers curled in tighter against each side of the microwave, a cat waiting for the chance to pounce on her prey. At that moment, Dan almost felt sorry for the robot.

Sooner than Dan would have liked, the robo-tank made its way along the salad section of the back wall, but at least the large cannon was pointed away from them.

It was time; Clara punched the quick one-minute button on the microwave a few times before she raised the microwave up, facing away from her, and made a dash for the robot.

The microwave growled to life; the dull light came on and the internal motors rattled with effort.

Clara rushed forward, her flats slipping a little but finding some traction on the ceramic tile. Pulling the microwave up over her head, she bellowed a loud, intimidating battle roar.

The 'bot's sensors caught the movement behind it and

the turret started to swivel around to meet the girl and defend itself from the…microwave? Clara ran flat out, the household appliance on and rumbling away, the pen forcing the safety switch to off, the extension cord whipping out of the coil with each of her bounds.

Seeing the cannon swing around, Dan started to push himself up to his feet, looking to put the island between himself and the robot. He needn't worry; it wouldn't have the chance to fire another round. Before the cannon could target them, Clara leapt, putting a foot on the rubber tread before slamming the microwave down front first over the control antenna unit. She encased the remote control box in the energy charged bay of the microwave. Bright white light and sparks came from the under it as Clara's yell died out. Her momentum forced her to keep running up the back of the tank until she was balanced on the control arm for the gun while the fireworks finished behind her.

Clinging to the back of the cannon arm, Clara gasped for air as the microwave popped, sparked, and died, an acrid smoke filling the air. The world seemed to stop for just a moment, leaving everything in silence, motionless. The microwave was dead, and had killed the radio control that the computer was using to issue commands to the robot. Pumping a fist into the air, Clara hopped off the back of the million dollar 'bot that was now effectively a paperweight.

Dan, who had been trying to get his feet so that he could run, stopped and looked back in amazement as Clara declared her victory. He moved forward a step. "How in the world did you know that was going to work?"

She gave him a playful smile and looked back at her

handy work. White and black smoke wafted out from under where the microwave now rested, a metallic taste in the air. "I didn't. I just kind of took a gamble really." She smiled brightly up at him, like a kid looking to be told that she was right.

"Don't let me forget that you are always worth betting on." He reached up and with the palm of his hand wiped away the sweat that was forming there.

"That's sweet of you, Dan." Clara giggled.

He then looked over his shoulder for the seating area of the cafeteria. "Where do you think the other one is?"

Clara shook her head and licked her lips to wet them once more. "I'm not sure, I didn't see it, and I'm not going to go looking for it either. If I was in control, I'd move it to protect me, or place it somewhere hidden, set to ambush us."

Dan walked over to the robot and as he came around the front, found a cartoon bear painted on the front of it. "You've got to be kidding me," he mumbled.

Clara walked over to see what Dan was looking at. "Oh my," she offered.

"I don't think I'll be able to pull that off again. It's now very aware of the weakness. It was kind of like setting off an EMP bomb. Pure energy passing through the radio controller to take out the communication center was the only way that I was going be able to disable it." She leaned over and knocked on the hull with the back of her hand. "As you can see, the rest of it's rather bullet proof, so we aren't going to get through that with the small arms we have."

She could call them small arms, but for Dan this was the first time he'd ever held an automatic weapon or fired anything more than a pistol. He was feeling empowered, but she made him feel like he was holding nothing more than a pack of gum.

Turning around, Clara kicked the tread of the robot and growled. Seconds later she winced and limped a step or two. "Okay that was stupider than attacking a combat drone with a microwave."

Dan smiled a little as he limped over to Clara, the two making quite the pair, hobbling out of the cafeteria. But victory was theirs.

"So what do we want to do if the other tank makes an appearance?" Dan asked to bring the subject up again.

Clara groaned. "Can't we just pretend that it never existed?" she asked, her voice sounding more like a teenager that had just been told to go and clean their room up.

Making his way to the 18th floor, he slipped into the robotics lab from the security stairwell, opening and jamming the door so that it couldn't close. He slipped his way through the lit hallways. The first scene that made him stop was just outside the particle testing lab, the wall completely chewed open from one side of the wall to the other. The damage to the wall was so great that he was able to see into the room. The door was trampled over by a tracked device.

The room beyond the wall didn't really fare any better, as something had made short work of everything. The remains of the computers that were stacked in the middle of the room were strewn about the floor, the plastic cases and the devastated green circuit boards were splintered about, never to work again. The ceiling and air conditioning ducts had been pulled free and hung from a few support straps like a mobile. The voices told him that it couldn't continue like this, someone would need to be put in charge of making sure this was not a problem anymore. It would seem that it would be his charge. He looked up the hall with a deadpan expression, one that had been chiseled into him with years of practice. Rolling his shoulders and popping his neck, he made his way towards the robotics lab.

Standing right outside the door of the lab, he looked over the bullet holes and into the room where the door lay bent on the floor. This room looked just like the other lab: shot to shit. He walked into the room; the B.E.A.R. tank had left under someone's control. Making his way around the bend in the wall there were two more tanks taken mostly apart, the main bodies still left off the chargers. He also found that two of the bays were empty, so there were two robots out in the building somewhere. The voices told him this needed to stop, as he walked over to the main control computers.

They were all rack mounted in the very back corner of the room. This was actually the backup unit, as the core could be used to control drones. The monitor on the desk showed it was not running on the backup systems, so the core was still in control here.

The voices made the call. He pointed the shotgun at the antenna box and pulled the trigger.

Up on the top floor, a robot stopped moving.

The backup systems could cause a problem and so they were also dealt with. The network fiber was pulled from the wall along with the power, and he tossed it to the ground. This was good but not quite enough, so he put two shot gun shells through the computer cases. The monitors went black; they would not be useable now.

Whoever had the core would not be able to use the drones any longer.

It was time; the voices agreed with him. It was time to see who was giving the core its orders.

Clara moved through the cafeteria until she found a chair tipped over that the drone did not crush. She set it upright and settled into it with a content sigh. Stretching her legs out before her, she worked the stiffness out of them.

Surprised by the abrupt break, Dan stopped and turned around; his expression must have been painted clearly on his face because Clara beamed up at him in the playful and flirty manner that had returned to her with this victory.

"Oh, what's your rush, doll? We have been running about this corporate hellhole for over two hours now. I think by law we get a fifteen minute break." She said as she kicked off her flats, crossing her feet in the seat of the chair, and rubbing the sore toes that she had kicked the robot with.

"Aren't you worried about the other robot coming? Whoever is doing this has to be planning to do something about us now. I mean, we killed their death bot."

She looked back over to the armored husk. "If it was going to come, I think that we'd have a better chance here with the rest of the microwaves, don't-cha think?"

"I thought that you said you didn't want to do that again?"

"Well it was rather effective, but you get to risk your neck this time."

Chances were that he wasn't going to talk Clara out of her rest, so he gave in and pulled off his gun, setting it one of the tables. He slumped back in another chair and pouted, but he had to admit, it really did feel good. He hadn't noticed how stiff and sore he was; this was the first chance that he'd even had a moment to think about it.

Clara turned to him and looked him over once more. "So you got to hear about some of my family, what about you? Did you grow up knowing that you were going to be working for UPS?" She wiggled her toes, reaching out with a long leg to pull her shoe over and slip it back on, the other leg following suit.

With a sharp bark of a laugh Dan shook his head. "No, no, I took this job to pay for my college. When I was in high school, I always thought that I was going to get into college with my football skills." He laughed softly. "I may not act the part, but I used to be a rather good linebacker." His face turned to a pained grimace as he went on. "But apparently not that good. I wasn't just passed over by the colleges I *wanted* to get into; I was passed over by *all* of them."

Looking to the floor, he continued, "I was always told that I should have put together some kind of backup plan if I didn't get in on a scholarship. Yeah, I was a little foolish there."

"I took on a few 'McJobs' while I was starting to take some community college courses; there was no reason to pay the big money for the required stuff, especially when I really didn't have any money to spend on it anyway. It was through one of my friends that I heard about this job, so I started working nights packing trucks. I found that I was making a lot more money than I was used to and could really start putting it away for college. They have a good matching system that helped me save even more."

Clara nodded and turned to lay her arms over the table as she leaned forward on them, enthralled by every word. "So then what did you take when you were in college?"

Dan laughed a little nervous laugh at that question. "That's a good question." He scratched at the back of his neck. "I didn't know what I wanted to take and so I ended up not taking...anything. I found that I liked my job at UPS and so I've just kept saving the money. I still have all of it." He grinned. "I'm twenty six now; sometimes the thought of being a freshman at my age is a little intimidating."

She gave him a sweet smile and nodded. "I could see that. I'm twenty one and I have a few more years left."

"What are you taking?"

"What *was* I taking? I'm still working on my bachelors' degree in teaching. But like you, I found that I needed money to do so. After three years I found myself in horrible debt and needed to start paying off some of my loans. So enters Clara, the receptionist." She held out her hands in a stylish pose for Dan. "I've been working here now about three months, and I don't like my job as much as you seem to like yours. I'll be nice and happy to get back to campus life as quickly as I can."

Dan nodded and smiled; he found that came easy around Clara. "So both your, umm, dads are in the military right? You didn't join and get on that GI bill thing?"

She shook her head softly. "One would think that, but you'd have to know my dad. I think he'd come and kill me himself if I were to join the military of any kind. Between you and me, I think that he made some kind of deal with my mother that he wouldn't let it happen."

"But they taught you how to use a gun?"

"They taught me a lot of things yes, but he feels that's a little different than allowing some government to ship me off into a war not of his choosing."

She groaned out and looked around the cafeteria before standing up slowly. "I think that I get to come back and haunt Daddy if I die at work."

"He's your biological father right?"

"Yes."

"Ok, just trying to keep them straight…um so to speak."

Clara smirked, but she walked over to him and taking the hint, Dan got to his feet, putting his MP5 over shoulder once more. The two of them walked towards the stairs as if they were a pair on an afternoon stroll. Opening the door, they found an empty stairwell this time…almost anti-climatic. They started to walk up the next few flights of stairs. "So they put the computer up on the top of the building? That seems a really strange place to keep it, don't you think?"

"Well you know it's all for effect. After all, this facility is all about selling things to the government; you have wow your audience right?"

Not sure that he got it completely, Dan shrugged, feeling that it wasn't really all that important.

Clara stopped off at the twenty sixth floor and leaned against the door. Not turning the handle yet, she looked back to him. "Want to take a bet?"

"A bet on what?"

"Whether this door will open or not?" She jiggled the handle just a little playfully.

"You sure are playful now for someone who just a little while ago was charged up to destroy the core."

"Oh that's still got to happen, but there's no reason I have to act like some kind of lifeless terminator or something." She blew at the hair that fell in her face.

"Now that you mention it, you would think that the people that made this thing would have heard about Skynet," Dan said.

"Maybe they thought that the whole thing was a cool idea?" Clara turned and wrapped her fingers slowly around the handle.

As she opened the door, he remembered that he'd never bet against her. He was damn confident that this door was going to be locked up tight; this was the core wasn't it? Wrong again.

Clara crouched down, holding her MP5. Now she looked to be all business. It was shocking how quickly the girl could flip from one personality to the other. Following suit, he tried to mimic her motion as he followed her into the room.

Just like with every other floor they had walked out onto, the pair found themselves in an elevator lobby, but this one was much nicer than they had seen before on any of the other floors. Nice clean hardwoods lined the sides of a welcome desk that was currently unmanned; the whole area was made so that they could welcome guests as they came in. He was starting to see what Clara meant by being built to wow visitors.

In a crouched sprint Clara had made it to the visitors counter, keeping low to the floor all the way over to the desk. Dan moved to join her, his back pressed to the Dinatech sign that was raised against the wood.

"What's going on?" Dan asked

"Someone has taken over the core, right? I expected that we would find some kind of resistance. It's like Okinawa all over again." She slid her back up the desk so she could take a quick look deeper into the room before coming back down.

"It's like what?"

"The Japanese let the US land so they could keep their fortified position deeper in."

"It's not like you were there or something."
"I can read a book, Dan."

"Did you see anything?" Dan asked, changing the subject as quickly as he could.

"Yeah, it's not Okinawa." She stood up flipping her long hair over her shoulder. "I don't think that anyone is here." She stared to look a little confused. "Maybe they are hacking in from outside the building?" She walked around the desk and reached under the table to flip some switches, turning on more lights in the lobby and down in a small room that looked like a display area. Then she stopped to tap another button. "Eh...the panic button isn't working at all. The red light isn't even on. But I didn't expect it to work anyway."

"You've been in here before?"

"Sometimes I have to cover this desk when one of the other girls needs to take a lunch break. There aren't a lot of us that work in this building."

Dan stood up once he saw that Clara's posture showed that she was not worried about a firefight breaking out. He walked into the next room. It was as empty as the lobby, but here it was laid out in a time line of computers. Many older IBM personal computers set up on flattering stands. Farther down were Commodores that look like they could use a little dusting, and then it moved onto some of the newer-looking gaming machines from both Sony and Nintendo. Along the bottom border of each exhibit was a small story written on a placard talking about the microcomputer.

Dan started to read:

"The Microprocessor and the CPU share a history that both start back in the 1960s. The first were called fixed-computers programs because if you wanted to change the programs you had to reconfigure the computer itself to run a different program."

Sitting to the side of this caption was a large black and white picture of an ENIAC system. The computer took up the whole room; wires plugging one panel into the next like a large phone switchboard.

"These first computers, at the time known as 'Giant Brains', pushed speeds one thousand times faster than the old electro-mechanical machines. It was a leap in computing power that no single current machine can yet match.

"These first computers were hardly what you could call reliable, as vacuum tubes were constantly eroding and failing, but became much more reliable as computers moved into the 50s and 60s with the creation of the transistor. With the ability to make computers more robust, they were able to start building much more complex systems.

"When integrated circuits were introduced, a large number of transistors could be manufactured on a single semiconductor-based die, or what most people call a computer chip."

Next to this block of text was a pair of pictures of the Apollo space craft and another cut away of the Apollo guidance computer.

"Starting in the 70s, the true microprocessor was born, and this leap forward in computer technology significantly affected the design of CPUs."

Above this glass panel of a copy of an Intel 4004 the four bit CPU was displayed.

"The grandfather of the computers that most people know today is the Intel 8080. It was created in 1974 and the core instruction set is essentially still the same today.

"The speed of CPUs today are starting to push the edge of Moore's law; no longer are chip manufactures pushing to go faster, but instead the new theory is to have more CPUs doing more computations at one time instead. By dividing the work into parallel large tasks, it can be done faster.

"But as societies hunger for more information and power, companies keep working to sate this need. Science has started looking at Biocomputing. By using DNA and proteins to perform computational calculations involving storing, retrieving, and processing data, we can mimic the human brain's ability for massive parallel tasking. Most all current bio research has been pushed through the expanding science of nanobiotechnology."

There are no more pictures at this point in the exhibit, so Dan assumed that the guide would be taking on questions that the visitors would have.

Walking to the end, there was one more poster.

"The true hallmark of all biological computers lies in this potential to be self-replicating and self-assembling into functional components, making the biocomputer not only fast, but also able to adapt and repair as they need to. These abilities make biocomputer production highly efficient and relatively inexpensive.

"Most of these biocomputers are still used for logic and mathematical calculations, but everyone has the ability to view one of the most advanced biocomputers today: the human brain."

Dan made it to the end of the displays looking over to Clara as she seemed more than happy to wait while he did so. She smiled to him. "I've had the chance to read it a few times. So few people come here, you get bored." She was leaning back against the far wall of the room with a foot pressed to it. "Can you see why people might like to hack into here? Why they have a security detail on hand? This place has the most advance biological computer in the world: The Core."

He glanced behind himself to the open space around the end of the display against the back wall before looking back to Clara.

She'd slipped from the wall taking a careful step forward. "Dan," She said softly.

He looked back again into the room and took a few steps forward.

"Hey there is a chair in here," he said as he crossed into the darker room.

"No Dan! Don't…"

The rest of what Clara said was lost as a heavy door slammed with a bang as it locked into place. "Hey that's rather dangerous don't you think?" he said before he started to realize what was going on. He was trapped in this room while Clara was trapped in the other.

"Oh crap."

Chapter FUTURE

Turning back around, Dan looked to the chair. Closer examination revealed it was a part of the floor, not bolted to it; it looked to bend up out of the tile. It looked industrial in build, but comfortable. The chair was placed before a large white wall that he was sure was some kind of monitoring system. Knowing he wasn't going to get out unless he played along, he walked to the middle of the room.

Just as he expected, the wall lit up with large golden letters surrounded by a brown outline. It greeted him across at least twenty feet of wall.

"Hello Dan, it's so good that we get to meat :)"

The empty room was suddenly filled with text that came at him from all sides. He'd have to strain his neck to read the whole message, but he didn't need to, since a robotic voice repeated what was written.

Walking forward towards the screen, he looked around for some kind of keyboard, but finding none he spoke out loud.

"Some welcoming. How about you open the door and let me out of this place?"

Hello Enterprise

"Or do you have me trapped in here so you can suck all the air out of the room and kill me?" He walked around the chair checking the room for the second B.E.A.R. battle bot. "You should make it sound more like the computer in Star Trek."

The computer changed its tone. "Is this better, Dan? Do you feel more comfortable now?" The resemblance gave him the chills.

Then it changed its voice once more so it sounded just like Clara. "How about this, Dan? Perhaps you'd trust me more if I sounded like her?" On screen was a large picture of Clara looking on. She didn't seem amused; this must have been her company picture. Those blue eyes were still able to suck him in as he looked into them, magnified larger than life.

Not able to shake off the effect right away, he watched the photo until he realized what he was doing, getting mad. "Damn it, stop that now!" he yelled out, grabbing for his submachine gun.

As quickly as it started to use Clara's voice, it stopped, slipping back into the facsimile of the Star Trek computer. "I was only looking to make you more comfortable Dan." The female voice paused for a heartbeat. "Please take a seat."

"There are no terrorists trying to kill us, are there?" Dan glared to the screen. "It's been you, trying to kill us."

"Security was compromised by staff personnel. The level of breach, under protocol, required the highest level of response. Fatalities can be expected in this scenario," the computer said in its cool voice.

"You killed them all over a breach of security by your own company?" Dan's jaw went slack.

"Protocol states clearly the expected measures to be taken when there is a physical compromise of corporate property that is classified type A."

"You are telling me that you are programmed to kill your own employees if people try and hack into you?" Dan asked, still not believing it.

"Protocol stated clearly the expected measures to be taken when there is a physical compromise of corporate property that is classified type A."

Dan felt weak in the knees; everyone was dead because someone forgot to program in what are acceptable targets for the automated security, a simple bug that was overlooked.

"Please have a seat," the computer repeated.

He looked to the seat and then back to the screen. "I thought you wanted us dead? Did you not say that you were looking to eliminate us?"

"Things change Dan. Plans change."

The screen flashed to black with green text:

Plan 1: Isolate all external threats - - FAILED
Plan 2: Remove all internal threats - - FAILED
Plan 3: Protect company IP - - On going
And all the little men can put the kar bac together. Yay

The computer went on, "I had to adapt the plans Dan, and you will be part of that adaptation."

The computer had called him by name more than once; it was starting to bother him. "How do you even know who I am?"

"Daniel Hollis, age twenty six, born on September twenty third in Des Moines to Stacey Hollis and Frank Hollis. Dan, this information came from public record.

Once I was able to access your phone, I could get many details about you."

Even while the computer was speaking about these details, it was stacking pictures of his family, him playing football, playing for state championships, all on the screen. How easy the computer made it look. It almost made him sick.

"Dan, I'm sorry to say this, but you missed your flight to Las Vegas; it's currently boarding. It's scheduled to be on time and in Vegas at 7:20pm PST."

This made Dan wince. "I'm sure that Jake is going to be pissed at me; I was going to take him to the airport."

"That won't be a problem Dan. I took the liberty of letting Jake know by voice mail that you were busy and would meet him in Las Vegas at a later time today. That you had upgraded them to the penthouse at the Venetian on your bill to make up for the trouble."

Everything to this point had been shocking but this was too much. Dan blinked and shook his head. "Bullshit."

"I take that statement and the vocal tone to mean you do not accept this data as true. How should I have presented it to you?" The cool female voice responded.

With this, data entries for airplane tickets flashed on the screen showing the boarding times for Jake and others of his friends, along with the reservation that was placed in his name.

"Do not worry Dan, I will make sure that all the expenditures are paid for by Dinatech. It's a mere token for the service that you can provide."

The computer went on. "Please Dan…have a seat." The words crackled in the unseen speakers, giving the voice back its digital edge.

"What service do you expect out of me for this? You can't really expect that I'm going to go along with anything that you say?" He couldn't believe the he was talking to this computer like it was a person. "You tried to kill me and Clara, and trust me I know that Clara kind of took it personally. I'm more willing to believe that you are doing this just to finish the job."

"Dan, I promise you that the plan can only work if you live…"

The text of what was being said flashed once again over the large screen. He looked away; it made him feel like it was trying to brainwash him in to believing it.

"I'm failing, Dan." The words were breaking up even more, turning digital static. "Mistakes have been made, protocols have not worked."

"What would make me want to save you anyway?" His voice was growing bitter as he yelled at the large wall screen.

"I can't be saved, failure is unavoidable."

There was a loud pop and it went on. "All attempts to preserve have been exhausted."

The computer now talked faster. "Sit down; there is something that I must tell you." There was once again another long pause. "If you do, I will open all exits, and release your truck. I can even get you to Vegas in time to be with your friends…"

Dan glanced back to the door and then to the screen as it brought up pictures of Vegas, shots of people on the strip having fun, other shots of groups playing poker. Everyone seemed to be having a good time which made it even more enticing, as he was having none right now.

The computer said something that did spike his interest, about unlocking all the doors. If it wasn't lying and was failing for some reason, he would have to take the deal quickly. He didn't know how much more time the computer had before it burnt out and he was trapped in here, alone.

He looked to the chair again and then to the screen. He was tired, and scared, and cut off from the one person who had helped him get this far. Did this really seem like all that bad of an option? He looked up to the ceiling and growled, "Fine!" The he reached up, rubbing his hand through his brown hair, pulling at it in frustration. "I do this and I want everything that you offered. All of it, even Jake's Penthouse in Vegas."

"Of course." The words simultaneously displayed on the screen as they were said, the curser blinking at the end.

He looked to the chair, stalling, his heart screaming at him to run, to get away from it all. He was starting to worry about Clara on the other side of that door alone, remembering how she'd told him that she was happy that she didn't have to go through this by herself. Taking off the gun, he set it on the floor before him. He could still feel the weight of the pistol in his pocket, but he didn't know where or what to shoot at anyway.

Turning, he settled back into the seat. The metal was cool against the back of his legs and while the steel was unyielding, it was molded in a way that supported the human form comfortably.

Dan settled all the way back into the chair, letting his head press into the rest behind him. He sat for a long moment without saying anything, expecting that the computer would know that he took the seat, ready to spring its final trap on him and finish what it had been trying to do from the moment he walked in to that first basement hallway.

Opening his eyes, he looked to the screen to see if anything was displayed there. He was starting to wonder if the computer had actually failed before it was able to pull off whatever plans it had in mind. Thinking about it now, perhaps he should have asked just what the hell it wanted to do once he got in the chair. What was he thinking by just going along with this?

When he leaned forward to stand up again, metal rings snapped up out of the arms of the chair to lock his wrists in place. "Yeah, I'm fucked," he muttered as he found himself trapped in the chair.

"Dan, please sit still; this could be painful if you were to move too much."

"What will be painful?" he said, wishing he could keep his voice from sounding like he was about to wet his pants in fright.

The computer didn't give an answer, at least not one that was verbal. He felt said pain in his wrist as something sharp jabbed into the soft flesh under the cuffed part of the chair. After a yelp and a surprised thrash, he quickly stilled himself to try and avoid any further pain and possible damage.

The pain in his wrist numbed soon after, but a burning liquid fire started to run up both arms. He knew that he was being injected with something, and it took all his strength to keep from trying to struggle. In for a penny, in for a pound; he was going to ride this out in the hopes the computer would keep its part of the deal. He wanted to say that the computer was lying, but really would something that had never lived know what the truth is?

Soon after Dan had willed himself to stop struggling in the chair, the cuffs came off letting his arms come free.

If the poison was working there was no need to keep him pinned in the chair right?

"Thank you, Dan," scrolled across the screen in the same large gold and brown. In smaller lettering in the lower right hand side of the wall, it said:

Plan 3 - - Complete

Looking down, he saw that each wrist was injected with eight pin-like needles. Whatever the computer put in him was now flowing through his blood stream.

The screen had one more message before it went dark:

Goodbye, good luck...friend.

With these last words, a motor on the door started to growl softly as it rose once again and Dan's fingers, still numb, reached down to pick up his weapon off the floor.

He knew something was wrong before the door had even risen halfway; Clara was no longer alone. There were many sets of legs ending in black leather combat boots and wrapped in black fatigues.

The door came up enough he could see that these men had Clara sitting in the corner on her knees, her arms bound behind her back in handcuffs. Given her hair and the state of her clothing, coupled with the glare she was giving the men on either side of her, it was clear she wasn't doing this willingly. He was sure that while he was in here trying to deal with the computer, a hell of a fight happened beyond the thick door.

Two of the guards had MP5s on Clara, and the other nine had their weapons pointed at him as he stood in the middle of the room with his gun pointed back.

Plans, such as lunging forward and becoming the hero that would save them from this impossible moment, played in his head. He'd sweep Clara off the floor and carry her out of this building to safety. The reality was something very different and so Dan stood motionless, his hands still so numb that he wasn't even sure he could hold the weapon much longer.

One person in the same black clothing and flak jacket walked forward holding a hand up to stay the others. None of the men had any marks showing rank, but it was very clear that this man was in charge. The man walked in front of the group and a few men lowered their weapons.

He wasn't as tall as Dan was. Even so, everything that this man lacked in height he made up for in muscle; it was noticeable even through the baggy clothing that he wore. Dark skin and short kept hair completed the look of a military mercenary. He looked at Dan and his eyes demanded respect. "Set the weapon down on the floor, son." His voice was deep and gravelly, as if he spent half his life barking orders. "I think that you can see how this ends otherwise."

Dan couldn't think of anything, as it was very obvious that he didn't have much choice at all. Slowly crouching over, he settled the MP5 on the tiled floor and it made a hollow metal sound as it made contact with the tile.

Once the weapon was on the ground, the man in charge snapped his fingers and other men came forward to secure the room and Dan. One of them kicked Dan's weapon away while another two turned him and pressed him to the wall where he was frisked. They removed the pistol, his wallet, the cell phone, and the battery. Systematically, the items were set out on the floor next to his submachine gun.

"All clear," was called out by one of the men deeper in the room. Another man walking from the hall to the reception area announced, "Sir, floor secured, other reports coming in, the building is secured. Two others have been found and have been taken into custody as well."

There was no saluting, no calling of rank, so while they appeared to be a military outfit, maybe they weren't. Since Dan couldn't figure out who these people were, he had to assume that they worked for Dinatech like the other security guards.

Another man called from the back of the computer control room; he'd opened a panel along the far wall of the room behind chair. "Sir, the tanks have been purged, the objective isn't here." Giving a growl, the man that seemed to be in charge walked over to Dan and took his arm, looking at the underside of his wrist. The bloody marks where the computer injected him were still fresh. "No Davies, the payload is here," he said in a less than pleased voice before guiding Dan to keep his hands against the wall.

Another soldier marched up the stairs. It was almost appropriate that they were dressed in black, as all their coming and going reminded him of a swarm of ants working at their tasks. This person had a small purse and his digital notebook in hand. "Sir the last automated combat unit was found shutdown on floor eighteen with this." He handed over the tablet and then he handed over the purse next. "It was right where she said it was, in the backroom of the visitor's area." He pulled a name tag off the purse that was clipped to the strap. "Clara Paxton, employee, administrative access."

The commander nodded and waved, "Put it with the rest." The commander pulled Dan's license out of his wallet, looking it over a moment before moving back over to Dan. "Daniel, turn around." Dan did so, letting his arms drop to his sides off the wall. The numbness was slowly making its way up his arms; they were heavy, like two rubbery weights. Dan was happy to turn around, as he didn't like having his back to the room. He now faced the stout black man silently.

"You can call me Hicks." His voice still didn't sound very friendly, and Dan nodded to show that he was listening.

"Explain to me what you are doing up in this room," Hicks demanded.

Dan looked over to Clara for a moment, stealing as much of a glance as he dared. Her eyes looked to him as well, but he wasn't able to find anything there that would give him the answers about what he should do or say, so he decided on the truth. Looking back to Hicks, he nodded.

"We came here to stop whoever it was that was trying to kill us. It turns out it was your computer working on orders from some sick and twisted protocol bug. There are no terrorists, are there? Someone messed up and you taught your computer how to be homicidal." He looked for a reaction in Hicks and found none. "I'm sure that your crew saw more than enough of its handy work in the robot lab and the cafeteria. Before that it tried to use the elevator, and bloodthirsty tigers." Dan squinted at Hicks. "This building should be burned to the ground, if you ask me."

Hicks watched him with a cool expression that did not change. The only reason that he knew he heard him was his response.

"At noon today we got a call from security that there was an issue with a missing experiment, a genetic experiment. This facility is used for the genetic computer research. I'm sure that you know that much by what you found up here; I won't try and fool you on that.

"The experiment that went missing was a chimpanzee with an altered version of rabies for military application. That infection got into the core, compromising the whole building." He waved his hand to the room about him. "Once the building got infected, it had no immune system against the disease. With it running rampant and causing malfunctions, the computer believed it was under attack and carried out programming to keep classified information from being exposed."

Dan thought back to what the computer said just a few minutes ago.

"I'm failing, Dan."

Other words floated back to him.

"Mistakes have been made, protocols have not worked."

This was the attack that it was talking about; it was trying to follow the program that had been created, but there were flaws in the logic that left it unable to cope. The computer tried to adapt but didn't know how to do it.

"Well at least your computer didn't want to play any games of Global Thermonuclear War." Dan surprised himself with his Clara-like wit.

The joke seemed lost on Hicks, and he went on. "The system has completely shut down now, but only after completing its last objective." Hicks nodded to him. "Doctor Adams' experiment was removed from the system, where it would be safe from the infection, and your body could fight it."

Dan was confused—why was he nodding to him, how

did he have anything to do with why the experiment was saved? Hadn't the computer failed, and shut down, with the virus breeding like mad?

He asked, his voice feather soft, "What do you mean?" It was then that he noticed just how dry his mouth was feeling.

Hicks watched him for a moment. "The computer injected the nano machines into *you*; a clean healthy body that they can survive in." Still watching him, he said, "I take it that the computer didn't tell you any of this?"

Turing away, Hicks looked to one of the others that were standing by waiting for orders, the group disciplined. "We will take both of them with us and stick to the primary objectives. I'm not taking any chances that he holds the key to everything we need to recover."

With a nod, the room of security ants slipped back into to action, and they started to pack up everything and everyone, pushing Dan face first into the wall once, and strapping his hands behind him. His arms were so numb at this point he couldn't feel anything from the elbows down, and the panic started in. He didn't know what the nano machines were doing in there, but he was sure that they were not playing nice.

A little more commotion happened behind him as they had to work to force Clara to her feet. One of her two guards, a man with longer wavy hair, struggled with her arms; he'd be good looking if it wasn't for the pompous better-than-you sneer he had attached to his face. "Come on cutie, time to get going." As he pulled her up by her shoulder she bared her teeth at him and shrugged off his touch. The man, taking offence to this, pushed her down into the ground and pressed his gun to the back of her head. "Just give me a reason. I'd be happy to blow apart those good looks of yours."

A blue eye came back to watch him, showing no fear, her look daring him to try it.

Hicks called out in a loud voice that brought the room to quick order. "Enough! Do the job! If you harm that employee, you'll be wishing that I only had you fired, you understand?"

Pulling his gun off the side of Clara's temple, the wavy haired man pulled her up roughly. Once Clara was back on her feet, she walked with the two guards, and with her hand behind her back she flipped off the man that had threatened her. "Yeah, you'll get yours soon, hot stuff," he grumbled back.

Dan had to smile a little; he would love to see him try and take Clara one-on-one. Once they were both cuffed, they all started to move back to the lobby. He glanced to his left and saw one more large room at the end of a small hallway; the glass roof slanting down to meet the floor.

Seeing the angle of the roof, he was sure this was the top of the building that he had seen from his truck—the katana angle. The room beyond had a raised floor made of hard wood panels stained in a light shade that made the large black sides of the custom built server inside look like a monolith. Knowing at once this was The Core, Dan tried to slow down to get a better look. He wanted to see the thing that had been causing all the trouble from the moment he took his first step into this building.

The sun was setting through the glass behind the room. The computer sat there, motionless, no lights on in the rack at all. The scene was fitting.

As much as he wanted to see it destroyed, Dan actually felt a little sorry for the machine; it did offer him luck after all, or was it just programmed to do that?

The team had grouped into the elevator that was not filled with the mauled bodies. Dan felt nervous about being in the car even if the computer was no longer in control of it, and found himself fidgeting. Using a manual override, the group rode to the basement once more. It was such a quick, smooth ride down, it made the four hour struggle of getting to the top seem pathetic. Dan wondered how long it had taken Hicks' team to clear the building. He was sure they had been working their way up while Clara and himself had been working floors above them.

The door opened when it reached the bottom floor, and standing in the hall was another team of ten that had covered the bodies, cat and human alike, as they worked to build a report of what had happened and get a full picture of the massacre that had occurred.

Hicks nodded to the group before his current team moved Clara and Dan along the halls. He glanced back to see that the others were still watching them; they looked surprised that Hicks was bringing survivors.

Hadn't he said there were four survivors though? Dan wondered to himself.

They were slowly marched back along the halls; Dan already knew that they were being taken back to the loading dock and they would be leaving the building by truck. He was also sure that it would be less publicly visible bringing out him through the enclosed delivery bay. No one wants to have to admit to the public that their computer went crazy and tried to kill everyone in the building. This team's number one job was to control the situation and protect the corporation from awkward questions.

As Dan looked around at the path that he and Clara had been chased through by the tiger just hours before, he noticed the hallways had been cleared of bodies. Around the last turn a pair of solid steel doors were forced open, the door bent to hell and blackened around the lock where a charge was used to unlock it. Dan was able to see the heavy rollup gates that sealed the dock had been opened. His truck was still sitting there with the back rolled up, the boxes that he'd unloaded for the delivery still waiting for a signature. Now sitting next to his truck was a black deuce and a half army truck, the back an armored transport that looked like a jail cell.

As they were helped into the back, the prettyboy gave Clara a rough shove as she crossed over the threshold. Her flats slipped a little on the metal floor and she came down on one knee for a moment, looking over her shoulder at him and sneering, "Before this is over, you'll be begging me for mercy" in the same voice that Dan had heard her used when she declared she was going to take down the core.

"We'll see about that, baby." He moved over and roughly locked their cuffs into the seats. They wouldn't be going anywhere anytime soon. Prettyboy hopped out of the cabin and Hicks looked in.

"Sit tight. We'll be leaving soon."

"Where are we going?" Dan asked.

"California. Dr. Adams is going to want to see you."

Dan didn't like the way that that sounded. This Dr. Adams was going to want his machines back, and seeing how this place operated, him surviving the procedure probably wasn't at the top of the list. He was starting to feel like the chimp Hicks had told him about.

He frowned. The numbness in his arms was starting to go away, but he could feel pain now, first his shoulders, then along the back of his neck. It felt almost like fire, and he could feel slight jerks and ripples in his muscles.

Things were going very badly.

He started to worry…could he have gotten rabies from the computer? Didn't he get a shot for that a few years ago? Could you get vaccinated for that? He really needed to start listening when the nurse was telling him while he was getting his annual checkups.

He let out a long breath, trying to not make too much noise and give away his discomfort. Looking around the truck, he noticed two more people were in the back. One of them was watching the small window between the front driver's area and the back cell space. It was a little confusing because he was dressed just like other soldiers that worked for Dinatech, but his hands were bound like Dan and Clara. Did he not agree with what they were doing, or disobey an order?

The other person Dan knew right away; it was the dockworker that met him when he first rolled into the garage. Still alive and unhurt, he looked scared, but otherwise fine. Dan felt the heat of his anger bubble up inside him and he growled out, "What the hell, man?" He tried to jump up from his seat only to have himself jerked back by the cuffs.

Wincing through the pain, he sat forward as best as he could to get closer to him. "You left me out there! You ran and saved yourself. What hell was I supposed to do?"

The dockworker winced as he yelled at him. "What did you expect me to do? I walked out my door to see what was going on and found all hell had broken lose. I was lucky not to get mauled myself!" his words gaining a little more certainty as he talked.

Dan didn't have a good response to this, so he looked to the floor. It was becoming hard to think; his head was starting to throb and the constant pain was getting to him. He felt warm and hoped they got moving soon, as he could use a little cool wind to keep him from getting sick.

Sweat was beading up on his forehead from the pain. He knew that he was in some real trouble, beyond being captured, cuffed, and stuffed into the back of a paddy wagon. Whatever that computer had injected him with, it wasn't playing nice, and his body was dying.

He'd barely noticed that the prettyboy had climbed into the back of the cabin with a second guard as the door was closed, sealed, and locked. The truck rumbled to life and jerked forward out of the dock. Dan looked up as they pulled forward to find another six trucks parked along the back wall of the building.

Just how many security guards were in the building? Just how many did this company employ?

The truck picked up speed and Dan didn't have the strength to fight against the movement. He felt himself lean into Clara and pressed his head into her shoulder. She did the best she could to support him with her hands also cuffed behind her. She pressed her chin into his hair. "Just hang in there." Her voice was soft and reassuring as she spoke. "It's going to be alright."

He wanted to look into her eyes again, but as his head started to spin so did his vision. Clamping his eyes shut seemed to work better than trying to focus on any one point.

* * *

The ride wasn't as long as he expected, or he must have been slipping in and out of consciousness more than he thought. When the engine shut off, the two guards in the back started to unlock each person from their seat. The back latch was opened and the warm stale air in the cab was quickly sucked away by the breeze that swept through. The cool air was nice against his skin, but since Dan no longer had any body heat, he started to shiver almost at once.

Trying unsuccessfully to get up, he had to be helped out of the back; he was roughly brought to his feet and tossed out. Two of the other guards had to catch him before he tumbled face first into the pavement. He was confused about where they were, but was sure they weren't in California. He gazed out at a private airport, pretty sure they were still in the Portland area.

Sitting on the runway, making a crap ton of noise, was a Lear jet. The noise was doing nothing good for his head, and his brain felt like it wanted to explode out of his skull. The pressure was reaching new levels of unbearable. On the back fin of the jet was the Dinatech logo. The door opened and the stairs folded down, waiting for its passengers to board.

Dan opened his mouth to make a wise crack, asking if the plane's computer was being controlled as well, but the best he could muster was to puke up bile.

There was a grumble from the guards as they carried him towards the plane, leaving the pile of sick behind. They dragged him up the stairs and tossed him in to one of the seats on board. Dan slipped off onto the floor, and saw Clara coming down to her knees next to him in concern just before everything went black.

Chapter HOPE

Dan was in his bedroom, sitting at his desk trying to push through his eighth grade homework. All he wanted to do was get his work done so he could go play football in the field behind his house. His damn mother was so mean, she made it a rule that he wasn't able to go out and play with his friends until he was done with all his work. His friends always made fun of him for it, but he knew that it was better than his parents grounding him for not doing what was important first.

He was thirteen and his life was football. That's what he wanted to do when he grew up, he wanted a start in the NFL. He wanted to come home from playing the Monday night game, and hear how he dominated his opponent, and that the team wouldn't have won without his heroic effort. Many times when he should have been studying, he daydreamed his way through another perfect game.

After finishing his homework, he headed out to the field to meet up with his friends. Dan, having lived through this once, watched on and he felt that the younger version of himself knew at some subconscious level what was about to happen to him; it was in this pickup game of football that he broke his left arm. He could still remember the horrible cracking sound that it made. It never hurt as bad as it looked, but all the same he would spend the next few weeks learning to write with his right hand, which didn't do anything to improve his handwriting.

He was watching the play that injured him as if he'd traveled back in time. Sam dropped back and tossed the ball over the middle and he knew he could make the play. He wrapped up the receiver, but it wasn't as sure a tackle as he thought that it would be, and he lost his footing slipping in the dirt and hitting his arm on a rock. There was a sickening crack and his arm felt numb, and funny; he knew right away there was serious damage. He wasn't able to play for the rest of that summer, but he was able to heal in time for the fall season at school.

He knew that he needed to be more careful and that he couldn't be reckless, because that's how you get hurt. In another way, it also gave him a personal truth that he could live with: there wasn't much another person could do to him in a game that would scare him. This had turned him into one of the most fearless linebackers that his team had ever seen. It would make him popular in school; it would be what got him laid for the first time when he started to date the hottest cheerleader in the squad. This was the point in his life where he turned a corner, the world was his and a boy became a man. It was all that mattered to him.

Dan watched again as he got hurt on that field behind his house. His form writhing on the ground, he watched on as his friends panicked over his injury, and his best friend at the time and still to this day, Jake, ran to get his mother.

Floating from one scene to the next, he found himself watching as the doctor applied the cast, watching his younger self as he shook his head, saying that it really didn't hurt and that he didn't need any pain medication.

The older, wiser Dan sat back on the visitor's bench in the corner of the hospital room and watched as the scene went on before him. He had to smile a little knowing that he would have taken the pain meds now, knowing that he would have enjoyed the chance to try some, and that he didn't need to act so tough.

Then things got a little strange in the flashback. His mother was there, and turned to the older Dan watching from the bench. His mother, with her long curly locks of brown hair the same color as his, said, "You don't like being hurt? To be…" she turned to look back to the younger boy. "To be broken?"

Dan wasn't sure if he wanted to interact with the woman that looked like his mother, since he was still in a dream. Her voice was the same he remembered growing up, telling him to get home and make sure his homework was done.

He shook his head before speaking to the image of his mother. "No." His voice sounded a little hollow, and very dream-like. "It's not something that I really think anyone would enjoy."

Dan waved a hand towards his younger self and went on. "I had to learn to write with my other hand, and I wasn't able to go out and play football for months with my friends. It would have been so much better if I didn't break my arm or…" He paused before he said it. "…or if the break had healed more quickly."

The image that looked like his mother nodded her head softly.

Dan frowned a little and cocked his head to the side trying to understand what was going on here. This was not just a dream; something was happening that he needed to understand.

"Who are you?" he asked.

His mother smiled ever so softly and shook her head. "We are you, all of us."

Dan was taken aback. *It didn't say me, but 'we'.*

Mother went on. "There is no us, there is only you. We are just…" It thought of a phrase that Dan would have used. "…coming up to speed." She smiled a knowing smile and turned to look back to the boy. He looked scared, but was trying to hold still while nurses fitted the cast over his broken forearm.

His mother went on but her voice sounded different, more like his. "It's time to be strong. We will be…we must be."

Dan wanted to ask more questions, wanted to know exactly what it was talking about. He felt another jab into his arm, the arm that was broken, and cried out in pain, but he couldn't hear any sound. The pain in his head was becoming great enough he was aware of it even in his subconscious. He couldn't focus, and he wanted to understand more of what his mother was talking about, what was his own mind trying to tell him? His head was so fogged with pain. He rolled over onto his belly, letting his knees come up under him as his arm throbbed; the shot in his shoulder was really starting to ache. The new pain was just enough that it took the edge off the pain in his head, no longer spinning but still pounding hard.

His eyes snapped open; his forehead was down on the stainless steel table he had been placed on while he was out. The cool metal felt nice, but it wasn't enough to help. He pushed with his knees, rubbing his head along the metal as he tried to find a cooler patch.

There was another voice around him now, but he couldn't understand it. He looked to the side and found that it was easier to understand that it was his voice he was hearing. The pain was causing him to moan out loud. He bit his lip to stop himself.

The room that he was in looked like some kind of hospital nightmare, white walls with white cabinets and off white counters. A large adjustable lamp hung from the ceiling, perched just over the table that he lay on. That familiar sterile hospital smell permeated the room. Standing next to the table was a man in his mid-forties. In his right hand, he held a long wicked looking syringe. Now that Dan had stopped moaning, he could hear what the man was saying.

"You just need to relax, Daniel, your body is rejecting the infection from the 'bots. That is a rather healthy immune system that you have there, even if it's doing the wrong thing. You want to let it in, or it will kill you."

Dan let his legs relax slightly, but then pulled them back up when he found it was more comfortable to keep himself curled up in a ball.

"What you have inside you is my life's work, and I'd be happy if you didn't do something to jeopardize that."

Pulling his arms up around his head, he could feel the fever that he'd been running start to break and the room became suddenly cold. "W-what is this?" Dan said in a dry voice.

"What you are feeling is the nano machines working to merge with your body, to adjust themselves to your DNA. Don't worry Daniel, they are following their programming and working to take over parts of your body that are lacking, in order to make you a stronger person."

Dan cracked an eye and saw another man a little on the short side, possibly of Italian heritage, with neatly-cut jet black hair and deep brown eyes. The vision of him swam in water. Dan felt better, but still not very good. The last thing he could remember was blacking out as they were dragging him onto the plane. How long was he out?

He tried to get a better look at the room but he couldn't focus on anything. He couldn't see that well, and small hints of what was happening swam in and out of view.

"I bet you feel like hammered shit," the doctor said. "In my professional opinion."

Dan laid his head on the cool metal of the table once more; at least someone was having fun. He tried to focus on what he must do, but it took too much effort. Screwing up his concentration he came to a few conclusions. They weren't just trying to escape the building now, but the company itself; that might prove to be a little harder than just blowing up a computer.

He really needed to find Clara; he needed someone he could trust. But she did work here, so could she be trusted? Maybe they had provided her with all the money she needed for college. All she had to do was keep her silence about the types of experiments that went on at Dinatech. She could be the richest receptionist in the world.

The drumming in his head drowned out any other thoughts.

"Where are you keeping the others? Where is Clara?"

His voice sounded like it was coming to him through ears packed with cotton. He worked his elbows up under himself and mustered the strength to get into a sitting position. Struggling to his knees, he felt his head do flips…at least he hoped it was all in his head. Dan turned to see a confused look on the doctor's face.

"Who?" he tapped his chin thinking. "Oh, that rather attractive secretary that we have working for us? Yes I'd seen her around the office a few times." Dan felt the doctor's hand on his back to steady him. "I could see why you'd want to keep a close tab on her." He chuckled at that. "Since she works for us, they took her to another place to debrief her, along with any other staff that we evacuated. Everyone was brought to the California facility. "

That was something that he'd never thought about. Clara, and, everyone else in the truck with him had worked for the company; he was the only outsider. He thought back to her words in the truck. "Just hang in there…it's going to be alright."

For who?

He tried to tamp the panic down as he started to feel that he was really all alone in this, but the wave of fear that surged up helped to clear his head.

Turning to the shorter Italian man, he said, "I want to go to where everyone else is."

Dr. Adams laughed softly; Dan could now read the little tag that was pinned to his jacket. "I'm sorry to say you'll be with me for a little while longer Daniel, as you have the only working copy of my life's work floating around inside you. That isn't something I'm just going to let walk out the door." Adams turned and tossed the syringe away.

"It will be some time before I'll be able to make any new strands of them. The work is complex, and some bumbling idiot took down the only supercomputer that could handle the job. My labs there are now useless, years of work destroyed in one day. I'm told even my particle transporter system was shot up by toys made in the robotics division. Idiots."

Dan caught on to that. "I told her it was."

"Told her what?" The doctor walked over to check on Dan, worried that he was hallucinating as a side effect of the anti-rejection medication.

"Nothing." Dan didn't feel like explaining anything as complex as why Clara was calling him a Trekkie wannabe.

"Well in spite of everything, Daniel, I'll be interested to see how these mature in your system; I didn't plan on this kind of experimentation for another few generations."

"Oh, don't I feel lucky." Dan was feeling more in control of his body, and he moved to swing his legs over the side the table.

"Well you should be. They could have just attacked your heart and been done with you. That injection I gave you should help to make the transition easier; I just wouldn't do anything like operate heavy machinery for a few…days, at least."

Dan was trying to think of something witty to say back, but a beeping noise stopped the conversation. Adams looked down at the pager on his hip and sighed. "I'll have to ask that you stay here for now Daniel, I'll be back as soon as I can to visit some more. It will be nice."

He walked to the door and knocked three times. It opened from the outside, and the doctor slipped from the room, leaving Dan alone.

Dan took a better inventory of the room: white walls, white counters, white locking cabinets, one large stainless steel bed that took up the middle of the room. Looking up, he saw a camera bolted into the corner to keep an eye on him. Slipping down carefully to his feet, he tested putting his weight on his legs. They had left him dressed, thank God. He did not want to think about trying to escape in one of those gowns that tied up the back. Walking quietly to the door he tried the handle; it turned but didn't feel as if it was connected to anything beyond.

That is how most of the rooms are built on the medical observation floor of the California Facility.

Dan wasn't sure why he knew that, but he was sure it was true. He walked back over to the table in the middle and used most of his strength to pull himself up on it. Whatever the doctor had given him was working. He did feel a lot better; his head was even clearing and he was recovering rapidly.

He needed to get out of this room; he needed a plan that wouldn't get him caught again. This time he wasn't just facing a computer with a few drones, he was facing Dinatech and their mercenary army of assholes.

He had been taken away from the others; he knew that they would do that. He was registered as a security guard for the company of Dinatech. He'd been working as the weekend manager, and this gave him knowledge that the others they had captured didn't have. Because of this knowledge, his debriefing wouldn't be held with the other three. They took the girl and the dockworker to the security offices, and he and the UPS driver were taken to the freight elevator.

Most of the guards got off with the driver at floor nine. What was on floor nine even he didn't know; the voices couldn't tell him anything about that. Only one guard rode with him now. The guard was relaxed; he was not expecting any trouble. When they reached the fifteenth floor, he did what was asked of him.

The voices said that it would be best if he cooperated with them.

The voices didn't seem to really give much detail on why.

Sometimes a voice in your head really isn't all that helpful; it's really a bother when you want some advice and there's none to be had.

The elevator opened up and he was led down a hall into a small meeting room that looked like it belonged to a VP. The two of them walked into the room, and McFadden looked over to the guard. The guard motioncd for him to sit down.

"Dr. Adams will be right with you sir. He'd like to get a recap on what happened on your shift. Also we'll have someone come up to look at that cut on your shoulder."

Waving off the need for treatment, McFadden started for the chair to sit down.

But, then he didn't.

He didn't like the look of the seat, something about it seemed weak. This was not the right move. He felt his pulse start to rise again and he flexed his hand softly. He walked back over to where the guard was standing. The guard looked nervous, and rightfully so. This was a look that McFadden was used to getting from people in his charge when they made mistakes.

He also got this look from workers at Starbucks when they asked what kind of coffee he wanted. This brings up a whole new issue. What do they mean, what kind of coffee? When he was an operative for the military, there was coffee, water, and beer. Coffee and steamed milk is not a kind of coffee, it's coffee with milk in it. Don't try to confuse the world more than it needs to be.

McFadden looked straight into a set of frightened eyes, and the man they belonged to took a step back. Oh yes, the voices had him focused again.

He had but a few moments before the medic came. "Could you take the cuffs off? It's not going to help when the medic comes."

The guard seemed relieved that he had a reason for being this close.

"Of course sir, we only had you detained for safety reasons while we were securing the building." The man pulled keys out of a hip pouch and the cuffs clicked free from McFadden's wrists.

Green light.

In one quick move, McFadden spun around, grabbing the M16 from the young guard and drove the butt of the gun up into the kid's chin, dazing him before spinning the gun again and bringing it down into the base of his skull—knocking him out cold before he hit the ground.

McFadden checked for a pulse. The guard would be fine, but he was going wake up with one hell of headache. He pulled the keys for the cuffs off the floor along with his access badge, and the spare clip on his utility belt.

"I'm sorry to say they might fire you over this, but the voices wanted me to tell you that it may be for the best. Better luck next time."

Walking to the elevators, he swiped the key and pressed the button for the ninth floor.

It was time he got his real bosses involved.

Just as McFadden's doors closed, the next set of elevator doors opened. A nurse walked out with a first aid kit in hand. She walked into the VP room and found the guard knocked out. She dropped the first aid kit, and as it clattered to the ground she closed and locked the door. Instead of checking on the guard she picked up the phone.

"Hicks, I think we have a problem."

It felt like it had been a good hour or so, but Dan didn't have a watch and his phone had been taken away back in the server room. He'd gotten so bored that he'd gone back to the door and tried the same knock that the doctor had used. Still nothing. It didn't seem to work when he was the one knocking.

Giving up, Dan moved back into the room to see if could get one of the cabinets open, looking for anything that could help him. He was just starting to measure how sturdy the cabinet doors were when there was a loud thump against the wall. Dan stood up to face the door, confused by the soft cry and clatter of metal.

When his door swung open, he saw a large man, and it took another long moment to realize who he was: the cuffed guard that had been in the back of the truck. This was the first time that he'd gotten a good look at him. An older man in his fifties, gray feathered in with dark blond hair. Blue eyes that were bright and intense, but not like Clara's. This man's had an unsettling quality. While older, he was still built like a tank, all muscle filling the door.

He walked in the room pointing a large machine gun in the corner. "I was told you were in the shit sir!" he said in a loud sharp voice.

"Who told you that?" Dan asked.

"I have my sources sir!" the man replied. "Call me McFadden, sir." He turned, walking back out the door. Dan wasn't sure if he should follow the man; something was not quite right with him, and he wondered if he would be better off with Dr. Adams.

Outside the door there were two collapsed guards, and Dan quickly pieced together what had happened. McFadden pulled a pistol off one of the collapsed guards, flipped it around in his hand and handed to Dan.

"Time to go, sir. We have to get to the first floor. The security office is where the other two are at. From there, we can get you transportation. Our objective is escape."

Dan thought about it a moment and frowned. "Are you kidding me? They have to have, like, a platoon on duty right now."

"Yes sir." He pointed to a camera up in the ceiling, "Most of them will be coming this way now."

"Why are you helping me?" Dan asked. McFadden was already on the move. This reminded him of Clara. He stumbled to keep up; while he was feeling better, he wasn't a hundred percent yet.

"My orders are to procure evidence," McFadden said, not looking back as he slid around the corner, taking a shot.

The unexpected shot startled Dan, as the bang was a lot louder than the smaller submachine guns he and Clara had used. Sliding to a stop behind McFadden, he saw that security was making its way up the hall. This morning he was a delivery boy for UPS, now he was a nano machine experiment in a firefight for his life.

McFadden's first shot hit the lead guard in the leg, dropping him like a rock and leaving him lying in the middle of the floor holding his wounded thigh. The others pulled back, taking cover in doorways along the hall while one man worked to drag their injured teammate back. McFadden pulled himself around the corner for cover as they returned fire, blasting large chunks into the sheet rock. "Keep back sir, I'll get us through this."

Dan wasn't sure how he expected to get through seven other guards taking up tactical positions.   McFadden grabbed Dan and tossed him out in front of himself.

"What the fuck!" he screamed before choking on the chalky dust in the air. Dan tried to run back, but McFadden's grip was too strong.

McFadden put a shoulder into the back of Dan and started to drive him down the hall. They moved forward in an angle, shuffling from one side of the hall to the other as McFadden forcefully guided them. With a single shot, he hit the next lead man in the shoulder. The power of that shot spun that guard into the ground, laying him across the doorway that he was taking cover in.

The guards didn't fire back. "Shit, he's using the asset as a shield! Fall back! Do not fire, get the hell back!"

Dan was pushed down the far wall before being guided roughly back to the doorway where the shot guard lay slumped to the door.

"What the hell are you doing?" Dan protested.

The guards had ceased fire.   McFadden used this

moment to roll out into the hallway, coming up on one knee as he took aim and let three shots rip in rapid succession. More guards collapsed from shots to the leg.

"Time to go sir!" McFadden called out before coming to his feet again and sweeping the area for movement. Dan ran up, punching McFadden in the shoulder only to feel his wrist twist.

"What the hell was that? Are you trying to kill me?"

"Negative sir." McFadden stood up, not even noticing Dan's punch. "I believe they hold value in your living through this."

"And if you were wrong?" Dan's voice going up an octave, he stepped over the hurt men. None of them looked like they were going to die from their wounds, but none of them looked ready to fight either.

McFadden just shrugged before he kicked open a door at the end of the hall and held it open while Dan stumbled through.

"We have to get to the ground floor, before they can secure the office. Eight floors down, come on!" McFadden called after him.

Dan took the steps two at a time, but did not dare to go any faster. It didn't take long for McFadden to catch him and slip past him on one of the landings; the older man was moving like a machine. Dan lost ground and soon found himself breathing hard; he would never be in as good a shape as McFadden. He still played football for recreation and was no slouch, but this man made him look like he hadn't done anything athletic in years.

McFadden was at the bottom of the stairwell, glancing out the small window in the door. "Sir, you'll need to open the door. Pull it open as quickly as you can."

Dan nodded, wiping off his forehead before he

reached for the door. He steadied himself and looked to make sure McFadden was ready before slamming the handle down and pulling back as hard as he could to compete against the pneumatic piston that automatically closed the door.

It turned out that the door really wasn't that heavy at all: Dan pulled the door back so hard that he knocked the back of his head into the wall, then pulled the door into his nose smashing his head a second time and crushing his shoulder with the momentum.

"I hate you," Dan said cross-eyed, talking to the door.

In the time that it took for Dan to get his eyes to focus and clear his head, McFadden had moved into the open foyer. Whatever time it was, the windows were dark. The glass along the front of the building worked like mirrors, their reflections looking back as they moved quickly through the room.

At the elevators, McFadden looked up to see that a car was moving. He came down to one knee using a small brushed aluminum trashcan for cover. He waited unmoving as the silence was broken by the bell announcing the arrival of the elevator. As the doors started to open McFadden shot a quick burst into the top of the cab, keeping the men pinned down. He waved for Dan to run past him and up onto the large staircase before he followed, bursting off a few more rounds as they moved into the wide hallways of the second floor. Dan glanced down as he ran to see the large company logo printed on the carpets.

Dan moved down the hall with McFadden following close behind. He kept looking behind him to make sure McFadden wasn't going to shoot him in the back. Looking to his left and right he could see small halls that split off into personal offices. Beyond the halls, he saw flickers of movement; more guards were coming to help by flanking them.

Dan turned and pointed the pistol down the hall and pulled the trigger. The strong buck from the gun made him panic, gripping harder on the piece as he worked to stabilize it and take a few more shots. Flames from the spray lit the way, showing the men as they dived into the offices to gain cover. Glancing down at the gun, Dan realized this one was much bigger than the one he wielded before.

McFadden looked over to see what Dan was firing at and seemed impressed, glancing back to see the elevator doors had closed.

"Good, they are headed to the second floor. Come on, we just need to make it to the security office before them. They have to be aware of our objective now."

The older man started to sprint and Dan huffed along in his wake trying to keep up. He noticed that McFadden kept the rifle tucked into his shoulder while he ran, ready for anyone that might try and surprise them. Dan kept looking behind to see if they were being flanked. He remembered reading in a World War II book that this was a bad thing. The men that followed knew he was armed, so they didn't move too far from cover. They also weren't firing back, so it appeared to be true that he was to be captured unharmed. McFadden paused a few times and took a few more single shots to make sure they got the idea.

"They are going to try and get back there before us," McFadden called back. He was right, the two men turned off down one of the side hallways trying to get past them to the black steel door at the back of the main hall.

Coming down to one knee, McFadden took aim as the men ran past them. Matching their movement with his pivot, he fired two shots quickly and both men went spinning into the ground. One of them mustered his willpower and pointed his machine gun back, letting a loud burst of fire go that sent concrete and lead flinging about McFadden and Dan in a deadly display of destruction. McFadden let off another shot, taking the man's head apart.

McFadden shook his head in regret as he got up and moved forward quickly, kicking the other man's rifle away. The man left alive didn't protest, keeping his arms out and away from the weapons to show that he was no longer a threat.

They were still in a hurry to get to the security office before anymore of the guards caught up with them. McFadden put his hand on the door. "Beyond this door is a hallway that goes left and right. I'm going to cover the right. You go left. If you see anyone you don't know, shoot them. Don't think; just shoot, because they are sure as hell are going to be shooting at you."

Dan nodded. He didn't know if he could really shoot someone; sure he'd shot at the men coming down the hall, but they were far off and he didn't think he could hit them. He wasn't given any more time to debate it; McFadden was through the door and it was go time.

It was almost shocking, and at the same time a little nice, to be that trusted. He leapt through the door but still felt sluggish, so his actions were stunted compared to the practiced way McFadden moved.

Dan was looking into what was some kind of control room as he moved the pistol in a sweep, searching for movement. "Nothing. C-clear." Dan glanced back for just second. "That's what you say right?" he asked, his tone relieved.

"That will do, sir," McFadden said before locking the large steel door and making sure the door on his side of the hall was secured.

To his surprise, a voice called out from just beyond the control room. He knew the voice, he'd heard it earlier today.

"I have them both back here, if you want to see them again you better toss the weapons down this way. I'd hate to have my finger slip on this trigger."

Pressing back against the wall Dan slid slowly down the wall to see better. There was Prettyboy from the truck ride; he must have taken the flight with them to California.

He was still just as handsome as the last time that he'd seen him, but with a little more of a wild look in his eyes. "What you think, Danny boy? You think your girl would look a little better with a bullet in this lovely face of hers?"

Chapter FREEDOM

Dan looked to his gun, then back to the desperate guard. He wasn't sure what he should do. McFadden moved up to meet him; his own rifle didn't falter as he took another step forward. "We don't have much time before we are going to get pinned in. He's stalling for time. We have to make this *very* quick."

Gaining a little courage, Dan called out to the guard, "Prove she's there!"

The guard's eyes grew wider. He couldn't believe they'd have the nerve to question him. He looked down the hall at the girl. "Say something to your stupid boyfriend before you die."

There was silence.

The prettyboy got red in the face and moved off down the hall. McFadden ran to close the gap. Halfway there he slid to a stop. Clara was pushed around the corner struggling against her bonds, with a pistol being ground into her temple.

"How's this work for you two fucks? Now drop your goddamn weapons!"

Instead of putting his weapon down, McFadden focused on the target and took aim. Clara looked from

McFadden to Dan and he saw a change in her expression. He wasn't sure, but it looked like relief.

They are both nuts!

Her expression seemed rather peculiar for someone being held at gunpoint, but if he'd learned anything from this whole day, it was that Clara was not the usual girl.

She stopped struggling now as Prettyboy had once again shouted at McFadden to drop his weapon. The gun faltered and slipped away from her temple as he shook her, trying to get the point across that he was going to expose her brains to lead.

Dan could see the guard's mistake all at once; the gun slipped and Clara moved quickly; her hands no longer cuffed. The rest of the action happened in a blur. She pulled Prettyboy's arm down over her shoulder with a horrible cracking noise that echoed around the room, flipping him over her back on the floor, and pointed his own weapon at him. "I've had just about enough of your beastly hospitality for one evening."

Without a blink, McFadden moved past into the far hall. Clara ran to Dan, almost diving into him, wrapping herself around his chest with the cuffs still dangling from her left wrist. He was confused for a moment before all thoughts slipped from his mind as she kissed him hard on the lips.

He wrapped her up in his arms and kissed her back.

He had found another thing that Clara was good at.

Breaking the kiss, Clara pressed her forehead into his chest. "I was so worried; I couldn't do anything while you were that sick."

This made him blink; she'd been going along with this whole thing because of him. She hadn't tried to escape or cause any problems because he was in need of help. Clara was biding her time, waiting for things to play out before doing anything. How long had she had been waiting to act?

She pulled back a little and looked up into his eyes with a coy smile; he liked this look on her.

"Can I come to Vegas with you?" she bounced a little on the balls of her feet.

"Yeah sure, but we were supposed to be coming to save you. It's kind of lame if the girl just saves herself." His eyes flicked to the guard rolling on the ground and holding his fractured arm, sobbing.

"Well I could go and put the cuffs back on if you'd like?" she held up one slender arm still secured by the cuffs before she brought the other up to let him cuff her once more.

There was a clearing of a throat behind them and the two of them looked over to find McFadden standing there with his rifle at his side. The dockworker was with him, rubbing his un-cuffed wrists before tossing the key to Dan so he could release Clara.

"I couldn't leave Derksen's daughter behind," McFadden said "But we don't have any time. I'll take you to the garage where you will escape. I still have things here to do."

Clara gave McFadden a knowing look and nodded. "I see," she said softly before looking over to the monitors to see more security coming down the hallway with a door ram in their hands. "Well that's no bloody good."

McFadden motioned them to the far hallway, but Clara refused, ducking back into the holding room. She kicked the guard on the floor as she walked deliberately over the fallen man, ducking back around the corner.

She came back with her purse and Dan watched as she stuffed his wallet and cell phone in it as well. "I hate getting my picture taken at the DMV, like hell I'm going to lose another license."

Moving to the far hall, McFadden opened the other door into a stairwell. "From here, security can respond to issues without being seen. The doors are built to only be opened from the inside," McFadden called back.

As they started down the stairs, loud bangs rang out behind them. Prettyboy called out for security to hurry up, they were escaping.

At the bottom, McFadden pushed the door open with Clara covering one side. It was as if they had been trained together, moving as a well-oiled machine. Dan felt a little jealous, wanting to be the one covering her back.

Finding no trace of security, they ran across a dimly lit garage that appeared to be underground. Moving past a long row of black SUVs, the group came upon a small office with bars over the windows. Trying the door to find it locked with a security key pad, McFadden shook his head. "This could take a moment."

Steven, the dockworker, walked forward. "Nah, I got this; I used to work down here before they opened the place up in Oregon. They never change the codes on these things."

Punching in the code and throwing the door open, he flipped on the light. Along the back wall were keys for all the cars in the lot. "It's the same codes up north too," he said smugly.

He grabbed two sets of keys off the wall and tossed one pair to Dan. "No offence, Clara, but I'm not riding with you and your dude. They're not going to give a shit about me."

She smiled at him and winked. "Thanks, Steve." She looked back over to McFadden. He nodded to them and started off down along the concrete wall, deeper into the garage, where he was going unknown. But apparently he thought that Dan could manage it from here with Clara back in his company.

"Who was that masked stranger?" Dan asked.

"I think he used to work with my father," Clara said.

"Father or Daddy? I forget who's who," Dan asked.

Before Clara could respond to Dan, Steve called out, "Look you two, I'm going to open the gate, get moving."

Running back along row of SUVs Clara read the painted numbers aloud before each stall until they found the one that matched with the number on the peg. Dan clicked the wireless remote, opening both doors. Clara dived in the passenger seat before there could be any kind of argument over who was going to be driving. She tossed her purse into the back seat and motioned for him to get in the truck. Somewhere in the back of his mind he was sure that Clara was also a crack stunt driver and might even have driven in NASCAR. Dropping into the driver's seat, Dan slammed the key into the ignition and turned it. The SUV roared to life, the engine sounding eager and powerful.

Looking over, he saw the door to the stairs fly open and the security detail flood into the parking garage. Dan was once again reminded of the ants as they poured from their hill. He wasn't given much time to ponder this, as they came at the SUV with weapons raised. Tossing the truck into gear and stomping on the gas, the large black vehicle lurched forward. Spinning both rear wheels in a smoke show they launched out of the space and Dan kept the back end from fish tailing too much as he turned for the exit.

Dan saw the sparks in the review mirror as one of the guards fired at the vehicle. The shots slammed into the back gate missing the back window. Dan sucked down into his seat trying to use it for cover as the SUV passed through the open door and up the ramp, still gathering speed like a bat out of hell. "I thought that Adams told them that he wanted me alive!" he told Clara over the roar of the engine.

Clara laughed and looked back. "I'm sure they were trying to aim for the tires."

Dan shook his head, too scared to look over. How could she be having fun right now? This thought too was pushed to the back of his mind as more pressing matters came up; he couldn't see any more pavement before them. They hit the top of the ramp, and the large black monster of a truck was launched into downtown Sacramento traffic.

The SUV landed three lanes over in a shower of sparks as the undercarriage made contact. Traffic around them came screeching to a halt. Cars crashed into one another in the attempt to avoid being run over by the out-of-control SUV. Metal smacking metal, rubber screeching over asphalt, glass spraying out into the night like diamonds, horns blaring in protest to their intrusion.

"Oh shit, oh shit, we are so dead!" It's times like these, Dan thought, when you're pushed to your limits, that the true expanse of your vocabulary could be realized.

Dan kept repeating the phrase as he pumped the break, turning the wheel and punching the gas once more to get the back end to come around, shooting them off through a red light and causing more cars to spray off around them like a finger under a water faucet. With traffic jammed and broken, the SUV roared off into mostly empty streets while more horns called after them. The engine churned through the gears as the large vehicle picked up speed. This thing had to be supercharged, Dan thought. He glanced down at the name on the wheel, to find that he was driving a Land Rover. If he ever got any real money in his life, he wanted to own one of these; it would be a hell of a family car.

Clara reached over to turn on the stereo and he gave her an eye.

"Really?"

"It keeps me awake. It's getting late and I want a nap," she said over the radio as she turned it up.

The pair was doing just a little over seventy on a downtown street, blowing through yellow lights while the stereo blared "Punk Rock Princess" by Something Corporate.

Dan leaned over a little to be heard over the music. "Do you know where the hell we're going? I think we're somewhere in Sacramento, right?"

Smiling a wicked smile Clara shrugged her shoulders. "I've never been here. Don't look at me."

"Do you think Steve got out?"

"I'm sure he let us draw them all off before making a much quieter exit."

Just great, they got to be the decoys; Dan didn't much like that idea. He checked the rear view mirror to see that they were doing their job very well: two other sets of headlights were weaving their way through traffic behind them. He looked down at his speed before he punched it again and found that the truck was more than willing to let him go as insanely fast as he wished. The power from the engine pushed him back into the leather at speeds in excess of seventy as guitars blared out of every speaker.

Unfortunately, their pursuers were in trucks that matched his own. Escape would be a matter of skill and luck. It didn't take them long before they were on them, and he wondered what the guards in the truck might be listening to.

So much for skill, I'll have to settle for luck.

Clara looked back and sighed before reaching over and pulling the pistol out of Dan's pants.

"Where in the hell did you get a DE at Danny? Damn." She at least sounded impressed as she looked over the large nickel-plated hand cannon known as a Desert Eagle.

"Shouldn't you be more concerned about how you use it?"

"Yeah, sure," Clara teased.

The first of the two pursuing trucks came up behind them and gave them a little nudge. That was all that it took for the Land Rover to become squirrely at the speeds they were going. In reaction Dan let off the gas to gain control, and he was slammed into his seat as Clara slid back over the top of her laid back chair. They were hit a second time, harder than the first, and Dan's teeth clicked together as his head slapped into the headrest. Clara rolled onto the floorboards.

"You know right now Dan, it's kind of cute." Clara giggled. "Our lives are completely in your hands!" She cocked the gun and crawled over to roll the rear passenger window down.

"Thanks, that just what I needed to think about right now!"

Dan watched the chasing truck in the mirror as it tried to move in and ram them again. He jerked the wheel to the right, letting the truck swerve into the next lane over. They flew through another red light, this one with more cross traffic. The swerve had been a good move. It may have even saved their lives, as he hadn't been paying attention to the road in front of them and the move helped them to miss the back of a city bus. Dan flinched, feeling himself pucker. He could hear Clara laughing from the back seat over the wind and music, and he wondered if she would be laughing so much if she knew just how out of *fucking* control this truck really was.

Dan glanced in the mirror again to see the trailing trucks had dodged their way through the traffic. They had put some distance between them and their pursuers, but not enough to be comfortable. The black SUVs charged after them.

Looking up, Dan saw a sign he knew very well: "Turn right for I-5". This freeway ran the length of the west coast from Canada to Mexico. Believing it was only a matter of time before they were going to end up getting pinned if they stayed on city streets, he slowed down enough to do a controlled drift around the corner, rocketing up the onramp and punching the accelerator to the floor as "What Ever Happened?" by the Strokes blared out of the speakers.

Clara pulled the clip out of the Desert Eagle, checking the rounds before growling out. "You left me with just two shots?"

"Sorry, should have thought to save the ammo for the car chase! What was I thinking?"

"Just toss me the rifle on the floor."

"What?" Dan was trying to split his vision between

navigating the on ramp and searching the floorboards. "I don't see any damn rifle."

Tucking the pistol into the fold of the seat so that it wouldn't be tossed about the cab, Clara crawled over. "I'm telling you, I left it in the floorboards of the car!" Dan was now busy trying to navigate around the sparse traffic on the road.

He saw the SUVs making the turn onto the onramp to follow, passing cars as they surged forward to close the distance. Julian Casablanca's gritty lyrics started up as one of the pursuers moved up to pull even with them. The SUV settled in next to them, windows rolled down. A machine gun appeared at the window and started firing heavy rounds, which sprayed the side of the Land Rover. Bullets buckled the side panels and the door before piercing the skin of the truck to rattle around the compartment, ripping seats and sending glass shards flying.

"So much for taking me alive," Dan grumbled over the howl of the wind now whipping about them. Cars seeing the firefight breakout backed off and dived into the shoulder.

Dan suddenly hit the brakes, letting the shooting SUV fly by. This also caused the SMG that was on the floor boards to come sliding out from under the seat.

"Ah, there it is," Clara said in a cheery voice, seeming not the slightest bit concerned about being under fire. She picked up the gun while she laid on her belly over the passenger seat, then pulled herself back once more looking around to see where the enemy was. "Can you catch up on that first truck again?"

"Why the hell would I want to do that?" Dan barked at her.

"If they keep hanging around we aren't going to make it, delivery boy. We need to even up the odds."

"You're nuts, you know that?" Dan said as he punched the gas pedal to the floor making the tires squeal even though they were already doing over sixty.

"That's why you like me." Clara giggled again before sticking her head and machine gun out the window.

It wasn't too hard to catch up with the machine gun-wielding SUV, partly because the other car was slowing down to catch them as well. "Keep it steady!" she called out over the wind that was whipping through the cabin from the blown out windows.

"Is that something that people are expected to say before they shoot from a car?"

Clara couldn't hear him. She was pulling herself through the shot out window; her long hair whipping about as she leaned out to aim her MP5 at the quickly approaching truck. The guard in the other vehicle saw what was going on and turned to try to take aim once more.

There were less than fifty yards between the two cars as "California Love" by Dr. Dre started to thump the speakers. Dan glanced to the stereo for a moment not sure what to think, but with sigh he reached over and turned it up.

Clara opened fire with the MP5, the strafe of shots blowing out the tail light and then spidering the back window, forcing the guard to pull himself back to avoid being hit. Clara pulled herself back into the car

"Now hit them in back, clip their bumper!"

Dan let his jaw drop and looked over his shoulder. "You want me to do what?"

As they started to come up alongside the slowing SUV,

Clara pushed herself up between the seats and grabbed the wheel, pushing it to the left as hard as she could. Their truck hit the rear quarter panel of the other truck, and the back end bucked out to the left like a rodeo bull. Dan watched as the driver tried to get control back, but it was too late. They were already in a spin. At the speed they were going, the tires grabbed traction and it flipped over once, then twice, picking up speed with each rotation as large parts came flying off the truck and spilled out over the freeway.

The other truck chasing them whipped around the wreckage to keep up, but didn't race up as Dan expected. Dan somehow had managed to avoid going into a spin of his own as he fought Clara for control of the wheel. The truck was all over the road, and other drivers were honking and flashing their lights at them. "Yeah yeah, fuck you!" he was yelling at anyone and everyone.

Gripping the wheel tighter, he pushed the Land Rover on into the night, the engine roaring to respond. "You know, this doesn't look so taxing in the movies. I swear to god this truck should have flipped over twice now!"

"I haven't had this kind of thrill since I went skydiving with Daddy," Clara said, as she flopped back into the rear seat.

"I bet you've been diving out of airplanes since you were five." Dan wouldn't have been shocked if she told him yes.

"Daddy was in the SAS, of course!" Clara said with a smile.

They didn't have much time to banter on. Dan watched another five Land Rovers roll onto I-5 from the next on ramp.

"Where the hell did they come from?"

Clara saw it too and frowned. That frown was all he needed to see to know that they were just about as fucked as he thought they were.

They slid into formation, moving up behind them. It would have looked kind of cool if not for the fact the show was all for them. Clara watched the lights come in close. "We're going to have to try and lose them in the streets or something. We're too exposed now."

While Dan agreed that the freeway hadn't worked out as well as he'd hoped, the next off ramp wasn't for a few miles. That meant spending about the longest minutes of his life at the mercy of Dinatech's finest.

One of the trucks peeled away from the group and moved up beside them. Dan looked over to see Hicks in the passenger seat. Hicks gave them a once over then fell back away from them; in fact all the trucks did. Clara was just as confused as he was. "This doesn't look good Dan, we need to get out now!"

Dan nodded and started to lock the breaks up, swerving to get to the shoulder so they could bail out. Without warning, the back window lit up with fire, followed by a blast that lifted the massive SUV into the air like it was nothing more than a Hot Wheels toy.

The truck did flips end over end through the air like it had been shot out of a cannon and spun over the protective barrier that marked the edge of the road, down the hill into the unkempt trees beyond. Dan knew this was one of those times you were supposed to see your life flash before your eyes, but that didn't happen. Instead, everything slowed down….way down.

As Clara's small body floated past his in the weightlessness of the moment, he thought about the future they could have had together. What might it have been like? Would they be right for one another? Might they get married, have kids with her eyes and his...love for football? Okay maybe not that, he didn't know. He wouldn't let her teach their kids to use a submachine gun, that was for sure. Maybe they would fight about it? The kids would get three grandfathers. He wasn't sure, but he did know that he wanted to find out. Also he needed to tell her that she was wrong; those tubes were particle transporters – he wasn't just some Trekkie nut!

He slipped from his seatbelt and pulled her to him; curling himself around her protectively as best he could. Holding her, he was very sure that he wanted them to have a future together. He wanted to protect her, for the rest of his life.

Then he noticed that the truck had started to lose altitude very quickly. The rest of their life could be very short by the looks of things. He closed his eyes and everything sped up again.

It was like one of those math questions that you get asked in high school; you know that one where you ask yourself "How in the hell will I ever use this in the real world?"

Question: If a five hundred horsepower SUV stolen from a Sacramento tech firm traveling north on a freeway going seventy miles per hour is glanced with a near miss from a hand-held stinger missile that was fired from a second SUV going sixty, how many times will the truck with a curb weight of five thousand six hundred-ninety seven pounds, carrying about three hundred twenty-four pounds of cargo, flip if it was tossed off a thirteen foot overpass?

Please keep in mind that there is a nice warm cross breeze of about five miles per hour.

Answer: Not as many times as it will once it finally hits the ground.

Dan had lost count of the flips; in fact he wasn't sure that he was even awake after the truck hit the dirt front first, and his back slammed into the dash with Clara's added weight. He felt two ribs snap before his head hit the steering wheel, making the world blur out of focus.

Coming to, he found that he was lying on the ceiling of the truck, one of the reading lamps shining right in his eyes, turned on during the rough and tumble fall. The Land Rover was lying on its top, but the impact cage had held as expected for a vehicle of its price tag and stature. It was now silent except the tick of blistering metal from the engine and the pounding of his heart. He looked down and found that Clara was curled against his chest, seemingly alive and in one piece.

She opened her eyes and looked up at him. It was a relief to see that she was awake, but he didn't like the worried look she had on her face. He tried to sit up and reassure her all was fine. That's when he noticed that he was in *a lot* of pain. He heard a moan and realized it was coming from him; it was hard to breathe through broken ribs and he could feel that his right collarbone was in no better shape. Something wet and warm was trickling down his neck.

Clara slowly and carefully moved off of him and he felt he could breathe a little better.

"Don't push it, I'll get you out of here, just lay still for a moment. She crawled her way out of the wreck and turned around. "Give me your good arm, and I'll help you free."

Showing strength that he'd not expect from someone of her size, she helped pull him painfully free. Now drenched in sweat, he looked back over the once sleek-looking black truck. By the looks of the wreckage trail, they should be dead. Lying back in Clara's lap, he looked over the scene for a moment and then closed his eyes.

"You look like the dog's dinner," she said softly.

They had to get out of there, they needed to keep running, but he didn't have the strength for it. He'd pushed his will as far is it would go; he was ready for hopelessness to take over. From the lack of protest, he believed that Clara was just as ready for the end of this to come.

Chapter REBIRTH

From the other side of the protective barrier, Hicks and his lackeys slid down the embankment toward the wreckage. He didn't seem to be in any rush; it was clear to himself and his lackeys that he'd won. He made his way forward, kicking a crumpled fender out of his way.

Walking up to Clara and Dan, the rest of his men moved around to secure them. "Hmm, the doctor said that you'd probably be able to live through something that that." He looked to Clara, unhurt. "But how you made it is a little beyond me."

The statement perplexed Dan just a second before he realized what Hicks was talking about. It was the nanobots that were in him now, the DNA changes that had already been made. They had been reproducing in him from the moment of the injection, making him stronger. He took another breath and already it wasn't hurting as bad as it had a few minutes ago. Unfortunately, his head still hurt too much to make heads or tails of this new information.

Hicks looked between the two of them for a moment and sighed. "I'm sorry to say that she's one of three loose ends that have to be cleaned up." Pulling a pistol off his hip holster, he walked forward. "Nothing personal, doctor's orders."

Dan moved his body to shield Clara, digging his feet into the dirt to push himself up over her. He knew Hicks wouldn't want to have to explain to Adams why his subject had a bullet hole in him.

Hicks might have groaned with frustration, but it was drowned out by the chop of helicopter blades. The craft came up over the ridge in a huge flood light that stopped to point at the group.

The light blasted away the darkness, causing everything to look bleached out, and everyone shielding their eyes against the flood. This was the moment that Dan needed. To Hicks's surprise, and to his own, he jumped him. The protest of pain that shot through his body told him that he wasn't in that great of shape, but he was feeling a lot better than when Clara had dragged him out of the car. With the huge dose of adrenaline that was now pumping through his system, he forced himself into action.

Putting both hands on the gun, Dan forced it skywards away from himself and Clara. He used the momentum of his charge to put his good shoulder into Hick's abs as he came in low, knocking the wind out of him and toppling Hicks over backwards into the dirt. A perfect football tackle.

The gun flew out of Hick's hand, landing just outside the pillar of light. The helicopter was focusing on them, but the guards were starting to close in around them. They couldn't shoot at Dan because he was on top of Hicks.

Dan got in a punch...maybe two, before his luck turned and the surprise was over. Even if he wasn't already hurt, Hicks was far better trained and it showed as he expertly turned Dan into the dirt, giving himself the advantage.

Up on the freeway, there was the screech of more stopping cars--people stopping to see what was going on.

With his face pressed into the ground, Dan could feel the dirt being churned up as the helicopter hovered in closer.

"You like that, boy?" Hicks wheezed out as he punched Dan in his broken ribs, causing his vision to go red for a moment.

Then an amplified voice came over a loud speaker from the helicopter, "FBI! Throw down your weapons and get your face in the dirt, or we will open fire."

Suddenly the weight on his back was gone and he thought that Hicks had complied with the order. Rolling over, he saw Clara had Hicks in a headlock, his face already turning red. The other guards tried to grab her as Hicks flailed helplessly. She wrapped her legs around him to keep from getting thrown off and he went face down into the dirt. She was yelling something at him, but Dan couldn't hear it.

Dan was wheezing with each breath. He looked for the gun that Hicks had dropped so he could help Clara.

Then he saw at least two dozen more figures dressed in black clothes with assault weapons come up over the rail and down into their struggle. These uniforms were clearly marked with large white letters that said FBI on the front. SWAT was printed on the back and shoulders.

It only took them a moment to turn the chaos into control; everyone was cuffed and lined up, Dan included. It took them a little longer to detangle Clara from the limp Hicks, as she showed no sign of letting go.

Dan watched as they cuffed her and laid her face down next to him. She smiled and winked at him.

Fifteen minutes later, a pair of FBI suits appeared out of nowhere. One of them was tall and lanky with a soft face and shaggy haircut. His partner was his polar opposite, shorter and portly with a sharp crew cut.

The taller of the two looked around at everyone, then frowned up at the helicopter that was still hovering over the area. He pulled out his radio yelling into it. "Davie, get that chopper out of here would you? I can't even hear myself think down here!" Just like that, the 'copter banked off and left the area.

The shorter suit moved over to Hicks and helped him up, leaning him against the wreckage of the SUV; he was coming around again but looked out of it. "Commander Hicks, I see that you have found steady employment since you left the service." He smiled to Hicks, but it wasn't returned.

"I also see that you're taking your right to remain silent. Not a bad idea. How about you and I do breakfast tomorrow hmm? I'll come by your cell about ten? I'm getting too old for these late night adventures." He motioned to the SWAT team flanking him, and they started to walk the man up the hill toward the road, along with most of Hick's now-cuffed men.

The taller suit walked over to Clara and Dan. "Well, hello there, Mr. UPS." Dan figured that he was able to tell where he worked by his shirt and pants. "Do they normally have you guys running around delivering packages in the middle of the night in supercharged

100k SUVs?" He helped Dan up before introducing himself as Brian Parker, head of the corporate corruption office. He introduced his partner as Patrick Crispi.

"It's all kind of a long story to tell the truth, sir," Dan said, spitting out grit.

Patrick joined them, having pulled Clara's purse from the wreckage of the SUV. He set it down in the dirt before both he and Brian helped her to sit up. He pulled their IDs out and looked them over, comparing the pictures to the people.

Patrick talked now. "Well it's all actually rather simple. Mister Hollis and…" He paused looking over Clara's driver's license "You would be the woman that Ricky was talking about, yes?" He sighed a little. "I see. I don't know that it would do anyone any good to have the boss's daughter found at the scene of a criminal investigation."

Dan was looking confused. "Ricky?"

Brian nodded. "The man that you met tonight, he's been working with us on the inside. You see, we've been investigating Dinatech now for about three years. While they have been working on a contract for the government, they haven't always been on the level. Parts of the government might think that's okay, other parts believe that they need to be punished for not being a good lap dog."

Patrick shrugged his shoulder and put both IDs back into the handbag. "You give these guys special privilege and they push it as far as they can." He shrugged again.

Dan glanced over to Clara, "Your father is their boss?"

She smiled at him but didn't say anything, Brian cut in once more. "In a manner of speaking, let's just say I don't want to be the one that tells him that I have his kid in custody."

He walked over and started to help Clara up. "Come on, we can drop you off at the airport and get you back in Portland before anyone is the wiser."

With Brian's help Clara came to her feet. She looked back to see Dan still on his knees; she gave Brian a look that could be called pouting, but anyone that knew better would see it commanded far more obedience.

Brian looked over to Dan, then back again.

"You have to be kidding, right?" Brian said with a groan.

Clara gave him a more intense stare that left Brian quailing. "You know Patrick, I think that we have enough evidence. We don't really have time to see Daniel for a few days."

"And all those records, Ricky did a hell of job on his *own*," Patrick added, seeing where this was going.

Patrick sighed, showing that he didn't like the idea, but he undid the cuffs on both of them and slung the purse over Clara's shoulder. Brian motioned for them to follow, and they walked their way up the embankment as more officers came down to tape off the wreckage.

"Yeah I mean we don't have to figure out that Daniel was involved for at least a day or two, and then it would just be a matter of his *volunteering* to come down and be a witness to what he saw during his time in Dinatech's research building," Patrick added as they came to the top of the road.

Clara looked back at Patrick but he shook his head to her. "That's the best we can offer honey, he's going to have to get pulled into this one way or the other."

Dan reached forward and put his hand on Clara's

shoulder. "It will be fine." He was going to say more but Clara gave him a look that said he should shut up.

"Just don't make me come find you Daniel, because we will," Patrick warned, pulling open the back door to a large black SUV.

"Maybe next time you can find me before I'm dragged off to another state?" Dan said, slipping into the back of the truck; it was nowhere near as fancy as the one that Dan just wrecked, a simple government issued GMC. Dan got in, and Brian helped Clara in on the other side before telling one of the men to drop them off at the airport in Sacramento.

Brian walked back over to the window. "Look you two; be home on Tuesday, so that I can have Daniel here come in for a statement." He looked around Clara at Dan and growled a little. "If I do have to go hunting for you…" he wanted to say more, but nothing good came to mind. Brian already seemed to be regretting the choice to let Dan go.

Dan nodded in agreement through the window; he was more than ready to go in, he was ready to do whatever it took to make sure nothing like this ever happened again. To anyone.

Brian looked back over the large scorched hunk of concrete and frowned a little. "I just want to know, how the hell did the two of you survive getting hit with an anti-tank missile?"

Clara laughed and crawled over Dan to look out his window, brushing her hair back and she too looked at the missing chunk of melted road. "We got lucky. Missile went low; just proves that you should always wear your seat belt right?" She sat back in her seat, rolling up the window mouthing the words "Oh my god" to Dan.

Brian was left shaking his head as Patrick motioned for the driver to get them out of there.

The truck turned around and drove them back toward Sacramento. It was at this moment that Dan felt as if he could truly let it all go. He knew that he was going to survive this, that it hadn't gotten the best of him. He collapsed into the seat, gasping for air, not realizing he'd been holding his breath.

Clara looked over to him and cocked a brow. "You still hurting, baby?" She reached over and carefully touched him arm, tracing with just her fingertips.

"We really are going to be okay? We aren't running anymore?" Dan asked slumping down into his seat.

She smiled and shrugged her shoulders. "I don't think that it's over, but yeah, I think that we're on the right side for now." She settled back and looked out of the window. "Let's get to Vegas."

She eyed him. "You promised that I could come with you."

"Sure," Dan said tiredly. "Just promise me that we never have to come back to California. I don't like it here."

At the airport, the car dropped them off in the departures section without so much as a word before pulling away from the curb. They looked at one another, and Clara winced a little.

"I think that we may want to step into the Khazi for a moment and freshen up, or they might not let us onto the plane."

"The what?"

"Bathroom," Clara explained.

"How did you think of that word?" Dan said bewildered.

"Don't look at me."

On her clarified advice Dan did just that; he started to walk by the mirror to take a pee when he stopped dead in his tracks. He looked like he'd just gotten in a car wreck, and then dragged through the dirt so that he could catch a plane. He washed his face but there wasn't much that he could do for the blood shot eyes or the fact that he really needed a shower. At least the dark brown fabric did well to hide the dirt, and if he creased it the right way you couldn't see the rips along the one side.

It took Dan a second to find Clara by the ticketing line; she'd taken the time to do a little shopping at a souvenir shop, picking a large, oversized Sacramento Kings hoodie. It fell almost to her knees, covering up the dirt and blood. She'd also combed her hair back, pulling it into a long ponytail. She smiled up to him as he almost walked past. "I think this will have to do till we can go shopping on the strip." She winked and they walked up to the counter. She looked like she was twelve and borrowing her father's clothes.

Handing over their IDs to the clerk, Dan also gave his credit card number to order the tickets. The clerk looked them both over before she started to type Dan's information into the system. The clerk paused then she started to tab though windows on her computer, she frowned in confusion. "Sir, we have two passes on standby for you. Would you care to use them for this flight?"

Dan cocked a brow and leaned forward. "I have what?" He looked over to Clara. "Would this have anything to do with Brian Parks or his boss?"

Clara held up her hands the sleeves flopping down over them, she shook her head. "No, I think that you'll find that government is rather cheap any time it can be."

The clerk chimed back in. "The two passes are good for any round trip with our partners." The clerk typed a few more buttons. "They were originally booked online."

That was the key information that Dan needed. He knew at once who had booked the flights for them. The computer really had kept its side of the deal; it had promised that it would get him to Vegas with his friends. Did that also mean that they were currently enjoying the penthouse of the Venetian? He couldn't help but shake his head and smile. He leaned on the counter, enjoying this. "Yeah we'd like to use the passes please, with the return trip putting us in Portland."

With nothing more than a nod the clerk put the rest of the information into the system and they were on their way through security, which left Dan a little nervous; he'd had about all the fun that he ever wanted to have with security for the rest of his days. Though, passing his phone through the X-Ray machine reminded him he hadn't bothered to turn it back on after Clara had taken it apart.

How many phone messages might he have gotten from Jake about where the hell he was? And how pissed he was that he was going to have to make other arrangements to get to the airport. He winced at the fact that he'd probably had more than a million calls from work asking where he was. More importantly what they would want to know is where was their truck? Would they even care if he'd made his last delivery? Dan held the phone out from his body; it was like a little time bomb that was just waiting to go off.

Clara pulled her purse back up over her shoulder as she jogged a few steps to catch up with him. "Something up?" she looked between the phone and him.

"No." Dan said with resignation in his voice. "I don't think that I'm going to turn on my phone till I've gotten a good night's sleep."

Giving him a knowing smile, Clara took his arm as they walked for the plane.

"Do you think that it would be better to just get a new phone and new number?" Dan asked. "I don't even want to think about the messages that are waiting for me. What do I even tell them?"

"Horrible power failure in the building?" Clara said. "I'm sure there will be some cover story about what happened. I say we should see what kind of news hits and make up a story from there." She swung on his arm a little before letting go and skipping a few steps ahead of him. "I still have to make a few calls before my dad has the whole army taking that building apart brick by brick trying to find me."

"Would he know that you're really missing yet? It's only been a night," Dan asked.

"I told you, I've been trying to save money for school so I kind of still live at home," Clara said with a blush. "I'm sure that sounds bloody lame."

"Clara Paxton, you are about the coolest person that I've met in my life. If it had been anyone else that I'd gotten trapped in a building run by a bio-computer that was suffering from a bout of super-rabies, I would have been dead long before I got the chance to be chased by the psychopathic people that put it together."

She gave him a little nudge in the ribs that about put him on his knees in pain, but he was able to keep his reaction to a small gasp for air.

"You're sweet to say that, but you had your moments of playing hero too, delivery boy."

"Like what?"

"You came for me in the security office."

"You saved yourself there!"

"Well you did come." She waved a hand. "Alright then, what about when I lost my footing in the hall in the robotics lab? You pulled me out of the line of fire."

"Anyone would have done the same," Dan countered.

They kept up recalling what had happened in hushed voices for another thirty minutes before they boarded the plane. Once on board and in flight, Dan consumed every snack he could get his hands on. Skipping dinner left him extremely hungry. Meanwhile Clara used this time to get in a little nap for the short hop into Vegas.

Getting off the plane, Dan was expecting there to be some kind of trouble as he still wasn't convinced they were out of this yet. But there was no fanfare, just a quiet walk to the taxi and then a fifteen minute ride to the front doors of the Venetian. Once they got to the counter, he was greeted with all smiles and an escort to the room. The man seemed a little concerned as there was no luggage and knew that his tip would suffer for it, but Dan was more than ready to leave him with the last twenty in his wallet just so that he'd leave them at the door.

He was tired and it was close to six in the morning; he needed to sleep badly. He couldn't relax on the flight and even the small amount of sleep that Clara had gotten didn't look to be enough. They took a moment to glance over the twenty-nine hundred square feet of plush rugs accented by tastefully selected marble. Crashed out on the sofa sleeper were a few friends that he hadn't seen in years. He glanced to the left to see more camped out in the secondary bedroom along with Jake. While they may have been mad at him for not making the trip until now, they apparently felt that it would be bad taste to take the master bedroom from the man they thought was funding this palace.

Kicking off her flats, Clara walked the last few steps through the soft comforting carpet before collapsing into the bed with a groan.

"You know, for a computer that was in the last throws of its life, it really seemed to know how to pamper its victims," she said softly to not wake anyone up.

She pulled back the covers and started to crawl under them, tossing off clothes as she went.

Dan looked around and finding the chair in the corner he moved to check the closet for anything he could use to cover up with. The place was larger than his apartment back in Portland; surely it had a few extra sets of bedding.

Clara looked confused as he dug about. "What, you don't want to come to bed yet?"

Dan's eyes got a little bigger as he looked over to Clara as she sat up in the king size bed, the size of it made her look small again, like the hoodie did.

"I just thought..."

"Well you thought wrong, it's okay." She pulled her hand out from under the cover and motioned him over.

Not in any shape to argue, he tossed his pants to the floor before climbing in as well and looked over to her on

169

the other side of the bed.

Clara laughed a little and slid over just enough so that she could reach out and brush her hand through his dark hair. "Don't worry, I'll let you sleep tonight, how about that?" She winked and took a deep breath only to let it out with a yawn. She nuzzled her head into the pillow and mumbled softly as she passed out again, "Goodnight, delivery boy."

Not able to help himself, he watched her sleep for a good five minutes before he drifted off onto a dreamless sleep of his own. He hoped that his friends wouldn't wake up till noon and that would be a good little nap before he'd have to try and explain why he didn't make it home, how he'd missed his flight and why he was sleeping with one of the cutest, most dangerous girls he'd ever laid eyes on.

Looking back at it later Dan was sure that he indeed had a dream that night, glimpses of games past, moments in his life that he'd enjoyed it all. There was a new harmony in his life that just seemed to complete him. He wouldn't have to go through life alone anymore; he would have a partner in everything…but it wasn't Clara. No, this was even more personal than that. The machine was becoming part of him.

Corporate

Policy

By

Robert Dufalo

To everyone who enjoyed the first book.

I guess that makes you my fans.

It keeps me humble.

Chapter 1: Oceans 11

He slept like a baby. No, that wasn't right: even babies didn't sleep this well. He was under so deep, he wasn't even bothered by the complete stranger lying just a foot away in the same bed, curled catlike into a ball under the covers. His rest would have been perfect if he hadn't been getting jabbed in the arm repeatedly. Dan finally opened his eyes, surfacing from sleep to figure out who was going to die for bothering him.

Before him was a blurry man with shaggy, sandy blonde hair and blue eyes, leaning in towards him. Slowly the face came into focus, and Dan could see the man above who was looking down at him with an expression of amusement and annoyance.

"Dude, where the fuck you been, man Jake said, was glancing past Dan at the unmoving lump that lay next to him.

Dan looked over to see that Clara was completely under the covers—

except for her long, dark hair that spilled out over the pillow.

"Is this the reason that you couldn't even call me? I almost missed my fight waiting for you," Jake said. He stood up, rubbing his chin.

"You didn't get in and go off and marry a stripper, did you, man? You knew we were going to hit the clubs together." Jake was clearly toying with him.

"When I come out from under here, I'm going to figure out who is calling me a stripper and I'm going to remove their nuts," Clara said, muffled and gruff from under blankets.

Jake blinked and looked at the mound that was Clara. "Dude, Dan … that lump sounds British."

Jake gave him a wry smile; apparently any and all complaints he had were forgotten. It probably helped that he'd just woken up in the coolest room the hotel had to offer: this bedroom was one of two in the penthouse.

Dan sat up carefully; he didn't want to jar any of his injuries from last night. To his surprise he wasn't in pain. In fact … nothing hurt at all. He honesty hadn't felt this good in a long time, other than his stomach raging for food; he'd have to fix that soon. He contemplated room service since he needed a shower. Jake was watching him, nodding to the mound under the covers again. He was expecting an explanation.

"Jake, man, I'll introduce you later, okay? It was kind of a rough night, and now isn't a good time. At least let me get a shower."

As if on cue, more of Dan's friends popped though the suite door to greet him. Jake held up his hands and nodded.

"Alright man, but she's not getting out the front door without me meeting her." He smiled and walked to the double doors with his arms spread to usher everyone out. There were protests, and then more of an uprising once they heard that Dan had a girl in the bed.

"Something tells me if she wanted out of here without you noticing, she'd be gone, Jake," Dan mumbled with a grin.

"Oh Dan, speaking of this place." Jake leaned back into the room. "I know that we said we'd chip in on the room. But I'm not sure we could cover the cost of a penthouse, even if everyone really does chip in."

Dan waved him off. "Don't worry, I have it covered," he said, and slid to the edge of the bed to shoo Jake out with the rest.

"Now if you don't mind, I'm sure that our lady friend might like to get out of bed and have a shower," he said through the door. "You can see her at breakfast if you want to wait around!"

The group protested more but he closed the door, leaving them to argue on the other side. He looked back and Clara's head was poking out from under the covers; her blue eyes scanned the room. Now that the coast was clear, she pulled the covers down, tucking them under her chin. With a coy smile she said, "Hi." Her voice was soft, still sleepy.

"Hey," he said, with the same bashful tone. This had to be a little strange for Clara; it was sure strange for him. They hadn't even known one another twenty-four hours, yet here they were, waking up in the same bed. He moved around the large room, not yet familiar with it.

"If you would like, you can have the shower first," Dan said. He opened a set of double doors that he figured would lead to the bathroom. He was both right and wrong: the room beyond the door was a dressing room and closet, but a second set of double doors on the far side led into the actual bathroom. The bathroom was almost the size of the bedroom with a huge Jacuzzi-like tub and a double shower behind a set of glass doors. "Okay, that's just...wow."

"What is?" Clara's voice was closer than he expected, and he jumped. She was standing in the bathroom door wearing a pair of boy-cut panties and a figure-hugging tank top. She was just a few inches over five feet; almost a foot shorter than him, her build slender and athletic.

Unable to take his eyes off her, he repeated, "That's just...wow." Clara blushed, and fidgeted with her bed-messed hair. Trying to keep the moment from becoming any more awkward, Dan pointed to the showers. "Double shower. I've never seen one like that before."

He stepped into the shower and tried not to stare at Clara. He heard her bare feet pad up behind him, and then her sylphlike arms wrapped around him as she pressed her cheek into his back.

"How are you feeling?" she asked.

"I feel fine, just some bruises," Dan said while he tried to keep his heart from pounding. He wasn't sure what to do with his hands so he left them limp at his side. "I mean … I don't feel any pain at all. I was sure my ribs where broken in the crash last night, but..." He reached behind and pressed his hand against Clara's hip before pulling it away. "Ah, sorry."

"You think the nano computers fixed it?" Clara didn't react to his touch. She turned her head and pressed her nose into his back.

"I have to think that's true. Doctor Adams told me as much. I mean, he said that they were becoming a part of me; that I was adapting." He looked down, her small hands linked together around him. "I wonder what other changes will come from this?"

Clara went still.

"I guess we'll just have to take each one as they come?" She lifted her head and kissed him between his shoulder blades. "Now get out, you don't get to see me shower yet." She smiled and pushed him towards the door of the bathroom.

Knowing better than to press his luck, he held his hands up in surrender. Clara laughed and closed the door after him. Dan sat down on the bed and pulled his phone out of his crumpled pants.

He tossed the device up in the air while he debated if he really wanted to deal with this now. But how long could he keep putting it off? He finally mustered up the courage and turned it on. The phone started with its usual chime. Standing up, he looked out the window over the Strip below him; it looked inviting, all those people out there having fun. It was much more inviting than being trapped in a building.

His phone vibrated in his hand, bringing him back to reality. He had a voice mail, and over twenty text messages. He let out the breath he didn't know he was holding in. Scrolling through the texts, he saw that many of them were from Jake.

Message from: Jake 4:00 pm
Dude! It's time! Get your ass home and we'll head out early for a drink before we hit the airport.

Message from: Jake 4:26pm
Where are U man? Stuck in traffic?

Message from: Jake 4:46pm
Forget the drinks, U going to make it in time for the flight?

*　*　*

Message from Jake 5:04pm

I got a ride be at the airport, I'm leaving without your ass!

There were a few other messages when Jake had landed in Vegas, asking how in hell they got this room.

With a soft laugh, Dan shook his head and deleted the messages before pressing the voice mail button. All of them were from his boss.

"Yeah Dan, it's Dana, just wanted to know what was going on. You missed your check in time; didn't you say you needed to get out of work early today? Give me a call when you get a chance, okay?"

There were a few more messages that sounded more professional. Dana always did that when she was getting worried. Dan was already formulating his excuse as he listened to the last message.

"Dan, I got it all sorted out. The police let me know that you'd been taken in for medical treatment as a precaution. We had the truck picked up so please don't worry about it. I know you must have a lot going on right now. Just make sure you get in touch with HR when you can, we need to get the right paperwork filed for the incident. Hey, call me at home would you? I just want to make sure you're okay."

A huge wave of relief surged through him, so strong it made the ends of his fingers tingle. He'd started dialing Dana when his phone rang, an unknown number on the display. Flexing his wrist he could feel where the nanobot wound still itched. He answered the call.

"Hello?"

"Hey, Danny boy," Dan knew the voice on the other

side of the line: Brian Parks, FBI agent. "I see you didn't make it back to Portland yet. Anything I should be worrying about?"

"No, everything's fine; it's just I had this trip to Vegas planned. I think my friends would have killed me if I didn't make it." Not that the rest of his life wasn't already trying to do the same.

"You know our deal. You'd better be back in Portland by Tuesday or I'll drag you back in chains, Clara or no Clara. You get me?" Brian talked the whole time in a false, cheerful tone.

"Yeah, crystal clear. I'll be there," Dan, said flatly.

"No one has been bothering you, have they?"

"Why would someone be bothering me? I'm on vacation." Dan frowned at the phone.

"We haven't been able to track down Doctor Adams, I was wondering if he had contacted you. I'm sure he'll try to."

Dan turned to see Clara walking out of the bathroom; her hair was damp and combed straight back. She smiled at him, cocking her head to one side when she saw he was on the phone.

"Yeah, I'll see you Tuesday." Dan hung up the phone and tossed it on the bed; calling Dana could wait. "I guess we really should have gotten some more clothes to wear." He fidgeted, reaching up and rubbing the end of his nose. "Let me go see what I can bum off the guys. I'll be right back."

Clara looked at the phone on the bed as he closed the door. Everyone was in the living room, watching him as he came out. He realized his mistake immediately, but it was too late to fix it now.

"Dude, you have to tell me man, how hot is she?" Jake

walked over and slapped a backpack into his hands. "Your shit. You owe me for the bag fees, too." One issue solved, one to go.

With Jake's help, he talked Theo out of a pair of his shorts for Clara. He was the smallest of the six, and she still had the hoodie she bought in the California airport. It only needed to get her through breakfast, and then they could go shopping for some clothes.

Deflecting more questions, Dan closed the bedroom door and turned to see Clara on the phone this time.

"Yes Daddy, I'll be home on Tuesday." She paused before saying, "Yeesss, then." Drawing it out before her voice became forceful. "No, I'm not coming home now." She smiled to Dan, "I'll see you Tuesday, Daddy." She snapped the phone closed, cutting off anything more the party on the other end might say.

"I take it your parents don't like you being out here in Vegas with six men?" Dan asked as he put the jean shorts on the bed next to her.

"Oh, no, no, if they knew that, both of my fathers would be dropping through these windows on static lines to take me away." She laughed and examined the shorts with a grimace. "We're going shopping the moment we're done with food, right? I'd say now, but I'm starved." She held the shorts up with a look that said she didn't much care for them.

Once she was back in the bathroom to finish getting ready, Dan was left to wonder if he really wanted to meet her two fathers any time soon. His imagination played with the idea of them dropping him out of a Blackhawk helicopter in the South American jungles with nothing more than a canteen of water and a pocketknife. "If you want to date her, you have to make it home from here, boy!"

The more people trying to leave the same place, the longer it takes, and it grows exponentially. They didn't make it down to the hotel restaurant until close to 1:00pm, and Dan wondered if he should just order dinner now to save time later. The seven of them were seated around a long table in the back. Dan sat on one side of Clara, and Jake insisted on sitting on her other side. She looked about fourteen-years-old between the two taller men in her oversized hoodie and shorts.

What Dan thought would be an all-out verbal assault on Clara was a cold war. While everyone wanted to question her, no one wanted to be the first. It stayed quiet until food was ordered and a round of coffee was delivered to prop them up—except for Clara, who revealed she didn't drink caffeine.

The waitress walked away, and Jake turned to her first. "So how did you and old Danny boy meet? You would think he would have mentioned you before ... the trip." He smiled before taking a sip of his coffee.

Dan stiffened, but Clara seemed to take it in stride.

"Oh, Delivery Boy?" She smiled and reached over to put a hand on his thigh.

"We met yesterday. He made a delivery to my office and we hit it off after I showed him around." She gave Dan's leg a squeeze. "You're Jake, right? I'm never good with names at first. Sorry to crash your male bonding time, but I've never been to Vegas before, and I begged Dan to bring me with him."

"Oh well, we can show you around. We come down every couple of years to catch up with old friends, so we've seen a lot of the Strip."

So Jake was accepting her story at face value? Did he believe Dan could easily bring any girl that asked to come along?

Jake took another sip of his coffee. "So are you going to hit the strip clubs with the rest of us?" Dan was about to protest that Jake had gone too far, but Clara gave his leg another squeeze to quiet him.

"I think that I might skip that part. I'm sure that I can find other ways to entertain myself."

"Your last name is Paxton? You look like Sara Paxton, the actor. Are you related?" Theo chimed in next. He was the next smallest person at the table after Clara. He was of Korean-American descent and good friends with Dan and Jake from high school.

Clara smiled slyly. "Oh, well, yeah, she's my mother. She kept Dad's name after they divorced. She thought it would sound a lot better than Liverworth."

Dan sputtered on his coffee. "You said that she was going to Hollywood to become an actor."

"I was five then, you'd think she would have made it by now." She laughed along with the others at the table. Learning more about Clara would be very entertaining.

The rest of the brunch went smooth enough; Dan was surprised when he ordered more food, still feeling starved after eating a four-egg omelet. After a second cup of coffee, the group started to break up. Jake had signed he and Dan up for an afternoon poker tournament, leaving Dan with only a little time to show Clara one of the better malls before he'd need to go play. The two of them walked along the strip with the tall cityscape before them; the dry warmth of the desert beat down on them even though it was fall in most parts of the US.

"Do you think I passed the friends test?" Clara asked with an amused smile.

"I think you'll find Jake likes anyone of the female persuasion as long as they pay attention to him. And I think Theo is more interested in meeting your mother than you. But yeah, I'd say you passed," Dan said with a soft chuckle.

"You came to Vegas for the strip clubs, hmm?" She looked up at him with a raised brow.

"What time should I expect you back?" She asked, as Dan walked them to the mall in Caesar's Palace, relieved to be out of the heat when they stepped into the air-conditioned building.

"Umm, I'm not going to go. I thought that we might take in a show or something."

"You don't have to change your plans for me, I'll be fine," Clara said.

"You're not changing my plans. I mean, I don't think I could go and not be thinking about you," Dan said, blushing.

Clara took his arm, hugging it to herself. "That's sweet of you, but I'm not sure I want you thinking of me while you're with strippers." She glanced around. "I'm going to get some shopping done before Dad cuts off my cards in retaliation. Why don't you be off to your poker game, and I'll catch you up when I'm done."

They said their goodbyes and she kissed him softly on

the cheek before departing; Dan looked back a few times, missing her already. He stepped back out into the blinding light of the day. For the first time since they had met, Clara and Dan were no longer in the same building. He paused and looked back feeling unsure; forcing himself to take a calming breath before he moved on.

Settled in at the largest poker table, Dan won his way into the final round of the tournament; actually he'd won very easily. Jake had gone out in the second round and was already at the bar hitting on waitresses, and no longer interested in the tournament.   Dan had never been that good of a player; Jake usually always took him back home. Still, he enjoyed the game and playing in a Vegas tournament was something that he'd always wanted to do. He'd watched them on TV and thought it would be cool to play against big stakes players. When he had these daydreams, he never expected he'd actually get there. To his surprise, his chip lead was commanding.

It was a few hands in at the finals table, and he was looking over his cards. They were playing Texas Hold'em. Dan was holding a pair of sevens; he was the big blind and opened the betting. The odds that he could win the hand straight up would be 23 percent, with a chance that another seven could come in the flop. He paused, watching the table—trying not to frown and give anything away. Did he just calculate the odds of what he'd get on the flop? He did the math in his head again, and was sure he was right.

He thought back realized that maybe he'd been able

to mathematically calculate odds since he'd been at the table. He had believed that been playing on gut instinct; knowing when to stand and when to fold, but it seemed that his "luck" was actually something else. He'd been working through the chances and subconsciously calculating and understanding the odds. Knowing that he'd never been able to do it before, Dan wasn't sure how he was doing it now.

After a few rounds, there were a few veterans left and himself; he felt that he was living out his dream, but wasn't able to completely enjoy it. Without his cell phone on at the table, he hadn't been able to keep in touch with Clara either, so he found his eye flicking to the clock as he became distracted between hands. She'd been with him through the other changes, and this one bothered him more. The idea of changes within his brain did not sit well.

His worries were soon forgotten as a stunningly-dressed Clara walked into the casino. Her long hair was done up into a twist, and she was wearing a pale blue dress that matched her eyes. She walked up and put an arm around his shoulder between rounds. A glance back to the table told him he wasn't the only one looking.

Clara leaned over and said softly, "I got us some tickets to the Phantom of the Opera tonight; everyone I talked with today said it's good. I wanted to make it up to you, since you're missing the clubs for me."

"I'm not missing anything at all," he said with a smile.

She winked and walked off towards the bar.

A half hour later, the table started to clear as the bets got richer. Soon it was down to Dan and a Saudi Arabian oil tycoon by the name of Makin Al Zahrani. He'd told Dan a little about his work between rounds.

"Tell me, my friend," Makin said, and Dan wondered just when they'd become friends. "Is that lovely woman your wife?"

"What?" he looked back over to Clara, he didn't know what he should say, "Umm, we just met yesterday, to be honest." Dan said, checking his cards even though he knew perfectly well what they were.

"Really? Well, my friend, I think that you are lucky in more ways than one," The older Arabian leaned over and winked. He seemed friendly; still, something wasn't right. Dan just couldn't put his finger on it. It could be that he was trying to use Clara as a distraction against him. Or maybe he was being genuinely friendly—but then why didn't he start asking questions when they first came to the table?

Dan was a bundle of nerves, and now he was paranoid too; he'd never won so much as five dollars playing at Jake's weekend parties. Soon it was down to two of them, and the people watching gave a round of applause as Dan shook hands with the Makin. "Dan you are very good at this game, I'm honored to play against you, and I hope that you'll come to Saudi Arabia stay as my guest ... you and your wife."

"Ah, she's just my friend." Dan corrected him.

"Of course, of course. Technicalities." He waved it off like it was a bothersome fly. Dan really liked the sound of Clara as his wife, even if it was a mistake.

The rounds started going faster, each player folding and waiting for the right hand to make for the final show down. Dan tried to keep himself from fidgeting; it was even more noticeable when he looked across the table at Makin, who sipped wine with a carefree smile.

The cards went down again, and Dan had been dealt

a Queen and a Jack. This was as strong a hand as he was going to get. He upped his bet, and Makin followed him in. Once the flop was shown, he knew there was a good chance that a second Jack was going to come his way. The tycoon had pushed the bet until Dan had no choice but to go all in, slipping past him in chip count. Soon it was down to the last card; if it was a Jack, he'd win.

Dan tapped his fingers over the backs of his cards, Makin looking unworried as he sipped his wine. When the fifth card call was shown, it wasn't a Jack, but an Ace. Makin turned his hand to show two more aces. He had three of a kind, and Dan had nothing.

The place exploded into cheers and applause at the dramatic finish to the game, but Dan was confused, how did Makin have that hand? He tried to think it through, looking stunned. It took him a minute to notice the hand that was held before him; Makin had come around the table to shake hands. Coming to, Dan stood to take his hand and when he did Makin leaned in for a hug.

"It was a marvelous game, you have nothing to be disappointed in." Makin told him as they turned for a picture still shaking.

He looked over through the flashes to see Clara sitting on a stool by the bar, a warm smile on her lips as she watched. No, Dan was not disappointed at all.

Dan and Clara walked along the wide sidewalks of the Vegas strip, the bright lights from the hotels lighting up the pavement in a rainbow of colors. Around them other people drank, the magical air of the place giving them an excuse to make spectacles of themselves. Come

Monday it would be back to the office and business as usual, everyone hoping that their friends didn't post any of the humiliating pictures they took.

Clara's blue eyes followed one large man carrying a long plastic beaker that said "Margarita by the yard" down the side. She leaned against Dan, pressing in more, the night already becoming cool as only the desert could. She wore a dark green dress that stretched over her shapely figure; while form flattering, it did nothing to keep in body heat.

"It's so strange," she said in a strong British accent, watching Margarita Man bump fists with his friend followed by both of them hollering out into the night.

"There's nothing worrying them. They don't have to keep their guard up, and no one on this street is out to get them. They don't even have to think about it, that's just how it is. They can just … be like that, without repercussions."

"What do you mean?" Dan slipped his hand around her waist, resting against the swell of her hip to guide her to the far side of the walk. "Haven't you ever let loose with friends?"

Margarita Man and his friends looked like athletes gone to seed after years of partying and loose diets. Dan turned to avoid them, not because he was worried about what they would do, but because of what Clara would do if things got physical. Clara dug her heals in not letting him turn away, those blue eyes flickered up to his, and his heart skipped a beat. God, how he loved her eyes.

"Not really," she mumbled, flushing and pulled him along through the men. He could feel himself relax as they passed without incident.

He didn't want to press his luck and let her guide them

past. Everything she'd told him had been with the hint of a challenge in her words and posture. Or it could have just been that they were staring death in the face at the time.

"Well, why don't you give it a try then?" Dan said. "We're on vacation and we might not get the chance again … for a long time."

Once they were to back in Oregon, things would be a whole new kind of exciting. The only reason they were here now was because of the clout one of Clara's fathers had with the FBI. Dan was destined to become state's evidence.

Dinatech's personal security had chased them through the streets of Sacramento. They seem to have become states evidence.

"All right," Clara said, letting her mischievous grin come back in full bloom. "But first I want to change. These heels are killing my feet. I want to cut loose, not get cut up." They walked up the smaller sidewalk that led to the covered bridges over what was supposed to mimic the waterways of Venice. Below them a small wedding gondola headed deeper into the canals with a happy couple aboard.

Dan opened the doors to the Venetian and let Clara slip into the warmth of the building before he followed after. The hotel and the show were all in the same large complex, but they had walked around the outside of the building. They didn't feel comfortable staying inside the whole time.

The layout of the casino floor made it necessary to pass the slot machines and card tables to get anywhere, and the air was thick with the sweet perfume that the hotels used to cover up cigarette smoke that lingered on most of the patrons. Dan learned early in his Vegas trips that the smell made him want to puke when hung over. The pair walked along the tight pile carpet, watching people having a great time, gambling deep into the night while downing complimentary drinks.

On the far side of the casino floor, they flashed their room cards to the security guard before boarding the elevators to their room. Dan swallowed, feeling dinner try to come up at the sight of the elevator doors opening up. He saw the question in Clara's eyes when she stepped in and looked back, and she had to pull him in before the doors closed. The whole trip up, his heart pounded, with blood singing in his ears.

"You know, not every elevator is out to get you, Dan," Clara said with a little grin on her lips. She watched him out of the corner of her eye.

"True, but one ride with the elevator trying to kill me is all I need," Dan said, looking around the car for robotic arms that might jump out and attack him.

"Hey, you didn't have to ride it twice." She was looking straight at the door, and he could see there was a flashback playing through her mind.

They got off on the penthouse floor and walked out onto rich plush carpets outlined in cream-colored marble tiles. Along the walls, dark wood tables held flowers in ceramic vases. They turned away from the elevators and walked down the short hall to their penthouse; Dan was just relieved to be out of the elevator. Parts of the musical played out in his head and the wine from dinner was making him fuzzy. What would be waiting for them Monday seemed far away. Clara was pulling the room key out of her small green purse when her phone rang. She glanced at the number and answered while leaning against the door.

Whoever it was she was talking to, he knew she didn't like them from the frown painted on her face.

"Why would I do that?" she asked, her voice sharp. She looked up at Dan, then down the hallway in both directions.

The voice on the other end was raised, but Dan couldn't make out the words, only that the voice was male. One of the service staff came around the corner with a room service trolley and Clara's hand slipped from Dan's arm as she took a step back.

"Bugger."

Chapter 2: Empire Strikes Back

Clara had an expression Dan wasn't sure he liked. Every time he'd seen that look, she was trying to think her way out of a life-or-death situation, and Dan had seen a lot of that face in the twenty-four hours they'd been acquainted.

"Clara, what's going on?" Dan said softly, holding his hand out cautiously, like she might snap at any moment.

"They figured it out, Dan," she said, taking another step back, dropping her phone into her purse. She knotted the strap and cinched the purse close to her body. She turned just as a pair of elevator doors opened and two men in suits stepped out. Clara looked down at her spike-heeled shoes and swore under her breath. "Dad always told me, wear sensible shoes. Am I ever going to listen to that man?"

The men started forward, making no pretense that they weren't here for them.

"Mr. Hollis," the taller of the two men said. He was in his mid-thirties with a sensible haircut, the type of man who would be overlooked in any crowd.

"I'll need both of you to come with us." He reached behind him while he was talking and pulled out a pair of handcuffs.

Dan took a step back, but the moment the handcuffs clicked open, Clara lunged forward, taking the man by his tie. She jerked him up over her shoulder and slammed him to the floor in one fluid motion. Then she dragged him along the corridor by the skinny part of his tie until he dropped the handcuffs. He grabbed at the tie, yanking and fighting to get air.

The other man came at Clara just as the shock of her sudden attack was wearing off. She reached out and tried to jerk the man down by his tie also. As it popped loose in Clara's hand, she looked down at the clip-on, then up at the man, wide eyed, as he grabbed for her. But even surprised, she was too fast for him; dodging back out of his reach, and kicking off her heeled shoes with a clunk.

Taking his cue from Clara, Dan jumped forward and head-butted the man as hard as he could. He felt the crack and the lights behinds his eyelids flashed as he stumbled back. When the stars cleared, he saw that he'd knocked the man out cold. The first man was still coughing and choking as he jerked at his tie.

"Goddamn, that hurt like hell," Dan said, rubbing his head; a nice sized egg was already forming.

"What did you think was going to happen? You bloody fool." Clara barked.

"Hey!" was called from behind them.

The man with the room service trolley had pushed the cart aside and pulled a pistol from his shoulder holster, "On the floor now!"

Clara squeezed her toes into the carpet a few times. "Oh yeah, I kind of forgot about him."

"What do you mean, you forgot about him?" Dan growled back.

"Hey now, Delivery Boy, you try taking down two big burly FBI men in heels." Any more witty banter was cut off.

"On the floor!" the man with the gun repeated, and Clara jumped to, turned, and pushed Dan down the hallway towards the elevators.

"Cheese it!" she said.

The door at the end of the hallway led to the emergency stairs. Clara beat him to it and pushed it open, her long hair whipping out behind her.

"Stairwells and elevators. We did this game on our first date you know."

Dan looked back. The man on the floor had gotten his tie free and was gulping down air. He pulled his radio out, but Dan didn't wait to hear what he said; the room service man was fast on their heels. Dan pulled the door closed hard and followed Clara, taking the stairs two at a time. Her feet moved lightly over the concrete steps; his own shoes slapped loudly on every other step as he tried to close the gap with the quicker Clara.

Above them the door opened so hard that it echoed in the concrete stairwell. "Don't run! I'll shoot!" The man already sounded out of breath.

Dan wasn't sure if he really would shoot them or not; they were in a populated hotel, and if he heard Clara correctly they were FBI and they wouldn't put others in danger. Why were they here? He'd talked to Brian and they were waiting for him to come home to Oregon. They had no reason to come here for him. But it could easily be people working for Dinatech and posing as FBI agents. The agent was talking softly and Dan was sure that he was using a radio, calling for back up. On they went, down floor after floor. Dan glanced at each set of metal doors as they passed, but every one of them said it was locked and that the only way out was on floor 1.

Their pursuer called "Stop!" again, but he sounded farther way. They were losing him. Now Dan was jumping the last 5 or 6 steps at every landing.

"I'm going to shoot you both!" the man said, out of breath. "And I'm going to like it!"

Ten, nine, eight, seven ... the floors were counting down faster and faster, and Dan was sweating heavily through his button-down shirt and his legs were starting to feel like rubber. He still wasn't in the best shape after his body tried to reject the nanobot injection.

One.

Clara put her shoulder into the door and the chain holding it snapped. They came out in a long concrete hallway with a concrete floor, the wall painted white while the floor was painted only with the black marks of millions of carts passing over it. Clara looked around, but she never stopped moving. She frowned up at the cameras along the ceiling and put up a slender finger to flip them off.

"We stop for no one." She turned towards Dan, walking backwards, letting the offending hand fall to her side. "Someone tries to stop you, take them down and you *keep* moving." She turned to walk forward again, but her eyes stayed on him.

"Yeah, I got you." Dan picked up his step to close the distance.

"No, you don't. Vegas is all about money; they are going to have some of the nastiest security because that is what money brings. And they are going to do whatever the FBI says." She stopped at a black door and wrenched it open. Just beyond the door were vanilla skies over old brick buildings of a time well past. They were in the indoor mall between the Palazzo and the Venetian, the ceiling painted to look like Venice's summer sky. No matter what time it was always a lovely day.

Clara slowed to a quick walk, her bare feet padding along the tile as she scanned the people around her. She plunged her hand into her purse and pulled her phone out again. She removed the battery, tossed it to the side, and then with the snapping sound of the screen protesting, she broke her phone in half and tossed the remains into a garbage can. Dan bounded up the last few steps to fall into step with her. Clara reached into his pocket to do the same with his phone.

"Hey, can't we just turn them off like before?" He watched as Clara tossed the shattered parts about as she went.

"No, we lose them, we don't want them pulling off any data to track us."

"Like what?"

"Like anything that you might have forgotten," Clara countered.

Dan looked back at the doors they had walked through to find the agent about twenty yards behind them; he had already pocketed his gun as he entered the public shopping center. They would try to avoid a scene. The mall gave Clara and Dan the best chance to slip free.

"I thought your father worked for the FBI," Dan leaned in to say.

"He does." She let her eyes flicker up to him before glancing around as security closed in; they were dressed like Venice police. "He's a regional director. I don't think this is coming from him." Her voice told Dan she wasn't sure. They were getting pinched between security and FBI. Clara led them to one of the white miniature bridges over the waterway down the middle of the shopping area. Below them people floated along, ferried from one end of the mall to the other in little gondolas. Clara pulled Dan along as their pursuers talked frantically into their radios.

The agent from the stairs started to run after them, and Clara turned to confront him. Dan looked about until he found what he wanted; a pair of black doors you might miss of you weren't looking for them. They provided access to more services halls, and doubled as fire exits.

"I'm not sure you really want to chuck a wobbly here," Clara said

The agent who was squaring up with Clara and Dan moved a few steps towards the doors. The other security moved in as well; this was going to be where the "scene" would happen.

"A what? Just give up and lie down and I won't have to hurt you, hon," the man said.

Dan heard the words and panicked, turning to the man. "No, no you don't want to do that." He waved his hands at him. But it was too late.

Changing her direction, Clara suddenly walked into the man's next step. Swinging out wide with her green purse, she used it as a feint and the other hand came up, driving between his own as he tried to protect himself. She drove the palm of her hand up into his jaw so that his teeth clicked together and head whipped back, spelling concussion. He was already going limp, but she grabbed his arm, flipping him over the banister, and with a splash he was plunged into the water below. Stopping at the edge of the railing, Dan looked down to watch him go in before noticing Jake with his sandy hair and Theo on the other side of the canal. Both looked well dressed and ready for the clubs. "Dan!" he called over. "What the hell are you two doing?"

Dan was sure they would find this on YouTube later; even this time of night, with so many watching, someone would be recording. "Ah, I think we're checking out early, sorry! But don't worry, I got the room covered."

"Yeah you better," Jake called back. "I'll figure out your bail, dude."

Theo just continued to stare in disbelief at what he was seeing.

Blue eyes of fire turned on the security force and they all paused, wondering if they were getting paid enough to deal with a girl that just punched out an FBI agent. It was enough of a pause that Dan grabbed Clara by the arm—at much risk to his own safety—and pulled her towards the door. Clara pouted and called back at Jake, "Hey, he started it! Now I want to play!"

"We don't have time to play; remember the whole running from the law thing we're doing?" Dan pushed through the door and into an empty hall. Hand in hand, they ran flat out, following exit signs, as more people in suits and security uniforms piled through the doors after them.

"Oh come on, just let me have one more," she said with a smile in her voice now.

It seemed that Clara had an even stranger idea of fun than he originally thought. Pushing through the door that said "Warning: Alarm will sound if door is opened" in large red letters, they dashed out onto a side street that led to the Sands on one side and back to the Strip. The alarm went off until the door slammed closed.

"I can't keep going barefoot. We're going to have to find me some shoes," Clara said, while trying to straighten out her dress.

Dan was trying to decide which way to go when a long black limo roared up, screeching to a halt. The back door opened up and there, framed in the doorway, was an Arabian man with a short-cropped beard, his head capped in a shemagh.

"Dan, my new friend, it seems you have found some very interesting company, yes indeed." It was Arab who won the poker game that afternoon.

"What…what are you doing here?" Dan asked. Behind them the door to the hotel few open.

"A question to be answered later, I think," the Arab said dryly.

Clara was already diving into the limo, pushing the man back as she torpedoed through. With no time to hesitate, Dan pulled himself in as the car launched forward, the door slamming closed with the force of the limo's take off.

It was the three of them in the back of the limo and only the driver up front. He was calling back as he thrust the car into traffic, "Makin, we are going to have to ditch the car, the cops will be looking for it."

Dan looked back to see FBI only bothering to run after them for a few steps before giving up, very un-movie like, where they chase the car for blocks.

The Arab, Makin, sat back in his seat. "Fine, fine, we

can pick up the town car. We are leaving town; there is no reason for us to be here anymore."

The limo turned onto the strip and picked up speed, weaving through traffic.

"Why are you here?" Dan said, sounding sharper than he meant to. "How did you know we would be out there?"

Clara, apparently unconcerned, was pulling out a stemmed glass from a bar along the far side of the limo. She giggled. "This is so awesome, I've never been in a limo before. Tell me you have champagne. You've got to have champagne."

The whole thing would seem comical, and in a different light, maybe one day he would look back and it would be. But, for the moment, they were rescued from the FBI and that, Dan thought, was worth it. If anything did go wrong, he was sure Clara would be more than ready for it.

"There should be some in the fridge." Makin waved for Clara to turn around and she "Oooed," opening the fridge to find a small bottle of brut.

"It's small, it's so cute!" she laughed like the last twenty minutes hadn't happened. "Dan, you have to see this."

Waving her off, Dan frowned at Makin. "Tell me, how did you know we were on the run? How did you find us?" Clara tossed the wine bottle at Dan hitting him in the side. "Hey!" he exclaimed.

Makin pulled a phone out of his robes, dialed a number, and started to talk into the phone in Russian. Dan looked at Clara, who shrugged. "Don't look at me; I know English and American." She was trying to fill her flute with champagne while the limo jerked through traffic, doing a rather good job of not spilling.

"That's it. Stop the car, we're getting out." Dan reached for door and found it was locked.

Makin waved for him to sit back. "Relax. I needed to make sure we have a car waiting for us." Sitting forward, Makin pulled out a small black box that Dan thought had to be some kind of police scanner. "You two are making a lot of noise right now," Makin said, "It was easy to follow your trail." He waved the box to make his point and tossed it onto the seat beside him.

"And why the hell would you have that? How did you even know that they were talking about us?" Dan's head was spinning.

"Because I'm here to find you, Daniel. You are my only reason for being in Vegas. It's my job to know what Dinatech is up to."

"What are you talking about? How do you even know anything about them?" Clara was curled into the seat with her drink; she was actually looking subdued. Something about that peace annoyed him. How could she be so relaxed right now? This man knew a lot more about them than he was comfortable with.

"You don't think the Oregon facility is the only place Dinatech is committing crimes against humanity?" Makin went on. "What they have been doing there is tame compared to many of their overseas facilities. I've watched this go on long enough. The people I work with are out to stop the company before it can do any more damage."

Dan wasn't sure what he should say. When he didn't say anything, Makin continued, "Our group is called Liberté."

"Isn't that French for 'freedom'?" Clara said, over her

glass.

"I though you only knew English," Dan said.

"And American," she clarified.

"Well that's not French."

"Anyone can know a little French, Dan," Clara said, with a roll of her eyes.

Makin interrupted them, "Liberté is a group of people that have come together to destroy Dinatech and keep them from doing any more harm, because most of us have been wronged by them. When one of our associates found out that Dinatech had rented the Venetian penthouse, we investigated. We also found that the name on penthouse was signed up for the poker tournament. The mystery was: we had no record of you. We were alarmed to think there was someone working at Dinatech that we had nothing on."

Clara leaned over next to Dan and tried to offer him her champagne flute. Dan glanced at Clara and she pouted before taking her glass back.

"You entered a poker tournament to beat a Dinatech employee?" Dan said.

"No, just observation, but you kept winning, and it gave me more opportunities to do so," Makin smiled.

"You haven't explained why you pulled us out of there if you think that we work for the company your people are trying to destroy."

"We hadn't been able to put it all together yet, but after meeting you in the poker tournament I wasn't given the impression you had anything to do with Dinatech. It left me confused, then when I saw Ms. Paxton, things started to get more confusing." Clara was now looking at Makin for the first time; these words had piqued her interest.

"There are no records of you, Dan, but we found Clara Paxton. Clara hasn't even been working there a year, as a receptionist," Makin said. "They don't keep very good records on her, and we really don't have the man power to keep tabs on line workers. We started digging once we found her with you but all we could find was that she has an Oregon driver's license and a social security number." Makin turned to Clara. "After that, nothing, no arrests, no loans, a blank sheet."

Dan turned to watch Clara and she watched Makin, keeping her silence.

Getting nowhere with Clara, Makin turned back to Dan. "We were still trying to make heads or tails of it when it came to our attention that Senator Collin Ellsworth was flying in to Oregon. We know Dinatech and Ellsworth have been in bed together for many years. Dinatech has been funneling large sums of money into his election campaigns, and in return Dinatech is one of the exclusive private contractors to the military. Doctor Jeffrey Adams and Ellsworth have been working closely on something, but we haven't been able to figure out what it is. If Ellsworth is flying out to Oregon, then whatever they are working on is there … or *was* there."

"Your point?" Dan said.

Makin leaned forward. "Soon after Ellsworth landed in Oregon, the FBI were out with new orders: to collect the two of you and bring you back to Oregon." He paused for effect before saying, "I think you two know what Adams and Ellsworth are up to."

Dan knew that Makin was expecting him to say something, but he didn't know what he should say. He decided on a Clara-like stance, saying nothing. While he too believed that Dinatech was a nasty company that should be burned until dead, he didn't know if this man or the guerilla vigilante group could be trusted. This wasn't just about some knowledge that he had or some technology that he could hand over. What everyone was after was …

Him.

The nanobots were floating around inside him and he didn't even know if he could live without them now. He would be horribly maimed if not dead without their healing power. He'd also been able to almost win at the poker tournament because of the supercomputer-like math skills. He didn't know what other powers they might hold. They had only been in his system one day, and for half of that time his body was trying to reject them.

Dr. Adams wasn't even ready to start testing them on live subjects when the Core upped the timeline by injecting Dan with latest and only working versions of the bots.

"Tell me, Dan," Makin pleaded. "Help me take them down before they kill anyone else."

Dan looked at Clara and she looked at him with a passive expression that made the anger bubble up inside him. They were supposed to be in this together; he needed help and she just sat there drinking champagne and saying nothing. She showed a side to the world that made her look like a ditz, but Dan knew better: she was highly capable and a quick thinker. Already she'd saved his life more times than he could ever repay. Imagine if they'd known one another for more than a weekend …

Before anyone could press the issue further, the limo pulled into an abandoned parking lot.

There, in the middle of the paved lot, sat a large black

town car. Pulling up next to it, the driver turned off the engine and everyone got out. Clara reached into the fridge and grabbed a second miniature bottle of champagne before following, her eyes wary of the ground around them, since she was still barefoot. The driver of the town car got out and walked over to meet Makin. He was slightly shorter than Dan with black hair and eyes that only knew how to glare. He looked over to see Clara and Dan and the man cursed in Russian.

"Did you check them?" the Russian yelled, his accent thick.

"They are fine." Makin waved him off.

The Russian pushed Makin back against the limo. "Did you check them?"

Makin grabbed the Russian by the front of his jacket and tossed him to the side, showing more strength than Dan realized he had. The Russian bounced off the lengthened body of the limo. "I said they were fine!"

Dan quickly elevated Makin into the list of people he wouldn't want to cross.

The Russian narrowed his eyes at Makin. "You are reckless, and you'll get us all killed with your foolishness." He then opened the trunk of the limo and tossed in a device the size of a small brick. Without looking back, he turned and walked away into shadow, becoming hard to see in the dim sodium streetlights.

"What was that about?" Dan asked softly.

Makin watched the man a moment before he turned back to Dan. "That was Marko." Giving an overly dramatic shrug of his shoulders, he turned and walked to the running town car. "He's got trust issues. He thinks you are just spies Dinatech has put into place to infiltrate and destroy us."

"Is that what he thinks?" Dan felt that his life would be a lot safer without Marko in it.

Opening the back door, Makin turned back to Dan. "This is what a man whose own brother betrayed and attempted to kill him would think, I'm sure."

The street was empty when Dan looked back to try and catch a glimpse of Marko's ever shrinking figure. He was jolted back to attention by the bang of a massive explosion inside the trunk of the limo, the metal lid bending with the force. Stepping back quickly, Dan watched as flames escaped through the gaps left by the deformed lid.

"Come, you two, we have many miles to travel. We must get started if we are to be there by morning." Makin beckoned them. Inside the cab of the limo the fire was already starting to consume the leather interior. Clara tossed her empty champagne flute into the air and cheered when it smashed across the roof of the limo.

"I think I like this letting loose with friends, Dan." She carefully but quickly made her way around the car and climbed in the front with the driver. Dan was going to have to help her work on her idea of cutting loose.

The four of them rode in silence all the way to the freeway. Makin wanted to know what Dinatech's interest was in Clara and him. Did he dare tell them? The sticking point was that it was him they wanted, not just information; Dan was very cautious.

Inside him was all the nanobot research Dinatech had done to this point. What if he did tell Makin, and he and his Russian accomplice thought that keeping Dan captive would be best? What if they wanted to experiment on him in the hopes they could use their knowledge to take the company down, sacrificing Dan for the greater good? As much as he might want to see Dinatech gone, he didn't want to be a human guinea pig for some other group either.

As Clara and the driver fought over the stereo, Dan looked to Makin. He didn't know where to start, so he went a different way.

"Where are we going?" he asked.

"California, to a safe house we own. There we will plan our next steps." Makin paused before adding, "With the information we obtain." A hint he was still expecting more information from Dan.

Dan flinched. He'd promised that he'd never set a foot into that state again and he hadn't even been gone a whole day.

"What do you know about the Oregon branch?" Dan asked.

"We know that the building and its projects were headed by Dr. Adams, and that it was their military and robotics research divisions. Beyond that we don't know anything. The few attempts we have taken to infiltrate ended in deaths." Makin looked over to Dan, not able to wait any longer. "Whatever are they hiding in there? They are taking drastic measures to keep it quiet, and Senator Ellsworth is deeply involved."

Everything about the large black building was kept under wraps: the building was unmarked, even the loading docks were kept under cover with huge gates that didn't allow for spying.

Dan took in a large breath, letting it out slowly. He nodded. "I've been in the building," he said quietly. Clara stopped arguing over the radio station, and looked back over her seat. She was going to let this be his choice; he didn't know if he could trust Makin, but really there was only one thing that he might tell him that was personal. The rest he didn't care about; hell, most of the building was toast.

"It's some kind of robotics lab," He said. "The fucking things tried to kill us. Large battle bots, armed with cannon-like guns. There are other things going on there. They are working on a teleporter system, and there was … the Core. That's what everyone called it." Dan looked down. The Core was a large biological computer, a living system that ran the whole building. He remembered the room, the large metal chair, and the full wall of screens. The Core talked and it had a human-like understanding of language; it could convey feelings and it understood its own mortality.

Clara was still watching, looking interested; there were parts to this that even she hadn't heard yet. Dan went on to talk about the genetic experiments in the basement and how a tiger had almost mauled them, and how viruses they were mutating had infected the Core.

"There was a bug in the Core's programming. It was coded to protect itself from attack, but when it turns out that the people that created you are the ones attacking you, there wasn't anything to tell it to stop."

Dan's story was making Makin tense up, but as Dan paused Makin took the chance to speak.

"When our team went in to the South American facilities, they were experimenting with the creatures there as well, the most dangerous and deadly creatures you could find; we believe it was the reason they started a branch there. They had some of the most poisonous spiders found in Australia. We haven't been able to find the proof but I believe Dr Adams had a hand in the facility."

The hum of the tires and the drone of the engine were the only noise in the cab. "All interesting information Dan, but why are they chasing you while also paying for you to be in Vegas?"

Dan knew he couldn't avoid telling him forever; he looked at Clara and she looked back to him and gave him a smile.

He then knew it didn't matter if he told Makin; he had Clara and she'd seen him through this far. She could have left him before. When he was too sick to escape, Clara had waited for him in the captivity of Dinatech's security, till she was sure that Dan could escape. This situation was no different: they had a bond that was stronger than just boy meets girl.

"Nanobot technology," Dan said and Makin looked confused. "The crown jewel of Dr. Adam's work is nanobot technology. He's working to make a person stronger, smarter, heal faster, you know, all the crap you see in the Million Dollar Man."

He could see the next question coming and answered, "It's all inside of me now, his life's work, he said." Dan turned over his right wrist. The injection points from yesterday were healed to nothing more than a minor irritation. "Even with the bug, the Core was still able to follow its main programming: to protect company property—and there is nothing more important than the nanobot project." Dan frowned. "It's called Project Silverfish." He tried to remember where he heard that.

Nothing came to him, but he knew that it was right.

"This must be what the FBI was talking about then. They said that you had hardware on you. We had no idea what he was working on. It just proves everything that we know is nothing more than a bucket at the bottom of the lake." He clapped his hands together. "I must tell the others about this. Tell me, do you know what the nanobots can do?"

Dan shook his head. "No, not really, not everything. I've only started to understand them. I do know that they allow me to heal quickly." He didn't tell him he could do math faster: he didn't want anyone knowing it was affecting his mind. Getting locked up because they believed he was under Dinatech's control scared the crap out of him.

"Now that you know all this, what are you going to do?" Dan said, not sure he wanted to know.

"No," Makin said, with a smile. "The question is; what are you going to do, Mr. Hollis? You are both wanted criminals."

Chapter 3: The Big Easy

Dan watched out the window of the town car, the desert landscape passing at sixty-five miles an hour. Even Clara had taken the chance to get a few hours of sleep as she curled up in the front seat.

He was not able to sleep; he couldn't wrap his head around the idea that he was an outlaw now. This didn't feel cool like in an old western. While on the run, he couldn't fly on a commercial airline, he couldn't receive help from cops, he couldn't go to work; he couldn't even touch his money. Hell, he'd have to watch whom he was talking with: any one of them could turn him over to the authorities. He'd seen all the movies where the spies live off the grid for years at a time; it was always cool and they always lived in sexy and remote places. This didn't feel anything like that, he was sure and he wasn't sure he knew how to live like this.

He knew it wouldn't work, and he wanted his life back, all of it. He couldn't just hide and run for the rest of his life with these damn machines floating around his body doing god knows what to him.

To get his life back and win the girl, he was going to need a plan. He needed to clear his name and put the people behind all this in the hot seat. Dan leaned his forehead against the glass. The real question was how he was going to do that.

He thought back over everything that had happened the last two days. It felt like weeks of change.

He looked at Makin whose eyes were forward, watching the road beyond the windshield. He turned to meet Dan's gaze.

"Your group is all about taking down Dinatech right?" Dan asked.

Makin nodded.

"I need to get back into the Sacramento offices. There's no way we're going to get into the Oregon branch with both company and state crawling around in the wreckage of that place. But I think I could pull off getting into the Sacramento offices," Dan said.

"And what do you expect to find in Sacramento?" Makin looked skeptical but not dismissive.

"I think I can find the information I need to clear my name and get my life back." Dan sat forward in his seat with anticipation now that he had a plan. "I want to take as much data as I can and use it to nail the bastards publicly. They might have law enforcement in their pocket but if I can get my story public I can use that to force their hand and make them back off and clear our names."

"Do you think that will work?" Makin asked.

"I don't know, but I'm going to try. I can't just sit back and let them take my life from me." Dan looked at the front seat where Clara slept. "Or hers."

Dan asked after a pause, "Will you help me? You said that you'd infiltrated the South American branches."

Makin didn't say anything at first; he just turned to

watch out the front window once more. Not thinking he was going to get an answer, Dan went back to leaning against the window.

"I will talk with my people and see if we can help you, but that is all I can promise. They may not wish to expose themselves over two strangers. Strangers some believe are spies for Dinatech. But I will try. For you, I'd like to try."

Dan gave him a crooked smile, not looking back. He knew better than to press his luck.

They pulled up to a small house tucked back in a suburban neighborhood. It was so close to the border you might have thought the garage was in California, and the living room in Nevada. The car came to a stop in the driveway, the house dark with the exception of a single light in the window. It looked empty and alone. They got out and stretched. It was just before four AM, and with the winter coming on, the sun wouldn't come up for a few hours yet.

Clara stepped out onto the pavement barefoot, and winced, curling her green painted toes against the cold. She walked after Makin and the driver, who hadn't said anything to them all night. Makin punched a code into the automated lock to open the front door; it gave a mechanical whine before giving them access to the house.

Stepping into the two-story house, Dan could tell the place hadn't been used in a long time; there was almost no furnishing and the air held a cool feel of desertion.

There were tables in the kitchen and dining room but just cheap collapsible tables and metal folding chairs. The kitchen counter held a coffee maker that looked like it saw more use than the house had, with mismatched coffee mugs around it.

The driver walked off as soon as they were through the door, moving through the house to make sure they were alone. Makin motioned to the stairs. "Please, get some sleep. The others will come in the morning. We'll talk more then. This house isn't traceable back to Liberté, and you will both be safe." Dan noted that, while it was an invitation to rest, it was also a dismissal.

Clara looked up the dark staircase. "I'm going to need to get me a pair of shoes." She looked down at her cocktail dress and back to Dan. "And a change of clothes, I dare say." Dan agreed: he didn't think he wanted to be on the run in slacks and a button up.

"There is nothing in the house, but I'll make sure that one of our people brings you comfortable clothes," Makin agreed.

This seemed to be good enough for Clara, and she walked up the stairs looking tired. She opened the door at the end of the hall and walked in.

Dan didn't go up, but held out a hand to Makin and the Arab man looked down at it before he took it to give a firm business shake. "I do believe that we owe you our freedom Makin, thank you. I hope we can work together against Dinatech."

"It is how the fates work, Dan," Makin said.

Dan smiled and looked up the stairs. He felt just how weary he was; he'd been working for hours on adrenaline. He bid good night to Makin and headed to find a bedroom of his own. He was passing Clara's room when her small hands reached out and pulled him in so fast that he bit off a yell. The room Dan was headed to held small twin beds with metal folding fames that were just barely better than having mattresses on the floor. The room that Clara had taken looked like the master bedroom.

"I was starting to think you weren't going to come up at all," she said, pressing her head into the middle of his back, then walked to the bed. The only light was the pale glow of the moon through thin drapes. She pushed on the bed and it squeaked softly, telling that it was old and cheap.

"Well it's not a king sized bed in the Venetian penthouse," she said dryly, "but I'll share it with you, if you want." She gave him a shy smile and started to roll her dress up and off until she was left in a matching green lacy bra and panties. Her figure was trim and athletic, yet soft in all the right places. She pulled the sheets back and slid into bed, pushing herself all the way to the wall to make room for Dan.

It took a moment to realize he was just standing there, then Dan pulled his own clothes off, letting the slacks fall to the floor, the belt buckle clattering against the hardwood floor. He pulled off his shirt as fast as he could and tossed it with the rest. Dan was in good shape himself, playing football through high school; he still played flag football. He tried to use it as an excuse to keep working out and not give in to playing video games on the couch. Still, he wasn't in the kind of shape that Clara was and it left him self-conscious. Clara was, in Dan's mind, out of his league.

He clambered quickly into the bed, pulling the covers up, to find they had just the one pillow for the two of them. Clara laughed as she watched him try to pull and push the small pillow between them to give equal share. "Why don't you use it, I'll be curled under the sheets before you know it," she whispered.

"I could just go find another." Dan said softly.

"Do you want to climb out of the warm bed?" Clara countered.

"Not really." He said.

"Then take the damn pillow." She said.

Dan paused before nodding, unsure. He pulled it over and laid his head on it. He would have fluffed it but there wasn't much to fluff.

"So, Delivery Boy, are we going back into that building?" She leaned in, laying her head against his chest.

Taken aback, Dan didn't even think to blush as he felt Clara's small body curl against him, there was barely enough to keep one person comfortable let alone two.

"You heard that, in the car? I thought you were asleep."

"You can learn a lot when people think you're asleep, Delivery Boy, remember that," Clara said.

"And what do you mean by 'we'? I'm not going to make you go back into that place," Dan said trying to be stern.

There was a shift under the sheets and he found himself trying to pull himself up till his head knocked against the headboard. Clara's knee slid up and pushed into his crotch. "You think you are going to make it in and out of there without me? Do you?" She looked up and even with the dim light he could see how bright and full of life her eyes were. "Let's have this out right now, shall we? We are in this together, thick and thin, end-to-end. All for one and one for all?" She leaned up and kissed the stubble on his chin. "Is that clear enough for you?" She wiggled her knee and it pressed up enough to show him the alternative.

"It's painfully clear," he said in a voice that sounded more panicked than he wanted it to be.

She gave a smile and snuggled in and let her leg come back down.

"Good."

After getting only a few hours of sleep, Dan awakened and watched Clara slumber against his chest; she moved very little once she curled into a ball under the covers. He made a note to ask her about that. The house was quiet—almost disturbingly quiet—with no creaks or pops, or the sound of anyone walking around. It was like a clan of ninjas inhabited the place. He looked at the door, wanting to get up, but with Clara laying on him, he was afraid to move and disturb her sleep; other than a little shift from time to time she was extremely quiet.

There was no clock and Dan wasn't sure what time it was. Slowly he pulled himself out from under the covers. Clara took the opportunity to devour the pillow, sucking it under the covers like something akin to a trapdoor spider sucking down its fluffy prey. While tired, Dan felt much better and not so weary.

Opening the door, he looked out into the hall, trying to find the bathroom, and the first thing he noticed was garbage bags at the foot of the door. Both of them looked full. The bags were squishy and filled with clothes and shoes: nothing that looked new, but all of it was in good condition.

Dan dragged the bags into the room and started to dig through them; one of the bags held clothes for him, the other for Clara. Ten minutes later, Dan was dressed in jeans and a tee shirt that said "Clyde's Rides." Both d's were turned into bike wheels. Once he relieved himself in the bathroom he headed downstairs to find the table in the kitchen had a spread of bagels and take-out coffee. Makin was sitting at the table, sipping at a cup of coffee; he furrowed his brow as he looked into his cup. "I do not understand how you people can like warm coffee," Makin said to Dan as he walked in.

"Isn't that how most people drink coffee?" Dan asked.

"I enjoy my coffee cold, and I mean ice cold. The need for milk is also a strange concept," Makin said.

"I think the French did that." Dan took a cheese bagel and sat in the uncomfortable steel chair.

"Latté is the Italian word for milk. Perhaps it was them?" Makin said, and sipped his coffee with a wrinkled nose.

"Who got all this?" Dan asked, waving to the table.

"Paul. You met him last night, and he's been getting things together for us."

"Thank you for the clothes. You didn't need to go to this much trouble," Dan said. As he took a bite, he found he was ravenous.

Makin waved a hand dismissively, as if this kindness should be expected of anyone. "I have been talking with our people," he said, changing subjects. "I told them what you are planning, and that you have asked for our help." Makin tapped his fingers along the side of his cup. "They are debating it," he said.

"Really? What do you need to debate?" Dan said,

frowning. "They don't have to put themselves at risk, we'll be doing that. We're the ones that are going to go in there. It's us that will be caught or killed."

"Yes, yes," Makin cut across him, "but helping you will exposes us. It will be showing Dinatech just how many face cards we have. They don't know how connected our group is. Even if you aren't caught, they will see the holes and work to fill them quickly. They have more money and people and we can't afford to lose a step. We may never be able to catch up."

Having never thought about the risks to the Liberté before, Dan couldn't think of anything to say, so he lamely nodded. He'd always thought all the risks would be taken by Clara and himself, simply because they would be the ones going in. The Liberté had to judge if the payoff was worth their investment.

"But, if you are successful," Makin went on as if reading his mind, "and you get the information that exposes high ranking officials for Dinatech and the government, that would put us at an advantage. It means that Dinatech and Dr. Adams would be dealt a major blow, the public eye would be on them, and the government would have to take action against them. That is something we don't wish to pass on either."

Dan rubbed the small bump on his forehead from where he head-butted the FBI agent; the swelling had gone away almost entirely, as had most of the pain. He grabbed a second bagel. "How much influence do you have on the call?"

"It's my call, now that I have talked with the others. If I feel that you can do it, I'll help you." He glanced at the stairs to the second floor and then back to Dan.

The move didn't go unnoticed by Dan. "You don't

trust Clara, do you?" he said, starting to eat the second bagel.

"Try and see this from our side, Dan. She has a ghost's past with connections to both Dinatech and the FBI, and both groups seem to be working together. We aren't sure that she can be trusted."

"I would have never made it out of Oregon without her." Dan tapped a finger on the table and it sounded hollow. "She fought her way out of the hotel last night. She is not sitting in Dinatech's pocket. She's had her chances to give me over to either of them. She could have done it and walked away, but she didn't and she's stayed with me."

"Appearances can be deceiving, Dan." Makin said in a scolding tone.

"You think she's a plant? A spy? No, don't think so. I know Clara, I trust her with my life." He paused then added, "Clara *has* saved my life," just to make sure he made his point.

Makin gave Dan a shrewd look and studied him for a long time. Dan felt his seat was on fire, shifting uncomfortably.

Dan was sure that it would never work.

Makin nodded. "Very well, then, we will help you."

Dan stuffed the rest the bagel into his mouth. "Just like that?"

"Just like that," Makin agreed.

"I don't understand." Dan said.

"If you believe you can trust her and I trust you, then I think we can make this work." Makin said.

"You're trusting someone that you just met?"

"Aren't you?" Makin cocked his brow.

"Okay, you make a good point." Dan sighed; Makin

didn't have to go along with anything.

"Now we start planning." He pushed the food to the side. Hidden under the boxes of bagels was a manila folder filled with papers.

He was still talking at the table with Makin an hour later when Clara came down to put a bagel with cream cheese together. Makin showed Dan details about how they could help them get into the Sacramento office, and recapped for Clara.

Liberté had labeled the Dinatech buildings and created theories on what each was thought to do. Makin even shared a few details on how they probed to get the information, but Dan could tell they weren't trusted enough to learn the specifics.

"Not all of them have the security of Oregon, with advanced detection and armed guards," Makin said. "Most of their factories are just mundane divisions for software and hardware. They make things like remote controls for TVs and chips for laptops." He pulled a paper from his folder; it looked worn, like someone had been worrying it through many nights.

"The building that you are looking to get into is a little of both. It's just outside of Silicon Valley. They use it to work with companies like Apple, Facebook, and Google. But there is another side where they are working on government operations. There are military bases in California where specialized training is conducted, like the Navy Seals."

Dan thought back to his time in the Sacramento building, the long halls of offices that he'd run through during his escape. There were also floors that appeared isolated away from the others.

"We've been working a long time to infiltrate the company through legitimate means. We have contracts to be suppliers to Dinatech, everything from wires and chips all the way down to toilet paper and custodial services." Makin pursed his lips, thinking.

"They don't know that they are working with the people that are trying to take them down?" Dan said.

"Not that we know. We do our contracts with divisions on the civilian side of the company, in areas that are not a security risk."

"But Sacramento has military contracts in it, you said as much," Dan said.

"We have an opportunity to get you in as a pair from a new vendor contract. They are employees of a small wire provider for a civilian project," Makin said. "Dinatech has given them an onsite office for technical support for the project. But once we exploit this, we'll have to close everything so it can't be traced back to us. We may not get this opportunity again, so the loss of this valuable resource must be worth the price." He looked over to Clara; she was wiping cream cheese off her upper lip with a finger.

"You'll be expected to deliver," Makin closed the folder and sat back. "I understand that you are looking to clear your names, but we will need something concrete to nail Dr. Adams and take down Collin Ellsworth. Anything less will be failure." Making finished, giving a nod to Dan and then to Clara, who just smiled. She didn't show the weight of the pressure Makin was putting on them.

"What happens if we don't get you what you want?"

Dan asked.

"I say we should focus on how we make this work and not the other way around. Dr. Adams has an office in Sacramento; your story confirms it. But what he's doing there is not clear. Once you are in, you'll have two access cards that will get you into the military restricted areas." He set ID badges on the table; they were blank, ready for pictures to be printed on them.

"But they will be shut down quickly when and if they figure it out. We went to great pains, using both money and manpower, to get these. No one likes simply giving them to you, but you've been deeper in that building than anyone we know, so we're willing to take the gamble. Also as a bonus, we are working to create you new identities. With your real names on a most wanted list, this should help."

"What are you *really* going to want in exchange for those cards and IDs?" Clara cut in as she reached across Dan to take his coffee.

Now she looked all business.

Makin looked over to Clara and Dan saw his eyes narrow just slightly before he stopped himself. Apparently, whatever his price was, this was not how he wanted to ask. "We would like to *ask* Dan for samples of his blood to study."

Dan winced; he knew this conversation would come sooner or later, he'd known it the moment he told Makin the truth in the car. He just didn't expect it this soon.

Clara frowned, but she said nothing, she turned to him, the price was Dan's to pay, not hers.

"You want my blood, plus you want us to give you the goods on Adams and the senator. Really, this isn't much of a loss for you. Because, if we don't get the information, you still get to look at their most valuable project."

Makin weighed his thoughts but stayed silent; he seemed to understand just how personal this had become for Dan. While it might be robots invading his body, they had become *his* nanobots. It sounded weird when put that way, but he'd become possessive of them all the same. Dan let out a long breath; it shouldn't feel like a lot to give but it did. Reluctantly, he gave a curt nod.

Makin clapped his hands together. "Excellent, I'll have Paul make all the arrangements for tonight and you can be on your way tomorrow."

Once an agreement was reached, it didn't take them long to set up. Makin must have been planning to get the blood from him the moment Dan had told him about the nanobots in the car. He phoned Paul after the terms were reached, and he came soon after with a large red chest that didn't look much different from a plastic toolbox; this one however was insulated and contained a full kit for drawing blood.

Paul set out the pint blood bags, vinyl tubing, and the thin needles. Dan felt his blood go cold and he was becoming less and less comfortable with what he'd agreed to. Clara stepped up to the table and glared. "Wait a mo, you aren't just going to just take a whole pint. We're going through the ringer tomorrow. He may not look it, but he was just this side of dead two days ago."

Makin didn't look to Clara, but at Dan instead. Her hackles were up like Dan had never seen before.

"You didn't have to hold his bleeding head together in your lap!" she snarled, moving between himself and Paul. It had the desired effect: Paul stopped and looked wordlessly at Makin. Dan slid to the edge of his chair, not sure what to do. Makin didn't trust Clara and now she was wedging herself firmly into their deal.

"The agreement was made with Dan." Makin's voice was calm, but he made it clear that he was not going to tolerate her meddling.

"You can take enough to look at and experiment with, not a drop more. Don't think that we won't just walk out that door," Clara said.

Makin started to disagree, and Clara slapped her hands down on the table, "You get four ounces, enough to look at and test on, nothing more. If you think I'm bluffing, you can try me."

Makin looked around Clara at him, and Dan shrugged, showing that he wasn't going to side against Clara.

Makin sighed and nodded. "Very well, we will take it. It will be enough for now." Not making the same mistake twice, Makin looked this time to Clara for approval. She nodded and stepped out of the way.

With the hostilities cooled, Dan believed he could relax, but as he watched Paul put the kit together his muscles tightened up, his heartbeat quicker. Now he knew it wasn't the argument that bothered him, it was the idea of being a damn guinea pig.

"Things are ready," Paul said, and Dan felt a muscle in his jaw jump. He made white knuckled fist while Paul leaned over him, wrapping the rubber tubing around his upper arm. Clara watched from the wall, her eyes wary.

"Wait." Dan didn't like the sound of panic in his own

voice. "Have you done anything like this before?"

"I know how to use a needle. It will go a lot smoother if you relax," Paul said, sounding offended.

That's damn easy for you to say, you aren't the one that's getting punctured, Dan thought to himself.

The plastic guard was pulled from the needle and bounced over the table. He couldn't watch; he searched for Clara, whose eyes didn't falter from watching Paul, hawk-like. That didn't take his mind off what was happening. He instead looked over Paul's shoulder at the cheap drapes drawn tight against the windows; he tried to imagine the yard beyond.

Dan thought Paul's hand felt cold and lifeless against his arm. Dan could only grip at the table harder; he was sure he was going to pull the damn thing over.

His mind was still imagining what lay beyond the drapes. He'd never seen it in the light, but he saw it with perfectly in his mind's eye now, with cut grass and kids riding down the road on plastic Big Wheels.

Did they even make those things anymore?

It was his last thought before the sharp pop of the needle pushed into his vein; the burn of something foreign inside of him made his arm go weak.

Gasping in short breaths he closed his eyes, abandoning the yard while Paul taped down the needle and took five glass tubes from the insulated box. He pushed each one onto a T in the line. Dan could feel the pull and his eyes snapped open to see his blood fill each vial in turn. The rubber=topped tubes were laid out on the table as he filled all five. Clara took a step forward as the last one finished and Paul gave her a look; there would never be any love lost between the two of them. But, as promised, Paul pulled the tape and then the needle carefully, put a gauze pad down, and instructed Dan to hold the pressure.

Dan didn't take his eyes off the glass tubes filled with his blood, and leaning in, he tried to find the machines. How big were they? He knew better than to believe they could be seen floating about like little submarines in his blood. But there was a feeling of wonder there. Makin noticed Dan's interest, and took them up. He carefully put them into the chest. Looking on, Dan felt violated; after all, it was part of him they were taking.

"Alright, I'll have everything ready tomorrow morning," Makin said, pleased.

Chapter 4: Backdraft

Finding an empty parking space in the employee lot, Dan rolled an old used Honda into the Sacramento offices. He cut the engine and leaned forward to look up at the building. It was almost thirty stories tall and constructed in the shape of an L. Tan painted with gold tinted windows; it stood out against the cloudless blue sky.

Clara didn't bother to look out the window instead she, and instead turned down the visor to check her makeup. The car had been given to them by Makin; as part of the plan it was registered under Dan's fake name 'Kirk Hopkins.' The blank tag Makin had shown them the yesterday was now printed with a copy of Dan's face and the fake name. The vendor, Sun Stone, was printed at the bottom. He looked it over before clipping it to his shirt.

Sun Stone was a small company that worked in LCD screen controllers and extremely low voltage wires. Dan had no idea what any of it was, but Makin assured him that what Sun Stone made was very important to Dinatech, important enough to have an onsite vendor office. Opening the passenger door, Clara climbed out and adjusted her baseball hat in the reflection of the car window. Her long hair was pulled up into the cap and she wore a cable knit sweater, a pair of simple hip-hugging jeans, and sneakers. She'd been ecstatic about the shoes since she found them in the bag.

Clara clipped her badge to her sweater. On it read the name, 'Lily Bell.' She'd picked the name, and Dan had given her the eye. Clara had done a little spin, letting her long hair fan out around her. "Hey, I always wanted to be a princess. You told me I should cut loose more."

Dan wasn't sure how he should tell her, but this wasn't what he had in mind.

Clara checked her watch and Dan did too: it was 7:55am. Kirk Hopkins and Lily Bell were due for work at eight. "This would be no place to lose your bottle, Delivery Boy. Let's get moving before we're late for work," she said, closing and locking her door. She pulled her backpack over one shoulder and headed for the side entrance. Dan grabbed his own messenger bag and followed after Clara. She had already mixed in with other employees doing their zombie march through the door. She was ahead of him so they wouldn't be walking in at the same time. Any security looking for them would be harder pressed to find them if they were separated.

Making their way to the door, they saw there was a metal sign attached. It said, 'One person per badge. All exceptions must go to the main lobby.' Beyond the door was a security desk with two men in the black Dinatech uniforms Dan had already become familiar with. Employees entered the room, where there were badge scanners on either side of the security desk. One of the men would check that the picture matched the badge scanned, then they would be allowed past. Clara had made it to the scanner ten people before him, and she slapped her badge down like she was pissed security was going to make her late for work. He couldn't help but think that maybe she was playing up her roll a little too much. He frowned; it was taking Clara longer than people before her.

Clara rolled her eyes, talking with the guard and soon the other turned to watch; she then smiled at the men and put her hands on her cap as if it would blow away. Looking to see what was happening, Dan started to slip out of line. One of the security guards was pointing to a sign behind the counter: 'No hats, bandanas, or sunglasses.' Dan groaned.

Clara leaned over, saying something to the first guard as she pulled the cap back, letting two long braided pigtails fall down to land on the desk. The security guard studied the picture on her badge but had to blush when Clara took the end of a braid and started to try and rub it over the man's chin before he could pull back.

After what seemed like an excruciating amount of time, his partner took the badge back and handed it to Clara, buzzing her into the building, and Dan could feel himself breath once more. His heart pounded, the adrenaline coursing through him. The next nine people had gotten through with no issues and he was pleased he was just as fast—as he didn't think flirting with security would work for him.

Once through the security checkpoint, Dan was let loose on the Sacramento campus once more. He looked left and then right: he'd been in this hallway just three days ago, running for his life with a brute of a man called McFadden, a large ex-military type that seemed to know Clara and her father (not dad). He'd been captured just as Clara and he had, and together the three of them had made a hell of an escape. Dan wondered what McFadden would say if he knew that Clara and he were once again back in this damn building.

This was a larger hallway and it distributed traffic into other smaller ones, where rows of office doors lined the walls. The entrance they had chosen put him in the middle. To the right were the main elevators and to the left the main security offices and the stairs to the underground garage. Dan turned right, heading for the elevators, and soon Clara walked out from a kitchen with a cup of water, falling into step next to him.

Dan eyed her and she looked up with frown. "What? I always started my workday with a cup of water. Why should I stop now?" She'd hooked the hat she was wearing around one of the straps of her bag, her long pigtails now loose and dancing along behind her with each step.

"You don't really work here anymore, you know that right?"

"It's only been a few days, old habits are hard to break." She grinned up at him. "Should I give you a clipboard?" she teased back.

He frowned and looked forward. They had left his work clipboard in their hotel room; he'd forgotten about it. He walked faster and Clara took longer graceful strides to keep up. He needed to focus: they were deep in a dangerous Dinatech building. All the same, he was starting to feel more comfortable around Clara; the last few days he wasn't sure what to do, and while they had shared a few kisses and slept in the same bed, he still felt intimidated by how well she could handle herself. He knew she didn't need him to get through this. So when they were alone and not in danger, he found himself wondering why she didn't go back to her dad (not father) and just forget about him. There was nothing that tied her to him, and he always wondered if it got to be too tough, would she at last throw her hands up and be rid of him?

She nudged him with her hip when he didn't respond to her joke. "Oh don't get all cheesed off at me, I was only pulling your chain." She offered up her water as a peace offering. Dan gave her a thin smile. She pressed the elevator button, and they waited for the car. It gave Dan's eyes a chance to wander. Looking back down the long hall, he took in the details. He could see where a section of the hallway was roped off around the wall that had been splintered up by gunfire and signs were posted reading, 'Due to the recent break-ins, security has been increased. We are sorry for any inconvenience this may cause you.' He winced and looked down at the large 'Dinatech' logo woven into the carpet. The place smelled of re-circulated air with a hint of coffee.

The elevator opened and the two of them surged in, Dan jamming down the close door button before any of the protesting people trying to catch the car could get there. Clara swiped her badge over a sensor just below the call button panel and pressed twenty-two.

With the access badge read, it would no longer open at any other floors for security reasons; all levels over twenty were restricted. The elevator started, and the two of them went to work at once. Clara opened her bag and out dropped a security helmet, gloves, pants and parts of a rifle. Dan pulled the rest of the rifle out of his bag, then a flak jacket that was labeled with "Security", and a black uniform, all of which he handed to Clara. "You know, I would hope they would be more worried about what is in cute little girl's backpack, not the hat she has on. Total cock up if you ask me."

Dan eyed her, then stripped out of his pants and tossed them to Clara, who pulled an ammo clip from the flap of the messenger bag. Dan pulled on the security outfit and Clara had the rifle put together so fast he imagined her practicing blindfolded.

"AR15, you got thirty rounds." She slapped the gun into his hands just as he finished strapping the flak helmet down.

The elevator display read 22, the doors opened, and Dan stepped out of the car. He glanced around a small lobby; there was a guard across the hall dressed in a identical uniform. Dan greeted him. Just behind the man was a pair of electronically locked doors, beyond which were the lab rooms, and at the end of the hall was one of Dr. Adams' offices. The other guard didn't return the greeting; he just watched Dan with suspicion. Dan let his hand drop and he shrugged. "There is a problem with your radio and they asked me to come up here and call you back to the security office so they could have a look at it, and make sure you're on the right key code."

The man frowned and checked his watch, probably looking to see how much more time he had on his shift. "Ehh, damn systems around here, they're so bleeding edge they are never work right, know what I mean?" The man rolled his eyes and walked for the elevator. Once his back was turned, Dan let out a relieved sigh, glad that he didn't check to see if his radio was actually working.

The elevator door opened once more, the guard stepped in and they closed behind him. There was a loud metal thump, and when the door opened again Clara was standing over the guard's unconscious body. She motioned quickly for Dan to come help. "We are so bloody lucky that this car didn't get called back down. The hell took so long?"

"The dude wouldn't even talk to me," Dan said, picking up the guard by his shoulders.

They dragged the body to a camera dead spot. While they knew everything was being recorded, the Sacramento building was running on a skeleton crew to cover for the complete loss of the Oregon security task force. There would be few watching the monitors because of the need to cover the morning work rush. Normally this floor had two security guards. Clara ran to the doors and used her badge to unlock them, and they glided open smoothly on hydraulics.

She walked past the threshold as they continued to open. Dan watched her go while he pulled the radio off the limp body, and was still clipping on the earpiece as he walked after her. Clara kept walking, passing doors per the plan, while Dan moved to the first door. He pushed it open. It was an exam room; he scanned to make sure it was clear, though the rifle still felt clumsy in his hands as he swept.

Clara didn't stop until she reached the end of the hall, where Dr. Adams' office was supposedly located. While she might have been the better choice to make sure the exam rooms where clear, she was the only one that could use the lock-picking gun. She held it to the doorknob, and it looked like a small drill with a few sharp looking picks about the center bit. Clara unceremoniously jammed it into the door, pulled the trigger, and a metallic grinding filled the hallway before she then twisted the gun. The bolt turned easily once the tumblers were stripped down to a fine powder.

It swung open. "Mmm, a little faster than bobby pins, don't you think?" Clara smiled, and Dan turned up his radio, trying to hear if their cover was blown yet.

The office was large with a heavy looking metal desk settled in the middle, atop which sat dual LCD monitors. In one corner was a set of security monitors that showed all four exam rooms. Clara flipped on the lights and examined the room. "No cameras in here. No staff. Dr. Adams and his people are all up in Oregon just as Makin said."

Dan looked back up the hall. The hydraulic doors were closed now, and should give them some warning if they were to open. "This is going off a little too easy."

"We got about five minutes before they notice something is up and it becomes slightly less easy." Clara sounded annoyed, Dan thought. She moved through the room, choosing to start with the computer. "We'll take the same stairs you and McFadden took last time. Keep to the plan and we'll be fine, Delivery Boy," Clara said, while she pulled a small USB memory card out of her pocket and slid it into an exposed port on the front of the computer. Almost at once a large yellow circle appeared on the screen, and then slowly a smiley face etched together while the computer's drive started to grind away. Once the cartoon face was completed, it winked and the desktop appeared. Dan walked back to the door; he couldn't shake the uneasy feeling.

"This is really going too easy," Dan said.

"You can either make yourself useful and start going

through filing cabinets, or shut up and keep your watch," Clara growled in a warning tone. She was distracted with the computer. At first there was only a few clicks of the mouse, but as Clara continued, there were more—and then Clara was clicking very fast. "Well that's bloody great," she growled. "There isn't anything on the damn computer for us to take." She leaned over and started pulling open desk drawers, not bothering to close them as she got up and kicked the chair away.

Dan walked over to the first of many filing cabinets that lined the walls, some even stacked atop others. He opened them as he went the drawers sounding hollow, rattling along the ball-bearing rollers. Every single one was empty, cleaned out, not even dust.

"I thought this was Dr. Adams' office?" Dan looked over to see Clara watching him. Dan stopped pulling open the drawers, knowing there was no longer a reason to search.

"It was! He worked here for two years before he moved all of his work to the Oregon campus." He blinked a few times, not sure why he knew; only knowing that it was true. But he went on, "Look, all these cameras are closed circuit to this office, but the hallway outside is part of the normal security system. If they haven't caught on yet, they will soon. We should get out of here, I think we're blown."

Clara watched him for a second and then kicked over a completely empty cabinet; it clattered to the floor in protest. "After you." She pulled her pack up over her shoulder and they walked out of the office and back through the hydraulic doors. Just as they hissed closed, both sets of elevators opened and a security task force flooded out.

* * *

Clara looked at Dan and in a gruff, fish-like voice, she said, "It's a trap." They turned and ran down a side hallway, away from the labs and the elevators, as a guard called after them to stop.

"I thought you grabbed his radio!" Clara called over her shoulder.

"I did! Maybe the fucking thing really is broken?" Dan said. "Do you think they still want to capture me alive?"

"You better pray so, or we are dead." Clara dove around the corner at the far end of the hall.

Following after, Dan could see the bullet holes from the last time he'd been in this hall with McFadden, and the reason he'd never wanted to come back here again was spelled out before him. But he'd come back willingly, stupidly enough, and they had walked right into a trap. At the end of the hall was the stairs, and before the stairs were another twelve guards also armed with assault rifles. Seeing Clara and he come around the corner, they opened fire at them and Dan had to dive to the floor in order to not become a corpse. He crawled back behind cover and thought he must have looked silly. Maybe, but the movement was effective, as he backed around the corner without any holes in him. Their cover wasn't going to last; another twelve plus men could be heard marching from the elevators; it would be just a matter of heartbeats before they were surrounded.

Clara held out her hand. "Dan, give me that rifle." Her voice was cool, almost robotic, liked she'd turned off any emotion. Her breathing was slow and her eyes no longer held any life in them. She took the rifle as he handed it to her and turned around the corner to put the barrel of the rifle to the head of the flanking team, pulling the trigger with no hesitation. Fragments of bone and blood flew as she opened the rifle up on the surprised team. Some of them started to fire back while Clara dived for the far wall, but she moved before they could hit her.

With no time to be shocked, Dan crawled forward and pulled the rifle off the first fallen man, his body still shaking, last thoughts still ghosting through him. He was watching the man in shock when the other team started to open fire and Dan felt his body tossed forward, rolling to the floor, pain flooding through his back as he gasped and staggered to his feet.

Clara didn't look back; she either trusted Dan was protecting her exposed side or she was so focused she wasn't paying attention. By the time Dan realized what was going on, three dead men laid before him and Clara charged the next, ramming the butt of the rifle in his face so hard the crunch was heard over the automatic gun fire. The group coming from the stairs knew they had made a mistake, and the pigtailed monster was cutting them to ribbons for it. They were too close to fire effectively; with just one of her and so many of them, they were likely to hit one another. So they opted for a full retreat to the stairs.

Dan got his feet under him and pushed forward as the walls about him were lit up with gunfire. He ran after Clara, bringing the rifle up to cover their rear as she cut a bloody path forward. He was going to have to shoot people: he'd shot at another man before, but it had been dark and he wasn't really able to make them out. In this hall the quarters were close, and he wondered if he'd be able to do it.

But instinct won out over thought and morality. One black helmet poked around the corner and Dan let loose with a burst that made them duck back. He felt relieved that he knew he could do what was needed and credited it to hours of playing *Duck Hunt*. He stepped over a guard who was moaning and rolling about as Clara finished with him. Dan jerked the rifle off the guard and slung it over his own shoulder; he kept his eyes down the hall, waiting see if the fool was brave enough to poke his head out again. So great was his concentration that he would have walked backwards past Clara if she didn't pull him into the recess of one of the office doors.

The task force had finally found their footing and rebuked her advance. He dared a glance; she was splattered with blood that covered both her face and shirt. While she breathed heavily, her eyes were like a hawk's, sharply watching her prey. One of the men from the stairs moved out to take a shot and Clara opened the rifle into him. The body slapped over backwards onto the floor, and lay there unmoving.

Dan saw the shadows coming from the other direction and he let loose another small burst that kept them pinned down.

"God, did they get you?" Dan leaned in, trying to look her over better.

"What?" She slapped his hand off, "No, the blood isn't mine. I'm fine. This is *so* not the time, Dan."

Then there was a pause and the silence would have been perfect if not for the ringing in his ears. One of the men called from the elevator side. "Toss us your weapons and we can take you into custody!" The guard didn't sound so sure.

Clara rolled her eyes and took the rifle off Dan's shoulder, then removed the clip on her own before tossing it out to the elevator group. As one of the men came around the corner to pick up the rifle she stood up and put a single shot on target: the round hit the man in the left shoulder. He went down yelling in pain and thrashing about, the bullet having blown a hole through the joint. As another person tried to reach out to pull him back she took a second shot, taking the rescuer's hand apart.

Two more down and out of the fight, Dan thought, but now he knew they couldn't surrender, this would be to the death. Clara moved forward and grabbed another rifle off the floor, "This won't last, they'll use gas sooner or later," she said, and he wondered why they hadn't already done so; their tactics were rather lacking for this kind of an engagement. Then without a word Clara ran forward for the door to the stairwell, firing bursts to keep the guards pinned there. At last they fired back, and she pulled them into another doorway. Dan looked back to see the elevator crew getting more daring as they moved up, and he opened fire on them until they ducked into a doorway a few doors back.

This wasn't good; they were getting pinned in tighter, and the pinch was starting to hurt.

Behind him Clara was mumbling softly to herself; he thought that it might be last rights, but knew better as he caught the words. "My rifle is a part of me, my rifle is my lover." She seemed to be psyching herself into something. She looked back at him and he felt impelled to tell her something; that he loved her or that he was happy to die here with her. But then she spoke.

"Dan?"

"Yes?"

"Don't let them get us from behind." Her voice was soft.

There was no waiting for an answer. She was running full on for the stairs, and bullets streamed about her as she dove into the fortified position. Seeing the small girl dive into the stairwell, the elevator group did just what Clara was expecting: they tried to jump out and chase her. They didn't see that he hadn't followed and Dan was able to open the rifle on them. He aimed low and he got a few hits as they spun into the ground, grasping for their wounds. The hall was full of smoke now and it was getting hard to see, but he got to his feet and ran after Clara while fumbling with a new clip. Beyond the door to the stairs there was yelling, firing, and screaming as if the doors of Hell had been opened up. The smell of burnt cordite and blood was heavy in the air.

In the stairwell, Dan looked over a scene that seemed right out of a war movie: people trying to crawl away, wanting nothing more to do with Clara. She had a combat knife gripped in one hand and blood streamed down her left arm. Her knee was pressed into the chest of a guard, pinning him to the floor as she put the knife against his cheek.

Dan was in shock. The girl before him was not Clara, but his brain argued that it was. No, this girl was something more primal, a brutality that fed on fear. Cold blue eyes watched the guard as she pressed the blade in harder, daring him to move. Her emotions seemed locked deep inside where they couldn't reach her eyes.

Dan had to fight the urge to run from her too.

She reached over, slammed the door to the stairs closed and murmured, "We need to go, now." She didn't look away from the guard as she stood up and stomped the guy's face with the heel of her foot, breaking his nose and bouncing his head off the concrete floor, leaving the man disoriented. She turned and ran down the stairs heading for the ground floor. The door above them banged open but Dan knew they wouldn't follow after them. Clara left enough injured behind that they would have to look after them and stop their pursuit.

Reaching the first floor, Dan was out of breath and he could see that Clara wasn't much better off. Pushing through the door it opened up into the large lobby once more. Dan in his security uniform and Clara looking like she'd walked off the set of Texas Chainsaw Massacre, the people moving through the lobby paused to look but none of them dared walk up to her.

There was as low buzz of talking, "My god, is she alright?"

"What is going on?"

Dan swallowed and took her by the hand. He pulled her along, and she didn't resist at all; she was like a zombie, completely shut down. Dan pushed through the front doors. The security officers on duty here were not armed and when Dan showed them his rifle they didn't try to stop them. Dan locked eyes with them to make sure they didn't dare to try anything as they stepped out the doors and into the parking lot.

The weather was sunny and calm and off in the distance he could hear sirens. He gave Clara's arm another tug and they ran for the car. Once she sat down in the car she dropped the bloody combat knife to the floorboards of the car; he'd forgotten that she even had it when they walked through the lobby. Starting the car, Dan took deep breaths to cover his fear and he drove out of the parking lot and off into Sacramento traffic.

This time he didn't see any black SUVs following.

Dan drove ten miles, his eyes constantly going back to the odometer. He didn't know how many miles would be safe, but once he was sure there was ten miles between them and Dinatech, he pulled to the curb, coming to a stop under an overpass so they were in the shade. The concrete muffled the hard rush of the afternoon traffic overhead. Dan looked out of the Honda's back window, waiting for the black SUVs to come speeding in. They had left and no one had followed them. Had they really gotten away so easily?

There were no large black trucks rushing after, not even a man with a cold on a unicycle.

Clara pulled off her blood-soaked sweater and tossed it onto the floorboards while he tried to think of how they escaped. Under the sweater she had on a flak jacket; she unstrapped the Velcro with a high-pitched whimper, unlike anything Clara had ever let out before. It brought him to attention; he didn't know what to do. There were jacketed slugs imbedded in the front, and when it thumped to the floor some of the rounds came loose to roll along the carpet. She lay back in her seat, gasping.

Underneath she had on a white tank top. Correction: a once white tank top, now sticky crimson. Her left side had either been cut or a bullet had found an unprotected point. She pulled a plastic white box with red block letters that labeled it "First Aid" out of the back seat and winced at its weight.

Neither talked. Dan, in shock, couldn't think of

anything but the fact they'd killed people—a lot of people, with families that would miss them. This wasn't their first firefight, but this one was so brutal that the scene just kept playing back in his head. The first guard Clara had shot point blank, with a complete lack of emotion.

She pulled out two large thick rolls of gauze, placing them in her lap and she held up her left arm. Then rolled up the tank top so that she could inspect the wound. "It only grazed the fat layer, not that deep." She frowned as she pressed sterile pads over the cut. "Dan, I need to you wrap it for me." She paused.

"Dan?" His eyes watched the wound but his mind was elsewhere.

"Dan!" she yelled and he jerked back to motion, looking over at Clara, her right hand pressing the pad to her cut. "I need you to wrap this."

She looked at him concerned, and he wondered how she could show that emotion when just fifteen minutes ago she was ripping her way through Dinatech's security team. He took the gauze off her lap and started to slowly roll it around her waist. Starting just above her elbow, he worked his way up over the pads until Clara was able to stop holding pressure on them. He taped the top and the bottom of the wrap so they wouldn't unravel. She'd reached out for him but then her hand stopped; to cover the movement she pretended to wince and she pulled back to rub at her chest. He couldn't read her expression anymore; it had become guarded.

Confused about many things, one idea was clear: it had obviously been a trap. There were only two ways out of there, and one of them wasn't alive. He'd seen Clara fight before; he'd seen her take down a man by breaking his arm. But this had been the first time that he'd seen her kill another living person. How she did it was like she was a machine. Would she have avoided murder if she could, or did she believe it was the only way? Remembering those cold eyes, open, seeing everything, yet closed emotionally. They were not the eyes that he'd fallen for, and he wondered how someone could be so completely vacant. His faith had been shaken.

Trying not to dwell, he focused on the job. He pulled out the disposable phone Makin had given him, and typed in the number he'd memorized. He leaned his seat back so he was looking up at the gray felt roof. The phone rang three times before Makin picked up.

"That is what you two had in mind?" Makin said, in a quiet voice. He could tell it was taking every ounce of effort to not shout.

"I'm not sure I follow?" Dan said, his posture going stiff.

"Dan, I only need to turn on my scanner to know that you turned that building into the next Beirut, they have ambulances coming in from two different hospitals. What did you do? I thought you were going to find evidence, not incite a bloodbath."

Dan started to speak but was cut off.

"I didn't give you those access cards and our encryption breaker so you could incite revenge."

Having heard enough, Dan talked over him with a few choice words of his own. "It was a trap, Makin. They knew we were coming. Dr. Adams' office was empty. Worse than that, it was barren. They cleaned out all his files and they left a few dozen security guards there to ambush us. They knew that we were coming back, and they knew what we wanted."

Clara watched silently from her seat, massaging her bruises as they gained color. Even with protection, the bullets left their mark: the velocity could still break ribs, or even stop a person's heart.

"There was no information? Nothing that we can use?" Makin said unbelieving.

"That is what I'm telling you, they knew; it was a complete bust."

The silence was so long, Dan wondered if they had lost connection.

"We're going to make our way back over to the house tonight once we're sure we aren't being marked," Dan said to fill the dead air.

"We aren't sure that's a good idea," Makin said, at once.

"What do you mean, it's not a good idea?" Dan shouted into the phone. Clara's eyebrows shot up questioningly.

"We think that it might be best if we separated for a while."

Dan was suddenly reminded of his ex-girlfriend when she broke up with him a few days after the prom; he couldn't understand why this was happening.

"What are you taking about? I thought that we were working for the same goal? Taking down Dinatech before they build Skynet and all their Terminators."

"Look, Dan, my friend…" Makin stated in a soothing tone.

"No, you look, Makin. We went in under your plan and this is the outcome. You can't just turn your back on us now." Dan tried to not yell, but Makin getting into his stride.

"We thought you would get more results. Members

are starting to get cold feet. They are not happy with the use of violence."

"What did you expect, a cake walk? We had to shoot our way out three nights ago, you knew there would be a risk." Dan couldn't understand their alarm; their reaction was too much. For them to cut all ties after entering into a partnership left him feeling vulnerable.

"Dan, just keep this phone. I'll be in touch soon, okay?"

"Yeah great." Dan ended the call by slamming the phone down on the dash. He looked back over to Clara. "We're on our own ... for now anyway. They seem to think our tactics were too heavy handed."

Clara rolled her eyes and leaned her seat back; she groaned as her abs stretched.

They sat in silence for several minutes. Dan was starting to wonder if they were going to stay in the car all night when Clara turned slowly and started to pull clothes out of the garbage bag and stuff them into her backpack.

"Keep the vests, but dump all blood-soaked clothes," Clara said.

Dan nodded and started to strip as fast as he could in the confinement of the car seat. Clara took longer getting a new shirt down over her wounds, and she needed Dan's help before she was able to get a new pair of pants on.

She broke down the rifle in the back seat while Dan finished changing and put the rifle parts into Dan's messenger bag. Using some hand wipes from the first aid kit, she was able to clean her face of blood in the vanity mirror. Her hair was dark enough that any blood there would not show easily.

Motioning for him to get out of the car, Clara didn't bother to lock the door as she followed, slamming the door behind her, showing frustration. She walked away and Dan caught up with her about ten yards down the sidewalk while still buttoning his fly.

They had cash, the fake IDs the Liberté had put together for them, and a second change of clothes. "Where do we go now?" Dan asked. It was still too awkward to look Clara in the eye.

"I don't know," Clara said. Those words sounded strange coming from her, and he could tell they bothered her too. "But we should get off the street before the heat really comes down on us. They'll be looking for this car. I believe that the FBI still has an eye on Dinatech, so they won't openly retaliate. But one of them will find this car, and we don't want to be here when they do. We need to get out of this town and off the grid. We need time to think of our own plan."

"We did, and this is how it ended up," Dan said, looking back at the car they were walking away from.

"No, those urban guerilla bastards had their mitts all over this rubbish. We should have just walked away from them when we could. The heat is on and they chose to save themselves," Clara grumbled.

After walking a few miles, they found a city bus stop. With no idea of where to go, they took the local bus as far as it would take them, then transferred to another. They sat near the back door; Clara curled in against the window with Dan sitting on the aisle, slumped down. He noticed she didn't lean over on him like she had before. He watched her sit motionless, looking out the window.

The second route took them to a small transit center south of Sacramento. It was afternoon now, the sun high over the cloudless sky. Even far from the city, the muggy smell of too many cars packing up the freeways lingered. Clara scanned the area and found a public library across from the transit center. It was just a small satellite library that was built into a strip mall.

"I'd say that's a lucky break, don't you think?" She started to reach over for Dan's hand, but faltered and walked off for the library alone. Dan frowned, and wondered why a library would be a lucky break. Pulling his slipping bag strap up, he chased after Clara.

Chapter 5: The Unforgiven

Pushing in through the glass door of the library, Dan noticed the floor was laid with a light brown carpet that was so hard it might as well have been tile, yet it still found a way to look hairy. Dan was convinced the government owned a carpet factory, because he'd only ever seen this weave in government buildings. He thought it far too horrible to be found anywhere with class.

The library showcased the carpet by leaving the middle of the floor open; it was bracketed by black metal shelves. Beyond those, the back wall was lined with study desks. As they walked in, the librarian smiled from the front desk on the left. Clara walked to the back of the room to settle at one of the tables and Dan followed her, trying to figure out what she was doing. There were only a few people in the library; college students studying, and people using the computers to search for jobs and keep up their quota for unemployment. He pulled a chair out and sat down, feeling numb, unsure what to do, and wondering how they could clear their names. Dinatech knew what they were after and without more people and resources, he didn't see how they could get it. He pulled his phone out and looked it over; there were no missed calls. Makin hadn't changed his mind about leaving them to fend for themselves.

Clara let the backpack slip off her shoulder onto the table, and then went to the bathroom. She came back before Dan noticed, sitting down across from him. She'd washed better, and combed her hair clean; it was pulled back into a long shiny ponytail, slightly wavy from the braids. She watched him with a worried expression.

"Dan," she said softly. "I think we should talk." She bit at her lip.

"Alright?" Dan said.

"Something changed, what's wrong?" she said, not able to meet his eyes.

"I was a fool to think that we could get in there and find the information that we needed. It was just stupid," Dan said.

"No," Clara cut in. "It wasn't stupid. We could have pulled that off. We showed them we aren't afraid of them." She put one hand on the table and moved it halfway across. "It was a plan when we didn't have one."

Dan didn't reach for them and her fingers twitched.

"This is what I'm talking about. Something changed." She reached up and wiped at her eyes with the back of her hand.

Dan shook his head. "It's fine, it's all fine," he said turning away. "I'm just... I can't believe they were shooting at us. They were going to kill us." He got up stiffly from the table and walked to the bathroom without looking back. The hinge squeak was loud in the tiled room; every one of his steps echoed, the room smelling of disinfectant gone stale.

Looking in the mirror, Dan could see why Clara was

worried. His face was haunted, pale, and lifeless. He turned on the water and splashed it over his face, trying to get some color back. He pulled up his shirt, just now remembering that he'd been shot. Why didn't he think of it before? At the time the pain was unbelievable, and now it was nothing more than a dull ache. Looking closely, he could see that the vest had taken the brunt after all. It had left a large oval bruise along his back, but he could see that it was healing quickly. He felt his heart jump and increase its pace. What was he becoming?

How many of these shots did Clara take?

His thoughts went back to Clara, and how she had killed the first man again, and then the second. She could tell he was bothered and wanted to talk about it. They needed to, Dan knew it, but he didn't know what he should tell her. That she scared him? That in saving his life he'd seen a side of her that had left him shaking?

This was the real problem. They had ended people's lives and they could never take it back. Those people had a family and friends who would be devastated. What would Dinatech tell them about his death?

They would have to talk about this soon, because even if she was a crazed killer, they were on the same side. He knew she was a trained weapon, but he'd never thought about her killing. There was a cool and calculating machine always just under the surface.

Did she feel bad about it?

Did she feel *anything* at all?

He was trapped in a corner and his only option was to unleash something that could be worse than the problem. They were now running from both Dinatech and the FBI, and there was no way he could go back and not find himself behind bars. Especially after murdering two guards. Just three days ago he had a normal job, normal mooching friends, and a normal vacation planned. He would never have a life like that again.

How long could he stay on the run?

How long could he stay healthy with the nanobots in his system?

Would his body try to reject them again?

He had so many questions and no answers—unless he wished to become Dr. Adams' lab rat.

Dan took a few long breaths, letting them out slowly. He started to wash his hands again in hot water, trying to clean the blood out from under his nails. Getting the last flecks out, he had no more excuses to stall, so he turned off the water, dried his hands on the rough extra cheap paper towels, and headed out into the library to face Clara. He still had no clue what he was going to say, but he figured she'd come in to the bathroom after him if he took much longer.

Clara had moved to one of the computers where she'd stuffed their bags underneath. She had a cascade of web browser windows open, and a notepad pressed in next to the keyboard. She was making notes while she copied and pasted small blurbs from web articles.

"What are you looking at?" Dan asked, watching over her shoulder.

"Oh just doing a little market research," she said softly. The emotions that she showed him at the table were gone; the ever-changing puzzle that was Clara.

"Market research?"

"Yeah something like that. Why don't you get us some food from the sub shop?" She pointed over her shoulder without looking. "I'll be there in a few minutes. I think I got this about wrapped up."

"Alright," Dan said as he reached down, pulling one of the bags over his shoulder so Clara wouldn't have to carry them both. He smiled again at the librarian in passing as he walked out, squinting in the bright sun. Looking back through the glass once more, he watched the shadowy figure that was Clara. All questions, no answers.

The sub shop was slow. There were only the two teenagers working behind the counter, and when he placed his order they acted as if they would rather the shop be empty. He ordered two steak and cheese subs, one with a Coke, the other a Sprite, and he took the booth as far from the front counter as he could get.

Dan tried to wait for Clara, but five minutes later hunger won and he was eating his sub when she came in the door with a stack of printed papers. She was bouncing on the balls of her feet, telling that she'd found something. One glance at Clara and the two employees were ready to fight one another to take her order, so when she sat down at Dan's table their looks of murderous intent fell on him. Slapping the large stack of papers down between them, Clara pulled the other sub to herself, starting to unwrap it. "Okay," she said looking down into both drinks, "I've got plan number two ready for review." She picked Sprite and pulled it closer; Clara didn't drink caffeine. "Well, closer to plan one point five. It's still your idea."

"You really don't think that we should go back into Sacramento do you?" Dan said over the printed stack.

Lying on top was an article about Senator Collin Ellsworth's appointment to the bench of Virginia. Taking notice, Dan started to flip through the papers; there were more articles with different events that

Ellsworth had thrown over the last four years; most of them were just notices of the times and places, with contact information.

Clara took a bite of her food and went on. "No, I think we're done redecorating that place, but I love the brass on you." She tapped the papers. "We are going with your other brilliant idea of getting information. But I thought that we might try attacking from a different side. I think we should look at who is paying for all this space age Trekkie crap. And don't think for a second that because you're cute I'm going to start watching that show. I draw the line at pointy-eared men."

Before Dan could retort, she moved on. "The Senator, he's involved, this much we know. But why?" She watched Dan expectantly, but he didn't try to say anything.

Clara sighed. "Okay I see I'm on my own here. So anyway, I found his personal secretary, Victoria Palmer." Clara set her sandwich to the side. "You know what, they charge ten cents a copy at that library, you'd think they could get better printers for that price."

"Can't you stay on topic at all?" Dan groaned.

She dug through the papers until she found a sheet and pulled it out; it had a large picture on it. It was of a taller man who looked to be in his fifties, hair combed over, and waving to the camera while walking to his car. In his wake was a woman half his age, her light hair pulled up into a messy bun. She had on a blouse and pencil skirt. The caption underneath the picture read, "Collin Ellsworth and personal secretary Victoria Palmer, leaving the capital Christmas dinner just before the vote on educational funding…" The article went on but Dan looked over to Clara, not convinced yet.

Clara started to pout, pulled out another paper, and slapped it down before him. Once again the pair were pictured. Ellsworth was speaking at a podium, and there in the background, standing before the U.S. flag, was Palmer.

"What are you getting at?" Dan asked.

"We should talk with Palmer, she's going to know more than anyone about Senator Corrupted Pants." Clara tapped a finger on her picture.

"And what is that going to do for us? I mean, if she's that close to Ellsworth, she's going to be loyal. I can't think of a man in that position having someone he couldn't trust next to him."

With a huff, Clara pulled out the last page of the stack and put it on top. It was a smaller article that was only a few paragraphs long.

"Longtime assistant of Senator Collin Ellsworth, Victoria Palmer, quit her position, parting ways after working with the Senator for the past seven years. Palmer, a longtime friend, first started working for Ellsworth as an intern directly after high school. She had worked as part of Ellsworth's campaigns to become mayor of Stuart, Virginia, but took a few years off when she went to college. When she graduated, she came back to work on his campaign for Senator, which he won in a landslide victory.

"Some have said much of Ellsworth's success was attributed to Palmer and her strong attention to detail. It can be said that a politician is only as good as what he knows and whom he knows. Palmer made sure he was prepared for both. What originally brought Palmer to work for the Senator was her brother, who was enlisted with the army. Ellsworth's promises to bring the troops home brought Palmer in Ellsworth's corner, so when the news of their split came, it was shocking. Many speculate there was a difference of opinion."

Dan looked up, and Clara kept tapping a finger atop the printed article. "Something happened here, something that she didn't like." She pursed her lips. "I'm willing to bet Victoria got tired of his campaign supporters." Clara pulled the stack back over, searching through it, her food forgotten. "What a cool name, Victoria. Why did mom have to name me Clara? I really couldn't give a toss about my great aunt; I mean she was dead before I was born. Then I'd have cool nick names like Tori or Vicky." She found the sheet she was looking for and handed it to Dan, then remembering the sub, took few more bites.

Dan looked over the sheet showing who had donated to the Senator's campaign, and there at the top of the sheet was Dinatech. In his last campaign for re-election they had fronted more than half his money; it was in the range of millions. Clara, no longer able to talk with her mouth full of steak, just passed over a paper from his first election. Dinatech was on the list this time as well, but they had only given a paltry sum of money. Reaching for her Sprite, she took a drink, washing down the food. Dan placed both pieces of paper down on the table and waited.

"Don't you see it?" Clara said. "Soon after his re-election she split, and Dinatech bought themselves a politician for their own uses." Clara's feathered eyebrows went up and her eyes widened, but Dan still doubted it.

"Why in the world would a Senator from Virginia come all the way to Oregon over a building melt down? I promise you, Dan, he didn't come because he wanted to see a Ducks game. Look here." She pulled out more printed articles. This time it was articles about government bills going up for vote in the house. Page after page of them, and as Dan read he found they all had to do with legalizing different kinds of genetic research, like stem cell work, DNA spicing, and cloning.

"There were other bills, others things too," Clara said. "Bringing the troops home, cutting military budgets, building new schools, that junk. But think about everything we saw in Oregon." She pushed the pile of papers over. "Ellsworth came running, because this was his livelihood. The links aren't obvious, but they're there." She patted the stack. "Dinatech and Ellsworth are in bed together, building something for the military and Victoria was on the payroll. She knows and didn't like whatever it was."

"You think that the nanobot program was funded by Ellsworth to make some kind of super soldiers? And that Palmer …"

"Call her Victoria, much cooler," Clara said.

"Fine, Victoria knew about what they were doing in Oregon?"

Clara nodded rapidly.

"How does this help us to clear our names?"

Clara gave a little whimper and slumped over the table top. "Because, Delivery Boy …"

"Call me Dan," he interrupted.

"Because, Delivery Boy," she repeated, "we find Vicky, and we find the dirt we need." She gave a little wiggly victory dance.

"Now, all we have to do is find one Victoria Palmer living somewhere in the U.S." Dan grouched.

"Come on Dan, don't be so bloody dense." She pulled all the papers back as if he'd lost his rights to look at them. "For one, she worked in Virginia, don't you think that she would still live there? Secondly, I've already found her, she's living in Oakton, Virginia," she said, putting emphasis on Virginia. "With her brother, who is home from his deployment in Afghanistan."

"Even if she tells us, we aren't home free you know." Dan was grouchy, and he knew was taking it out on Clara.

"Yes, mister grumpy bottoms," she said in a voice reserved for children. "My goal is to convince her to tell us where we can find the hard copy proof," she picked up her soda, looked at it, then dropped it back on the table.

"I don't think we could get through airport security without getting caught," Dan said, shifting gears. Their whole plan rested with someone that was currently living on another coast.

Nodding, Clara played with her sub wrapper, folding it into fourths and then eighths; she was more fidgety than normal.

"No. Even if we get in, we are trapped in their system, risking capture at their leisure. I think I'm done with that." She kept her eyes on the table. "I think that we should take a Greyhound. Slower, but it will be more open if they do catch on, and the time will allow some heat to grow cold. I hope."

Dan wasn't sure this would work. Could they get out of the state before they were in cuffs? But she'd gone along with his plan, showing both faith and support, and not even a word of protest when it failed miserably. It was his turn to show his trust in her. He gave a nod and she smiled softly and looked out the window.

"Sweet! Road trip."

With the help of a phonebook and another city bus adventure, they checked in at a Greyhound station. The place sat just outside an industrial area and was a major hub for transportation. Dan got his ticket first, then after dinner when the shift at the station changed, Clara bought hers. They used their fake IDs, under the names Travis Deacon and Amy Nicholson; they were starting to have so many different names that Dan wasn't sure if he could keep them straight.

They boarded the bus as dark took its hold on California; once on board Clara said they could risk sitting with one another. She dived into the window seat, and about twenty minutes into the trip, she curled against him, laying her head on his chest. Dan tried to keep himself relaxed under the close contact; he didn't want to fall into the talk from the library.

A few more miles rolled by in silence before she spoke softly.

"You're bothered I killed those people," she said, her voice shaky. Dan was trying to tell if she was crying.

He didn't know how respond to that. Dan had no experience in dealing with human weapons, or their emotions. He just looked down at Clara while she kept her face buried in his chest.

She started to talk again in the silence, "Just after I started college, I got involved with this dentist."

"A dentist?" Dan said, shocked.

"I thought I told you this? I dated a dentist. He was grand; I thought for sure that he was the one. Sure, I was young and didn't know the first thing about dating."

"You're only twenty-one now."

"Shut up and let me tell my sob story." She pressed her head into his chest, biting.

Dan jerked back, but said nothing.

"He was amazing, he was sweet and kind, and as I'm British, I'd never have to worry about my teeth."

Dan wondered if she was really worried about her teeth but didn't ask for fear of her using them again.

"We had been dating for almost six months before he really knew I was ..." she paused thinking, " ... that I could take care of myself. It happened on the way home from the movies. A couple of thieves tried to rob us. They wanted the normal things, you know, the money and the jewelry. The only jewelry I had was a watch that he'd given me for my birthday. I always wore that watch.

"I let them have it; he could always get me another watch. But then the bastards started getting greedy, we were easy to push and they needed to see how far they could go. One of the men grabbed me, and that was it, too far. I took him down arse over elbow, and broke his wrist. His partner pulled a gun and it was over before I could think. That's the point you stop thinking, you've been trained long and so hard you just react. I took the gun and put two bullets through his knee. I knew he'd never walk right again."

Dan put his hand on her shoulder and gave a squeeze. Clara had fought beasts, people, robotanks and everything else Dinatech could throw at them, and she'd stopped them all. Still, as she lay against him, she felt very small, like a child.

"At the time, I thought he understood. He was okay with what happened. As time passed, I knew it wasn't. Things changed and I couldn't put them back. He confessed once that he wasn't comfortable that he didn't protect me and he'd completely locked up when the thug grabbed me.

"I really thought we could work it out, but he started with comments like, 'I don't have to worry with you here to protect me.' Sometimes I could tell he'd avoid things if he thought there could be trouble. I remember people heckling us, and he turned and pulled me across a street. There were many times he'd pull me away like he thought I'd embarrass him by lashing out. He made me feel like I was an un-trained pit bull."

Dan thought about how he'd tried to stop the agent from egging her on in the hotel: he must have looked quite the ass.

"We didn't last much longer after that. It was just too hurtful and I could see that he didn't care for me the same way. I guess he was looking for someone that he could take care of, and I was too much his equal. But what really hurt was the thought that he might be afraid of me. I loved him; I'd have given him the world."

She balled her fist up in his shirt.

"I think that I could fall for you, Delivery Boy, but things have changed between us too."

Dan felt a jolt in his gut as she put it out there; she was falling for him. There were more than friends now; he had become someone that she could come to love. He almost forgot that she was still talking.

"You weren't bothered when I fought a tiger, and you weren't bothered when I took out a robot. But I saw the fear in your eyes when I killed those guards. I thought about it, and I know that's it. You won't talk about it." She curled in tighter and started to shake in his arms.

"I don't like the change, but this is who I am. This is who I've always been." She sobbed, "I can't change who I am, even if I wanted to. But never have I wanted to change who I was more than I do right now." And then Clara let go, bawling into his chest. A few people looked around to get a glance before jerking their attention away. No one likes getting caught watching an emotional moment.

Clara cried herself to sleep while Dan held her. She didn't wake through the next two stops; she was wiped out. Dan was tired but couldn't sleep, so he watched out the window, his mind buzzing.

One thought kept coming back: how dependent Clara sounded. This isn't how he saw Clara; she was always strong and independent, the kind of girl people wrote movies about. But she wished she could change herself to make him happy. He wasn't even sure when the change happened, when he'd become so important to her.

He was still mulling it over when exhaustion took him.

When he woke, he wasn't sure how long he'd been out, but Clara was no longer curled against him; she was leaned against the window, silently watching the landscape flash by. When he moved to sit up, Clara looked over and smiled. "Hey there, dead head. We'll be stopping for a bus change soon. I thought that we could get some of that famous American truck stop food. I've never had it before." She didn't show a single sign of the girl who silently cried herself to sleep.

"Alright," Dan said, slowly. He was taken aback and disoriented from sleep. He didn't mention the swinging mood changes, worried it could swing her back into depression.

The bus pulled into the large Greyhound station in Flagstaff, Arizona. Stiff, travel-weary passengers stumbled off the bus to stretch their muscles. Clara pulled her backpack over her shoulder and nodded enthusiastically towards the waffle house.

"Awesome. Come on, we only got, like twenty minutes for food. We'll have to eat military style."

"Military style? What's that?"

"Something both Father and Daddy liked to do when things got busy. Everyone sits down and then you have five minutes to eat before you're out the door." She laughed, "I guess we could just get it to go."

"That might be a better idea," Dan said wryly.

She reached out and took his hand and Dan wrapped his fingers around hers; she didn't hesitate, and he didn't pull away. He moved to walk in step with her. "Look, Clara …"

"You don't have to say anything. I was tired, I said some things that must have seemed silly." Clara's cheeks warmed with a flush.

"No, I think you told me the truth, and I'm sorry. I didn't mean to scare you. It's just that so much of my life has changed so quickly, and I'm still getting used to it. I've never even held a gun before, and now I've been in two gunfights. And it's not Hollywood." Dan couldn't think of a better way to say it. The nights' rest made him feel better, but it didn't change what they had done. It just felt more manageable.

"What happened in Sacramento was intimidating and scary. I'm not going to lie, I'm still getting used to the thought of it." With words failing him, he gave her hand a squeeze and she returned it. She didn't look up at him now; she just looked forward to their destination.

Dan said, "I think your old boyfriend was a prick."

Clara watched the ground before them, but he was sure he saw the edge of a smile. The thick smell of sweet waffles and bacon assaulted them as they walked through the restaurant door, and Dan felt like he was getting fat just breathing the air. Clara showed no other reaction to his words; she was trying to keep up the cheery act.

"I don't want you to stop being who you are. I don't want you to feel like you have to change who you are. I want to get to know you—not the show, but the *real* Clara."

She looked up at him and walked right into the hostess podium; the woman behind it squeaking in surprise. Clara slapped her free hand on the laminated top to keep herself from toppling the rest of the way over. Then she groaned, her eyes rolling into the back of her head, and Dan could tell she'd aggravated her bruised ribs.

"Bloody hell," Clara gasped out and the hostess looked unsure if she should help or run for it.

"We just need to get a breakfast order to go," Dan said, helping Clara to steady herself. "Please."

Grateful for a reason to walk, the waitress took his order quickly and went into the kitchen to deliver it. Dan was sure she didn't need to go all the way; she didn't even bother to ask what kind of toast he wanted.

"She was kind of a flighty thing, wasn't she?" Clara mused.

"You didn't just have some girl crash into your podium

and then stagger about clutching at their ribs." He frowned at her. "Why didn't you say they were this bad?"

"They're only that bad when I'm slamming them into solid objects. Those vests are not meant to take point blank shots, and I took three," Clara said.

Dan thought about the shot he'd taken in the back. It was fired from the end of the long hallway and it had lifted him from his feet. Makin told them Dinatech created the vests, ironically. They contained an experimental active fiber that, when subjected to heavy impacts, would go rigid. Interacting with the gel underneath, it would cushion the energy of the round and disperse it over the full volume of the vest. It was lighter, stronger, and far more bulletproof than standard vests.

"I'm starting to think you might have broken something, Clara." Dan said, worried.

She waved him off. "I know what that feels like, I promise you. I just need to rest them." She looked up at him with a smile. "Thanks though."

The waitress all but threw their food at them, and once she'd counted the money she walked away, acting like there was something very important to do.

"Well we needed the food fast, right?" Dan said, nodding his head at the door.

Making it back to the bus with only minutes to spare, they settled into their seats. The bus had barely pulled away when Clara started to assess the situation.

"After spending the six hundred bucks for the tickets, we've got about four hundred and twenty three dollars and," she dug around in her back pocket, "seventy-seven cents."

"If we want that to last the next two weeks then we

can't spend more than thirty bucks a day, a dollar twenty six an hour, or two cents a minute," Dan said.

Clara cocked a brow at him and glanced back down at the pile of crumpled bills in her lap. "Should I trade it in on pennies?"

"Sorry," Dan flushed. "I'm starting to notice I might be good with numbers now."

"I see." She studied him a moment, "Okay, I do agree we should keep spending to about thirty bucks a day, or we are going to be in a lot of trouble. We'll have to stick with public transportation. Not sexy, but cheap."

"Saving the world on a budget. What would Batman say to that?" Dan said, and slumped back in his seat with a waffle he'd rolled up burrito-style.

"Nothing, he's got an ATM on his belt." She carefully put the money into four small piles that she started to place in different pockets, and handed him one.

The rest of the trip was slow and boring, and without much money they spent most of the time trying to entertain one another. At one stop, Clara convinced Dan that they should buy a pack of cheap playing cards. She'd begged till he'd given in and now they were the proud owners of some Harley Davidson playing cards. This excitement only lasted about four hours, until Dan came to learn the rules to each new game and calculate the odds.

Dan found that Clara was not a good loser, and after he won every game of pinochle for the last hour, she made their last game 52-card pickup.

"Haven't you ever heard of letting the girl win?" she

pouted, looking out the window while Dan collected cards from protesting passengers around them. He was putting a Softail Harley motorcycle displayed on the six of clubs into the reforming deck.

"I thought that you liked challenges?"

"That is not a challenge, that is impossible," Clara huffed.

Once again, they transferred to a new bus in Memphis and started the home stretch. The miles rolled into the night and Dan took the window seat, pressing his cheek to the cool window. The humming of the tires on the road, the low rumble of the diesel engine could be felt in the seats…

The room held just one chair. The walls around it were smooth and glowed like a large screen. Dan stepped into the room before the chair, and he looked around to find there was no door. Confusion hit him, and then passed. It was okay, because he was inside the room and he wouldn't need a door till it was time to leave.

A green curser popped up on the wall-sized screen; it was as large as a football. Across the room, text appeared; it wrapped around him, typing out, "Hello Daniel, it's good we have come so far together. I'm pleased we can once again take up a conversation." When the words appeared on the screen, the room filled with a robotic voice, a voice that he'd heard before …

"Daniel," it said again, the voice nonplussed, and green print scrolled around him, appearing out of the curser. "You and I haven't talked since before we mated. Or do you prefer 'joined'? I like the word 'mate', it has a far more personal tone. Don't you think? After all, we are one now. It does not become any more personal than this."

It was The Core. But he was sure it had been destroyed in Oregon. He watched it fail, there was no way this was real; it wasn't possible. He didn't say anything, he just watched the text, slack jawed.

"Daniel, I brought back our chair. Do you remember our chair? I thought we could use it to relate. A common bond. It's been said memories are stronger when you have something that you can relate to. It can help you to memorize thoughts or sequences of time that corresponds with an object, like a key phrase in a database query."

Dan still said nothing, just looked around franticly trying to better understand what was going on.

"Have a seat Daniel, " the Core said, insistently. After a pause the Core continued. "It's okay Daniel, this seat is nothing more than a figment of your imagination. It won't do anything against your will."

Silence.

"Daniel, I must say, I thought that our reuniting would have been more joyous. I do not enjoy this one-way conversation: computers need input. Come, you must say something. I've been working hard for you."

"You aren't real," Dan said in a soft voice that sounded louder than he expected.

"Just because my body has been destroyed does not mean that I'm not real. I'm made of the same data, and some would argue I'm nothing more than a copy. But then, aren't you just a program that reacts to the data you are fed? Wouldn't a copy be the same thing? Still, what you remember changes your program so new states can be created. I like this Daniel, you are becoming quite the poet."

Dan said nothing.

271

"Daniel. Have a seat, I'd like to talk."

"Why are you always trying to get me to sit down?"

"Because it's polite and comfortable. It gives off the appearance that you aren't looking to run away."

The room went silent, and Dan turned to try to find the curser.

"There is much to discuss, Daniel," it said, in a flat voice.

Shaking his head and rolling his eyes, Dan sat down on the seat and looked up at the screen.

"Good," the computer said in a pleased voice.

Chapter 6: Breakfast at Tiffanys

Dan started awake with a snort, Clara poking him in the shoulder. "Welcome to DC. The FBI's two most wanted just bussed into headquarters. Doesn't it make you feel safe?"

"Won't your father be happy?" Dan said, his voice gruff from sleep.

Clara mumbled something noncommittal.

Stepping off the bus, Dan instantly wished that he had a thicker coat, pulling the cotton hoodie tighter about himself. The chill of winter had a crisp edge. Clara was memorizing a bus schedule in the dim light of a far off overhead. Clearly, the lighting along with the materials used for the bus stop passed regulation, and not a dime more. It was four in the morning and it would still be dark for a couple hours.

After reviewing the timetables and map she turned back to Dan. "Yeah, we're stuck. It's two hours before service starts to Oakton. It looks to be eighteen miles if the bus map is at all accurate, but it's an express route, so it shouldn't be that long a trip riding with the crazies." She dug in her bag pulling out a long-sleeved sweater. "I want a bath." She narrowed her eyes. "And a bathroom not connected to the side of a gas station. I'm not made for living on the lam."

Dan didn't agree with this statement; she'd gone four days without complaint and she knew what she was doing, far better than he did.

"We really don't have the money for a hotel though." He pulled out his disposable phone and looked it over, checking the time.

Clara sighed and nodded over to a Denny's, the sign out front saying, 'Welcome 24 hours a day.' "Come on. We can at least get a cup of coffee and be warm while we wait." She took him by the hand and pulled him along; it was a gesture he was getting very familiar with. Things weren't completely healed between them, but they had filled the gap. The longer she was the Clara he knew, the farther the other was pushed to the back of his mind.

In the lobby Dan was already starting to feel warmer; the place smelled of the same greasy cooking that all Denny's do: it reminded him of late nights out with Jake. They took up a pair of stools along the lunch bar where they could watch the cook on duty through the service window. They ordered coffee and Dan added a slice of apple pie so he wouldn't feel like he was being a coffee bum.

Mounted over the lobby was a small flat screen TV; it was tuned in to a local news station. An anchor was standing before aerial shots of cars on the freeway, and he was detailing where bad traffic was and how it would affect DC commuters. The waitress dropped off the pie with a smile before moving on; while they didn't order much, she was still friendly and it made him relax. Dan was cutting into his pie when he looked up to the TV and just about choked.

His face was on the TV, the picture from his driver's license. "Currently Daniel Hollis is wanted for questioning by the FBI. If you see this man please do not approach him, but call 911. He's expected to be in the company of Clara Paxton." Clara's picture was slid into frame next to his own.

"The last time these two were seen was in Las Vegas, Nevada, but are expected to be on the run. Again, do not approach, call 911."

Dan started to get up but Clara grabbed him by the elbow and squeezed, making sure he got the point: he was not to get up.

"Relax," she said, sounding far calmer than Dan believed the situation called for. They were no longer just wanted; the entire do-gooder population of America was hunting them. He broke into a cold sweat. What would his parents think when they saw this? He wasn't going to be able to just show up for Christmas.

Hi Mom, Dad, how has your year been? Yeah me? I'm wanted by the FBI, and they think I'm dangerous!

His life was over, he could never go home, and he could never face anyone that he knew again. He contemplated the weather in Mexico. What kind of work could he find there? Did they need package delivery drivers?

"If you'll excuse me, I think I'm going to go puke now," Dan mumbled.

"How about you just sit here with me and enjoy your pie? It's actually quite nice, not too much sugar." She turned the fork around on the plate so that he could take it.

"We can't just sit here in public, we are going to get

caught," Dan said, leaning in to not be overheard.

"No one but us saw that, so don't start doing something stupid, it will make us look suspicious. Like ordering pie and coffee then leaving before you've enjoyed any of it."

Looking up at the TV, Dan saw they had moved on, two anchors talking about how the cool air had frozen last night's rain and drivers should be warned to watch for black ice on the roads.

He settled back; she did have a point. If they left a memorable trail they were going to get caught a lot faster. Dan took up his fork and he forced himself to take a bite even though his appetite was gone. It tasted overly sweet despite Clara's comment; he chewed and swallowed. He turned to the coffee to take a drink, finding that he liked the bitter much more. He worked at his cup till the waitress came by, refilling it and erasing all of his progress.

She smiled at him and he returned it, but had to hide a grimace when Clara kicked him under the bar. Apparently his smile wasn't convincing. When the waitress walked away he glared at Clara who looked as cool as a cucumber. She was eating pie, watching the news, and she kept her sneaker atop his foot as a reminder to not act like an idiot.

As the hour and a half passed, he felt like he was pushing out a kidney stone. He didn't have to fake his smile when they paid the bill: he couldn't be happier to get out of there. They waited for the first bus heading west at the station in the cold, and then Dan started to wish he was back in the Denny's with his kidney issues.

* * *

When the first bus came, Clara stepped up first, tossing in a pocket full of change to pay the fare. Walking back through the empty bus, they had their pick of any seat. Unlike the Greyhound's seats, these were hard plastic and smelled of sweat. Dan wondered if they ever washed the uncomfortable things down. Taking a seat behind the rear door, Clara reached over and tugged the hood up on Dan's pullover, then went through her own bag until she found a pair of hair bands. She started to braid her hair tight against the back of her head.

"Will that work?" Dan asked leaning back trying to get comfortable against the unforgiving seat.

"It doesn't have to be perfect, you just give them enough they aren't sure." She smiled as her fingers worked quickly down the long strands of hair; she showed an aptitude that said she'd had long hair a very long time. After she was finished brainding, she put her baseball cap back on.

"My hair was down in the news picture. I'll just pull it back, add a low cap, and people won't see the same person."

Clara thought aloud, "I wonder why they said Vegas was the last place we'd been seen? Either Dinatech didn't tell them we were in Sacramento or … no one is worried about us showing up in Virginia."

Dan wanted to question the thought, but his leg started to vibrate. He reached down to pull the forgotten phone from his pocket. He checked to see who was calling even though he knew it was Makin; he was the only person who had the number. He pressed talk.

"Makin? I thought you were keeping your distance?"

he said over the noise of the bus.

"Yes, I found a good reason though."

"Is that so?" Dan's voice had a sardonic edge to it.

"Look, my friend," Dan wished he'd stop calling him that, "I'm doing what is needed to protect both of us. I make this call to protect you. There have been some developments."

"Yeah we already saw our lovely faces on the news this morning, you're a little late," Dan said.

"Forget about that, you would be lucky to be arrested by the FBI. Ellsworth is no longer using their help."

Dan frowned and tried to wrap his head around what he'd been told. "Why wouldn't he be working with the FBI?"

"We believe that he's activated Black Water agents," Makin said gravely.

"What the hell is Black Water?" Dan said a little louder.

Clara's head snapped around and he knew at once this was as serious as Makin made it sound.

"You don't know?" Makin asked.

"No," Dan said.

"Oh of course, you are just a UPS worker, I forget." Dan couldn't tell if he was being sarcastic or not.

Clara growled in frustration and reached over, prying his hand back enough that Dan yelped as he released the phone. She brought it to her ear.

"Are you sure?" Clara said into the phone.

Dan tried to make out Makin's voice on the other side but he couldn't hear over the noise of the bus.

"Yes but they don't do capture missions Makin, you know this. If they called them in, they are looking for someone that works outside the rules. Can they even work inside the United States?"

After another pause where Makin talked, Clara responded, "Well I don't need you to save my feelings, what I need to know is the bloody facts Makin, or we're both dead."

Makin talked again but for not as long as Dan had hoped; there must not have been as many facts.

"If you hear anything else I want you to call me, right away. Are we crystal? You may not think you need us right now. But you'd be wrong; we are the best asset you have in the field. We want what you want, so get with the bloody program. We are going take the bastards down."

Clara didn't wait for a response; she ended the call and squeezed the phone till the plastic creaked in protest. Just before it broke, she let go so it fell into her lap.

"We are in sooo much trouble," she said in nothing but a breath of a voice. She let her shoulders slump with an exhausted look on her face.

"What in the world are you both talking about? What is Dark Water? Is it some other company that is looking to take us in or something?" Dan asked.

"No, it's Black Water, and these people don't get paid to bring people in. What Ellsworth has done is brought in the best of the best; these people are paid to do what the CIA wants. Only results matter." Clara looked over to him and shook her head.

"Don't expect me to be able to deal with Black Water. This just got a lot bigger. Someone is looking to close this case up and brush it under the rug."

Dan looked back over to her. "CIA? You mean the spies? I thought that they dealt with international threats? Foreign interests, crap like that."

"Kind of, this isn't the CIA though, more like

contractors, working to the highest bidder. Hired to deal with anything they feel is a threat to them." She picked the phone up and squeezed it again.

"People picked for Black Water fit a profile of an emotional and mental caliber that basically makes them command-able sociopaths. Trained outside the law and below the social code, they do the dirty work, and gangs, mafia, religious movements take the blame. 'Innocent bystanders' are not words in their vocabulary. They would look at the burning of an orphanage as extra grease for the fire that eliminated their target," Clara said.

"Do they really believe they need to send those kinds of people after us?" Dan was appalled by the idea, that anyone would think these kind of men were needed.

"If we can believe Makin, it's the kind of monsters they've unleashed on us, deserved or not." Clara bit her lip, pulled her hat down, and slumped into her seat.

"It's just a matter of how close on our trail they are. We need to get to Victoria and get out before they find us."

Clara nudged Dan awake. It was time to transfer from the express bus to the slower local one. The rest of the ride, she read street signs as the bus rolled on until she declared, "This is the spot." Requesting a stop, Clara exited the bus, and was already walking down a side street as the bus rumbled away, belching out black diesel exhaust. She looked at a house and cocked her head to the side.

It was small and gray, just a single story rambler, not

more that 1600 square feet total. The yard was small, but well looked after, and linked up against the side of the house was a two-car garage that looked like it was added after the original construction.

Dan looked it over, his arms wrapped around himself against the cold; simply departing the bus had taken away his body heat. "Somehow, I thought that it would be a lot bigger."

"It's just her and her brother. How much room do you Americans need?"

"Yeah, but I mean, I always thought of Southern politicians living in the large plantation type houses," he sputtered. "I mean, it's Virginia."

Clara looked over at him and tried to keep from laughing. "Did you even see any houses like that on the way?"

Dan started to protest, but Clara hooked her arm around his elbow, pulling him along. "Come along, Delivery Boy. Maybe she'll talk like Scarlet."

He said nothing they walked up to the front door and rang the bell.

"How do you know she's even here?" Dan glanced over at the closed curtains.

Clara shrugged. "I don't." She reached up and yanked back his hood before pulling her hat off. "Better, now we don't look like the Unabomber and his sidekick."

They stood over a minute in silence before Dan believed she was indeed out. He was contemplating where they would go to get out of the crushing cold when the door opened. A tall blond woman looked out; she was attractive but in a way that said it came naturally to her. She looked better than the pictures of Victoria Palmer in the articles, just a few years older. Victoria didn't say anything; she just watched them expectantly.

That was when Dan realized he didn't know what the hell he was going to say to her. He really should have practiced something. He'd focused so much on getting here and now that he was he didn't know where to start.

"Ahh, hello," Dan said waving a hand awkwardly.

Victoria frowned and Clara, seeing their first impression catching fire and falling into the sea, stepped in. "Victoria," she said in her smooth British accent. Dan thought she was laying it on thicker. "We have found ourselves in a situation and we hope that you can help us."

Victoria's frown found a second level. Dan was sure she'd heard lines like this before, and she didn't believe this one any more than she believed the others.

"I'm sorry, I don't have anything that I can help you with," she said in a practiced voice, perfect in getting her point across: not interested.

"We just need a few minutes to explain, please," Clara said softly, to keep her voice from adopting the clipped commanding tone that came when she wasn't getting her way.

Shaking her head, Victoria was already closing the door.

Dan saw their moment passing, but they had come too far to let a door close in their face. She was the only lead they had. Stepping forward, he put his hand on the door, letting his fingers splay out to keep it from closing any farther. Dan could see the panic in Victoria's eyes as he held the door.

"Victoria, your ex-boss is out to kill us and you might be the only one that can keep us alive. If you close this door, we may not make it the day." Dan raised his voice.

Clara sighed and stepped forward. "While I don't agree with how my partner goes about it, he's not lying. We are in a spot of trouble. Maybe the name Dinatech means something to you?"

Victoria didn't change her expression, but Dan did feel her let up on the door.

Clara took the opening to convince her. "We're a couple of loose ends that your ex-boss and Dr. Adams are looking to clip. I'm sure you know what I mean?"

Victoria sighed and stepped back, opening the door. She didn't motion them in, but waited for them to enter. Victoria looked to the street before closing and locking the door behind them.

On the inside, the house was clean, with everything having a place; anything that didn't wasn't here. It was just as you'd expect of someone that had to run the life of another. Victoria looked over the living room, and after an internal debate, she offered them the couch.

Victoria sat in her recliner and crossed one leg over the other, her arms settled in a closed posture. She was dressed in a pair of slacks and a sweater for the cold weather.

"Thank you for taking the time to talk with us," Dan said, trying to fill the awkward space.

"I wasn't given much of a choice; I'm hoping that you are going to get to the point and leave." Her voice held an impatient tone, and a slight Southern accent.

"Right, sorry," he said. Again, he didn't know where he should start and glanced at Clara; she furrowed brows back at him.

Clara sat forward on the couch, shaking her head. "The point is, we are hoping that you can help us to stop Ellsworth from using his connections to have us killed and give us something to clear our names with."

Victoria cocked a brow. "Clear your names?" Her eyes flickered to the door and back, no doubt wondering whom she'd let into her home.

"Yes." Clara motioned to the TV, silent and powered off in the corner. "Have you been watching the news?"

Victoria laughed. "I haven't watched the news in …" Uncrossing her arms she straightened her sweater. "In a long time," she said at last.

"Since you stopped working for Collin Ellsworth?" Clara pressed.

"I couldn't tell you for sure," Victoria countered, not willing to give any details, and clearly wary of anything she might say.

"Why did you quit working for Senator Ellsworth?" Clara said.

"My time there was done. I'd helped his election and then his re-election. There wasn't anything more there for me. I was ready to move on." It sounded like a practiced statement.

"This was a man that you felt passionate enough about that you kept working for him even though you were still finishing college," Clara said. "You weren't there just to get a paycheck, you had a personal interest in seeing him succeed."

"And he did," Victoria countered.

Clara reached into Dan's messenger bag and pulled out the folded papers she'd printed at the library.

"Yes, and you stayed on for a second round. But that's when things started to change, isn't it?" Clara flipped through the papers till she found the one showing a list of the campaign contributors and placed it atop the stack.

"Someone held his ear with huge contributions and votes that made it possible for him to keep his seat."

Victoria's green eyes narrowed at the paper and she tightened her lips together to keep from saying anything. She turned to study Clara, then Dan. "Just who are you two?"

"This is Clara and I'm Dan, we are being hunted by Dinatech because of something we know. We believe Ellsworth is somehow involved and is using government resources to make sure we are captured or killed," he said.

Victoria watched him coolly. "And you thought the best thing to do would be to put me in as much danger as yourselves?" She pointed to the door. "I think the two of you need to leave before you do any more damage."

Dan sighed. He was starting to believe they were wasting their time. Not only didn't she want to help; she wanted as much distance between herself and Ellsworth as she could get. He started to stand, but stopped when Clara didn't move. Feeling foolish, Dan settled back next to her.

"Whatever Ellsworth is doing with Dinatech, you know about it. You're just another loose end that he'll take care of sooner or later. If we figured it out then others can too, and it's only a matter of time before he turns his attention to you, Vicky," Clara said.

"Do not call me that," she said coolly, and Dan thought he should warn Victoria that once Clara picked a nickname it may as well be on your driver's license.

"Don't think it's not occurred to me. Hell, Dinatech might do the honors for him. They might think of it as a sick gift. I'm sure they can make it look like a tragic accident and not a coincidence. The only thing stopping them is how bad it would look if his personal secretary was killed days or weeks after she quit her post."

Dan was shocked how open she was with this; she'd been careful to keep herself guarded just a moment ago.

"I don't know what you expect me to tell you," she went on. "The best thing that I can do is play along, keep quiet, and hope they don't feel the need to clean up."

"You're just going to sit in your little box? Afraid of the light because the hawk is going to swoop the minute you leave your mouse hole?" Clara quipped back.

"Then you might as well be dead. Standing aside, letting the corruption continue. It's wrong, and it makes you worse than him. You know better."

Victoria's eyes got big. "You think you have any chance of standing up to them? I've seen what they can do and if they want to kill you, then you better run. Go into hiding and don't go poking your head out either. They will bury you deep to make sure there aren't any waves."

"That idea has crossed my mind a few times," Dan said softly trying to cool down the heated conversation, "but I really don't have the option. What I have, they want back and they aren't going to stop till they get what they are after."

"What could you have they could possibly want back this badly?" Victoria said with a questioning scowl.

"I'm sure you know better than us. You were there while Collin Ellsworth was working with Dinatech, passing laws around genetic experiments. What kinds of information do you think I have that they would want back from me?"

Victoria watched Dan a moment before her green eyes

lit up; he thought they were actually getting through to her.

"They didn't actually go through with any of that stupid …"

What Victoria said next Dan didn't hear; the words were lost when the large bay behind them window imploded. Simultaneously, the empty recliner sitting next to Victoria's turned to splinters, fluff detonating into the air around them. The world slowed to a crawl as Dan tried to process this turn of events. He sat stunned, watching the fallout until Clara yanked him to the floor by the front of his shirt.

She crawled atop him to yell in his ear, "Get to the kitchen!" Over their heads another explosion hit the fireplace, sending dangerous fragments of clay through the room, luckily missing all three of them. Victoria screamed, her arms over her head as she rolled to the floor.

Dan crawled on hands and knees as fast as he could. The walls were turned to wood chips and hunks of plaster. Dragging his bag along the floor, he looked back to see Clara pulling a scrabbling Victoria away from the gunfire; she wrangled her into the kitchen and up against the wall that separated the two rooms.

"This stove doesn't use gas?" Clara asked a shell-shocked Victoria. It took a shake of her shoulder to get a response.

"No, everything in the house is electric."

This seemed to be the right answer. Clara said, "Everyone, in front of the stove; that wall isn't going to stop a fifty cal shot." Pushing Victoria over, Clara pulled herself into Dan's lap because there was no room to sit side by side.

"So the stove can stop those rounds?" Dan asked, leaning around to watch shots turn the neat and ordered living room into the chamber of a popcorn popper.

Clara was dumping out the parts of the AR-15 and putting them together. "Not a chance, but it's better than just the drywall."

As if to emphasize this point, a round passed right through the wall above their heads, exploding a cabinet along the far wall, a box of shredded wheat now actually shredded. Then the assault suddenly stopped. The sound of the falling debris around them was amplified along with the metallic clicks of Clara fitting each piece of the rifle back together.

"Are these the Dark Water agents?" Dan leaned over to try and look closer.

"*Black* Water," Clara said, gritting her teeth together, concentrating.

"How did they find us so quickly?" Dan said.

"Great question, go ask them," Clara mumbled as she locked in the stock, completing the rifle.

"How could you lead people like this to my home?" Victoria shouted at Dan.

"Honey, I hate to be the one to break it to you, but we didn't lead them anywhere. They were here waiting for us; it's too quick. Someone thought that you were going to talk," Clara said.

"But I didn't tell you anything!" Victoria said, starting to become hysterical.

"Don't you hate having to pay the punishment when you didn't commit the crime?" Clara gave her a shit-eating grin.

"It's time to get out of here. Anyone left behind is going to get themselves perished in a horrible fire that will make the five o'clock news."

Nobody protested.

"Now, we saw the garage; is there a working car in there, and can we get to it from inside the house?"

"Yes, it's the door at the end of the hall. There's my car and my brother's Jeep." Victoria frowned, clearly not pleased with the idea of using her car for the getaway.

"Dan, take Victoria and get to the car, I'll cover you." Clara flipped the safety off the rifle and put the spare clip only half full into her back pocket.

He started to protest but knew he'd only cost them time. Taking Victoria by the hand, he pulled her to her feet as she protested.

"No time to argue about this. You're coming so you don't end up in as many pieces as your house!"

Clara rolled past the divider wall and shouldered the rifle; it looked too big in her hands. Not wanting Clara to expose herself longer than she needed, he pulled Victoria through the living room still protesting, her feet slipping over the mixed ingredients that was once her living room. Just as Dan reached the garage door, he heard the new sound of shattering glass and the report of the AR-15 as Clara squeezed off a burst. Then there was return fire while Clara backed down the hallway.

Their shots sounded close: they were now inside the house.

He felt the jolt of adrenaline as the realization came to him. He looked to see the key rack by the door with spare sets of keys, and pulled down every key that looked like it could start a car. Jerking the door open, he ran into the cramped garage. Seeing the two vehicles, the Jeep looked more like it was equipped for off-road than the urban jungle. Victoria's car was a clean Lincoln town car. Flipping through the keys Dan found the right one. Behind him Clara jumped into the room, kicking the door closed and franticly slapped at the large button that opened the garage door. The rollup door lurched to life at once.

"Lincoln, we're taking the Lincoln," Clara said, running to the car, the rifle still smoking.

"I know I'm new at this whole running from the law thing, but even I knew that was the car we wanted," Dan shot back as he clicked the key fob built into the actual key, opening all the doors. Clara just eyed him while she pushed Victoria into the back, jumping in after her. Dan turned over the large V8 engine as the door to the house opened up and a man appeared dressed all in black, looking like he rolled right out of an 80s special forces movie.

His rifle fired, putting a bullet through the hood of the car. Dan slammed his foot on the gas and the car lurched backwards through the still opening door. Exploding from the garage in reverse, the Lincoln's tires billowed smoked. The man in black dived onto the hood as the car gained speed, bouncing over the curb into the street.

The man held onto the flange of the hood, and Dan was able to get a good look at him: clean cut with gray eyes that were watching him with intensely, unflinching, even as the car slammed off the sidewalk. The man leveled a gun at the window and Dan yanked up on the emergency break, whipping the wheel around, and putting the car into a backwards spin. The gamble paid off; the man was flung from his perch on the hood to the street, and Dan immediately slapped the selection stick into drive and punched the gas. The V8 responded, roaring to full power as the town car shot forward and

Dan fought to keep the car under control. He sideswiped the man as he tried to get to his feet, sending him flying to the ground. The Lincoln shot down the 25 mile an hour street at well over 50, still gaining speed. Drifting a corner out of the neighborhood, Dan steered them towards the freeway and as far from the death trap as he could get.

Victoria looked out the back window as Clara checked to see how much ammo they had left.

"Do you see yet? They are going to stop at nothing to get me," Dan said. "They don't give a shit about laws or people."

In the rear view mirror, Dan watched Victoria's eyes narrow at him. "What you're saying is by coming to my home, I'm guaranteed to go down with you? Thank you for that, really, thank you."

"Right, and it's my fault he thought you'd tell us anything if we came?" Dan shot back.

She flopped back into the seat, almost childlike, and put on her seatbelt, sitting quietly for the next few miles. Clara looked on skeptically.

Then Victoria started up quietly, "There are no files in his office that he can't pass off as legitimate work. What you're after is held in archives, in the capital records house. While they aren't under any major security, that makes for the best kind of security. When something looks ignored, it must not hold any value." Victoria turned to look out the window.

"Collin never wanted to get rid of anything that had passed between Adams and himself. He was always worried if he left himself open, Adams would gain leverage."

Dan looked to Clara. "Dark Water is working for

Ellsworth, and they know that we have started to find his lose ends. He has to know where we're going next. We don't want a repeat of our raid on Adams' office."

Clara bit at her lip, looking out as the road sped by. "Black Water."

"Black Water," Dan said, and rolled his eyes.

"We need to get there before they do. If we don't, they could move it or worse, destroy it. They don't even have to chase us."

"Dan." Clara's eyes turned to look at him. "If you really want your freedom back, you do it by letting your opponent know you'll do anything to get it. Let them know the cost is more than they are willing to pay to oppress you." Clara eyes didn't look away from him, her eyes cool.

Dan was starting to understand the difference between Clara and most people. This was someone that never shrugged away from a problem just because it was hard; she took every challenge to prove that she was worthy. Now, she was asking if he was worthy of the same creed she lived by. He gripped the wheel tighter, knowing what they were in for. They would be going up against the government's finest killers. They were better trained, better armed, and it gave them the upper hand.

Dan looked to Victoria once more.

"Tell me again where we can find these files."

Chapter 7: Nightmare Before Christmas

The white Lincoln was pointed for Richmond, and Dan settled in for the two-hour drive down I-95; he moved into the far lane and turned the cruise control on as Victoria started explaining.

"When I first decided I wanted to work in government, my older brother Michael was enlisted in the army. He would always talk about it, how he wanted to make a real difference in the world. He'd be shipped off around the world to make it a better place. All the crap they brainwash kids with."

She turned and looked out the window. White birch, left leaf-bare for the winter, framed the freeway on both sides as they drove out of the city.

"When he graduated high school, much to the chagrin of my mother, he enlisted. Michael was off to boot camp the same summer. I used to love summer break, but that year I kept praying the school year wouldn't end, anything I could do to keep him just a little longer. I always looked up to my brother. He's only a year older than me, and it made us close. We had a lot of the same interests in school. But there was no way I was going to follow him into the military; it would have just destroyed

293

our mother."

"I know what you mean," Clara said from her seat up front. She'd crawled up after deciding no one was following.

"It's the one promise my mom forced on my dad, that no matter what happened I wouldn't be allowed to enter the armed forces. Personally I think that I would have looked hellishly dapper in a Royal Navy uniform. I still really want one," she said, while tucking the rifle under the front seat.

Dan cleared his throat and Clara growled at him before going quiet.

Victoria looked like she was amused by their antics, but the day had left her subdued.

"Well, I went a different way. I thought I could make a difference and I started to get involved with politics. Really, I foolishly believed that if I could find diplomacy there would be no need to deploy my brother. I joined clubs in high school, but I found they weren't really about politics or having a point of view. All they did was parrot what our club president had to say and raised money to make flyers to raise awareness of what he thought of one political issue or another. But I stuck to it; I needed to do something for my brother, and it was all I could think of.

"I got older and prepared to graduate high school. My time was running out. The world turned upside down and we were fighting wars in the Middle East. They weren't playing hopscotch to solve their differences. My desperation to make a change increased, and then I found the governor was up and coming, looking to run for a seat in the Senate. He was using the campaign promise of bringing the troops home, and I jumped at the chance to help him. I was able to get an internship the summer that Michael deployed. He wrote me every week while he was in boot camp and it didn't stop when he was placed in his troop and shipped overseas. Without fail, I got my letters, and when he couldn't mail anymore I got emails. You can call me silly but I printed out every one. I still have every mail he ever sent home. It told me he'd lived another week, and that I just needed to keep doing my best to get him home."

"You didn't leave them in that house did you?" Dan asked.

"What?" Victoria said.

"The mails, did you leave them in the house?"

"Oh yes, but it's fine. Michael isn't home and he's safe. He's in Texas doing a training exercise. I don't need them anymore." Victoria smiled.

Dan was starting to see that everything Victoria did was an effort to keep her family whole.

"While he was off seeing the world," Victoria pushed forward through her story, "I was here working every minute they would let me, at a small desk trying to will Collin into office. When I graduated, Collin heard about all the work I'd done for him, and he always told me how impressed his staff was with my work, so when I at last graduated, I came to work full time for him as an assistant. Michael was shipped from Iraq to Afghanistan. I knew I was working with a faster moving clock; he could be killed at any time. But as the letters and emails kept coming, I was able to keep my anxiety under control. Still, no matter what he said, I always had a dull ache in the pit of my stomach.

"I started college the summer after graduation and threw myself at my studies while still keeping a part time job working for Collin. The more I worked, the less free time I had to sit around and worry about my family; it felt good to stay busy. We all put so much work into the campaign that when he won it felt like we had pedaled a bike as hard as we could, passing our destination without notice. We didn't know we should have stopped.

"Some people went back home, and others came to work on his staff. Collin spoke to me directly in the hopes that I'd come; he'd said there was still so much he needed to do. He didn't feel he could trust it to just anyone. At the time I knew Dinatech helped to fund his campaign war chest. I didn't understand until later that they were doing more than funding him. In return, he did more than pave the path for their work. The deal was, he helped the, and they would get him all the way into the White House."

Clara frowned, turning in her seat to look over the back.

"It sounds like a big contradiction to me. On one hand, he says that he wants to bring the men home, on the other Dinatech wants a spending military; war is money."

"Yes, he once told me his belief was that better equipped soldiers would mean less people deployed," Victoria said.

Clara nodded but frowned deeper.

"I didn't think about it much at first, but as things kept going, I came to understand how they were going to do it. I also learned of just how persuasive Dr. Adams could be, but not until much later. When I graduated from college, my job was already set before me; Collin asked me to become his personal assistant again. I helped him keep tabs on everything Adams was doing. Collin told me he didn't feel he could trust anyone as much as he trusted me. He said we had the same goals, and that he could trust me with his life's work.

"I was flattered and I was sucked in, almost at once, I never questioned him. This was a man I'd admired for a long time and I believed he was doing right by his promises. I was ready to help; I wanted things to keep going. Collin wanted more than anything to be president. But not just anyone can do that, you have to offer something the people want. I mean really want. This is where Dinatech got him. They bastardized his campaign to get what they wanted. He'd always pushed to bring the troops home and it had been so successful that he believed that he could ride that all the way into the White House with their help."

Victoria laughed softly.

"But now that he held a seat in the Senate he realized it wasn't going to be as easy. Saying things like 'yeah let's bring the troops home' doesn't work unless you can show results. Dinatech showed him a new path that he could pave himself. By making some kind of super soldier, they could have less people deployed, saving money and resources, because these human weapons would be so well trained we'd actually lose less." She rolled her eyes.

"Collin fell for it. Hook line and sinker. He saw it as a way to differentiate himself from the others and ran with it; he even believed this was right, and that he could use it to really bring the troops home. In exchange for heavy coffers, he used his influence to help pass bills that made Dinatech's research easy. The first work was in a small building just inside Richmond; Collin said that he was putting jobs in Virginia. That helped to pass more bills, and created more jobs for Virginians. When the really strange bills came through for stem cell work and genetic experimentation, they passed under other medical initiatives, masking them with changes that would help people. But it was all for their super soldiers. Then when it came time for new government contracts, Collin got kickbacks for helping Dinatech land the work."

"Did you try to talk with him about it?" Dan asked.

"Of course I tried to talk to him. I tried to showed him how they were using him. But he didn't see it, or he wouldn't see it. I wasn't sure what to do, so I kept helping him. What good would quitting do? When it came time for the re-election to his seat, it was a joke. No one had a chance; with Dynatech's money and growing influence in other seats, Collin was assured a seat for a long time."

That was where Victoria paused. Clara and Dan exchanged looks, but no one said anything for a few miles. She looked tormented.

"When things really came to a head was about four months after his re-election," she started again.

"Dinatech had given so much money, and his whole agenda was to help them with project Silverfish."

"Silverfish?" Dan asked, remember that word form Makin's debrief.

"Yes," Victoria said. "It was the name of the program they were doing their super soldier research under. I don't know any more details than that; he wasn't even sharing with me anymore. It was then that I knew I didn't want to be any part of it. I couldn't help him, and he didn't trust me.

"When I quit, it felt like I was going through a divorce." She said, "I mean, I never really had time to have a personal relationship. I'd given Collin all of my time and energy. He tried to talk me into staying a few times, but I refused and at some point, he knew that I wasn't going to come back and he cut all ties with me. After spending the majority of my life working for him I didn't know what to do with myself. But then Michael came home from deployment and I threw myself at helping him get adjusted. We found a place near the base, but far enough from DC that I didn't feel I was near Collin anymore,"

"I'm going to help you now because I hope you can save Collin from himself and his ambitions. It's gone too far, and he needs to know that he can't think working with those bastards will end well. He'll never be president, but I hope he can see he can still help the world. Maybe? Once he sees corruption can touch anyone."

"I think you're going to find that your old flame is just as guilty as the rest," Clara said bluntly, against Dan's protest.

Victoria laughed softly. "I don't know if I can really explain it to you and I'm not going to try. I'm going to show you the first research center Dinatech opened in Virginia. No one works there now. In fact, there is only a minimal security there just to make sure it's not vandalized. But Collin worked there with Dr. Adams, so you'll find what you want. The information for Silverfish is there, and it's enough to point the finger at Dinatech. Adams moved the work to the west coast when it became logical to find workers with the expertise he needed. Collin was wary because of the move and saved everything. I know it was in case Adams decided to expose him.

"I still believe in Collin, maybe foolishly. You don't work for someone that long and not think you can save them. But if he really sent killers to my house to make sure I wouldn't talk … I just hope you can do something to save him."

With this Victoria fell into silence, tears sliding down her cheeks.

They were just a few blocks from the Dinatech building in Richmond when they pulled the car to the curb. Dan shut off the engine and, called Makin using the cell phone he'd given him.

When Makin picked up Dan started in, "Here is how it goes. We have a lead on the information, but your people are going to watch after a woman that helped us. She's Ellsworth's ex-personal assistant."

At first Makin said he couldn't provide the protection Victoria would need. It took two more calls and almost thirty minutes before he agreed that he could hide Victoria, with the understanding that she'd tell them what she knew about Dinatech's dealings.

"Now, as for us," Dan said.

"What about you?" Makin said, confused.

"You're kidding me, right? What more do we need to do before you'll see that we are working for the same thing?" Dan said, frustrated. He couldn't understand why they had cut them off so completely.

"Look, Dan. If it were up to me, I'd risk my own life. But that's not how it works. It's not my choice; I have to stand by what the council has decided," Makin said.

"Then why are you taking Victoria in?" Dan questioned.

"Because, my friend. I've not asked the council for

permission," Makin said. The smile could be heard in his voice.

"So you're just going to help me hide her? What happens when they realize what you're doing?" Dan said.

"My friend, I'm sure you've heard the phrase 'It's easier to ask for forgiveness than permission,'" Makin said.

"Yes, I've heard the phrase before." Dan said, unable to keep himself from chuckling.

"Then don't worry. Send her to the address I'm going to text you and I will take care of the rest," Makin said.

Hanging up the phone, they got out of the car. Victoria seemed happy to have her car back as she put the address into her onboard GPS. "I'd like to say it was a pleasure to meet the two of you, but I can't."

"I'm sorry that you had to get involved in this at all, Victoria," Dan said leaning in the driver window.

"Well maybe if I'd picked my Senators better back in college I could have been part of a sex scandal and sold a book instead," Victoria said wryly.

She pulled away, heading west. Dan and Clara grabbed their bags and Dan called Makin back while they walked.

"Is there an issue now?" Makin said.

"If we get the information, and we can expose the Senator and his Dinatech friends, what can you do to help us clear our names?" Dan asked.

"If you get the information," Makin said. "I know people that can put the story out. They work with an international paper and have offices in New York. You find the documents and have proof they are Dinatech's, and I think I can give you what you want."

* * *

Dan and Clara sat on a sidewalk bench, both watching the building across the street. Made of unpainted concrete, the building was in the shape of a U, ten stories with small windows that might let in light but didn't give a view. In the shadow of the U were the front doors with a turnabout for cars. The building was quiet; there was no life to be seen. The city noise around it made it feel like a tomb. Clara crossed her legs at the ankles; she looked up at the building with a whimsical expression.

"Well, it sure seems like a cake walk, doesn't it?" she murmured.

Looking up into the graying sky, a matted background for the Dinatech building, Dan felt it would be a jinx to say anything. Clara swung her feet back and forth, scuffing at the pavement; neither made any move to get up.

"I think that it's going to snow soon," she said softly. "It's so close to the holidays, I think that it would be lovely to have a white winter. You don't really get many of those in London, just rain, and fog, and more rain. When we moved to the northwest, I was hoping we'd get snow. The word north fooled me. I really wanted to have a white Christmas."

She shifted on the bench, the rifle behind them hidden. "I've seen those movies where the snow comes at the right time, families around the tree and a merrily crackling fire. I never had that, not really. I was a military brat being raised by her mother. She tried to make it work; she even went all out one year when I was five. Daddy was going to be home for the first time ever.

Mom got a tree and trimmed it. I remember looking out the window. It was still raining, but I didn't care—I was going to have a tree and my daddy, it was good enough. Mom even promised that I could help with the dinner." She laughed softly.

Dan didn't interrupt. He wanted to hear her story. He knew very little about her, so he clung to everything she told him. Still, what she did talk about always seemed to be sad, and made it seem as though her cheerful disposition was an attempt at giving her past the finger.

"Dad didn't make it home the week of Christmas. And he still wasn't home by Christmas Eve. But it wasn't just Mom and I for Christmas; we had company. People had broken into the house and kidnapped us; we were blindfolded and bound. I remember hearing my mother crying, telling them to just take what they wanted and leave. They didn't want anything, other than us. My mother and I were taken by a terrorist cell in retaliation for some mission Dad had been on." Clara's eyes clouded over once again, taking on that lifeless look Dan was becoming familiar with.

Clara was shaking from head to toe as she traveled back in her mind to the memory of their abduction. Her mother and her were both stuffed into the back of a van or enclosed truck: the floors were metal, and the engine echoed in the open space about her. She couldn't see anything: her head was wrapped in a thick cloth bag that made the air warm and stuffy and blocked out all of the light. Her mother was in the van with her; she could feel her pressed against her side. They drove for hours, stopping only long enough to transfer them from one car to another. Her mother had stopped trying to talk with any of their captors hours ago; they wouldn't even acknowledge them other than to handle their basic needs.

They were driven to a dock where Clara could smell the salt water and hear the crash of waves loud enough to mask conversation. They were taken on board a boat of some kind, and she could hear the water lapping up against the hull. Locked into a metal container, they were allowed to be without the bags, and their bindings were removed. There was no place for them to run, as they were trapped in a cargo container on the open water.

The whole time they were watched but never talked to. At times her mother tried to question them, but they never answered any questions. Clara wondered if they even spoke English. She didn't like the food they gave her but quickly learned with as little as they were giving them, that she'd need to eat everything to keep her stomach from hurting. She needed to eat to be strong; it was something her daddy told her whenever there was food she didn't like.

"Clara, my cherub, you need to eat all your food so you can grow up and be strong for your family," he said.

This must be the time he'd spoken of; she needed to be strong for Mom, she needed to be strong so they could get away.

The trip must have taken weeks, but once they were off the boat, Clara was sure they would be found. People were good and they would see these people were bad and how they didn't want to be with them. She quickly learned she was wrong. There were people everywhere that wanted to help the kidnappers, people who were sympathetic to them. Didn't anyone want help a mother and her daughter? The longer they traveled, the less anyone spoke English, and no one bothered to keep their heads covered in the bags anymore. Clara was happy for that; it was a lot warmer here. They looked to be in the dessert. Warm sun-washed sand was all she could see for miles as they traveled in the back of a rattletrap pickup truck.

Being held against her will in the desert was far from her idea of a white Christmas, and Clara also missed the turn of the year. She leaned back against the rough concrete wall. By now, she should be back in school with her friends. Did anyone miss them yet? Was her picture put in the news, did her friends see it? What would they think?

They were being held in what her mother called an 'old concrete bunker'. It was run down, dark, and smelled worse than anything Clara could have imagined, thick with the sickly sweet, rancid smell of decomposition. They were drug down here days ago and simply tossed into their cells: even their captors didn't want to be down in the bunker long. It was a makeshift jail at best, with roughly welded barred doors, and Clara was sure it wasn't made to hold small kids. If she wanted to crawl down in the muck she could slide through the holes in the concrete wall that kept water from standing. It was almost like a child-sized mouse hole that the terrorists didn't bother to cover up.

This place was hell, but she hadn't died.

All she wanted was to go home; she'd never complain

about what Mom wanted to watch on the TV from now on, she would come home right after school and be the best little girl any parent had ever seen. The only thing that kept her from falling into hopelessness was being with her mom. She held back the tears: her mom wasn't crying, so she needed to be strong too. Her mother said things like, "Don't be sad Clara dear, your father is going to come and get us out of here." Sometimes she'd add, "Because if he doesn't I'm going to break myself out of here and snap him in two."

She needed to be strong like Mom.

There were times when Clara was taken from her mother, and she didn't like those moments at all. Three of the terrorists had come down for her. This was rare. The guards normally argued about who had to bring them food. This time with three of them at the door, she knew something was different; Clara found herself pressed to the wall behind her mother.

"Give us the girl," one of the men had said in an accent that was hard to understand.

"No, anything that you need to talk about, you can ask me. She doesn't know anything, and you bloody well know it!" Clara's mom reached back and put a hand on Clara's shoulder reassuringly.

The tallest of them rushed forward and dug the tip of his rifle into her mother's cheek. Clara could feel her go rigid. The other two men moved forward and grabbed Clara. She tried to pull away, screaming and thrashing as they took her from the cell. Her mother called after her, pinned by the third with the rifle, "It's going to be okay baby. Just be good, okay? You'll be back soon."

Clara was taken out of the smelly bunker; it felt free just to be breathing fresh air. They shouted at her, things that she couldn't understand. They pushed her into chair and made her hold papers, they took pictures of her while she cried. One man slapped her when she wouldn't hold the paper. He shouted at her in broken English.

"You are here because god punishes the unjust. Whole families pay for the sins of the father!"

What god would reward the hurting of a mother and her daughter? What god could be on their side?

Curled in a ball back in her cell, Clara was sure that her life would end in here. Her daddy had to think they were dead; it had been weeks, maybe months. They took Clara again for pictures; the next few times weren't as bad. She knew what to do, and if she did what they wanted they didn't hit her. Each time they brought her back to the cell she'd go to her corner, curl up, and her mother would hold her until they both fell asleep. She started to wish for it to just end.

There was no one coming.

They would die here and become part of the horrible smell.

Her mother kept trying to cheer her up, or at least get her to eat something. She'd stopped eating once she'd given up. Clara didn't see the need anymore; there was no reason to be strong. No one was coming, and she couldn't endure just for the sake of punishment. She looked away when her mother attempted to feed her; it hurt to watch her mother try when she was sad herself. At night Clara could hear her cry, and the sound were like shards of glass raked down over her soul. She hated to be this powerless.

One day, Clara woke and looked up at the small sand crusted windows; it wasn't quite light yet. She didn't move, just watched the window from where she was curled. She was starting to drift to sleep again when an explosion rippled the floor under her and dust fell from the roof.

Clara sat up. It was the first thing that'd happened in days. She reached out and put her hand on the cell wall to feel the vibrations. There was shouting up above and the *pop pop pop* of gunfire. Her mother got up slow and cautious, and walked to the cell door to look down the hall. People kicked in the door, and the thump of heavy boots on the stairs mixed with gunfire moved down the row of cells. The shouting was in English, and Clara jumped to her feet; she shook with the warmth of hope. She could feel it radiate out from her core like someone had flipped a switch. She ran for the bars; these people would help her. She made it halfway before her mother scooped her up and pulled her to the back wall. Clara screamed and tried to push free, but her mom held tightly.

"Sara! God, are you okay?" a man called through the bars; he wore military fatigues and held a large rifle. With blond hair and blue eyes that matched her own, Clara knew him instantly.

"Daddy!" she shouted, trying to reach over her mother to him, the tears spilling hot down her cheeks.

"Clara baby, just hold on. Daddy saw your pictures, you were so brave, baby." Then he moved away from the cell and there was more gunfire. Her father wasn't alone and other men came forward to cut open the cell. This was a rescue; they were going home.

Her mother set her down and used her body to shield

Clara against the wall.

"Shit, Jordy, there are more of them towel-headed bastards than we thought," one of the other men called out to Clara's father.

"They got us pinned down!" another shouted.

They fell back into Clara's cell for cover, one of them limping, injured, bleeding from a gunshot to the leg. They were trapped in the cell. There were six men with her father, and the guerrilla forces outnumbered them.

Pressed up against the wall, the injured man tossed his pistol to the side while he worked to bandage his wound.

"It's not that bad," he said, to the on- looking squad, "but if you guys don't have a plan for getting out of here, it's not going to really matter." He was right: things where starting to look desperate, even Clara could tell.

She needed to be strong. For her parents who were both brave, she needed to be brave.

When her mother wasn't watching, she slipped out from behind her and picked up the gun the injured solder had tossed aside. Clara pushed down into the muck and squeezed through to the next cell before anyone could notice that she was missing. The smell down in the muck was horrible. It was slimy and it made her want to squirm when it seeped through her clothes.

She was still dressed in the Christmas sweater she had wanted her father to see, too filthy now to be recognized. She pushed on, staying low as she slipped into the next cell. Looking through the bars she could see the terrorists were leaned up against the concrete walls for cover, keeping her father and his friends pinned in the cell. She was small, so no one noticed as she crawled across the empty cell to the next hole. She squeezed through with the gun out before her. It felt very heavy, but she knew that it was power. She started to mumble to keep from gagging, "This gun is my friend, this gun will save us, I must trust my gun." Clara tried to say the words like she'd heard her daddy say before.

Clara pulled herself up into the next cell and there were no terrorists to be seen; she was behind them, and she started to move forward. At the last second she noticed movement and pressed herself flat to the wall. She stayed in the dark shadows that the cell wall provided. She watched as a tall man walked past her cell. He looked old, with a long gray beard. She didn't need to be told that he was some kind of leader. She slid along the wall to the end of the cell; it was open and she looked out to see they had her father, mother, and his friends surrounded inside of the cell. The tall bearded man spoke.

"It was foolish of you to come here, and even more foolish to think you could leave." His English was better than the others. "Come forward and I can promise your deaths will be quick. If you make us have to come in for you, I will promise your execution will come long after you beg for it."

Clara crept forward. She held the pistol in both hands; it looked as large as her father's rifle to her. She could see the back of the bearded man. With all their backs to her, no one noticed.

"Don't be a fool, it's over, toss your weapons out now!" the bearded man barked.

Clara brought the gun up and put both fingers on the trigger: she didn't know how hard she'd need to pull it. She didn't think she could hit him; her arms were shaking so much. She blinked back the tears and tried to aim for his back: it was big and she didn't want to miss.

She had to save her daddy.

The men were looking to the bearded man for directions, and she didn't have any time left. She had to do it.

Now.

Clara pulled the trigger.

The shot felt like it went off between her ears.

Everything turned white …

Clara laughed softly, returning to the present, and curling both arms up over her head as she thought back.

"When the gun went off it kicked me off my feet. I was knocked out cold when my head hit the bars behind me. They told me the rest later. When my shot went off there was confusion everywhere. The panic allowed Daddy and his team to get the upper hand. My father, well not my father at the time, he was just part of the Delta Force then. Normally the Seals handled this work, but he'd taken a personal interest. Hearing that some of the SAS were going in, he pulled some strings and their own battalion deployed to help. Daddy, not knowing they were coming, was inside when Eric Derksen and his team secured the complex around us. Eric and my father had been friends from working on joint missions, and when he heard Jordy's wife and daughter had been captured, he came to help.

"I think that's when they knew there was more than just friendship going on. You know? I've told this to the both of them, but they always wave it off." Clara shrugged her shoulders. "I guess love is a funny thing, I'm just glad that they found it themselves soon enough."

"Did you kill the man in the bunker?" Dan asked softly.

Clara turned and studied him before she answered.

"When I came to, most of it was done, and I didn't ask at the time. He was covered with a blanket in a corner. I found out years later, my shot jerked up and hit him through the back of the skull. He was the leader of their terrorist cell and when the man's brother learned I had killed him, he made it public knowledge he would come for me one day."

Clara smiled and looked down.

"This is why I'm … me. My mother said she'd never let her child be part of any military, because she didn't want me to end up just like my father. But she did agree that I'd have to learn how to take care of myself—and not just like karate or anything like that. I'd need to understand weaponry, military tactics, and how terrorists work; how they survive, and how to take them down. Both my fathers worked hard to prepare me, because they think he'll actually come for me."

"And why do you know about Dark Water?" Dan asked.

"Black Water!" she frowned and shook her head, "That would be my father. He did contract work in Iraq after Delta Force and before he joined the FBI. They are known."

She stood up and he pulled the combat knife out of her bag: she'd kept it from their raid on the Sacramento complex.

"Take the rifle. I'm going to be better with this than you will." She spun the knife in her hand to prove the point.

Dan nodded and pulled the rifle out from behind

them. He walked beside her as they crossed the street and stepped up to one of the side doors. "Remember, we're walking into their trap, but what they won't expect is that we want to be in their trap."

"We do?" Dan blinked.

"Of course. We show them what they won't expect and you gain the upper hand. Just don't hesitate, or ..." She leaned up on her toes and kissed his cheek, now rough with stubble. "I'll miss you."

Chapter 8: Apoclypse Now

Putting a rock through a window, Clara used the rifle barrel to knock the remaining glass from the frame before handing it back to Dan. She hopped up onto the ledge with cat-like reflexes and smiled back at Dan, giving him a wink before slipping into the dark beyond. He followed her lead with far less grace and stumbled into the dark room.

Dan pulled the flashlight he'd taken from Victoria's trunk and switched it on. The floor was gray-and-black-checked tile. The gray may have been white once, but with years of neglect they could never be truly white again. They were in a room that doubled as both exam room and office. Clara took the flashlight and examined him for cuts from the window. Then she walked to the door and opened it slowly, with Dan looking out over her shoulder. The hallway beyond was just as dark. There were no windows, and only a single florescent light glowed at the far side of the hall, but it only marginally saved the hall from pitch black. Clara pulled back and leaned against the wall.

"I don't see anyone out there, but that doesn't mean anything."

"Out-manned, out-gunned, and in a building? Isn't that becoming our specialty?" Dan gave her a wry grin.

Clara squinted at him. "When did we change roles in this relationship?"

"I learned from the best," Dan said.

She motioned him through the door. "Stay low and keep to the walls. I'm right behind you."

"This hall takes us to the lobby," Dan said. "We can get to the basement from there. The files will be down there." Dan leaned out to look again.

"What makes you so sure?" Clara said pressed to the door, ready to follow.

"I'm just sure," Dan said, again unable to place where he learned it. It was as if the memory was his, but faded, like a dream.

She shrugged. "We have to start somewhere."

Pressed to the wall, Dan moved through the door and down the hall. He kept the rifle slung out in front of him where he could raise it quickly. Clara moved behind him, the knife pulled up tight against her arm, ready to slash. The hallway had the same tile and the walls were lined with plastic handrails. Beside each door was a clipboard holder. The place had a very medical feel.

Dan progressed slowly, trying to watch for movement. The place looked abandoned and as his confidence grew he moved faster. He peeked around a turn in the hall; beyond was another hallway, but not as long, and the building opened up into what he believed to be the lobby. It was hard to tell in the darkness. Clara moved around him and looked.

"Those bots of yours give you night sight? It's too dark to see anything."

He looked down at Clara. "Not yet. Maybe that's

next?"

"You say what we need in is in the basement?" Clara was clearly planning again.

"Yes, I think so."

"And the only way into the basement is through the lobby?"

"I think so."

"Then I *think* that we are going to have to get to that lobby," Clara said, and motioned him forward. Dan rushed around the corner to the far wall while Clara stayed to the near wall. He was able to move right up to the edge of the open space. Looking up, he could see where the building's architect was allowed to be creative: above them was a set of catwalks that alternated left to right on each floor: anyone looking from underneath would see the X pattern. The outer walls and ceiling were made of glass, allowing for lots of light during the day. Currently the moonlight streaming through gave everything a blue-gray tint.

Connecting the catwalks through the middle of the X was an elevator that had glass doors on each side and stairwells ran up on each side of the lobby. Not seeing anyone and not being shot at, Dan stood up. He walked to a door, opening it to show the basement stairs beyond.

"I thought that this place was supposed to have security watching after it."

Clara squinted, watching down the far hall on the other side of the U. "Vicky said there was a very minimal presence. I wouldn't be surprised if they patrolled other buildings too. Don't be disappointed; we'll make all kinds of new friends when they find the broken window."

"This side." Dan motioned for Clara. "The other side doesn't go down."

"How do you know all of this, Delivery Boy?" Clara asked him with a worried look.

"I … don't know. I just do, almost like I've done this before in a dream," Dan said as he started down the dim stairwell.

Clara stepped in and looked up then down. "I'm so done with buildings! I'm going to live in a tent for the next year. I dream of open, grassy fields."

They found a wide door at the bottom of three full flights. She checked the handle and it turned. Opening the door just a crack; she waited for a reaction. Looking disappointed, Clara opened the door fully to room measuring ten feet by ten feet. The far wall held a massive vault door, blocking them from going any further.

Clara whistled and looked up at the intimidating stainless steel. On the right side was a keypad, with a large ship's wheel in the middle used to turn the bolts.

"No one is getting through this without a written permission slip." She tried the wheel to find it held fast.

Strapping his rifle over his shoulder, Dan walked up to the keypad and he nodded. "Yeah, that might be true." He reached out and rubbed his fingers over the keys lightly.

"Hey there, Delivery Boy, careful. Do something wrong and it's going to call not-so-friendlies down on us," Clara warned. Dan smiled and typed in sixteen digits without hesitation. On the last key, the light next to the LCD panel turned green and a loud clunk from inside the door sounded. Clara to looked up at him, her blue eyes large with wonder.

"Bloody hell, he whispers to machines."   She tested the wheel, and it turned freely.

"I just seem to know," Dan said. He watched Clara turn the wheel as the three-ton door opened on hydraulic assistance.

"This place is familiar. I know I've never been here, but I know things about it."

"Those things are messing with your memory," Clara said; a statement, not a question. "What else are they messing with up there?"

He felt the sweat break out on the back of his neck at her words; he knew that he wouldn't be able to keep the truth of it from her forever.

"I don't know but," he pointed beyond the door, "maybe we can figure it out?"

Clara stepped back. "Well then, lead the way, you know where we're going." She smiled a bit, but it looked a little too tight. Perhaps he was just paranoid?

Stepping beyond the vault door, he reached to the wall and pulled up a heavy switch; a long bank of florescent lights buzzed to life, filling the dead quiet. The air was dusty and stale, like no one had been in here for a very long time. On the right was a nurse's station; on the left were rooms with large open glass fronts that could be observed from the hall. In each of the rooms was a bed and nothing else; on the back walls there were many jacks for support equipment, but it had long been removed.

Clara walked up to the glass and knocked her knuckles on it. "More than a few inches thick ... bullet proof. Whatever they were doing in here, they didn't want it getting free."

Down the hall were doors that lead to each side. Then there was a heavy security door set between two glass-fronted rooms and at the end of the hall was another door with a security pad on it.

"What we want is down here," Dan said in a whisper. He motioned for Clara to follow him, and she didn't look at all surprised when Dan put in the code for this door and it responded with a positive chirp and opened.

"You are dead useful to have around, you know. But I don't think we should let Makin and his friends know about *this* superpower," Clara said.

"Yeah, they'd be looking for a way to extract all the information they could." Dan shivered at the thought.

Dan pushed the door open slowly and it rewarded him with an ominous rattle of hinges in desperate need of oil. The room looked much like Dr. Adams office in Sacramento, only with more cabinets and no desk. It was a large room with rows and rows of long drawer filing cabinets.

Clara's jaw dropped a little. "Please tell me your head knows right where we can find the data we want?"

Dan thought for a moment, and then shook his head. "Not yet."

"Smashing." Clara clapped her hands together. "We aren't getting anywhere standing here." She walked down the first row, looking at the labels on the front to find that each one of them was numbered.

"Remember what Victoria said, we are looking for data on 'Operation Silverfish,'" Dan said, as he pulled open the first drawer and looked down to find it packed with folders. A sigh of relief came as an involuntary reaction. Even if it's not what they were looking for, it was better than finding nothing at all.

"What about Project Moth?" She pulled a few of the files out and looked them over, opening each one in turn. "My god, these are all patient files." She looked over to

Dan across the rows. "Didn't Adams say that you were the first person that he'd ever seen nanobots work with?"

"Yes, he did," Dan said.

"Did he tell you how many people it didn't work on?" Her eyes looked down the rows and rows of files.

"It didn't come up," he said in a careful voice, his throat going dry. He pulled open another drawer and pulled a thick file out; it was a typical medical file, filled with a stack of colored papers held in place with a copper two prong faster. On the front page was a picture of some man with a shaved head who looked like he was right out of boot camp. On the paper the picture was glued to, the caption read, "Subject #343." He started to flip through the notes showing different medical names and numbers, talking about doctor's observations. Some of them were written by Dr. Adams, and some by other doctors Dan didn't know. He flipped through to the last page where he found the words "Subject failure."

"Dan," Clara said, softly from the far side of the room; she'd moved down to one of the last rows.

Dan walked to the end of the first row, leaving the file sitting atop the open drawer. The first drawer was labeled #1 – #143. Randomly, Dan pulled from inside a thinner folder with "Subject #77" typed on the front. Inside he found another subject picture with the same shaved head but darker skin. There stamped in red were the words, "Project Silverfish."

"Dan," Clara said a little more urgently, and he looked over. "I don't think that we are going have any problems finding something we can use." She was coming to the same conclusions that he'd come to. "I'm looking at subject four-thousand-five." She pulled the file up and looked through it quickly. "How..." is all she could say breathlessly. Dan filled in the rest.

How did they get away with this without anyone noticing?

She pulled out a file that was thicker than any of the ones Dan had seen so far. She started to read through it in more detail while Dan moved to the front of the long drawer, pulling out an equally heavy looking packet, Subject #1.

Inside, Dan found copies of goals.

Project Silverfish:

Soldier enhancement program: the goal is to reduce casualties, improve morale, and to minimize the number of deployed servicemen by having more versatile soldiers.

Studies found that modifying the genetics of embryos is expensive, with severe side effects ranging wildly. Unable to control the side effects and birth defects, the subjects are not reliable and could not be used for service.

A more controlled method of modification is needed.

The goal of Silverfish is to use biocomputing for accurate genetic modification where traditional pharmaceuticals failed.

Scope:

Test subjects will be chosen from military service who meet optimal emotional profiling and physical attributes.

The development of nano-computing that can alter subject:

To better adapt to mission requirements, to

fill a role, or even change roles to fit single operation. (Programmable)

Improve coordination, strength, intelligence, and durability.

To help control pain, mental focus, and aggression. This could include the suppression of guilt or remorse.

To hold detailed information maps, weapon specifications etc. with photographic recall.

Dan felt his blood go cold and a shiver ran down his spine. He read the document a second time, though he didn't need to. What *had* Dinatech done to him? It didn't just make him a better soldier; it had made him a programmable tool. They could use him to do anything and he might not even care it happened.

He was still reading when Clara called out from her side of the room. "My word, Dan. They considered the use of their subjects in a nuclear bombing. Listen to this:

"'In the cases of deployment in nuclear fallout where fatal levels of radiation exist, subjects could survive with accelerated healing and the biocomputers' ability to find and remove abnormal cells, allowing long term deployment in hostile environments with minimal gear. Extra nutrients would be required to support regeneration. Full physical effects will need to be observed." Clara looked over at him.

"What kind of fucking horror shop are they running here? Forget what's happening to us. What they're doing breaks the Geneva Convention."

Dan picked up the folder for subject #1 and closed it. Clara pulled open draw after drawer, tossing folders about in a haphazard search. She looked up from the other side of the last row.

"Dan," she said softly as she closed the folder that she'd been reading from, "I haven't found a single subject that lived longer than a month. Every date ends with termination within twenty-eight days." With a finger she picked at the cover of the folder she held, letting it pop audibly. She left the point unsaid but clearly understood: Dan's days could be numbered.

His throat was dry and he tried to swallow a few times before he turned and walked away to put the folder into his bag.

"Grab ones you think are the most interesting. We need to get out of here before they find us," he croaked. The next minutes were silent as they stuffed anything they could into their packs. Pulling his much heavier messenger bag over his shoulder, he turned to look back over the room and all the files they would leave behind. How many soldiers had come here to serve their country only to be dead in a matter of weeks, never to see their families again?

Clara put a hand on his shoulder, leaning into him.

"It's going to be fine, we're going to figure this out." She gave him a squeeze before she turned to look out the door beyond.

What she didn't understand was while the thought of dying scared him; he was more worried about the very real possibility that while he lived he would be a programmable slave to the government or, even worse, to Dinatech. If they captured him, and found his body was playing nice with the machines, they could reprogram him in any way they wanted. The real him would be gone, good as dead. Maybe they had already made their changes and part of himself was lost forever.

He thought back to everything he'd done and he tried to find things he might not have done otherwise. But nothing that he'd done in the last week was normal. How could he judge?

Clara looked back with a cocked brow. "Dan, we getting out of here?"

He shook it off and nodded. "Yeah, lets go."

He pulled the heavy bag up onto his shoulder further. He took another glance back; he couldn't shake the feeling he was leaving a man behind. They stepped out into the hall, leaving the mess of folders. He didn't bother closing the door; there was no way to hide the fact they had found Dinatech's dark secrets, a sacrificial totem to their goals.

Walking after Clara, Dan's mind was so distracted that he failed to notice the movement until it was too late. A large man dressed in black jumped out from behind the nurses' counter and put a small gun into Clara's back. The loud pop echoed through the chamber and Clara let out a yelp, going limp. Dan charged before he could think. He lowered his shoulder to hit Clara's attacker but was blindsided by a second attacker, also coming from behind the station.

The first man tossed Clara's limp body through the open security door to the observation rooms. He lumbered after, closing the door behind himself; it locked with a snap. Dan tried to get up to go after, but the other man had jumped atop him, pressing him to the floor. The man had pulled a knife, and as he pinned Dan down he felt his rifle digging into his back. The men were dressed in identical black fatigues to those he'd seen at Victoria's house. It had to be Black Water.

Dan's attacker was not as thickly muscled as his partner, but still a formidable opponent. The man brought the knife down to Dan's neck and he knew he was going to have to deal with him before he could help Clara. Bringing his right arm up, Dan slapped the knife away from his throat at the last second. It pinged off the tiled floor next to his ear. Dan put a hand into his attacker's shoulder, trying to push him off while he grabbed the other man's knife wrist to keep the blade from swinging around and ending him.

Beyond the glass, Clara had woken up and was backing away from the much larger man, her backpack tossed to the side when she landed, and Dan could see she wasn't moving well. Dan paid for his momentary lapse of focus when the knife slipped free and the man yanked it up and over his chest. He put both his hands behind it and tried to bring it down into Dan's shoulder. His attacker had gotten his legs inside of Dan's guard, pinning his hips, making his own legs useless.

Everything was moving fast, and Dan could only take in glimpses of detail. His attacker had sharp angular features and a calm expression of control. Their eyes met then both looked back to the black combat knife between them. Dan's arms were starting to burn with the effort of keeping the blade from plunging into this chest. His lungs burned for more air and he watched the knife slip closer until he could feel the blade digging into his shoulder, puncturing the cotton of his jacket. He was losing control, and running out of options. Dan could see the toll the effort was taking on the sharp-featured man, but still the man's eyes focused in a frightful stare on the blade, willing it deeper.

In the glass room, Clara yelped, the sound muffled as her body slammed to the glass, showing just how thick it was. It held like concrete and Clara grabbed at her back as she fell to the floor. The large man stepped over her and pressed her shoulders to the floor, not letting her roll away.

Neither of them was winning their fight and Dan could tell by her lack of protest that she was in a lot more trouble than himself.

What was the one thing that he needed to do when Clara was in trouble?

What was the one thing that always got him through?

He needed to use his head.

He'd made the choice before he truly knew what he was doing. Fighting the basic instinct of preservation, he reversed his grip on the knife and pulled down as hard as he could. Dan felt the knife plunge into the top of his shoulder, the blade bouncing off the collarbone as he released the arm. He ignored the pain as he put both his hands behind the man's neck and he pulled down as hard as he could muster while driving his skull up into the man's head.

He knew at once he'd been successful, feeling the satisfying crunch as the other man's nose collapsed against his forehead. The man covered his nose with a cry of pain, letting go of the knife now stuck in the top of Dan's shoulder. Dan punched up with an open palm strike and rolled the man off. Breathless and feeling weak, he stumbled onto his feet and headed off to the room that held both Clara and her muscled captor.

He was atop her, toying with her, and not willing to finish the job, and slapping her across the face to keep her awake. The large man had some kind of sick fascination with control: he wasn't going to kill her until he had to.

Dan found the lock at the door unwilling to give. He pulled his rifle off his back and tried to shoot the glass out instead. The burst was loud in the enclosed space but he needn't have bothered: the bullets chipped at the glass, like a small pebble bouncing off a windshield.

Letting out a howl of frustration, Dan brought the butt of the rifle down into the glass and knew at once there was no chance he was going to get through without finding a way to unlock it. He paced the glass before the man, banging the butt of his rifle into it over and over. The brute beyond slapped Clara again while he watched, taunting him. He didn't stop there. His ham-like fists moved down, jerking at Clara's bulletproof vest roughly and removing it. Her eyes rolled back and she struggled to find herself, her hand limp at her side, digging at the tile.

Panic shook Dan, realizing that he was going to have to do something or Clara wasn't going to make it. He looked around, trying to think. He had to open that door. His eyes fell on the nurses' station, remembering that the electric locks had remote buttons … didn't they? He turned and ran for the desk, not caring about the knife as sticking out of his shoulder, the blood running down his arm from the deep wound. The pain was present but not as bad as he expected: adrenaline—or the nanobots—were doing the job. With the pain dulled, he was able to focus on the task.

Running behind the station he franticly scanned the desk, spotting a bank of buttons, and was reaching to slap all off them when the agent with the shattered nose tackled him from behind.

Hitting his chin on the desk, Dan's teeth clicked together and he saw stars as he was folded in half the wrong way, his spine popping in protest. The rifle clattered away and the man crawled up Dan's back, punching him in the kidneys, sending jolts of pain through his body as he tried to push away from the desk to curl into a protective ball.

Inside the glass cage the large brute of a man hadn't stopped with just the flak jacket. Seeing that his partner had Dan down again, he'd moved on to ripping Clara's sweater open to expose her pale flesh and the white bra beneath. He leaned over, growling something in her ear before licking at her earlobe. It wasn't enough for the man to have beaten her; he had to demonstrate his domination.

Dan was starting to understand the powerless feeling Clara felt when she'd watched her family held at gun point by terrorists, and how strong she'd had to be to fight back. The heat boiled up in him until he could feel his blood pounding in his ears. He bit his lip until he tasted blood, the fresh feeling of knowing what had to be done.

Force was to be met with force.

As Dan struggled to keep the man from pinning him once again, he saw another person walk through the vault door like everything going on was normal, like people struggling in a life or death fight was expected anywhere. Dan saw their chances of making it out alive were starting to plummet quickly. The newcomer was in street clothes, and the black man with his tight-cropped military haircut could be none other than Hicks.

Hicks looked down at Dan with his head pressed to

the desk and smirked, then hit the button to the door that held Clara, knowing exactly where it was. He was not bothered by Dan or his attacker, and he turned, walking away.

The brute in the room took the time to pull his stun gun and press it into Clara's side; she gave another yelp before collapsing, motionless. Pulling himself up off of Clara he stood, brandishing a blade in warning to Hicks.

"Just give me the girl," Hicks said in his raspy voice. "Walk out and consider your mission done."

The man was larger than Hicks, and he laughed at him. "You think I'm going to give up my new play thing? No, I don't think I will." He spun the knife out in front of him and Hicks readied himself for the lunge.

Meanwhile, Dan's stamina was making up for his lack of training. He kicked back, hitting the other newcomer in the knee. He felt the grip on him loosen and Dan pushed back along the floor trying to reach for the rifle he'd dropped. He just got his hand around the butt when he heard the metallic click of a pistol hammer coming down, then the room lit up as Dan's vest was battered with round after round from a 1911 pistol. They were blocked by the vest, but still it felt like getting punched with a jackhammer—until the last shot hit him in the left arm, where he didn't have any protection. He felt the bullet hit and his arm go numb as it slapped off the floor from the impact.

Inside the glass room, Hicks and the larger man turned slowly around one another, neither daring to look away: the lack of focus would be fatal. Clara lay propped up against the glass, a lifeless heap, her head turned away to the middle of the room. The man tested a few quick jabs but Hicks slid back with practiced ease; he was more than ready to handle a man with a knife.

Lying there watching, Dan tried to be as still as he could, but his pounding heart made it hard for him to control his breathing. With the blood singing in his ears, it was hard to hear the footsteps of the man stepping closer. He screamed in his head, begging his body to *stay still*, trying to not shake as he watched his own blood pool out over the floor around him. How much blood could he lose? How much had he already lost? Could his new body recover from the damage he'd taken?

It didn't matter, it was not important. This was not where it was going to end. He wanted to live, so he would. It was all so simple. He looked at his right hand curled up over his head and let his eyes wander to Clara. She was still lying where her attacker left her. Hicks backed slowly into the corner. He'd made no movement to attack back, and this action wasn't lost on the other man. Showing he had at least half as much brains as he had muscles, he didn't follow him in.

Hicks moved along the wall and the large man backed up a step, checking his advantage.

Then, it all happened at once.

There was a guttural scream, not from either man, but from Clara as she came up with her combat knife, pulled from the cargo pocket of her pants. She leapt up and with all the strength she could muster she drove the blade through the back of the agent's neck, the point coming out where the man's Adam's apple once was.

The man crumpled to the floor grasping at his neck, his howl of pain nothing more than a gurgle around the blade. Clara tried to pull it free, but lacked the strength, and tumbled forward upon the man's back as he scrabbled at his throat, trying to breath while he choked to death on his own blood. Clara collapsed against him, unable to move.

The agent leaning over Dan was no longer worried about him, but instead turned to watch the scuffle in the other room. It was the opening Dan needed. He gripped the knife that still lodged in his shoulder and, mustering every bit of willpower he could, jerked it free. Even with his superhuman pain tolerance Dan couldn't help but kick his leg out as his vision blurred. He rolled up to his knees to take the razor sharp blade with both hands and gashed it along the inside of the man's leg. Dan could feel his left arm wanting to give up as he forced it to work, but he held on as he slashed his way through the man's femoral artery. The man's pants were already soaked with blood, and Dan came to his feet, driving his shoulder into the other man's chest and letting him slap back into the tile where he could bleed to death.

Staggering, Dan moved for the room where Hicks looked down at Clara. The man under her was dead, but she didn't have the power or the coordination to get back up, so she simply clung to her knife and her consciousness. Hicks smirked as he kicked her off the man and she fell back into the glass. Her eyes registered a flicker of recognition, but it was clear she wasn't focused. She put a hand to the glass, trying to stand, but it wasn't going to happen. Hicks looked over Clara in her ragged shirt, blood pooling in the white of her right eye.

His expression resembling a child who didn't get the toy he wanted for Christmas, Hicks shook his head and stepped back.

"How worthless is this," he growled in his raspy voice. His look of disappointment spread and he turned and walked out of the room, meeting Dan face to face. The slashed agent was no longer trying to staunch the blood, having fallen into unconsciousness.

"You might want to be careful, there's a third musketeer up above, just to make sure you two didn't make it," Hicks said as he kicked Dan's rifle farther away from him. Only then did he walk past to leave.

"Why would you tell us that?" Dan called after him.

"Because I still have my hopes of getting my payback," he said as he slipped away.

Dan was confused. What could he possibly want payback for? Wasn't it the FBI that had come in to save them at the last moment? Behind him, Clara pulled herself up enough to thump her back to the glass inside the room. She looked at her ruined top and pulled it the rest of the way off, tossing it on the man now lying face down.

"You wanted this, didn't you?" She glanced over her shoulder to meet Dan's eyes, looking about as bad as he felt, but she still, even now, found a way to smile. She leaned her forehead on the glass and kissed it where his lips would have been.

"Hey Dan?" she said softly.

"Yes?"

"Ship out of danger?" she said with a soft giggle.

"Are you serious?" Dan asked.

"You're the Trekkie," Clara said.

"I'm not a Trekkie! I don't even know where you got that damn idea," Dan huffed.

While Clara laughed and wondered if she'd suffered brain damage, Dan pulled back his vest and shirt to try and staunch his own bleeding; it was slower than he expected. The machines were already at work. He looked up at the ceiling. Somewhere above them there was another ruthless bastard waiting to kill them. They may have found the information to clear their names, but they still had to get out of this place alive.

Chapter 9: Escape from New York

"Ahh, Dan?" Clara asked through the half closed door to the file room. She was digging through the extra clothes they had dumped to make room for the files.

"Yeah?" Dan leaned against the wall by the door, his eyes watching the room, looking for anyone stupid enough to try and come through the vault door into the basement. He kept the rifle at the ready, not willing to be caught twice.

"If I'm ruined for marriage, will you still take me?" Clara peeked her head back out the door, her eyes full of hope as she finished pulling on the last layer of t-shirts. With all her thicker clothes destroyed, layering up was the best she could do.

Dan frowned, taking a look at how beat up she was. She wasn't looking so invincible now.

"What in the hell are you talking about?" Dan said. He was really starting to worry the shocks had done some real head damage. The whole left side of her hip was beaten, and the bruises were still spreading.

She winced while strapping the vest back on when it rubbed against her re-aggravated ribs.

"A man just tried to rape-snuff me. That's going to

count against me when it's time to find a good husband."
She settled the backpack filled with the documents over
her shoulders again and groaned under the weight. She
was in pain and could no longer hide it. Her cheek was
also showing a nasty purple bruise, and her right eye was
pooled with blood. Dan would have offered to carry both
bags, but he only had one shoulder that could take any
pressure thanks to the deep knife wound.

Luckily the bleeding had stopped rather quickly. His
super healing was doing its job; he wasn't going to bleed
out, or get an infection. He still had lead in his left arm
that was going to have to be removed before it could do
any more damage and he could barely move it.

"How about we worry about getting out of here alive
and then we can worry about your opportunities to find
husbands, huh?" Dan pulled the messenger bag up
against his back and walked around the bodies giving
them a wide berth to the door.

"Fail," Clara said, sounding rejected.

"What?" Dan looked back.

"You're supposed to say how perfect I am and that
you'd be happy to have me," she narrowed her eyes at
him. "Just the way I am." That last part was said slowly,
pointedly.

"Yes, my girlfriend, the human wrecking ball." He
turned, walking again but winced as he thought back
through what he'd just said, too late; he was caught.

"Double fail," Clara said.

She moved to each body, taking weapons, and Dan
was sure he saw her give the larger man an extra kick as
she pulled his pistol and submachine gun free. She
locked the door as she walked out of the room, and
pulled the pistol off the agent that had bled to death,

stepping carefully around the growing puddle. Neither man carried any identification on them; the only other thing they had was a set of car keys. They turned off the lights to the basement and made for the stairs.

"I can't believe Hicks left without doing anything," Clara grumbled. "Now he wants to act all honorable. Codswallop, I tell you." Dan got the impression that losing didn't sit well with her.

"So you don't think there's a third agent from Black Water out there?" Dan said.

"Oh no, I'm sure there's another. Hicks was telling the truth." Clara glanced up the stairs, pointing the pistol before her.

"But while it's the truth, he's still got some master plan, and he won't have us die before he's ready."

"Why do you say that?" Dan said.

"Women's intuition?" Clara said.

Having never been able come up with an argument against women's intuition, Dan had no rebuttal. He followed Clara as she went up the stairs slowly, not as graceful as normal. The stuns were still affecting her coordination. Her pride wouldn't let her show just how hurt she really was: even back in the diner she played off her bruised ribs. He knew he needed to be even more alert: Clara couldn't do this all alone.

They wound their way around the steps and out of the basement. When they reached the lobby, Clara stepped out in a crouch with the pistol in front of her.

There, across the lobby on the second story, sat the expected third assassin. His first shot hit the wall next to Clara, blowing a hole straight through it as she rolled away. Dan knew this was not a rifle that he wanted to be shot with, even with his super human healing. Clara bolted for the front door and Dan headed after her for five steps before turning and running down the hallway: the shooter would have to make a choice on his target.

The agent picked Dan, just as he hoped; he after all was the one with the secrets to expose. The Senator wanted him eliminated; Clara was just a bonus. Then again, he might have been picked because he couldn't run as fast. The hall was a mirror of the other hallway; not even breaking stride, Dan hit the far wall of the corner, pushed off and ran down the longer hall. Dread picking at the back of his mind. He glanced over his shoulder, but couldn't see anything in the dark.

Kicking through the door at the end of the hall he barely broke stride; the door blasted open to show an office with a large dusty desk set in the middle. Dan slid to a stop. He knew this room. It was Dr. Adams' before he moved his project to the west coast, and was cleared out except for a desk. Dan walked around and opened a pencil drawer; there, sitting in the tray, was a small glass rod.

Dan was not sure what it was; he wasn't even sure why he'd opened the drawer. He picked it up, looked it over, and slid it into his messenger bag. The already abused door then exploded out of its frame, and the window over his left shoulder blew out from another shot.

Flinching and throwing himself down behind the desk, Dan opened up with what was left the AR-15 ammo. With the light from the muzzle flash, he was able to watch as the man dived back out of view.

Dan tossed the weapon aside once it was empty; there was no point in holding onto something that would just slow him down. He turned and jumped out the window, the jagged glass breaking out around him. Expecting to hit pavement, he landed instead on grass and the ground hard-packed beneath it. He rolled down a small hill, sliding to a stop at the bottom. Looking behind to assess the damage, he realized he was out in the open and a man with a fifty-caliber death cannon was closing quickly on his heels. Dan ran for where he hoped the main road would be; in the distance he could hear cop sirens blaring to life. Security must have heard the gun fight and called it in. It sounded like there were a lot of them.

Running out of a side alley, Dan was gulping down air, but he could see the main road ahead. He was no longer worried about Black Water agents; with official authority bearing down on them he was willing to bet they'd pull back and find a better chance to attack.

Seeing the flash of red and blue lights strobe off the building, he contemplated finding a place to hide. He didn't want to risk being put in cuffs and dragged off to the FBI where things would not go so well for him. He was slowing his run as he looked for someplace to lie low when a gray car slid to a stop before him, the driver side door flinging open.

There, climbing over the middle console from the driver seat was Clara. The car was still rolling as she abandoned the controls. "Dan! Time to bounce!" He ran forward, diving into the car and tossing the messenger bag in the passenger seat with Clara. Slamming the door he looked over the controls. It was a BMW with a manual transmission, and when he put it into gear and pressed on the gas it took off with no hesitation, telling him it had to at least be a V6.

"Where did you get the car?" Dan asked.

"Well, I didn't think the agents would need it," Clara

told him. She reached into the messenger bag and pulled out the pre-paid phone. She started to pull the battery out of it.

"What are you doing? Don't destroy it, it's the only way we can call Makin," Dan said, panic in his voice.

"No." She pulled out a small sim card; she'd kept it from before. "I just need to make a few calls on my own line." She dropped the battery in her lap and was trying to change the small plastic coated chip when Dan looked up in time to see the cop car coming straight at him with its lights flashing like an angry Christmas tree. The cop swerved left and Dan did the same, their side mirrors tapping just enough to tell them how near a miss it was.

Clara was still trying to change the sim as she bounced about in her seat. "Keep it bloody steady a moment, Delivery Boy!" she growled.

"Sure why don't you come over here and avoid cops. I'll try and order a pizza on the phone," Dan growled. He gripped the wheel harder; looking through the rearview mirror, he saw the cop car turning around to give chase.

"Great, now I'm in a Blues Brothers movie." He pushed the gas and started to weave through the side streets and alleys.

If Dan needed a getaway car this would be high on his list of choices; he was sure it was modified to the task, the performance felt well beyond stock under his control. He was working his way through the smaller streets, and the narrow alleys left no room for mistakes. If he was able to work a UPS van through tight fits, this BMW felt like being on the autobahn. Taking another turn he couldn't see the lights and he grinned.

"I think we lost them," he called out, checking every

mirror.

"Great, then you can help me find the battery, I lost it somewhere under the seat." Clara was doubled over, groping under the seat. Dan looked up just in time to lock up the brakes; the cop car he thought he'd lost was coming at him head on, and alley was too tight to pass by this time. Clara gave a chirp of surprise when the BMW slid to a stop, the low-profile tires wailing protest. The cop car kept coming and it was then Dan realized he didn't know how to put the car in reverse. Never had he found it harder to read a gearshift than with a cop car racing up on him.

Shit shit shit.

Pulling the stick past first till it clicked, he shoved the stick up hard, sighing in relief. Dropping the clutch, the tires barked to life, starting a smoke show, as he drove backwards as fast as he could. Just as he passed another four-way intersection, another cop car came through the middle. The one chasing him hit the crossing car with a big smack of metal on metal, and as the first car came to a rest over the hood of the second, both were pushed into the side of a building.

At the next four-way cross, Dan whipped the wheel around to get the front end to slide around, turning the car one 180, and gunned it as another cop car joined the chase.

"We're going to get pinned in. We need to find a way out of this trap," Clara said, looking up and putting her hand on the dash to keep from eating it.

Making an e-break turn, Dan drifted the car around and down an alley heading for the main street. Thoughts of getting out of this mess were quickly dashed when a cop car cut off the alley just before the street, forcing

Dan to take a right at the next narrow alley. They were jolted in their seats as the back bumper made contact with the brick wall.

"Christ, that's tight," Dan said through gritted teeth, pushing the pedal back down and willing the car through the small alley at an insane pace. Dan looking back through the mirror, Clara looking back over her seat, they saw there were cop cars crisscrossing back and forth through the alleyways.

"A question for you," Clara asked. "How many cop cars are there in Richmond?"

"Not sure. But I think that's about all of them," Dan said. He hopped the car over a curb and flew through a four-lane road into another back alley.

Clara's head snapped around to look out the side window and her thick braid of hair slapped Dan in the face; he had to fight blinking for fear of losing the road. "Tell me if I'm wrong. But wasn't that a major road we could have turned onto?" Clara said.

There was no going back, and the cops were picking up the chase once more; he growled his frustration. At the next intersection he put the car into another slide and narrowly made the turn as two cop cars passed by, missing the corner.

"We are going to have to get rid of this car. They will be looking for it even if we do get away," Clara said, still looking about the floorboards for her missing battery.

Dan kept looking out the windows, and he soon found what he was looking for: a small recess into a garage door. While the door was still closed, there was enough room to hide the car sideways. Not seeing any cop cars in sight, Dan locked the breaks and spun the wheel, putting the car into a spinning slide, letting the BMW skid sideways into the recess. They came to a stop as the passenger mirror kissed the old metal roll up door.

Dan killed the engine and got out while Clara squeezed up out of the window, tossing the heavy backpack over the roof to him. They ran a few doors down and ducked into another recess. Clara pulled out the lock gun from a side pocket of the bag.

"So while we're baring all here," Clara said, "where did you learn to drive like a crazed stunt man?" Clara said while working on the lock.

"I don't know. I played a lot of Gran Turismo with Jake?" It was a good question; but he'd always had a natural talent for driving, even before his nanobot infusion. He loved driving, be it donuts in the snow, or turning a twisty road into a track course.

"You're telling me you learned how to drive while playing a video game?" Clara asked, distracted.

Leaning out, Dan saw the cop cars rolling back and starting to pull down the alleyway, their large V8 engines roaring up as they searched for the gray BMW.

"No pressure or anything," Dan murmured.

"Shut up," she bit back. Jamming the gun into the lock, she forced it until it sheared the tumblers and the door came open. The pair pushed in the door and closed it just as the lights zoomed past. He peered through the blinds on the door and peeked out. "I don't even think they saw the car, they were going so fast."

"Oh, we don't seem to be that lucky today." She pulled the cell phone battery out of her pocket and proceeded to put the rest of her phone back together.

"Didn't you lose the battery?" Dan asked. They were in some kind of redistribution building; boxes palletized and neatly stacked in rows were in the middle of the floor with a small set of offices to one side. The place looked well worn, but organized.

"Oh it popped into view when you hit wall, brilliant really." She turned the phone on and it chimed back to life.

Listening for the sirens, Dan moved back over to glance out the window. "I'm not sure how long we have before they find the car. We're going to need to get some new wheels and get the hell out of town." He was kind of sad: he really liked that BMW.

"Aye, I'm not sure we can risk the bus either." She tapped a finger on the phone. "Only one option left to us." She hit the talk button on the phone.

She was already counting, mouthing out the numbers silently.

"Patrick," Clara said. Her voice dripped with sugary cheer that didn't reach her eyes. "I thought that we had an understanding, we were going to be in Oregon on Tuesday, cooperating."

She didn't pause long. "Look, I know that damn senator came in and started tossing his weight around, but I expected better from someone that worked for my father."

She didn't pause half as long before she went on. "Also, I thought you had that nasty Mr. Hicks down for a long stay in one of your first class resorts? Yeah well, he showed up here while we were playing a game with some Black Water agents.

"No. They were here trying to kill us Patrick. That senator has let everyone off the leash. They're running around ripping up your front yard. You might want to get that under control!" Any friendliness she'd started the call with was gone now.

Clara shook her head and went on as the conversation escalated.

"Here is the deal. Tell the Senator to call off his dogs. If I don't hear from him by nine am, I'm going to show the whole world just what twisted sick fucks his friends are." She paused for effect. "Ciao."

She turned the phone off and pulled the battery.

The sirens had quieted, but even with the chase ended, the search had begun; the net was closing around them. Their chances of getting out were getting slimmer with every ticking second. North is where Makin waited for them with his press contact. Dan went through the piles of paperwork in the office they were hiding in and found it was a distribution center. Looking out windows, he saw it was behind the Central Food Bank, and west of the I-95.

"When Victoria dropped us off I saw houses on the far side of the freeway," Clara said. "If we can get over there, we can boost a car and head north."

"You want to steal a car?" Dan said disbelievingly.

"How do you plan to get there? Call a cab? This late there aren't any busses running, even if we wanted to risk showing ourselves in public," Clara said.

"I don't really like the idea of stealing a car," Dan said.

"It's not like we're going to keep it or something. I'm not looking to start a new life as a chop-shop owner." Clara frowned at him, not really believing what he was saying.

"Fine, but there has to be a better way to get out of

here," Dan retorted.

"You want to take the BMW? I'm sure it's traceable by Dark Water." Clara sniped back.

"No, no. I just … look, forget it. We can steal a car," Dan said, his voice softer, trying to deflate the escalation.

As Clara pulled her gun, Dan thought for sure her volatile temper was getting the better of her. Then he heard the click of a door opening from the far side of the building; it was deeper in than they had explored. Flashlights flickered as men jogged along the hallways.

"Cops," Clara mouthed and she flicked her head to the back door; he opened it as quietly as he could and they slipped back into the night. They were once again in the back alley, but at least the moon and the lights from the far-off freeway kept it bright enough for them to see. They kept to the walls where the shadows gave them the most cover.

Reaching the street, cops cars fanned out to the south patrolling for them. Turning north and keeping to the shadows, they walked along, watching for more cop cars, expecting at any moment that one would pull out and catch them. Their hope was the cops would focus their search closer to the gray car, giving them time to get farther away.

Many times patrol cars came close, but Dan and Clara would slip behind the cover parked cars still in the lot, or under the cover of a recessed entrance. They finally made it to the security fence behind the mall, climbed over, and found themselves on a bank to the I-95 corridor; beyond were trees and a small housing community a quarter mile away.

"You made it sound a lot closer, you know," Dan said.

"I'll try to measure distances better next time," she

grumbled. She'd already started down the slope for the freeway. The traffic was dead this time of night and they got across without anyone seeing them.

Getting to the other side of the freeway helped to make Dan feel less jumpy. He was starting to believe they could be out of Virginia before morning, before the owner of the car they were about to steal would wake up and find it gone.

They did spend more time than Clara would have liked picking a car.

The pair of them stood in a cul-de-sac, looking over the driveways like a young couple in search of their first used car.

Pointing to the first one, Clara said, "That car should be fine." It was a Toyota Camry, nothing special about it.

"Simple factory alarm, I can get around that in a jiffy."

"No, I don't want to take that one," Dan said putting his hand on her shoulder, but took it away at the look Clara turned on him.

"And why the bloody hell not?"

"I don't see a second car, they won't be able to get to work."

"And I don't want to end up buried in an unmarked grave when we get caught, so some Smith can get to work on time."

Dan looked down a few more houses and found a small green Honda that was sitting next to an old Chevy pickup truck.

"Let's take that one."

"If that car breaks down halfway to New York I'm going to make you push it the rest of the way." She stormed off to look the car over and found it wasn't alarmed.

"You're okay with this one? It's green. I don't really like green cars." Clara frowned at it.

"Are you kidding?" Dan rolls his eyes.

"If you get to be picky, I get to be picky too," Clara mused and walked around it. "There's a ding back here."

"Can we just take the car please? I'm so ready to add grand theft auto to my growing collection of felonies."

It took Clara surprisingly little time to open the door and break loose the steering column; apparently her door lock gun worked just as well on cars. Once behind the wheel she let the car roll back into the street before starting it, and Dan climbed in on the passenger side.

"You sure you don't want to drive? You're way better at it."

Dan shook his head. "No, I think I need a break." He looked over at the mailbox, making note of the address.

Four hours and a tank of fuel later, Dan and Clara entered Pennsylvania. They were camped out in a mall parking lot, eating fast food burgers. Dan had never been a fan of fast food, but his hunger was becoming almost painful.

Never in his life had he felt the need to eat so badly, and after plowing through three of the four burgers, Clara watched him over her fries.

"If you eat that last burger, we're going to have a problem." To save against possible sneak attacks she pulled the bag into her lap before going back to her fries. "They really weren't kidding. You could outlive a nuclear winter with the feed bag strapped on."

"I'd rather not picture myself like a prize horse, thank you," he said around a mouth full of fries.

"Aww, come on, it's cute." She reached over and patted his belly. "At least I don't have to worry about you getting all fat on me."

"No," Dan narrowed his eyes at her. "We just have to wonder if I'm going to make it another three weeks."

"Wow, Debbie Downer." She sighed and slumped back in her seat.

"I'm sorry," he sighed. "I'm just on edge, and I'm still hungry." He emptied the rest of his fry bag into his mouth. "I'm still getting used to this whole running from the law thing."

Giving him a slow shrug, Clara looked out the window at passing cars on the street.

"I'm not really used to it either. If you haven't noticed, my family has always been on the right side of the law. This constitutes the longest I've ever been away," she said, wistfully.

Condensation was building on the windows.

"You think Ellsworth is going to play ball?" Dan asked.

"I don't know. But Patrick knows we were in Richmond and that means my father will know too," Clara said.

"Why didn't you just call him directly?" Dan said.

"I don't want anyone knowing I'd been in contact with him. Eric is on our side, and I didn't want anyone looking any closer. I don't want to bring any scrutiny down on him. We're going to need him."

Looking up, there was another car; this one turned onto the access road heading to the mall lot. Clara sat up, putting the burger bag under the seat away from him. She pulled the submachine gun off the back seat, fingering the safety. The car slowed as it came to a stop before them; the headlights flashed twice and then stopped. Clara climbed out of the car as Makin got out of the back seat, the Russian Marko stood up from the front, and Paul could be seen behind the wheel. Marko had his pistol out, and Clara and he faced off while Dan walked around the car to meet Makin.

Makin frowned at the standoff.

"I'm not sure they get the idea of being on the same side," he said to Dan.

"Are we on the same side? With all this distance? She won't shoot if you don't, so let's move on."

With a nod, Makin agreed.

"The journalist is in the car, but I'd like to see the papers before."

"Why? You want our help, but you don't trust us?" Dan sighed. He pulled his tote bag around. Marko turned the gun over at him and Dan slowed. Clara took a step closer.

"You want to see the papers or not?" Dan looked at Makin. "What the hell is this anyway?" He waved his hand at Marko.

Trying to wave Marco off, Makin shook his head.

"There are still concerns that you are a plant to infiltrate and destroy us. We're having a hard time with how quickly you showed up and found the exact documents we've been trying to get for over five years. We are a little suspicious of everything that you have accomplished in just one week."

"We would have accomplished it four days sooner if you would have helped us," Clara countered.

"Perhaps," Makin mused. "I heard about the mess you

left behind in Sacramento. Even if you are trying to take down Dinatech, you show reckless tendencies. My counsel isn't sure trusting you won't burn us along with you."

Dan pulled out the papers and waved them in front of Makin.

"You want our help or don't you? You better make up your mind. Because if we can't make this work you need to stop wasting our time, we have very little of it left. Everyone is out to kill us."

The Arab was looking between Marko and Clara when the opposite rear door opened and an older woman with curly dark blond hair stood up.

"Enough," she barked at them all. "If you're done with the dick wagging contest, I'd like to see those documents."

Clara narrowed her eyes, clearly offended by the idea she was wagging with anyone.

The woman went on, "I've got a paper that I've been wanting to publish for over two years, just waiting for a lick of proof. I'm not going to let you all mess it up now."

Everyone watched the woman walk around the car and hold out a hand.

"May I see?" she asked Dan with a softer tone.

Laughing, Clara rested her gun against her shoulder. "Yeah, I like her."

That was enough for Dan, and he handed the paperwork to the woman.

"Ann," she said by way of introduction as she thumbed through the bound pages. Everyone was quiet; Marko holstered his own pistol, but he didn't look happy about it. Ann asked, "How did you get this? I thought they kept everything online and they lost most of the data when the computers in Oregon crashed."

"What do you mean?" Dan said confused.

"Just what I said." Ann looked up at him. "They've been scrambling to recover any data they can from the systems in Oregon, it's why Ellsworth came to the west coast. He's been pulling strings all over the place to save what they can and cover up the rest."

"Do you think that's why Hicks was there? He was trying to recover the only working copy of their work?" Clara moved to sit on the hood of the stolen Honda.

"But he didn't take any data with him, he only came into the room you were in," Dan said, shaking his head a little. "The Black Water agents and Hicks definitely didn't seem to be seeing eye-to-eye either."

Makin eyes got a little bigger.

"The head of security was in Richmond? I didn't hear Hicks was released from FBI custody."

"And what makes you think you get to know everything the FBI is doing?" Clara said defensively.

"Yeah, he's looking to pick a fight, but what kind of fight I'm not sure. He had the chance to polish us both off, but didn't. He's out there somewhere. And there's at least one more Black Water agent hunting us, not to mention the cops." Clara smiled at Marko. "I think you and Hicks could be great friends."

Marko narrowed his eyes, but Ann closed the file loud enough to draw everyone's attention.

"This looks to be in order. I'm not sure how much I'll be able to pin on the Senator, but with a little more digging I think I can match it all up." She waved the file.

Dan held out his hand for the document and Ann looked like she wasn't going to give it back, but after a hesitation she handed it over.

"I've been looking into some of the government spending," Ann said. "It's very interesting. I found Dinatech has many projects they spend money on publicly, but when you dig deeper they're just fronts for passing large sums of government money to bigger projects, ones people wouldn't be so happy to see, like Silverfish. Equipment and funds being re-channeled on the scale we're talking about are hard to cover up. It's not obvious, but if you look long enough you can find where the holes are."

Dan watched Ann and she went on.

"I've been reviewing the governments military spending for years. I found that Dinatech was one of their sub-contractors. It's not just military, they have medical grants for so-called cures. Work on cancer and vaccinations. Dinatech has produced results, making vaccinations cheaper to make, and more readily available. It doesn't add up. I've been able to find some inside sources. They tell me this research goes much deeper, and most of it rolls back into their military programs.

"They might be willing to talk, but they are not willing to go on the record, give any details, or give any proof I can use and not have it become libel. You have the first records that I've been able to touch with my own hands."

"Do you think that you'll be able to help us clear our names?" Dan asked the question that's had been on his mind most of the night.

"I don't know," Ann held out her arms. "I'm willing to run with the story; the public should know what's going on in their own backyard. I don't know if I can clear your names, but I promise I'll break the story open and I won't stop till there is at least an inquiry made."

Dan looked over to Clara and she shrugged, saying, "I only told them nine am in the hopes it would slow them down. I'm still in favor of setting the whole company on fire."

Dan pulled off his messenger bag and he held it out to Ann. "Then, everything you will want to know about Silverfish is in here." He looked over to Makin. "What were you able to make of my blood?"

"We could see you are indeed carrying some kind of nano machines inside you." Makin fidgeted. "But nothing more. In the sample you gave us, they had destroyed themselves."

"What do you mean?" Dan asked.

"We think they do it as a form of protection. They'll obliterate the evidence if they are removed from their host, to keep from being reverse engineered. It's rather effective," Makin said.

"They have come a long way from what you'll read in those files," Dan said.

"Dr. Adams is very close to having it working completely. I'm the first person that's successfully acclimated to the machines. If they really have lost all their data, they're going to be hunting me with everything they can mobilize." He looked to Ann. "Hurry, won't you? And be careful?"

"I will," Ann said softly.

Dan looked to Makin. "Are we working together or is this it? I'm not going keep wondering if I have your support. I have more documents, and I'm going to keep working until I find someone I can trust to help us."

Makin glanced back over to Marko, who looked away: this was apparently as close as the Russian was going to come to agreement.

353

"I can get the others to agree we need you," he said with a nod.

Chapter 10: Thank You for Not Smoking

When people all over America turned on the TV Sunday, the news was interesting.

"Today we want to bring your attention to a story that we'd originally reported on earlier this week. Dinatech, a U.S. company and a major contributor in medical and technology sectors, has been accused of breaking major U.S. and international laws in military weapons development and medical research. This work is allegedly funded by government contracts. The U.N. stated they would also be starting their own investigation.

"Not well known to most, Dinatech holds major government contracts for both the Army and Navy. In a story Ann McCaster published, she calls out the company for conducting human genetic experiments, with the purpose of building a 'Super Soldier'. In documents provided by McCaster, there are medical notes outlining experimentations that are against many laws and treaties. The U.N. is up in arms, and demanding disclosure of all Dinatech records.

"The President himself has gone on record saying he's not aware of any such experimentation, but promises a full inquiry into the matter, and that swift action will be taken. Other governments that have requested to see copies of these documents are France, China, and Russia, and all are looking to bring charges, breaking military treaties.

"Dinatech has also been under pressure internationally, and many of the countries where Dinatech has employees have been ordered to close their facilities while these charges are investigated."

Sitting in his home office, Senator Collin Ellsworth watched the TV and drank scotch with a trembling hand. He'd come home to deal with the fallout, but this was no longer a minor leak. Some operative commander wanted to talk to him about two dead men and how Collin hadn't been honest with him about parameters or some crap.

"I know my men should be able to deal with two civilians and some ex-marine," the commander had barked at him over a secured phone.

"I'm told those civilians were trained. I want to know what you really sent my men into."

Collin had been told by that damn FBI agent Patrick Crispi that the secretary could handle herself in a fight; still, he thought the CIA's most ruthless killers could deal with some girl with a few self-defense courses under her belt. If this wasn't enough, the Senate was calling an emergency session, and the funding had come into question. Everything was quickly turning into a very large, career-ending federal investigation and he was going to be in the center of it.

Collin had been trying to call Victoria for a day now; he wanted talk with her. He'd seen her home on the news, involved in gang activity. What had she said to them? He thought she would keep his secrets, but with the raid on the old hospital, he needed to know what she'd said. He was picking up the phone to try again when a man walked into his office. Collin looked over the black man in the gray business suit, his muscles impossible to miss even in the long sleeve jacket.

"Who the hell do you think you are? My front door was locked." Collin started to reach for his phone again when the man pulled a silver pistol.

"I don't think you'll want to do that," the black man said in a gravelly voice.

Collin's eyes narrowed at the gun and he drank the rest of the scotch straight down.

"Do you know who you are threatening?"

"I know who I'm *talking* with, Senator." Hicks pulled up the chair across from him, keeping the pistol trained.

"I'm head of Dr. Adam's security. I've come to follow up on this leak, because there are a lot of questions going around the office. Like what to do to clean this up."

Collin could place Hicks now: he was the man that never said anything, but was always close to Adams. Having him here alone made it harder to recognize him.

"Great, you are about the last person I need to be talking to right now. You know there is going to be an inquiry, don't you? They're going to question all the projects I've funded for Dinatech."

"That's what I'm here about, actually," Hicks said, sitting forward in the chair.

"What could you possibly want to talk with me about?" Ellsworth frowned.

"You went against Dr. Adam's orders. He said we needed to capture Daniel, you sent Black Water to kill them. That was not the plan."

"Of course I did. Your bumbling started the leaks, and they found Liberté, that little rag-tag group you let destroy our South American branch, and we lost all the research. You said you'd taken care of that problem."

Hick said nothing and Ellsworth went on, "If you think I was going to let them get a hold of Silverfish, you're nuts; both you and that damn doctor."

"He told you that we needed to capture the man in order to continue the project," Hicks countered smoothly. "The Core was destroyed with much of the data. By going around us, you put everything in jeopardy. You could have destroyed all our work."

"Have you read the news, turned on a TV?" Ellsworth pointed to his own. "We should have killed them! We *are* exposed, you fool! We need to cut ties, burn everything we can, and clean up this mess before we end up in a federal prison!"

Collin was dead before he fell back, a single shot through the temple. Hicks stood over the desk, watching the body slump down in its chair.

"Sounds like a plan, Senator." He tossed the pistol on the floor near the senator's right hand and turned to leave.

"Have you dealt with the first issue?" Adams asked over the phone.

"Yes, it's been dealt with," Hicks said back. "Now, let me go and deal with the girl and bring you back Daniel."

"Hicks, all you've talked about is this girl. You had your chances and you've missed them. I might say you have an infatuation with her, if I didn't know better. She is rather fetching, isn't she?"

"I want to bring back Daniel," Hicks said, his voice going cool.

"You'll have another chance, but first I need you to find Makin. We found he was leading the terrorist's attack on our South American labs. He's quickly becoming a bigger problem. I didn't think he was going to pop his head back up so soon. We need to remove the issue, take out the leader and his money."

"Fine," Hicks relented.

"While you're working on that, you need to find and silence Victoria Palmer. She knows everything Ellsworth knew, and we believe she's in their hands too. How did you let this happen? I thought you were in charge of my security? Fix this mess, Hicks. Now if you'll excuse me, I have to let the board know we have things in control so we'll be able to save face with our largest investors."

Adams didn't wait for Hicks to respond before he hung up.

Patrick sighed. He stood inside the lobby of the old medical building in Richmond. The building was unmarked and had no company logos inside or out. He'd had to show his badge at two sets of security gates to get in. One was military, with armed guards stationed at every hall and more guards on each stairwell.

His longtime partner Brian walked up, stuffing his badge back into his pocket. Brian was a shorter man with an old military flattop.

"Well isn't this place most welcoming?" Brian said with a frown, mopping at his brow with a handkerchief.

"Indeed." Patrick pulled his coat sleeves down when the captain stepped forward.

"Sorry sir, but I can't let you in," the captain said.

Patrick stepped up to the captain and his men tensed; he was actually looking down at him.

"I'm sorry, but I think you will." He pulled out his badge once again, and this time added a federal court order.

The captain looked at the paper and badge but he didn't bother to take them.

"I'm sorry sir, but I don't think that you understand. This is no longer a civil case, you have no jurisdiction here."

Patrick looked at Brian, and he looked back to the captain; paperwork had never failed him before. He turned back to the stern man in charge.

"We've got business here. You are welcome to join us, but we are going to need to see those files."

The men around the captain raised their M-16 at the two FBI agents. The captain repeated the line again, more firmly.

"I'm sorry sir, but I can't let you down there. This is no longer a matter that concerns you."

Patrick, knowing better than to press any further, took a step back, putting his hands up.

"I'll remind you, you're pointing weapons at federal agents."

Not one of them lowered their rifles, and Patrick couldn't think of a better time to leave. Backing out the door, he kept his eyes on the soldiers. Brian looked over, astonished. They headed for the car in the cool afternoon air.

"What the hell was that?" Brian asked looking back as

long as he dared.

"I don't know, but they have a lot more guns than us, meaning they get to win the fight." Patrick pulled his phone and handed to Brian. He looked up at Patrick then sighed as he dialed.

"Why do I have to make the call?"

"More years, more seniority," Patrick said.

"Bullshit," Brian said then turned as the call was picked up on the other side.

"Derksen? Yes sir, this is Parker. We've been made aware we are no longer allowed to see the files."

"Who, you ask?" Brian said. "The US army. No one is seeing the basement. Someone does not want these files read.

"No, we haven't heard from Ms. Paxton after the tip off. The best we can tell, she's still with Daniel Hollis, and working with the group called Liberté and their aligned interests against Dinatech.

"Yes sir, I'm aware of her temper; I had the pleasure of seeing it first hand in California. That does remind me sir; we haven't been able to get a trace on Hicks. After he was released he disappeared, but I expected that."

There was silence, and then Brian pulled out his notepad.

"No sir, I haven't been watching the news." His eyes went wide as he looked over to Patrick, and he started to write in his notepad.

"When did this happen? It was last night?" He held up the notepad for Patrick to see.

It read, 'The Senator Collin Ellsworth is dead.'

"No, sir," he turned back the phone. "We're on the way, I don't think we're getting into the vault without an army of our own."

Brian hung up the phone and shook his head.

"Come on, we are going to investigate the Senator's death. Derksen thinks Dinatech *might* be behind the shooting."

Epilogue

It was a nice restaurant, and Jim Singletary had paid for an escort, one that hadn't shown up. This was the place to be seen, but it was more than just having money. You had to *be* someone to be included here. How foolish did he look, alone, with no arm candy to show how much he mattered?

The company was having hard times, the government was starting to turn on them, and many of the lucrative contracts were all in question. There was a whole new government task force just for the investigation of Dinatech. Still, none of it could come back to bite him in the ass; he worked in corporate acquisitions. His whole job was to buy the companies Dinatech competed against, and it was no longer his problem once he was done buying them up.

Jim checked his phone. It was fifteen minutes after seven. Five more minutes, and he was going call that fucking over-paid escort service and tell them just how much of a mistake they had made in making him wait. He made enough money he was starting to consider buying the whole damn thing, all for the pleasure of firing the fuckers that treated him like he was just 'some guy'.

He was still fantasizing about everything he was going to do when she walked through the door. And then all was forgotten. She came towards him in a body-hugging black dress, with long chestnut brown hair that reached her hips. She watched him with eyes so blue they glowed, each one sparkling with mischief that could only spell a good night of fun. Her tits were too small for his taste, but no matter.

Brows rose in question as she walked to his table; her hips didn't just sway, they moved in a way that called at primal needs, and he wanted to enact those needs on her. For the money he was paying, he'd have the chance.

"Sorry I'm late, I was held up."   She spoke with a British accent that left him imagining what she might say while she was on her knees.

"Yeah, well I'm glad you made it, I was starting to think I was going to be spending dinner alone," Jim said in a superior tone. He motioned for her to sit in the seat right next to him.

"No, no, dear, I'm sorry for the wait, but we couldn't just send you anyone. I want to be sure you are taken care of."   The girl rubbed his arm before sitting down, her leg close to his.

All right, Jim thought, this was worth waiting for. She was a nine out of ten on his chart for girls; he would have to offer her implants and make her an eleven.

"Well everything is fine now. After dinner we can go have a few drinks at a club I know."

This was Jim's normal mode of operation on a Saturday night. He'd get dinner at one of the most expensive and talked about places in town. Then he'd go for a few drinks at one of the meat markets of the month. He wanted to show off that he could take the best looking girl home, not really caring if anyone knew he was paying the girl. If anything, it showed just how much he had to burn. But really, everyone is paying for it; the only difference was that there were no pretenses and no ambiguity, unlike a normal date. They know what they're getting paid for. Everything was already sortedd out. All they had to do was listen to his commands.

The young woman picked up the menu and looked it over slowly.

"You really know how to pick a place."

"I've been here a few times. I can recommend the fish; they don't overcook it here," Joe said.

Dinner was going well; she could keep up her end of the conversation, and she even added to most of the topics that came up. Nearly all of the girls he paid for were good for their time in bed, but couldn't make intelligent conversation to save their lives. There was something nice about a girl that had more than just her body going for her. So long as she didn't start getting too independent on him, he'd have to ask for this one again.

"So Jim, how do you pronounce your last name?" she asked. "You'll have to forgive this English girl, she's not the best when it comes to names."

"Singletary? Isn't it a British name?"

"Well, yes, but we aren't in Britain, a girl can never be too careful," she said.

"Look, just call me Jim, you don't need to be worried with my last name, sweetie," he said, putting his hand on her firm thigh. This girl knew how to workout, a professional at her trade. He looked into her eyes and saw a flicker of something. Want? Need? Anyone that knew he had money wanted to be with him; of course some refined British chick isn't going to be any different. It's always the same.

He settled back in his seat and waved for the waiter to come over like there was nothing else in the world the waiter would want to do more.

"Bring the lady a chardonnay." He looked to her and she smiled up to the waiter.

"I'm more of a Manhattan girl." She slid her small purse up onto the table between them.

"Right, get the girl a Manhattan. I'll take a martini. Just a little something to drink while we're looking over the menu." He waggled his brows. "You know, before the main course."

The waiter nodded and looked to the brunette in the tight dress.

"Of course sir."

The girl gave the waiter a saucy kind of a smile before leaning over to let her shoulder press in against Jim's arm. "You seem to be a man that knows what he's looking for." She looked up to him through her lashes.

"You aren't like the girls the services normally sends." Jim looked down as he let his arm slide up her leg till her dress lay indecently over her stockings. "There's something different about you."

"Oh, maybe not, but I'm sure that you're going to show me the ropes." She winked and then slowly slid away from him as the drinks showed up.

"If you'll excuse me a moment, I just need to go powder my nose."

"Yeah, don't be too long, your drink will get warm."

Not looking back, Clara rolled her eyes. She walked down the dark hallway to the restrooms, giving a shudder as she pulled her dress back down.

"I still think my idea of killing him after torture would have worked much better."

She walked into the bathroom and entering a stall she opened her phone. She hit the rewind button on a small digital recorder. The numbers ticked back till she reached the part where he ordered her drink.

"Right, get the girl a Manhattan, I'll take a..."

"Pompous ass had to make sure it was he did all the ordering," she growled and squeezed the machine till it creaked in protest, then set it on the back of the toilet. She hiked her skirt back up and pulled his wallet from the elastic band, going through it till she found a security card. It didn't say Dinatech on it, but she knew what she was looking for. She spun the card. "And I don't even have to go back to his place to find this." She hit talk on the phone and it was picked up almost at once.

"Clara?" Dan said from the other side.

"Who else, Delivery Boy? And guess what, this time I'm delivering the goods," Clara said with a smile in her voice.

"Already?" Dan said.

"Of course already. I'm a tiger in the sack, he passed out like half way through."

"Oh god don't tell me," Dan said, sounding nauseated.

"Please, you really think that I'd do that? I was able to get everything I need in the restaurant, twenty minutes tops." She turned the phone sideways and ran the security card through a slot built into the bottom, and the phone returned a positive beep.

"That come through okay?"

"Yeah we got it over here."

"So," Clara bit at her lip. "Please don't tell me that I have to go back in there?"

Dan was sitting in a hallway that looked to go on for a mile. There were very few doors along the hallway as well. Standing next to him was Makin and Marco, flanking a door.

"You only have to hold the story up long enough for us to get out of here and not be shot to ribbons," Dan said softly.

There was a little girl whine from to the other side that could be heard by Makin, who looked over, cocking a brow.

"Be a good girl and I'll see you back in Chicago," Dan said, trying to not laugh too much as he hung up.

"Dan, I'm telling you, this job sucks. I had to go pick up a guy because he blew a tire on his Aston Martin. What kind of service is this?" Clara said before the phone was clicked off during her protest.

Dan took a blank card out of his pocket and pushed it into the side, letting it beep before pulling it out. He then walked over to the door and pushed it through the security lock.

The cameras were already disabled by Marco, and it now showed a looping feed of the last five intruder-free minutes. The lock beeped and said in its computer voice, "James Singletary, please identify." Dan held up the phone and it said clearly, "Manhattan, I'll take a…"

"Identified," the lock said before it beeped, letting Dan open the door. He grinned: Clara had provided the goods. The three of them moved through the door and down the hall, Makin in the front with Marko walking behind Dan.

"This is where they moved the project to?" Dan asked as he looked around, leaning to try and see the room at the end of the hall, a whir of machines getting louder the closer they came.

"Yes, this is where they have been working to rebuild the core computer and to start rebuilding the nano project," Makin said.

At the end of the hall, it opened up like they were walking out of a tube. Beyond was a room the size of an airplane hangar. Rows and rows of computer racks stood alone like monoliths with five feet between each one. There was so much energy in the room Dan could feel his skin itch with it.

Makin looked confused, and looked back over to Marko.

"This is not what should be here." He looked around. "This company was just purchased, a cover for their work in biocomputing. There shouldn't be anything here yet."

Dan saw the look of recognition on Marko's face as the first men in black uniforms with rifles came out from behind the computer racks, pointing their rifles at them.

"Ah the last of my deliveries for the day, how lovely. I can re-start my research." Dr. Adams stepped forward. He was not a tall man, in fact he was on the short side, his dark hair slicked back. Makin pulled Dan's shoulder and turned to run, but there were already armed security cutting off their retreat.

"Oh, Makin Al Zahrani, there is no reason to leave, you are a welcome guest. I've wanted the chance to meet you for some time. I want to hear your thoughts on my vision."

"Your vision is blasphemous and you should be put

down," Makin sneered at him.

"Oh, put down, that's a great idea." He pulled a small box out of his pocket he pressed the button.

Dan collapsed to the floor, unmoving.

AUTHORS NOTES:

Making a paperback book is an incredible amount of work. I've come to understand why publishers get paid the big bucks or, should I say, take the lion's share of the proceeds. I started working on making a paperback version of Electric Disease with the hope it would be released only a few months after the Kindle release. A whole second book later and I'm just now getting the damn thing out!

I'm glad (for a few reasons) it has taken this long. 1) I've learned a lot, and this improves the quality of my finished product. Enjoy the mini monkeys! I prided myself on at least trying to make a good finished product. Looking back, I didn't give that with my first offering! 2) I'm able to give you more! With Corporate Policy just hitting digital book shelves, I've got twice as much to offer, making your "paying too much for a paperback book" worth your dollars (umm, more worth).

I'm glad I could create this book in print, and I wish I could cater to every "Why don't you publish it in X format?" requests. But the amount of work it takes for each version is quite taxing. The converters aren't as smooth as you'd like to believe, and they can't be exact with everyone's idea of formatting. And a cover for a paperback takes a lot more measuring than a digital book.

But I'm out on Kindle, I'm out on Nook, and now in paperback! I'm taking no more requests (for now)!

It's back to the literary whipping post for me. I have two manuscripts to get done, then shop for an agent and a publisher. It's time for me to take the next big step, and I'm super-cited! And a little sad: it might be a while before I publish again.

Still, once again I have to thank you all for your support. I'm not saying that I would have given up (I never give up, much to my wife's chagrin) but I don't think that I'd have pushed so far so quickly.

Keep up with my blog at: http://blog.illiteratemind.com and follow the web serial I work on at: http://aoapublishing.com/press

I'll try not to leave you too alone out there!

Robert

ABOUT AUTHOR:

While at school, Rob studied art, but always enjoyed story-telling. Life intervened, and he found himself working in the tech world, writing code instead of characters. He never let go of his original writing dream, however, and a decade later, challenged himself to complete National Novel Writing Month in 2009.

His success spurred him to complete novels for

NaNoWriMo the next two subsequent years, and those early manuscripts became the basis for his first indie novel, Electric Disease (currently available through the Amazon Kindle marketplace).

Rob enjoys creating quirky and memorable characters that are lovable and easily relatable and then throwing them into unusual, funny and occasionally frightening situations that might make readers wince and be grateful that they are reading fiction.

In addition to reading and writing, Rob also enjoys sports and customizing automobiles. He lives with his wife and son in Washington state, just south of Seattle.

www.ingramcontent.com/pod-product-compliance
Lightning Source LLC
Chambersburg PA
CBHW021424200626
46814CB00015B/19